Winter Sorceress

Book 2 of the Sorceress of Selvast Forest Series

E K Dobbins

Apellez Dreams Publishing

USA

EK Dobbins/Apellez Dreams Publishing
5343 Belleville Crossing Street
Belleville, Illinois 62226
www.apellezdreamspublishing.com

Publisher's Note: This is a work of fiction. Names, characters, places, and incidents are a product of the author's imagination. Locales and public names are sometimes used for atmospheric purposes. Any resemblance to actual people, living or dead, or to businesses, companies, events, institutions, or locales is completely coincidental.

Book Layout © 2017 BookDesignTemplates.com

Winter Sorceress/ EK Dobbins. – 2nd ed.
ISBN 979-8-9877350-2-2

Contents

The Fáidh of Desitana 4

Realm of Ice 38

Hall of the Ice King 62

The Plan 92

Reviewing the Troops 118

A Bold Snow Leopard.....................136

Tandon Attack 148

The Icebreaker...........................189

The Ice Dragon 203

Temple of Nag'teragiea 218

Queen's Return...........................249

The King's Attack 264

Ruins of Yedis............................280

The King's New Allies....................308

Queen's Revenge.........................339

The Departure 361

CHAPTER ONE

The Fáidh of Desitana

Once a booming village in the middle of the northern tropics, Pirate Island is now a is a barren rock populated by sea crustaceans. Many of the houses that stood proud upon the avenue are now skeletons of their former glory. When the visitors first landed upon the shore, they could not make out the distinguishable features of the island. They did find the remains of the mayor's home earlier in the day and delighted when they discover a room full of maps and charts. One of which points to the exact location of the Fáidh of Desitana upon the island with a warning that all who visit run a risk of going insane.

After a brief discussion and the rapid loss of sunlight, it is decided that two of the adventurers will take of the challenge of finding the Fáidh. The light from the setting sun turns the blue sky to amber. The colors overtaking the landscape as the glowing sphere sinks closer to the sea. Small crabs scavenge for food in great haste so they can fill up and get back to their burrows as soon as they can. A set of fast-moving feet causes the minor crustaceans to scatter. A second pair sent them retreating to their homes The ground trembles as the two explorers hurry up the hill to their destination.

Milea slides to a halt and glances behind at the large beast that is heading in her direction. The salty ocean breeze precedes it, stirring her hair and providing her senses with an overwhelming stench coming from the charging animal. From her quick assessment she sees that the pursuing beast is a pig-like creature with long tusks and equally long snout.

It has spike-like horns protruding from the tip of its nose and proceeding all the way back across the spine ending on the stubby mace-shaped tail. Milea notices a red, irritable, rash covering the spikes and is present in the spots where the black, greasy, bristling fur has fallen out. The sight of the rash indicates to her that it is way too close so she turns her attention back to the path ahead of her and increases her speed. The sound of the beast's low-pitched bellow of anger renews energy in both she and her fellow adventurer.

"Where in all Ublivorin did that thing comes from?" Milea expresses her question out loud.

"I don't know," Zaria answers, "but the sun is too high for me to do anything and I do not want it to eat us."

"I second that decision," Milea agrees.

The two continue up the steep hill at a rapid rate and nears the edge of a cliff. Zaria pours on more speed and outdistances Milea by several steps. She reaches the edge of the cliff and jumps high into the air, clearing the broad distance between the two sides with the grace of a feline. When she lands, she lets out a guttural grunt, sliding several feet to stop and turn. Milea sees the jagged edges of the cliff and locks her legs to slide to a stop. She is barely able to do so and gets an eyeful of the deep shadows below the cliff.

The sounds and smells of the ocean a distance below warn her that there may be jagged rocks awaiting her. The sorceress turns to face her pursuer as she hears it coming up the path. The seashells that are scattered around her begin to vibrate as the mangy boar rounds the bend. The beast's eyes gleam with murderous intent as it lowers its head and surges forward.

"Milea, are you nuts?" Zaria shouts out to the woman. "Get the hell out of there!"

"If we don't take care of the problem now it will be waiting for us when we return," Milea defends. "Thus, I am remedying the issue now."

Seashells shatter into dust and rise behind the charging animal as it hones in on its victim. The beast roars and foams at the mouth in anticipation. Milea keeps her cool as the ground around her vibrates violently. The winds around her starts to swirl at her command as she times the mangy boar's attack. The beast is inches from the sorceress and swings its tusk to skewer her as the wind explodes and blinds it. It does not touch Milea but instead goes through her image which surprises the boar. It is startled and tries to stop, locking it's legs.

The creature slides in an uncontrolled skid then fall into the deep ravine it fails to see. The beast's cries of surprise are short as it hits the bottom. There is barely the sound of a splash as the immense creature meets the water. The eerie silence is broken by the slush of the water against the stone. Zaria exhales in relief as Milea fades into view next to her.

"You are going to give me a heart attack one of these days," Zaria scolds. "What in all of Ublivion were you thinking?"

"Like I alluded to before, take care of the problem as it presents itself," Milea reiterates. "I'm not sure where that beast came from. I just hope that the cliff is tall enough and that there is a nasty surprise at the bottom to take care of it."

"Even though the shadows are deep I'm not going in there to take a look," Zaria said with a shake of her head. "I don't like this place; it is eerily abandoned, and it smells horrible."

"I too do not care for this place, but I feel that there is more to it than what we see on the surface," Milea agrees. "I just hope that the Fáidh of Desitana is worth this much trouble."

"From the information that I can recall, the Fáidh is a tad bit insane," Zaria informs. "We have to stay on our guard when we are around her."

After a few more minutes of looking over the cliff, Milea and Zaria begin to descend the hill and head to a cave. Unwanted shells of various sea animals make up most of the path they traverse. A large crab catches Zaria's eye before it disappears down a big hole. As soon as the two travelers pass the burrow, the discarded remains of the crab eject from the hole. Milea has a casual discussion with Zaria about the fate of the residence that once lived upon Pirate Island.

The settlement is far enough away from civilization to not be a threat unless you're a merchant ship sailing in the tropics. The current state of their world, Bri'al, may have a play in the destinies of the pirates that once roamed this land. Perhaps Tandon wiped them clean off the face of the planet. Zaria disagrees with Milea, citing that entrepreneurial folk like those of this island must have abandoned it and settled someplace else. Once they reach a known port, they will learn more about what has happened on Pirate Island.

The light of the setting sun lingers enough to keep strong shadows at bay. It is likely to last at least a few more hours in the tropics. The ocean breeze stirs the hair of the two women and accompanies them in their walk. Three large dragonflies buzz past the travelers, catching their attention. Milea focuses on them, noting that they are the only insects seen on the entire island so far. They reach the cave entrance a short time later and stare into the cavernous opening as it yawns in front of them.

A large row of stalagmites lines the floor of the entrance and resembles jagged teeth. Stalactites hanging above add to the effect of teeth complete with a strange green liquid dripping from them. The pools of the liquid give off an eerie glow that illuminate a short distance past the entrance. Zaria peers into the cave and reports that there is enough light from the green liquid to guide their way.

A foul wind exits the cave and slaps into both women. Milea takes a step back and covers her nose to protect herself from the stench that strikes her. It is worse than the mangy boar they just faced and disposed of. Zaria covers her mouth and turns away from the stench, then perks up when she feels the breeze switch, going into the cave. Milea feels the switch of the wind as well and again as it changes once again to exit the cave.

"Is this thing breathing?" Zaria inquires.

"It appears to do so," Milea responds. "Could it be the trick of the ocean?"

"I don't know. But with this changing wind and those strange teeth-like carvings it gives the illusion of being alive," Zaria said. "Do we still go in?"

"Let me see," Milea pulls out a map from Zaria's backpack. "According to the map. Yes, we do go in. It points to this as being the home of the Fáidh of Desitana."

"You're serious, aren't you?" Zaria inquires as she takes the map and scours over it. "Dammit. Then again, strange fellows live in strange places."

"That they do, dear cat of shadows," Milea said.

"The only good thing I sense about this cave is that I can use my capabilities freely," Zaria grumbles as she hands the map back. "Just in case there is trouble, I will go first."

"Considering this island is uninhabited except for the one we seek I should hope trouble is at a minimum," Milea reasons.

Zaria adjusts her belt of daggers and then heads into the shadows of the cave as the winds once again exit it. This time it makes an audible moan as it sifts through the stalagmites. Milea is careful as she follows the woman into the structure, being surefooted enough to avoid the green pools. Dripping water echoes from deep within the darkness, beckoning them to travel further. Zaria pauses to allow her eyes to adjust to the twilight of the cave and so that Milea can catch up.

A very narrow path cuts through the stalagmites and continues into the distance as far as they could see. Milea stops next to Zaria as the shiadokat takes in their path through the cave. The darkness is unusual, almost mischievous at times. Zaria takes the lead once again and tells Milea to follow her, step by step. The suggestion is obeyed as they traverse deeper and deeper into darkness.

The cave starts to lighten as the two move forward, making the explorers pause in their tracks. Milea looks down to study the ground and notices that it is bright pink with strange green liquid pools in the folds of the ground. Occasionally, the liquid bubbles but does not appear to eat the floor. The stalactites and stalagmites combine to make full columns of natural coral.

Several of the columns together form a cathedral effect within the great halls of the cavern. Small lizards scurry around and climb up the columns to avoid the intruders. Several of them flash their stomachs at the women as if to entice or warn them. Milea walks over to the column and touches it with a scowl. The texture is squishy and warm to her fingertips. She removes her hand and wipes it on her pant leg to neutralize the feel of the stone.

"I don't like the looks of this," Milea said. "I really do not like the feel. This place has either a very strong enchantment or very horrible curse upon it."

"It might be both," Zaria agrees. "Wait a second. I think the wind has stopped."

"It has quite a while ago," Milea informs.

"There's something going on around here," Zaria said as she observes the lizards scattering around.

"Let's not linger here then," Milea suggests. "I do not want to run into anything like the mangy boar. Especially in close quarters."

The dancing shadows on the wall catch Zaria's attention as she looks around to find the source of the movement. She peers up into the deep shadows of the ceiling and sees nothing so far. A deep animal-like growl emits from the shiadokat as she once again leads the way into the cave. Milea turns around to glance behind as she to senses something is watching and following them. She hesitates a moment before following Zaria down the path. Steam turns into fog as the humidity level rises around them and the foul odor that they contended with is replaced by the smells of the salty ocean.

The light of the cave changes to a tinge of yellow and the lizards all but disappear. The two stop at the crest of a strange hill to take in the rest of their path. The narrow causeway they had been following has open into a large, infinite cavern. The strange light is emitting from large orbs in the ceiling that resemble the perfect round spheres of a sea creature's eggs. They are dangling from strands of green slime that somehow keeps them from falling to the ground. Zaria's enhanced sight grants her the ability to see movement within the lights. Milea frowns at the news until she notices something speed across the floor.

"What was that?" Milea muses.

"What was what?" Zaria counters.

The lights flicker as the unknown stalker moves about with unnerving speed. The dangling orbs shift and move as a breeze from the stalker presses around them. Milea causes her sword to appear in hand as she follows the movements of the impending attacker. Zaria pulls her dagger and pinpoints on the figure with intent to bring it down. The stalker drops from the ceiling surprising both Zaria and Milea. The shiadokat cusses and then places a hand upon Milea's arm to prevent an attack when she recognizes the stalker.

The invader emits a strange primeval scream before dancing in place and barking a strange chant. Zaria hesitates a little then releases the sorceress's arm and stares at the being. Milea keeps her sword in hand and places her free hand upon her hip as she arches an eyebrow.

The stalker is now glowing a rainbow of colors, the height of which blinds Zaria for a short period of time. The air crackles with energy resulting with the unknown woman flies backwards and into one of the stalagmites. The stalker blinks several times from the blow and then hops to her feet. She starts to stomp in place in similar fashion of a toddler throwing a temper tantrum.

"How dare you reverse the curse that I wanted to place upon you," the woman scolds with an angry tone.

"I did not reverse it. I only shielded us from the results of you reversing your own incantation." Milea corrects in a calm way.

"Wait," the strange woman blinks twice then make a sound of recognition. "I know you! I really, really know you. You are the sorceress I saw in the glass."

"I'm glad you know me, but I have no idea who you are," Milea said matter-of-factly.

"Yes, you do know me," the strange woman protests. "I am the one that you're looking for. I really, really, am."

"Yeah," Zaria rubs the back of her neck. "I think we should cut this and go see if we can find Oswind. Maybe he knows where we can find the other half of that book."

"I think you are right," Milea agrees.

"Oswind! The Keeper of the Dead. The Eltis who never returned any of my summoning, the bastard," The strange woman interrupts the conversation. "Yes, yes, you will need his help. Oh! Follow me and I will show you my vision."

Milea runs her fingers over her eyes and massages the bridge of her nose in attempt to avoid a headache while she witnesses the strange woman does a bizarre dance. The madwoman then runs around her guests twice while laughing in hysterics. She stops in front of them, hops in place momentarily, then runs towards the back of the cave. She does not get far when she collides with another stalagmite. The blow sends her to the floor and flat onto her back.

The madwoman cusses and rubs her forehead a little. She stands up, shakes off the effects of the blow, then, quaking with maddened laughter, continues her run into the darkened tunnel. The sound of her hysteria echoes for several seconds and then quiets. Milea stares after the strange being, shakes her head, then turns to leave the cavern. Zaria is gentle as she takes hold of the sorceress's hand and encourages her to follow the madwoman.

"I think she may have hit one too many stalagmites in her lifetime," Zaria reasons.

"I don't think the cave is entirely at fault for her unusual behavior," Milea explains. "I am having a few second thoughts about this quest."

"Are you going to be the one to tell Keela that you changed your mind?" Zaria inquires in a matter-of-fact way.

"After this encounter I am very tempted to do so," Milea said in all honesty. "However, the wrath of Keela far exceeds any uncomfortable feeling I have at this present moment."

"I've seen her full wrath twice in my lifetime and I don't want to see it again," Zaria explains and puts her dagger away. "I will go into the shadows first and I want you to follow me just in case this woman is some sort of strange guardian of this unnatural place."

"Let's go before I have a foolhardy change of mind," Milea offers.

Mad laughter echoes around the two adventurers, making it hard to pinpoint the location of the strange woman. They locate a tunnel in the general direction of her travel and decide to follow her inside. Zaria peers into the darkness, yet even her enhanced eyesight could not penetrate the deep shadows within. Milea casts a light spell and directs it into the darkness in front.

The orb bobs and wiggles, illuminating the way as they take their hesitant steps into the tunnel. Every once in a while, the sound of laughter from their hostess greets them, yet they do not see the owner of the voice. Darkness soon starts to fade showing they have reached the end of the tunnel. The room they walk into is both well-lit and airy, causing Milea to pause, look around and then look behind her. She frowns when she sees that the tunnel they once exited is now replaced by a set of strong columns and a breathtaking view of the ocean. The Lady of the Night is sitting among the waves with sails down as the ship and crew await the return of Milea and Zaria.

"Our hostess seems to have disappeared," Milea said. "As has our way out."

"The Fáidh of Desitana was once an Eltis," Zaria explains. "I do not remember all her capabilities. I only remember that she fell into madness after she betrayed the trust of friends and family."

"Eltis, you say," Milea stares at her companion. "That is alarming. I do not want to linger in this space that she knows intimately. Can you track her so we can get out of here sooner rather than later?"

"When the wind blows you can smell her just up the way," Zaria nods to another tunnel. "I'll take the lead again just in case she has set some strange trap."

"Perhaps I should do so, considering she reversed her own incantation earlier," Milea suggests. "It looks like the tunnel is wide enough for us to go down, side-by-side."

"I won't argue with you," Zaria said.

They walk past a large altar-like stone and into the new tunnel following footprints they presume to belong to their hostess. The floor goes from the crunching of seashells to the echo of hardened stone. Milea pauses when she notices the change of flooring and looks down to see what appears to be castle stone under her feet. She looks up and around and calls to Zaria to pause when she sees that the tunnel has changed forms once again. It is now a regal hall associated with a structure fit for royalty.

A wind blows around as a name is whispered on the breeze. Both Milea and Zaria hear the voice and perk up, noticing that it is husky, masculine, and distorted. Milea listens to the language and realizes that she does not recognize it. A strong aura of power in the air urges her to increase her pace to the end of the tunnel. She did not want to stick around long enough to find out who or what is talking, nor did she wish to learn the language. Zaria swears and jogs to catch up with the sorceress.

"Hey, hey slow down," Zaria scolds as she catches up with her. "We don't know what the strange woman has in store for us. Let's use a little caution."

"I sense a powerful being behind the voice that we heard in this tunnel," Milea explains. "When it comes to choosing between the Fáidh of Desitana or this mystery man I'd rather face the Fáidh. If I had to face the owner of this voice it would end in a very bad way."

The hall that they are traveling starts to glow yellow, catching them off guard. The change of color is followed by vibrations shaking the hall. Zaria unleashes language unfit for young ears as she bolts for the other side of the hall. Milea is close behind and is soon running in stride with her. Moments later, they exit the hall just before it collapses. The two stop running in time to avoid a collision with a giant cauldron. They also get a better look at their mad hostess.

She is wearing animal skins to cover her body and she is more than seven feet tall. She walks in a slight crouch with her knees sprawled out and seems barely able to hold her trunk. She turns to see her guests and gasps in surprise. Her eyes shift and change into various colors, and appear animal like as she stares at them. Her thick white hair shifts in the breeze that wafts her pungent odor toward her guests.

Milea involuntarily turns her head and shakes it in order to clear her sinuses. Zaria lets out a strange sound as she covers her nose and backs up in order to protect her sensitive nose from the assault. The woman laughs hysterically at her guests' reactions and does a dance of sorts as she edges her way behind the cauldron and motions them to come closer. Milea looks at the cauldron first, then up at her hostess as she considers the offer. Zaria makes the decision for them to stay put and wait.

"I have many names, yet today I will go by Chaehi," the madwoman informs. "In recent times I have had the title of being the Fáidh of Desitana. I know all about the past, the present, and the multitude of futures that can affect all Bri'al."

"I am here to discover the location of a relic," Milea said.

"You are hesitant and skeptical of me, Milea Sirus, Sorceress of Selvast Forest." Chaehi corrects. "Do not fear, for I do not wish to harm you. I know why you and A'drianis, Daughter of Armels, are here."

"Since you know us and know why we are here," Zaria crosses her arms, "then why don't you let us know where to find it so we can be on our way?"

"You may be shiadokat, A'drianis, but sometimes you need to work on your feline-like patience," Chaehi scolds. "As far as the reason you two are here, you seek to know the way to awaken the sleeping children of Keela, the last great warriors of the Eltis."

"Then you are aware of the reason why I seek them," Milea interjects.

"Ah yes, however, they are placed in their state for a reason and they may be keys to unleashing a great evil," Chaehi informs. "Do you truly wish to usher in a new era that can be suffering or sanctified?"

"What great evil do you speak of?" Milea asks.

"One that will bring Bri'al to its knees, or it can lift us all to utopia," Chaehi said. "Either way, the item that you seek is the other half of the Book of the Eltis."

"You are correct, Chaehi," Milea agrees.

"Oh, good, good, good," Chaehi beams in happiness. "You had me going for a minute there. I thought you were going to asks for something else."

"Is it me, or did she just shift personalities?" Zaria whispers to Milea.

"She did," Milea answers in short.

"The other half of the book is well-guarded, deep within the frozen tundra of the North in the Temple of Nag'teragiea," Chaehi continues, unaware of their conversation. "It's a lovely place in the spring. Have you visited it lately, A'drianis?"

"Frozen tundra of the North, you say. Nope, I'll pass," Zaria shakes her head. "I've never heard of this particular temple, so I don't know where it is let alone visited there."

"I know that," Chaehi boasts.

"So where in Ublivion is it?" Zaria questions.

"Not there, I can assure you, but I really can't tell you any more information than that," Chaehi shrugs.

"But you can tell us how to get there, right? It is only fair since, as you are aware, we came here for the information," Milea reasons. She also has a hand on Zaria's shoulder to keep the shiadokat at bay.

Chaehi paces back and forth as she seems to contemplate Milea's reasoning. Zaria grumbles as she figures that attacking the Fáidh of Desitana is not a good idea. Milea releases her companion then waits as the strange woman talks to herself. From their vantage point, it looks as if Chaehi is arguing about a variety of topics with another, invisible, person.

Among the topics of disagreement is the unknown evil mentioned when they first arrived. Chaehi takes a deep breath as she stops pacing then once again takes position at the cauldron and peers inside of it. The Fáidh of Desitana shakes her head and focuses on her guests with a goofy smile.

"Sure, I guess," Chaehi answers the question posed to her. "It is located further north than anybody should go, just past the kingdom of Selcros. If you continue straight for twenty leagues and turn right, you won't miss it."

"Thank you, Chaehi, for your information," Milea nods in respect, then turns to leave.

"Do not be in a hurry to leave, Milea. There is more that I can help you with," Chaehi offers.

"Like what?" Milea asks as she faces her hostess.

"Finding the book is only half of the quest. You must also find a means to awaken the sleeping Eltis," Chaehi informs her. "For this you will need a key finder. You will need it and your half of the book to open the Temple of Nag'teragiea."

"What other uses does this key-finding device have?" Milea inquires.

"Very observant, child," Chaehi smiles. "The key finder is a means to awaken the sleeping Eltis by locating the items that unlock their chambers. Although shiadokat is very talented, it is easier and far safer to gather the keys and unlock the Eltis."

"I am no amateur, nor am I any kind of slouch when it comes to unlocking and locking doors, traps, and the like," Zaria said, feeling a bit insulted.

"How well I remember, dear shiadokat," Chaehi agrees. "However, you cannot find them, and if you do, I would not recommend you force your way into their chamber. You can end up in worse condition than I am."

"So, with the key finder and the book as a whole we will be able to locate the sleeping Eltis," Milea summarizes. "Where do I locate the key finder?"

"I have it," Chaehi admits. "However, there is only a specific person who travels with you that can use the key. She has the mark of a silver dragon and is pure at heart."

"I know the one that you speak of, Chaehi. Why does she have to be the carrier of this bracelet?" Milea inquires defensively.

"Because all others will be killed the instant they wear it," Chaehi answers in an abrupt manner. "Do you still wish to go through with your quest, Milea? If so, your time is running short."

"Is it, now?" Milea challenges.

"Oh yes indeed," Chaehi grins maliciously. "For you must reach your destination in the far North before the next full moon cycle. One moon cycle has passed while her twin is nearing it. But even on a good wind it is hard to make Selcros in a week, isn't it? You seem to have a dilemma."

"I can get to Selcros...," Milea starts.

"If you are thinking about using your teleportation abilities, my advice is that you do not. At least not all the way to your destination," Chaehi suggests. "It is very dangerous to teleport to ruins such as Nag'teragiea. You never know what is waiting for you or what could happen to you. It would be a shame if you fall into Oswind's lap because you are impatient."

"Then it seems that I have to get started on my journey," Milea said. "Give me the key finder."

"It will be my pleasure," Chaehi said with glee.

The lights in the room darken, catching the attention of both Zaria and Milea. They look around as voices ring out around them, some fair, some foul. Milea's attention returns to Chaehi when she feels a great increase of energy from the woman's direction. The shadow behind the Fáidh of Desitana has begun to shift and form a very different creature from the one represented in front of them.

The cauldron begins to bubble violently as the shadow reaches into it. A few seconds later a golden bracelet floats out of the churning water, gliding towards Zaria. The pure gold jewelry has the head of a lion grinning at the two women with sparkling dark green eyes. Various symbols decorate the bracelet, providing both instructions and warning for those who wear it.

Zaria uses caution as she reaches up. She catches the bracelet when the force holding it lets it go. An intense blue light fills the cavern and blinds all inside, causing more than a few unkind words from the two guests. The light fades and the two women find that they are at the entrance of the cave, looking out. Milea glances over her shoulder to see that the cave itself has been reduced to a few feet. Zaria also sees the strange phenomena and takes the lead back into the open air.

The sun is still hanging in the sky, as if time has stood still while they journeyed inside. Both take in the fact that Chaehi is nowhere around. Neither concern nor curiosity overtakes Zaria or Milea enough to find the Fáidh of Desitana. The two set their sights on the ship in the harbor and the long voyage ahead of them.

Seagulls squeal in glee while flying to their roost for the night. The sun has slip beyond the horizon to allow the stars to twinkle to life. A comet streaks across the sky, leaving a trail of dust in its wake. In the crow's nest, Sonja watches her mother comes down the steep hill towards the ship with Zaria. From their mannerism she figures that something disagreeable has happened during their search for the Fáidh of Desitana. Sonja heralds the return of the adventurers, catching the attention of those on the ship, including the captain, Neil. He perks up and turns toward the island in anticipation of leaving the lagoon before the Dragodu starts to prowl.

Dark clouds appear just beyond the entrance of the lagoon as Milea and Zaria board the ship. A deep growl emits from the clouds as they coagulate near the surface of the water and form into the Dragodu. Sonja lets out a small sound of fear when the ship appears.

The girl shimmies down the mast to avoid detection as the haunted ship drifts past. The Dragodu makes more angry noises as she seems to search the area, unable to locate its quarry. Milea watches the haunted vessel as it continues to move, a contemplative look crosses her features as she tries to figure out how to avoid it.

"The ghost ship is sailing around the island," Sonja informs her mother. "I don't like it. How do we get rid of it?"

"Apparently it's a difficult thing to do," Vicki answers, overhearing the question. "It is rumored that Ra'jil got rid of it many years ago."

"I'll have to let her know she missed," Sonja said.

"She may not have," Milea offers. "She may very well have destroyed the Dragodu and sent it to the bottom of the sea. There is a strong negative force aboard the ship and something otherworldly is keeping the boat animated."

"Why is the Dragodu stalking us?" Zaria inquires with a scowl.

"Good question," Neil said. "I don't have an answer for that at this time. My guess is that she is after one or more of us on board the ship."

"I don't want to think about that," Vicki remarks.

"I guess no songs or cooking fires tonight. We will be lucky if we can get out," Brion offers.

"We don't have time to wait for it to leave us alone," Milea said.

The sorceress stares off into the distance as Zaria relays to the crew the encounter with the Fáidh of Desitana. The next time one of the moons would be full is about three weeks from tonight. It takes at least twice that long, if not longer, to get to Selcros and perhaps another week or even a month to get to the Temple of Nag'teragiea. The warning about the speediest travel, teleportation, did not set well with Milea.

However, the Fáidh did sympathize and say that they might use mystical travels part of the way. Milea concludes that perhaps she could use them to travel at least ninety percent of the distance to her destination. She leans upon the rail of the ship as her mind drifts over to where that may be.

"Selcros, you say," Neil said as he sits down on the ledge above the cabin door. "I've gone to Selcros once before. It's colder than Oswind's touch up there."

"Eh, Selcros is not a bad place this time of year," Brion assures. "If I remember right, it's spring up there right now."

"Are you sure? Moreover, how would you know anyway, Mr. Sea-sickness? The only way up there is by boat," Vicki points out as she faces her traveling buddy.

"By boat, unless you know someone that can teleport you there," Zaria agrees.

"We went by boat," Brion explains. "It was the worst ride of my life. Charged to protect my sister, Eryn, while she was on a diplomatic visit. It turns out that she did not need me to protect her but I needed her for the same reason."

"What is the closest port to Selcros?" Milea inquires.

"I can think of a handful off the top of my head," Neil said. "Let me get my maps and I will narrow it down for you."

"Make sure the port is friendly, brother," Vicki reminds him.

"What was wrong with Churn?" Neil asks, then grins at his sibling's scolding look. "Fine, I'll make sure we do not go somewhere hazard-ous." He hops off the ledge and heads to the trapdoor leading inside the hull.

"It should be safe enough," Brion said. "Selcros controls all ports within seven days of their capital city."

"If you are thinking about using teleportation to get close to our destination, Milea. I recommend that you do so a league or two away from this island," Zaria warns. "Chaehi may still be around and I'm not sure if I trust her."

"I do not trust her," Milea admits. "However, it is going to take a little trickery to force the Dragodu to turn away. Let me contact Frey to see if she can lend us a little assistance."

"Either way we go, we will be going past the Holbek desert," Vicki offers as she finishes tying a rope.

"Isn't that the continent where Tandon and Cholbek reside?" Brion inquires. "It is a pretty place, so I've heard. Have you visited it?"

"I have," Vicki nods. "It is beautiful but I'll not be going back there for a little while."

"Why not?" Brion asks. He leans back against the mast as he watches her shrug.

"Let's just say personality issues," Vicki answers with a smile. "The family of the late governor and I are in disagreement."

"That's more than enough information for me," Brion admits as Milea chuckles and heads towards the sleeping cabin.

"Hey, did anybody else see the island move?" Sonja inquires.

Zaria, Vicki, and Brion turn to study the island as the door to the cabin closes behind the sorceress. The ship's cabin is large enough for five cots around the room. It is warm and dry for the most part as well as inviting. Usually, the ladies sleep in the cabin while Neil and Brion go below deck during the voyage. Zaria enters the room in silence and camps on one of the cots as Milea makes her way to the end of the cabin.

The sorceress glances behind and nods a greeting to the shiado-kat before sitting down at a desk with a mirror attached. She smiles at her reflection as she picks up a brush and uses it to tame her flaming mane. The mirror begins to wiggle as her reflection changes at her mystical command. Milea places the brush down and opens her eyes to greet her sibling. Instead, she manages to hold back a few unclean words as she jumps to her feet as the unexpected image solidifies.

"Mother," Milea apologizes. "I am sorry, I thought I contacted Frey."

"You were about to, but I decided to intercept," Keela admits as she focuses on her mortal daughter with humor-filled eyes. "How is your trip so far? Did you contact the Fáidh of Desitana?"

"A'drianis and I did make contact with her," Milea reports. "She gave us a bracelet, instructions on how to find the other half of the book, and a warning of a great evil should the sleeping Eltis ever awaken."

"What great evil does she speak of?" Keela inquires.

"She would not elaborate. She just said it could be great suffering or great salvation," Milea summarizes. "Either way, the sleeping Eltis are the keys to it."

"Without having a full conversation with her, I can hypothesize that her warning is dependent on which side of the coin you stand," Keela offers. "Where is your next destination?"

"I head north to the lands of snow and ice," Milea explains. "The Fáidh of Desitana has instructed me to head to the Temple of Nag'teragiea. It is located above the northern kingdom of Selcros."

"I do not take kindly to cold weather," Keela said. "The temple you are going to is forgotten and consequently abandoned. Yet old temples do have their ghosts. Are you taking Maya with you?"

"I do not have time to go retrieve her from Dorma," Milea reasons. "I have to be up north and at the temple prior to the next full moon."

"I see," Keela muses. "What did you want to contact Frey about?"

"We are still being pursued by the ghost ship, Dragodu," Milea answers. "Everything I have tried has not successfully knocked her off our trail. We need to get a few leagues away from this island so that I can teleport us to a seaport close to Selcros. I am hopeful that Frey could provide little more trickery for us so that we can distance ourselves from both ghost and island."

"A'drianis could not help with this?" Keela inquires.

"I am out of all ideas on how to throw that thing off our tail," Zaria speaks up.

"Hm, it is too bad that Oswind is upset with me at this moment, else your undead predator would be easier to deal with," Keela said and leans back a little. "But I do have a trick that I can use to assist you. I learned it from my sister, a shiadokat like her daughter. You will like this one, A'drianis, as it will suit you quite well."

"I am willing to learn anything I can, especially when it comes from my mother," Zaria perks up. "What does it involve?"

"You will see once you go back outside," Keela smiles with confidence. "Do you need any other assistance, Milea?"

"Not as of right now, Mother. Should I need more help, I will reach out," Milea assures.

"And I will be here," Keela said. "I sensed your twin's anxiety a few nights ago. I have yet to find her. Can you please locate and check on her for me?"

"The place that Maya is in makes it hard for locating her," Milea admits. "I will reach out to see if she is in her room as we travel to Selcros."

"Let me know either way," Keela requests.

The mirror returns to normal and Milea finds herself staring at her own reflection. She closes her eyes in order to get over the shock of communicating with Keela instead of Frey. She has a quiet conversation with Zaria before turning to the mirror once again in order to contact her twin, Maya. Milea ignores the sounds Zaria makes while getting comfortable on the cot as the surface of the mirror becomes wavy once again.

The room inside of the reflection changes from a ship cabin to the brick-and-mortar of a palace. The hair on Milea's reflection changes to coal black as her eyes become a shade darker. Inside the mirror, the woman drops a few unkind words as she stands up and takes a couple of steps back. Milea chuckles from the movement and the language her twin sister expresses opposite her. Inside the mirror, Maya calms down as she leans forward to examine the item and realizes that she is looking at her sister.

"Don't do that," Maya scolds as she sits back down.

"I'm sorry about that. I just want to let you know that we will be going to Selcros instead of returning to Dorma," Milea informs. "Also, Mother is worried about you. I will let her know that you are well."

"I am as fine as I can be considering the circumstances," Maya said. "Ice country, not a place I want to go willingly. How long will you be?"

"That depends on how fast I can get up there and how long it takes to find the relic," Milea answers. "How is your vacation going?"

"Vacation," Maya laughs a little. "Ah, I remember that word so well. Unfortunately, it will not happen this time around."

"Tell me, what did Amadahy do this time?" Milea requests.

"Well, in short, Amadahy and Ra'jil did get into a little battle. No clear winner as something hit me and I got irate," Maya explains. "From there I had a skirmish with Amadahy. When I realized what was happening, she hit me with a null magic spell. Since then, Ra'jil and I are caught in Amadahy's little game until you return."

"What?" Milea said in a slow and even tone.

"Yep," Maya nods and leans on an elbow. "So, no magic for me, and she sent us to the Temple of Krast as a test of skills. Without the use of my magic, I relied on Ra'jil and her mystical skills. That woman is a powerhouse waiting to explode."

"Yes, Ra'jil does not like to use her magic and I am glad that you're still alive," Milea agrees as she sits back and crosses her legs. "What else is happening?"

"The jungle itself is an adventure," Maya recalls. "I owe it to pure luck that we had Cain and Da'los to guide us through."

"They are the best guides for the jungle," Milea agrees.

"Oh, speaking of Da'los, he is currently possessed by Weyma," Maya informs.

"What!" Milea exclaims loudly as she gets to her feet. "How long?"

"From what I can attest to, less than a day." Maya explains.

"As far as Weyma, she has to be drawn out as soon as you can, we don't want her taking root into Da'los for long." Milea offers

"I know that, but how?" Maya challenges, folding her arms and sitting up. "No magic here, remember? When you destroyed my own puppeteer, it was a hell of a magical battle. I still have scars."

"Is Amadahy near you?" Milea inquires. "She really needs to lift that spell so you can get to Weyma without harming Da'los."

"Ra'jil and I both have talked to her about that. She is insisting on a 'test' before she lifts this spell." Maya explains. "We are going to talk to her again, but she does not have a promising record for changing her mind. Do you know of anyone with capabilities like mine?"

"Only one I know of is Zoe but I have not heard from her in a while. She lives in Sedur." Milea sits back down. "I will find Amadahy and confront her about this spell she seems humored about."

"I'll get with Ra'jil and we can come up with a plan." Maya stands. "It is good talking to you, sister. I wish you a safe journey out there."

"Take care, sister." Milea smiles in return.

The mirror goes back to normal as Milea contemplates contacting Keela to inform her of the current situation. Zaria recommends not doing so just yet, but instead try to locate Amadahy. Milea focuses on the mirror once again, causing it to shift and move as it settles on Amadahy's room. It is empty, which does not set well with the sorceress. The mirror shifts once again to focus on her trusted retainer Kay's room, to no avail. It too is empty, as is the home of Cain, the shaman of Dorma.

Milea stares at the mirror as if gathering her thoughts or her temperament. After a moment, she shifts the image to the home of the one currently possessed, Da'los. Behind her, Zaria holds her breath knowing that if the Tragin possessed man is there, Weyma will no doubt challenge the sorceress. Upon seeing the empty, messy, room the shiadokat lets out her breath in relief. Milea, on the other hand, whispers words of frustration for not being able to locate her quarry. The mirror returns to normal as the sorceress stands up and walks towards the door. Zaria hops off her perch and follows the woman outside.

The waves of the lagoon rush to the shore, creating a very relaxing sound. Sonja continues her post to watch the island while those around her go about doing their chores. Neil is standing at the helm of the ship with one of the maps unrolled. He looks up at the stars and then back at his charts in order to locate the ports requested.

The dark clouds from the Dragodu blot out a large section of the night sky, making it frustrating for the navigator to plot his course. Vicki leans forward on the ship's bow and focuses away from the ghost ship to ignore it. The door to the sleeping cabin closes as moonbeams pierce the murky clouds of the ghost ship. They bounce off the hull of the Lady of the Night as she sways in the water. Milea takes a couple steps onto the deck of the ship. She is approaching her daughter when, without warning, the entire vessel illuminates in a bright white light.

The sudden change in lighting causing more than a few sailor's oaths from Zaria as she holds her eyes and falls to her knees. Milea shields her own eyes from the intensity of the light. She hears exclamations of shock from those around her. The light dies down enough for all to recover from it. Zaria growls, then gawks at a white shadow of their ship and crew. The apparition starts to sail towards the ocean outside of the lagoon. Sonja makes the announcement of the second ship and Neil stares at it in disbelief as the image solidifies. The second ship continues to sail out to sea with familiar voices ring out. It disappears around the corner heading out to sea.

The Dragodu howls and goes after the imposter ship, clearing the skies of her evil presence. Brion shakes his head and rubs his eyes with one hand in the disbelief of seeing an image of himself standing on a replica of the ship. Vicki gawks at the now empty space as she recovers from her surprise. Milea gets over from her own shock as she recalls conversation from earlier.

"This is what Keela meant by providing assistance to us," Milea explains as the stars return to the sky. "It seems like she is using a shadow of the ship to lure the Dragodu away."

"That is one hell of a trick," Zaria said, clearly impressed. "I'll have to remember it and give it a try in the future."

"Safe to say that a little elder Eltis assistance has been granted to help us along our way," Neil speaks up and put his chart down. "Get ready to set sail, we depart as soon as we can."

"I'll keep an eye from the crow's nest," Sonja volunteers, before climbing the main mast to her destination.

An atmosphere of calm washes over the entire crew as they await the time to set sail. Milea leans against the rail of the ship and contemplates the next stage in their adventure. Vicki pauses next to the sorceress as she tests various ropes in preparation of the voyage. Neil announces that the closest port to Selcros is a fishing village called Kalb.

Milea tears her attention from the horizon and travels to the helm. Her thoughts and steps are disrupted when a set of sapphire blue eyes flash in front of her. Mad female laughter echoes in the still air around the entire island and is heard by all. The ship rocks violently as Sonja and Vicki both cry out in surprise when two giant tentacles emerge from the water. Zaria swears and dodges another tentacle as she announces that the lagoon entrance is now blocked.

Shrieks of a giant sea creature mingles with the expletives of all passengers on the ship. Ocean water and light gray fluid rains down on all. The ship rocks again from multiple blows to its side. Milea falls onto her backside and rolls out of the way as a tentacle slaps the deck. The sorceress gets to her feet as the ship tilts again from the attacking beast.

A shriek escapes the sea creature's mouth as it tries to bite into the enchanted wood of the vessel. Neil uses his blade to cut through a smaller tentacle then dodges its larger companion as he fights to keep the sea monster from destroying the ship's helm. Vicki calls out to the sorceress as Milea turns in time to be struck by a tentacle.

The sorceress holds on as it sends her over the side of the ship. The embers around Milea's body roar into flames right before she casts a lightning spell straight up the appendage that she is holding onto. The beast yowls and drops the woman that cause its pain and pulls the offended tentacle into the sea. Milea levitates back onto the ship and follows the string of attacking limbs to its source. To her amazement, it is the island itself. The shell of the sea beast somehow provides a path as well as shelter for the Fáidh of Desitana. Multiple giant tentacles shoot up into the air, waving precariously before slapping and attacking the ship. The scrape of the beast's birdlike beak against the wood seem to agitate it further when the ship does not splinter.

"Where in all Ublivorin did this thing come from?" Neil demands as he continues his fight.

"It seems that the Fáidh of Desitana has a previously undetected Guardian," Milea offers.

"The lagoon has closed off as soon as this thing started attacking," Vicki points out. "Any ideas as to how we get out?"

"Vicki, look out!" Sonja yells from above.

The warning comes a little too late. A tentacle grabs hold of Vicki's leg and hoists her hundreds of feet into the air. Sonja swears and hops onto the appendage, climbing it in order to reach her friend. While climbing, she notices the ocean swirling around the giant creature as waves push against the basin of the lagoon. The wall closing them off is somehow connected to the island and is slowly drawing toward the ship. Sonja takes her eyes off the sights below and climbs up to Vicki's location in haste.

"What are you doing, girl?" Vicki blurts out, her mind in a state of confusion.

"Trying to get you off this ride," Sonia answers. "Just don't look down."

"Not what I want to hear," Vicki said.

The tentacle that holds Vicki twists until the woman is upside down and she can see the ocean. Vicki takes in the height as she draws a deep breath. The ship appears a few inches long from her standpoint. Vicki gasps once more as the tentacle nearly drops her. She then unleashes a powerful terror-filled scream. Below, Neil looks up to see his sister and swears an oath to his father when he observes her predicament.

Zaria takes in the situation and folds the shadows around her form. She grows at least a foot taller before she crouches down and jumps into the air with a tiger-like growl. Her body shifts to that of a giant black panther with dragon-like wings. She uses her appendages to climb towards her companions rapidly, honing in on Vicki's screams.

Milea faces the wall that traps them as the attacking beast grabs hold of several parts of the ship to break or bend the vessel toward its mouth. A moan of agony escapes the ship yet it remains intact. Brion dodges and cleaves several of the tentacles at once then looks up when he hears Vicki's faint cry of terror. The lighting around the ship changes to a deep maroon glow as Milea concentrates. The attacking sea creature shrills in surprise and releases the vessel.

Milea gathers the energy around her form and stretches out her hands, aiming at the wall. A mighty yell escapes her as the concentrated energy roars towards the wall. The large column of flames hits its destination, causing it to explode and send pieces of wall, bone, and cartilage into the air. Those on board the deck of the ship dodge the debris as best as possible.

The tentacles of the beast shudder in agony. A geyser of blood gushes from the undersea wound as the beast shrieks in pain and drops its victim as it trembles. Vicki screams for a short time before hitting something dark, warm, and furry. Sonja manages to jump from her perch and land behind Vicki on the back of the shiadokat.

"Am I dead?" Vicki inquires as she touches her frame.

"No. Don't worry you are going to be okay now," Sonja assures.

"What happened?" Vicki runs her fingers through the dark fur. "What is this?"

"Shadow Eltis," Sonja answers with a smile. "That thing is not a Tragin, is it?"

"It would be interesting if it is such a beast," A'drianis answers, causing a sound of surprise from one of her passengers. "Hold on tight, it looks like this thing is getting a second wind."

Vicki gasps in surprise when the shiadokat whips to her left and then up to get away from one of the attacking tentacles. A slew of unkind words comes from the dark creature as the sea beast continues its assault on both ship and passengers. The Lady of the Night groans as she tries to free herself from the attacker. Ropes snap around the perimeter as Milea casts a second spell at the island. The incantation slams into the main shell and shatters it to pieces, yet the creature continues to persist.

Brion slices off yet another tentacle of the beast with his blade, defending himself from the attacks. His sword lights up unexpectedly, causing him to swear and let it go. Instead of falling to the deck, the blade floats then shoot straight up into the air. A'drianis sees the sword then swears as she dodges it and descends to the deck. She has very little time to set all four paws in the shadows of the ship's deck when the floating sword lights up the sky, returning daylight to the area. The shiadokat utter profanities again as the weight of Vicki and Sonja sends her to the deck. The air in her lungs leaves her from the unexpected blow.

"Get off..." Zaria manages with a groan.

Sonja hops to her feet and helps Vicki to stand as night turns to day. Milea shields her eyes as she looks up at the sword to witness it release a powerful bolt of lightning. The air crackles and roars as the lightning slams into the island beast. The sea monster hollers long and loud. The bolts of lightning continue to strike and boil the water around it. Those tentacles holding onto the ship melt into sand as the rest of the beast descends into the water. Neil calls out for everyone to hold onto something as he grabs hold of the wheel.

The water around the sinking island starts to swell rapidly. The tidal wave pushes the ship towards the exit. Brion's sword descends and lands, blade down, in the wood of the ship. Milea surrounds the ship in an arcane shield as it ramps through a part of the remaining wall that she did not destroy. A large amount of sand erupts into the air from the impact and slides off the protective barrier. The momentum from the wave propels the ship forward for a time until they reach calmer water. Brion uses extreme caution to touch the hilt of his sword. He exhales in relief when he notes that whatever powers had activated it are now once again dormant.

"All on deck?" Neil inquires as he looks around.

"We are all here," Milea answers and wipes sweat from her forehead.

"Good. Let's get the ropes repaired, hoist the sails and get the hell out of here," Neil said and properly put his weapon away. "I hope our doppelgänger is sailing in a different direction then we will be."

"What about you, Vicki? Are you okay?" Brion inquires.

"Shaky, but I should be fine," Vicki answers as her voice and body trembles a little bit. "I appreciate heights about as much as I do ghosts."

"You're freezing," Milea said as she touches the woman's shoulder. "Come on, we'll sit you down and see if we can get you some tea to calm your nerves."

"That will be fine," Vicki relents and allows herself to be led to the sleep cabin.

"Brion, take the wheel for a while. I'm going to check on my sister then I'll be back," Neil instructs as he walks away from the helm.

"I'll do my best," Brion assures and takes over the wheel. "The storm clouds went east so I will assume that the Dragodu went that way as well. I think we should head west for a while and then north until Milea wants to use her teleportation abilities to get us to Kalb."

"That will be in about an hour," Zaria said and focuses on the horizon. "Before she does, I'll see that she gets at least a couple of darkened dragonfruits into her system."

"Brion, you said it is spring in Selcros. Is it pretty in the spring?" Sonja inquires as she focuses on the elf.

"It's as beautiful as a pine forest can be in the spring," Brion answers with a little chuckle.

"Pine forests are good, filled with all kinds of shade and shadows," Zaria smiles a little bit. "Anything that we have to be wary of that you can remember?"

"If my memory serves me, the only thing we have to worry about in the spring is an occasional blizzard. But those are rare. I don't recall seeing one make landfall while I spent time there," Brion said. "It also might be a little cool even though it is still springtime."

"A little cool is not bad. I can handle a little cool," Zaria assures.

"How bad is a blizzard? I've never been in one before," Sonja asks.

"It depends on a lot of factors," Brion answers. "I'm told that in general, those in the spring are worse than those in the winter. To be caught out in a spring blizzard is suicidal and only a fool would venture out in it willingly."

"I think we should keep that challenge to ourselves and not test Neil," Zaria offers. "He is reckless enough to accept it."

"Noted. How do you think we ended up on these voyages?" Brion smiles at his memories.

The water splits as the bow of the Lady of the Night cuts effortlessly through the waves. Sonja decides to venture back up into the crow's nest to get a bird's-eye view of the path ahead. An hour later, Milea stands at the helm of the ship and relaxes as she brings up the winds to surround the vessel and all those aboard. Red lights swirl about as a large mystical funnel cloud whips around the ship. The winds increase and then die just as fast. Once the clouds dissipate, the ship and crew are gone.

CHAPTER TWO

Realm of Ice

The winds of a freakish blizzard whip snow and ice around in a punishing way. The sounds of the storm drown out the galloping hooves of a powerful horse. The snow pelts the rider as if the elements themselves are angry. The rider encourages his mount to go faster as they come around a corner and head deep into the large pine forest. The stallion bellows as he jumps over and clears a fallen tree effortlessly, landing without breaking his stride to continue his way. The rider showers the horse with accolades unheard through his thick fur coat.

The tall man ducks under a low hanging branch as his steed increases in speed. He utters a few words of relief that he did not take his own head off. In normal circumstances, he does not ride recklessly during a blizzard such as this; however, he also knows that this spring storm is unusual. He needs to get out of it as soon as possible with a package that he knows his daughter will love in an instant. The sight of the impenetrable walls of the city spurs him to dig his heels into the stallion's sides to encourage more speed; they are close to their destination.

Trumpets from the high tower sound off as the rider approach the gates. Guards gather in a rapid pace as they grab then yank on the chains to pull the gates open in time for the horse to run through. The horse and rider charge through the gates and continue up a steep hill, charging into the inner halls of the castle.

Once he reaches the throne room, the rider pulls on the reins in order to stop the stallion. The horse rears up and slides as he bellows to stop before he hits the stairs. The rider hops off his steed and quickens his pace deeper into the sanctums of the castle. Guards in the hall salute or bow to the man as he heads straight for the queen's chambers.

Small bits of ice tap the windowpane and the winds howl, demanding to be let inside. The crackle of a large flame within an enormous fireplace denies the cold entrance. The queen of Selcros stands in front of a mirror as she takes in her reflection and her situation. She is of average height for the women of this country, standing at just shy of six and a half feet. Her dark green eyes hold mystery and mysticism within them as she peers at her reflection.

The history of the people of Selcros is slowly being lost, however, it is said that they are the descendants of Car'ladens and elves. The people of Bri'al bestow upon them the name of Alnis for this far north tribe of hearty folk. Yet the queen looks different than the rest of the country's people. She rubs her hand and notices that she has a slightly darker hue than those around her, including her husband and stepson. Her black hair is darker than most in this country, leading her to believe that her mother may have been stranded here for a time. The wind taps at the window once again, catching the queen's attention, beckoning her to walk over. She stares out at the forest as she remembers her childhood running among the darkened paths of the pines.

Many adventures both real and imaginary trickle through her memory, causing her to smile a little. She will not admit it to her husband, yet she does miss freedom from the palace. Often times she would let her mind wander during important events. Perhaps she should walk among the forest occasionally, to satisfy her longing for adventure.

The queen turns her head slightly when she hears her door open and notices her adopted daughter entering the room. Unlike herself, the child is considered human. The young woman has a good command of her mystical abilities.

The queen faces her visitor and studies her, noticing that the girl is no longer a child but has blossomed into a full-grown woman. Her figure is hidden under a long red gown and robe. The queen focuses on the young woman's eyes, noting that they are still the color of a winter sky. The girl, now a woman, stands at a voluptuous five feet and seven inches in height.

"Mom, where do you think Dad went?" the young woman inquires as she sits on the bed.

"Your father likes the sport of riding into blizzards, as he feels it is best to hunt his prey that way," the queen explains in a gentle manner. "One day I will ask him to take you with him, Wyntre. You are old enough to go out on the hunt."

"No thank you, I'd rather not," Wyntre said. "I'd rather marry a strong king like father so I don't have to hunt."

"In order to find such a quarry, you have to be a little bit of a huntress," the queen offers.

"Is that how you and father met?" Wyntre inquires. "You hunted him down?"

"No," the queen answers truthfully. "I am the prey."

The door to the queen's chamber slams open. Wyntre jumps in surprise and the temperature in the room to plunge as the queen faces the intruder. The flames in the fireplace shrink to a minimum as the queen's abilities come to frosty life. The intruder hesitates as the two occupants look him over. The queen tilts her head to one side and then straightens up and allows her abilities to quiet once again.

The room gradually warms back up as the fire increases in size. Although his seven-foot height does little in identifying him, since most men of Selcros are that or a little taller, the queen can identify the intruder by his rash and bold behavior.

"What have we got here?" the queen inquires as she adjusts her posture and focuses on the intruder. "Are you a bear that can walk as a man or are you a man posing as a bear? Either way you should depart before my husband gets home. I am sure that if you are indeed a bear you will make a grand trophy."

"Trophy?" the man's deep voice rumbles as he laughs. "I believe you are a much finer catch than any bear, Dysis."

The intruder removes his hood and hat to reveal salt and-pepper colored hair and hardened facial features. A warm smile spread across his features as he gazes at the queen, taking in every curve that he knows she has. Queen Dysis stands her ground as he approaches her and pulls her into an embrace. He nuzzles her neck and whispered something in her ear before gently kissing her. An unexpected brush against her breast causes the queen to separate from her husband. She takes a further step back when she notices his shirt is wiggling unnaturally.

"Koro, what is that?" Dysis inquires, pointing to his shirt.

"Hmm," the king has a look of confusion on his face at first, then realizes her inquiry. "Oh, my little passenger that I found in the snow. He is almost frozen to death, but I kept him as warm as I could. He is a fighter, that is for sure."

King Koro finishes taking off the fur covering his upper body that had kept both himself and his passenger warm during the ride to the castle. A snow leopard cub shivers against his broad and battle-scarred chest. It is smaller than many cubs his age and his spots seem to run together into stripes upon his forehead. Dysis stares at the cub, noticing that the eyes are brighter than many animals his age. She barely hears Wyntre when the young woman stands up and gasps in surprise. A high-pitched sound of glee escapes the young woman as she runs past the queen and straight to the cub being held by her father.

"Oh, so cute and cold," Wyntre said. "Father, can I keep him? I adore him already."

"Of course, you can keep him, that is why I bought him here," Koro answers. "I did not see his mother anywhere and his siblings were already frozen to death."

"Koro, you know the laws of Nature, you should have left him there," Dysis warns. "If he is to survive, Nature will find a way."

"No need to revert back to your childhood, love," Koro assures. "You are in a more civil environment now. Besides, he is cute and I think he is something special. He will become a protector for Wyntre when he grows up."

"My childhood has nothing to do with the fact that this feline is a wild animal," Dysis assures. "In fact, it lends me the knowledge to know that to trust such an animal is foolish. Especially as he grows."

"Eh, he's young enough that he can be trained," Koro dismisses the worry and turns towards his child. "What are you going to name him, Wyntre?"

"How about Snowpuff?" Wyntre announces and smiles when the feline appears to make a face. "He loves it!"

"I don't think that is a face of joy, but he's too weak to protest," Koro chuckles and places a hand on the girl's shoulder. "So, Snowpuff it is."

The queen crosses her arms and watches as Wyntre bounces like six years old as she hugs her new pet. Koro smiles in satisfaction as his daughter gives him a hug and departs the room. Dysis features reflect her displeasure at the entire experience. She returns to her spot at the window and stares out at the distant mountain. Known as Oswind's Throne, the intimidating landmass is at the beginning of an impenetrable mountain range. There is an ancient city located at the base of the mountain that has borne witness to the death of Dysis's only child by birth.

The queen's shoulders sag a little as she recalls the day that a powerful evil sorceress came to Selcros and stole the newborn from her crib. The evil woman then took the child to the base of the mountain and sacrificed her. Dysis jumps a little when Koro wraps his arms around her waist and places a soft kiss upon the back of her neck.

"Not tonight, Koro," Dysis said and pulls away. "I am neither in the mood nor feeling well."

"Is it because tonight would have been Chastity's coming-of-age birthday?" Koro inquires.

"That is part of it, yes. I am also still displeased about Snowpuff," Dysis answers.

"Snowpuff can stay and you will see how easy it is to tame an animal, love," Koro assures. "As far as vengeance for the death of our daughter, her murderer will make the mistake of returning. Folks that evil tend to have very short memories."

"I hope that someone in all Bri'al has already dealt with her and sent her deep into the bowels of Ublivion so that she may never return to Selcros," Dysis said, her words dripping with cold anger. "However, if she does, I will deal with her and destroy her in the form of new fallen snow."

"A cold and well deserving end to such a foul being," Koro said and caresses the queen's shoulder. "Now I wish to turn your thoughts away from the pain caused on this night and fill your mind with warmer and more sensual views."

The queen closes her eyes and turns her head as the king plants his lips upon her neck. He pulls her close to his body once again. She could feel the temperature upon his flesh rise as his hands finds the opening in the back of her gown. Dysis knows that no matter what she says, nothing is going to discourage Koro tonight. A strong knock upon the door brings reprieve to the queen as her husband lets out an angry sound and separates from her once more.

The knock comes again before the door opens and a tall, proud, knight marches into the room a couple of steps then pauses. He takes off his helmet and reveals features like the king as he salutes the royal couple to show his respect. Dysis exhales in her relief and retrieves a robe to wrap around her form. Koro takes one look at the intruder and laughs hardily as he goes over to shake his hand and swat him on the shoulder.

"Father, sorry to interrupt," the young man said as he runs fingers through his dark hair to straighten it. The locks fall back to his shoulders.

"Qwest, my son, welcome back," Koro said with joyous tones. "What news do you have from the front?"

"The news is not good, I'm afraid," Qwest answers. "It appears that our enemy is more organized than they used to be. It's as if some of the chieftains have finally grown a brain."

"That is not what I want to hear," Koro frowns at the news.

"Perhaps you and your son should go to the war room and talk it over," Dysis suggests.

"That would depend," Koro said without turning around. "Qwest, is there anything that needs my immediate attention tonight?"

"No, father. All the information that I have can wait until tomorrow morning," Qwest answers. "My only mission tonight is to let you know that I made it back to the castle during this spring storm."

"Then I shall see you in the morning," Koro dismisses him and faces his wife once again.

"I also want to let you know that a couple of fellas and I have witnessed fighting among the ice dragons," Qwest informs. "Perhaps they are trying to establish a hierarchy once again. Their usual leader is missing in action."

"Really," Koro glances over his shoulder. "We will talk in more detail later."

The queen sits on her bed as she takes in the brief news provided by her stepson. The fighting among the ice dragons is a shock to her, usually they have stable leadership. Dysis lets her mind wander as she tries to remember the last time she saw an ice dragon. Koro's hands upon her abdomen bring Dysis back to her present reality. She closes her eyes as the king removes the robe that she had just wrapped herself in and once again starts to work on her gown.

A few hours later Dysis is awakened by the sound of the large clock located in the town center as it strikes, marking the hour of nine o'clock. The queen takes time to shift until she is sitting on the edge of her bed, noting that her husband is no longer there. He had left an hour and a half earlier, while she slept. Dysis dresses herself and pulls her robe back on, tying it securely to her waist as she approaches the door leading to the hall.

The queen opens her chamber door and listens. She hears the voices of her husband and stepson somewhere down the dark corridor. Dysis steps out into the hall and walks towards the voices. Her instincts cause her to hesitate when she comes to a window. She looks out to see that the spring blizzard is slowing down. The ships on the harbor bear the wrath of the storm and are covered in ice and snow. Large chunks of ice float up and down with the waves of the ocean as it crashes against the shore.

Dysis peers out into the ocean and is able to distinguish the outline of a small ship from the gloom as it makes its way into the harbor. It is moving in an odd way, as if against the wind, and faster than most the same size. The small vessel wins the fight against the elements as it reaches the destination and ties up to the pier. Dysis continues to watch the ship a little longer before she decides she is not up to arguing with her husband tonight. The queen tears her gaze away from the window and goes back into her room, closing the door behind.

The heavy door of the inn opens with a thump as Brion, assisted by the winds, enters the establishment. The door struggles to stay open as Sonja rushes through, sliding to a stop and stomping a little to warm up from her ordeal. The girl hesitates in her movements when she trains her eyes upwards to observe the permanent residents of the north, the Alnis. Sonja notes that the men are shaggier than the southern Car'laden, while the women are more muscular than their cousins. Vicki walks in next and touches Sonja on the shoulder to break the girl's self-trance. The L'vane woman then calmly continues to the large fireplace near the rear of the room and the empty table next to it.

Sonja lets out a whoop of joy as she hurries after Vicki. Zaria bursts in next and does not stop or slow down as she heads straight to the hearth. Milea then approaches the threshold and is hit by a strong gust of wind before she can pass through the doorway. It drives her against the doorframe, harshly, then allows her to proceed into the inn. Milea presses into the building and lets her hood fall as she turns to peer out the door at the storm, a frown gracing her features.

Several of the inn's residents glance up each time the door opens. The winds whistle as if angry at the strangers for invading this land of ice and snow. Milea grumbles and turns to glance around the room in search of her daughter and companions. She spots them as one of the larger men stands up and heads out the open door.

The sorceress dodges the man and continues to the fireplace to join the others already there. Neil dodges the exiting man as he enters last and helps Brion close the door. The winds catch the object once more and attempt to force it back open. The men hold on as the element yields to the strength of the two visitors. Brion and Neil then follow Milea to the back of the establishment as Vicki waves to them from the table she confiscated.

"Spring weather," Neil comments as he takes his coat off and places it on the back of a chair.

"According to the weather, spring is still sleeping," Brion agrees, sitting down in one of the large chairs.

"It needs to wake up," Sonja rubs her arms and pulls her legs to her chest. "Is it hibernating?"

"I need to be hibernating," Zaria grumbles and crosses her legs under with room to spare in her chair. "Never seen or smelt a hairy Car'laden before, though. Until now."

"They are the Alnis," Brion explains. "I'm not sure about the whole legend but the Alnis are the descendants of a northern band of elves and a shipload of lost Car'ladens from the south."

"Must have been more than one ship," Vicki observes. "You and your sister where here at one point?"

"Yes, diplomatic mission. I think either a trade agreement or some sort of meet and greet," Brion explains. "Lady Eryn and the Prince of Selcros, Qwest, were once betrothed but decided to end it. I don't think it would have worked out for them anyway."

"Arranged   marriages rarely do," Milea said absentmindedly.

Milea looks up as loud, barking, laughter erupts over the constant chatter of the tavern and drowns out the breaking of a few glasses by either staff or customers. A large, six-and-a-half-foot woman with ample breasts makes her way to the table carrying a tray full of beverages. The waitress's nut-brown hair has a few braids in it with the rest of it falling and flowing around her shoulders. The woman focuses on Brion and her features brighten with humor as she recognizes him. A grin lights up the woman's face as she arrives at her destination and puts her tray down.

"Lord Brion, welcome back to Selcros," the waitress greets with great excitement. "It's been a while, how is your sister?"

"Last I saw her, she's doing very well," Brion admits. "How is everything here, Colleen?"

"Business as usual," Colleen answers and places the beverages on the table "What can I get for you and your guests?"

"What do you have on the menu?" Vicki inquires.

"And," Neil adds as he pushes Sonja's beverage away from her, "what do you have with no alcohol?"

"Oh? A younger, I am sorry," Colleen apologizes. "We have the house stew and the inn mistress's hot chocolate. Both are excellent. One round will warm and fill you up."

"How much for the meal and a couple of rooms for the night?" Zaria inquires.

"Meals on me. I will ask father how much he wants to charge for the room," Colleen offers. "My mistake for bringing inappropriate drinks to the table."

The glasses rattle as Colleen finishes collecting them and hoists them back above her shoulder. Her muscular arm holds the heavy tray steady as she whirls around and heads back to the bar. Milea smiles a little when she hears Neil comment on the alcohol content of the beverage. Sonja assures him that she did not drink or even smell the glass, her fascination with the Alnis having distracted her.

The group falls into quiet conversation as a few more curious residents glance their way, occasionally. Milea meets a few gazes and notes that more than one of the men would react a little, then turn away. The exception is a very large seven-foot man lumbering toward the table. He is carrying two large trays, one in each hand, held up by massive arms above his head. The large man releases a belly laugh as he nears, noting that Brion is sitting between Vicki and Milea.

"Not a word, Leon," Brion warns, seeing the mischief in the inn-keeper's eyes.

"Of course, Lord Brion," the innkeeper manages to keep his chuckle to a low rumble as he speaks. "Welcome back, who are your guests and how long will you be staying?"

"We are not here for long, just enough time to rest, fill up and recover from our trip, then we'll be on our way," Milea informs the innkeeper.

"Eh," Leon focuses on the lady. "You look unfortunately famil-iar. Are you Maya Sirus?"

"No," Milea answers with caution, "Why is it unfortunate that I look like Maya?"

"An unfortunate event happened here in Selcros, and the anni-versary is tonight," Leon answers cryptically. "Maya Sirus's participation in this event was a heinous crime. I am glad that you are not her. A word of caution to you, many Alnis do not take a sec-ond look. Some fool will mistake you for your doppelgänger and attack without thought, be careful while you are here in Selcros."

"Thank you, Leon, I will be mindful," Milea said.

"You are very welcome, milady," Leon nods in respect. "Colleen told me that she is paying for meals due to an error tonight. I will one up her and give you your rooms on the house. Glad to see you again, Lord Brion."

"Well, I'm ecstatic," Vicki said in enthusiasm. "Thanks, Lord Brion."

"I'm happy too, means I don't have to work tonight," Neil grins. "Many thanks to you, Lord Brion." He bows playfully.

"Yeah, yeah..." Brion waves the formalities away.

Leon chuckles at the scene as he passes out the steaming bowls of stew and the hot chocolate to the table. He stacks his trays and walks away as the group indulges in their meal. Sonja sipped her beverage at first then starts to gulp it down at a fast pace. Milea scolds her child, preferring the girl to drink the hot liquid in a much slower rate. Zaria digs into her stew, a very thick meal, as the night's entertainment trips onto the stage.

A regional man, his build suggests that he is more a warrior than a bard despite the elaborate guitar he clutches in his hand. Milea watches as the man staggers to one of the chairs that is at the center of the stage and sits down, almost missing his target. The audience laughs without mercy as he gives a few drunken swears, denouncing the humor of his entrance.

Neil places a spoonful of stew in his mouth then just about breaks his teeth when the entertainer strikes a bad note on the guitar and starts to howl out a song. Vicki drops her utensil, in either shock or awe from the horrible way the entertainer sings. Zaria chokes on her meal and is swatted on the back by Milea to help clear her airways.

Sonja drops her own fork and covers her ears, unable to take this method of torture. Brion tries his best to ignore the man as he stares into his meal. Milea sees that the rest of the guests around the room appear to be reacting in a similar way to her small group. Many of the patrons just stand and leave the establishment altogether. Leon shakes his head as he endures the entertainer's torturous performance.

"Oh, for the love of all, shut up!" Neil stands and shouts above the noise. "Where did you learn how to sing? You sound more like nails scraping against a slate board than any type of singer."

"Neil, do not insult the Alnis. There is already enough tension in the air," Milea warns as many of the audience members turn to focus on the speaker.

"I know," Neil turns his attention to his employer, "but he is killing that song. I doubt if he knows the words, let alone the rhythm to sing it. In fact, he's so lit I doubt if he knows any songs right now."

"I suppose you can do a better job," the entertainer bellows out with irritation, setting the guitar to the side.

"Damn right I can do a better job," Neil turns his attention back to the stage. "Even if I were twice as drunk as you, I could do a better job."

"What happened to relaxing for the evening and enjoying the meal?" Brion inquires in a hush tone.

"I'm sorry, but Neil's right. This man is hurting an all-time favorite," Vicki stands up as well. "He must have heard us perform it in the South once or twice. I'm sure Ra'jil, rest her soul, would not like the way he's butchering her legend."

"What? You mean he is trying to sing about Ra'jil?" Zaria asks, flabbergasted.

"Yeah, Ra'jil would smack him good if she were here," Sonja acknowledges.

"If I had recognized it, I'd have done the honor myself," Milea volunteers.

"How do you know the song, shorty?" the entertainer challenges.

"Because I wrote it," Neil answers as he and Vicki make their way to the stage. "These good people deserve something more entertaining than the nightmares they will have from the howling you present."

"So, we are going to show him how it's done, brother," Vicki stretches as she walks.

"You know it, sis," Neil agrees and hops on the stage. "Let's see if we can get them out of their seats with the way this song is really supposed to sound."

"I'll take that," Vicki picks up the guitar and walks away from the entertainer to sit on the side of the stage.

Milea sits back while Vicki strums the guitar and tunes her confiscated instrument. Neil rouses the audience with a few cheers as well as accolades. The entire house thunders with the voices of the proud seamen of Selcros for several minutes. Neil stomps his foot on the stage, using it as a deep bass drum.

Vicki hits every note perfectly as her brother begins to sing the song. His voice carrying beyond the confines of the walls of the inn. Milea turns her attention to the bar when she sees movement there. Leon straightens up in shock, his jaw slack. Colleen whacks her father on the back in order to make sure he is still breathing. Her assistance just about causes the big man to stumble and hit the floor from the force of her hand.

Audience participation is at a high as Neil, now standing on a chair, leans his perch back at a precarious angle as he bounces and continues into his third song. Brion and Milea converse about the mystical way that the Dresden siblings take control of a room of strangers. Zaria disappears into the shadows to take advantage of the distraction on the stage. Sonja claps and bounces to the beat with the rest of the audience.

On the stage, the siblings artfully trade places as Neil retrieves the guitar from Vicki. A powerful high tempo melody exits the woman, filling the room and bringing a few passersby in from the cold. By the time she finishes her song, the audience is on its feet, clapping, and the entire floor of the inn is full.

"That turned out to be a bit of fun," Vicki said. "What do you think, brother? Give a little more of the show while we are up here?"

"I have an idea; however, we will need another instrument," Neil says and turns to the bar. "My good man, do you have another string instrument?"

The tavern is abuzz as Leon leans his head back and stares at the ceiling a moment in thought. After a few seconds he bends down and tells his daughter to go retrieve the instrument requested. Milea sips on her beverage as she witnesses Neil go over to Vicki and speak to her out of earshot of the audience. Vicki seems stunned at first before her features light up with glee as an impish grin spread across her face. Vicki turns her gaze, bit by bit, to focus on Brion. The elf meets the l'vane's stare and arches an eyebrow as he tilts his head to one side. Vicki chuckles a little and faces Brion completely, placing a hand on her hip.

"Come on up, Brion," Vicki calls out.

"Why?" Brion questions his companion.

"Might as well, Brion. If you don't, she will continue to persist until you give in," Neil coaxes, as he accepts the mandolin brought to him by the staff.

"He's right, you know," Vicki agrees.

"Tinc," Brion grumbles as he stands.

Cheers go up as Brion finishes off his beverage and places the tankard down. He then heads to the stage, encouraged by the audience. Zaria uses cat like stealth to retake her seat as Brion reaches his destination and hops onto the stage. The shiadokat places several cups of warm milk and hot chocolate on the table to share with

Sonja. The girl makes a happy sound at the sight of the beverages. Milea smiles at the enthusiasm of her daughter and the audience as Brion picks up the guitar and sits down on a barstool next to Neil.

The melody from the stage is slow and soothing, keeping time with the measured tick of melting snow striking a piece of metal outside a window. The lights in the room dim, alerting Milea as she glances over to Zaria. The shiadokat admits to dimming the lights and nods to the audience. Many of the members are enjoying the ballad that Neil is singing about love lost and found.

Vicki stretches and stands from her seat as the tempo of the music speeds up a little. She claps out a beat to which the audience members participate. Brion and Neil speed up the rhythm of the music even more. The music ends in abruptness bringing the audience to their feet with the thunder of applause. There are many who shout out for more from the new entertainers on the stage. The former musician curses and swears as he staggers off the stage, then out of the tavern. Milea lifts a glass in salute to the performers as the audience settles back down.

A member of the audience stands up and shouts out that he will pay five hundred coins and a round of ale for the entire house if they sing one more song. A second man rises to his feet and doubles the offer for two more songs. Neil sits back and considers the offer a moment before shouting out that he and his companions will play two more songs if the person funding them would also pay for two rounds of ale and a bowl of the house stew for the entire tavern for two thousand coins.

The two Alnis men bicker back and forth to the point of insulting each other before the second man wins the bid. Milea is gentle as she refuses the drink and food. Neil hands the mandolin to Vicki and goes to the edge of the stage to lead the audience in a loud, rambunctious cheer. The entire establishment shakes from the cheers as Vicki starts playing a fast-paced sailing song on the mandolin. Brion follows her lead on the guitar and strings a few extra notes together much to the amusement of his companions.

The staff of the tavern continue to bring out the beverages and food while Neil stomps the beat of his song on the stage. Milea notices that Neil's eyes are on the person paying for the services. That man has just finished off his first ale and is given the second. He is also done with half of his stew. Neil lets out a mighty cheer before shuffling over to his sister and, with the grace of a dancer, takes the mandolin away from her.

Vicki stands up and does a little 'sailor shuffle' to the front of the stage. Neil and Brion stop the fast-paced song, count to ten and then start playing a slower, more subdued melody. Vicki sways from side to side as she sings her tune, her voice captivating the audience. Milea jumps a little when Zaria elbows her and nods to the man paying for the songs. He is halfway done with his ale and all his meal is gone. On the stage, Neil picks up the pace of the music, which cues Vicki to quicken the lyrics. The sponsor picks up his mug, presses it to his lips and tilts his head back to drain the last contents of his beverage. As he slams it down, the music stops and cheers go off from those inside the establishment. Vicki hops off the stage and approaches the sponsor of the event.

"As agreed, we provided two songs," Vicki said. "Now we are owed two thousand coins."

"That's true and you dance divinely for a short lady. I think I want a little more for the money." the sponsor slurs as he stands and grabs Vicki's arm.

"You are making a grave mistake," Vicki warns.

The man's laughter is cut short and becomes a yell of surprise and some unhinged words as a sudden shadow fall upon him. The angry words turn to astonishment as he finds himself outside and without his clothing on. Leon glares in disapproval as he closes the door to blot out the man and his demands. The room lightens just as fast as it darkened and did not seem to faze the audience. Vicki shakes her head then jumps when she sees Zaria standing next to her and dusting her hands off. The shiadokat then turns to Vicki and smiles with thumbs up.

"Are you alright?" Zaria inquires.

"I'm fine, just did not expect him to fly out the door like that," Vicki assures her.

"Eh, he had it coming to him," Zaria said with a casual wave of her hand. "Lovely entertainment by the way."

"Thank you," Vicki acknowledges. "Although the show at the end may have been more hilarious than the one on the stage."

"I'm sure he will not forget it," Zaria agrees. "Milea and Sonja are waiting for us at the table. I'll go get the guys."

Milea continues to applaud, standing as her companions return to the table. Sonja cheers as her friends take a bow. Colleen sets out three fresh bowls of stew, accompanying each meal with a tankard of mild beer for each performer. Milea orders a glass of wine as the entertainers sit down to indulge in their meal. Neil sips on the beer and decides he likes the flavor. The laughter from the night's entertainment soon turns to plans of their northern trek. They have a little time to get there, however, each minute is precious on this journey. Neil offers to check the conditions for sailing in the morning once the sun comes up.

Brion volunteers to go talk to the king should they need the assistance of an icebreaker.

As the night wears on, Milea excuses herself and escorts her sleepy daughter up the stairs to one of the rooms provided for the night. As soon as the door opens, Sonja walks straight until she bumps into one of the beds and just collapses onto it. Milea goes over to check on her child and is relieved when she hears light snores. She pulls the covers up over Sonja's shoulder and plants a gentle kiss upon the girl's forehead.

Milea then takes in the rest of the room. It is decorated with two large beds and a dresser with a mirror. There is a rustic stool in front of the dresser. Milea sits down in front of the mirror and chuckles at her reflection. The wind has done an incredible job in tangling her locks. A brush appears in her hand as she thinks about the situation of her twin sister. She will inquire more about the circumstances Maya once faced in Selcros tomorrow morning. Right now, Milea decides to check on the situation in Dorma.

Milea hums a soft lullaby as she locks eyes with her reflection for a moment then closes them. The mirror appears to fall away as the reflection morphs to show a tacky, messy, room with a large, well-used bed. The sounds of peeping crickets performing a soft melody floating through the mirror. Milea opens her eyes and scans the image, ignoring the mess. She notices the individual she wishes to communicate with is not there. She makes a sound of curiosity and is about to check another space when the door to the room opens.

A tall athletic woman with dragon wings and dark hair grumbles as she walks into her room. It seems that something has happened that has agitated the tall woman. Milea watches as the dragonigena hastily prepares for her night and flops down on the bed. Milea finishes brushing her hair and waits for several more seconds as she watches the mirror. When it is obvious that she is not being detected, the sorceress places her brush down and peers at the woman in the mirror.

"You know better than to ignore me, Amadahy," Milea said in a matter-of-fact way.

The power level in the room Milea is watching rises in an expeditious way as Amadahy activates her gift, coming to her feet. Milea casually dusts her arm off as her challenger unleashes a lightning spell in her direction. The incantation crackles and spits as it nears the mirror then suddenly reverses, heading straight for the one that cast the spell. Amadahy curses and ducks the lightning, narrowly avoiding the singeing her wings. The bolt slams into the wall, bounces off of it, and strikes the dragonigena woman in the back. The blow sends her careening forward, stopping when she hits the dresser holding the mirror. A chair then slams into Amadahy's legs, forcing her to sit down. Milea calmly meets the agitated gaze of the woman on the other side of her mirror.

"Hello, Amadahy," Milea greets.

"Milea," Amadahy snarls, "What do you want?"

"What I want," Milea repeats. "I want you to use a little common sense. The games you are playing with the life of my sister and guest are unacceptable."

"What are you talking about?" Amadahy snaps. "Maya and Ra'jil are doing perfectly fine here in Dorma."

"Oh really?" Milea said and sits back a little. "Did you remove the nullification spell that you placed on Maya? What of Ra'jil, did you leave her alone so that she can recover? What about Weyma, did you find a way to destroy her?"

"How do you know so much about what is going on in Dorma?" Amadahy questions, eyeing the woman with a suspicious gaze.

"I talked to Maya a few days ago. This is my first opportunity to sit down so that I can talk to you," Milea explains. "I am waiting for my answers."

"I see where Maya got her haughty attitude," Amadahy observes. "So, the answer is no, I did not remove her confines. She needs to learn more respect before I do. As far as Ra'jil, she would die of boredom if she were not antagonized."

"I do not believe either of that, Amadahy," Milea interrupts. "My attitude has nothing to do with Maya's reaction to your bullying."

"It has everything to do with it," Amadahy snaps back. "She needs to learn to respect the Queen of Dorma."

"She respects the queen highly; however, I am not there right now," Milea said. "When I left, I reluctantly put you in charge as steward until my return. I would have given my sister the responsibility but she respectfully declined the offer. I should have been more insistent."

"I am the daughter of Avenshire the Great," Amadahy snarls.

"And I am her protégé," Milea responds in a calm way, "I also defeated you three times in a challenge to rule Dorma. If I recall, the last time was particularly humiliating for you. Considering the location, the public square with the whole city watching. Per the rules set in stone by Avenshire herself, that means that I am the undisputed Queen of Dorma."

"You cannot deny my birthright," Amadahy sneers.

"I see that this is a thorn in your side and we can discuss it once I return to Dorma," Milea said. "Right now, I want you to remove the incantation you have on Maya and allow Ra'jil to heal and recover from her ordeal."

"I will do as I please," Amadahy yells in rage and punches the mirror.

The glass appears to shatter and the mirror in Milea's room returns to normal. The sorceress leans back in thought as she considers returning to Dorma for a short time to settle the differences with Amadahy. The quick thought leaves her mind as she remembers the warning from the Faidh of Desitana about the timeline. Milea stands up to go over to the window and look out upon the snow. The moons are causing the powder to sparkle like the stars in the sky. A soft wind swirls the snow into a little twirl, playing with it.

The sorceress determines that it would best to finish her mission first so that she does not need to return. She will deal with Amadahy when she gets back to Dorma. She hopes that she can keep her temper under control and not kill the daughter of her mentor. Milea turns from the window to check on Sonja once more, then gets into the second bed in the room. The soft material of the sheets is coupled with a fluffy and warm down filled mattress, easing away some of the tension in Milea's shoulders. The sorceress takes a deep breath in and releases it as she lets her mind quiet down into a lulled and well-deserved sleep.

Hall of the Ice King

The red hues of dawn grace the halls of the tavern. Its light warms the wood and brighten the interior while welcoming the day. Vicki keeps quiet as she closes the door to the room she shares with Zaria. She turns and blinks against the brightness of the hall, a very stark contrast to the darkness she just left. She decides to not disturb the shiadokat and goes in search of breakfast instead. She will wake her brother then check on their employer after she satisfies her hunger.

Vicki hears other guests stirring while she makes her way to the stairs leading down to the first floor. The first thing she spots upon reaching her destination is the discarded guitar. A smile trickle across her lips as she remembers the night's entertainment. Hearty accolades to her left catch Vicki's attention to a table full of new fans. She engages in brief conversation with them then finds an empty table to sit down. The waitress, Colleen, sets a large plate of hotcakes, reindeer bacon, and scrambled eggs in front of Vicki. The recipient's eyes widen in glee as she thanks her hostess and digs into her meal.

"Well, aren't you a pretty little lady," a man complements as he sits down in front of Vicki.

"Thank you for the complement, but I am not interested in anything that you have or want to sell," Vicki said and continues her meal.

"I am not here to sell you anything, pretty one. I am here to purchase a service that you provide," the man assures her and places a large bag of gold on the table. "I want to hire you to take care of an evil menace."

"That is a lot of gold," Vicki said in a low tone. "Not many people know me by sight, how is it that you recognize me?"

"My first stop was in the village of Laurence. I spoke to the elder who recommended you," the man explains, also in a low voice. "He told me that you would be perfect for the assignment, providing I coax you out of retirement."

"That depends. Who is the target?" Vicki asks, and once again indulges in her meal.

"She is a powerful enchantress by the name of Milea Sirus. I'm sure you have heard of her," the man says. "My client, your employer, thought her dead but they did not locate a body."

"I see, that is a powerful and highly dangerous target," Vicki said. "That pouch you provide is not even close to being enough to tackle that mark."

"Bring me proof of your deed and you will get ten times more," the man said. "You will find me in Delveris." He stands and leaves the tavern.

"Still not enough," Vicki remarks to the now empty chair.

Vicki lifts the bag, feeling the weight of it, then moves it to an empty table so that she can continue her meal. She will discuss the situation with Neil prior to making any rash decisions. The sound of heavy and loud male voices penetrates the walls of the tavern as roaming merchants set up just outside the popular establishment. The noise reaches the very top of the inn and into the rooms of those just stirring for the day.

Neil grumbles as he exits his room and stretches while walking down the hall. He pauses by the room Vicki occupied, knocks on the door then opens it. The room is empty and the beds neatly made. Neil makes a curious sound, closes the door and continues down the hall to the stairs. He will check on the ship as soon as he finishes breakfast and the rest of the crew is awake. Since the sun is shining, the waters should let them sail up to the Temple of Nag'teragiea with no problem. Neil pauses at the top of the stairs when an unusual woman saunters up the steps and stops in front of him. She is human but Neil senses something strange about her and remains wary.

"May I help you, beautiful lady?" Neil inquires with gentle grace.

"There are a lot of things you can help me with," the woman coos in return and gets a little closer to him. "However, I am here for another reason."

"Oh really? What might that be?" Neil asks.

"Such a fine flirt," the woman touches Neil's chest then holds up his hand and places a small sack of gold in it.

"What's this?" Neil glances at the sack, then back at the woman as she presses closer to his form.

"I know who you are, my timely flirt," the woman whispers in his ear. "My client wishes to employ your services and thus had me track you down. The elder in Laurence told me that you and your sister will be perfect for the two jobs we have for you."

"The elder knows that we are retired," Neil informs her. "We may or may not be interested in the work you offer."

"I think this will pique your interest a little, especially since the target is rumored to be an excellent sword master," the woman said.

"I'm listening," Neil said.

"He is the exiled king of Solis. His name is Brion Kaiser," the woman explains as she runs a finger down Neil's jawline. "If you bring me his head, your employer will give you ten times the amount in that sack. I will be in Delveris, a town just outside of Tandon."

Neil watches the woman walk away and go into one of the rooms. He glances back to the room he shares with Brion, then takes the stairs going down into the tavern. Hearty cheers go up from those already enjoying breakfast. Neil pauses by the table of fans and leads them in another round of cheering and bantering. He ends the mild entertainment when Vicki calls to him to come sit down. He obliges his sibling and is greeted with a full plate and a glass of fresh forest berry juice. Neil sets his sack of coins on the table before he digs into his meal. Vicki takes note that the pouch is identical to the bag of gold given to her earlier.

"They approached you too, eh," Vicki says. "For who?"

"Brion. Apparently, he's the exiled king of Solis," Neil answers and starts to enjoy his meal.

"Really," Vicki says in surprise. "I often tease him about being a king but had no idea it turns out to be true."

"I am surprised too," Neil agrees. "What about you, who did they want you to target?" he places a fork full of food in his mouth.

"Milea Sirus, Sorceress of Selvest Forest," Vicki answers without taking a breath. Neil starts coughing as he almost chokes on his meal.

"Seriously," Neil manages, then coughs again. "Why the hell do they want to target her?"

"Apparently she is an evil menace and they tried to kill her before, but failed," Vicki explains in short.

"Nope, nope, nope," Neil shakes his head. "I can only imagine what happed to the one that tried to kill her. I love you sis; I don't want anything unnatural to happen to you."

"Me either." Vicki agrees and finishes off her meal. "So, judging from your reaction I can safely say that both of the assignments are, no?"

"Brion is a no. I need more information other than exile. Especially since Brion has become a good friend," Neil said. "Milea is a hell no, if they want someone to clean up after a failed attempt, find someone more temerarious than I am."

"You gave them a challenge with that statement, brother," Vicki teases. "Nonetheless, I think we should at least warn Milea so that she is aware. Brion is around us often enough, so I'm not worried about an attempt on his life anytime soon."

The loud voices of the traveling merchants drift up the walls of the inn. They are soon coupled by the booming sounds of arguments as customers barter for the merchandise. Milea stretches, then chuckles when Sonja pounces on the bed with a hearty greeting for the morning.

Milea sits up and playfully wrestles with her daughter before letting her go to stand and face the window. The mountain in the distance is still wrapped in shadow, despite the morning sun. A loud knock catches the attention of the room as Milea turns to the door. She beckons the visitor to enter and is greeted by Zaria. The shiadokat yawns and closes the door behind her.

"Good morning, A'drianis," Milea greets. "You are up early today."

"Folks yelling outside, can't sleep through all that," Zaria said and yawns again. "What'cha looking at?"

"The mountain in the distance. It is strange," Milea answers and turns back to the window. "The shadows are not leaving it, not even in this light."

"Eh?" Zaria goes to peek out the window. "That is odd. Maybe the way the mountain rises?"

"No, something else is keeping it in twilight," Milea frowns, then turns away. "Let's get to breakfast. We should reach the Temple of Nag'teragiea before nightfall."

"Once we get the book, can we teleport back to Dorma?" Sonja inquires.

"That's my plan," Milea agrees with a smile.

The hall is full of sunlight as the last of the guests make their way down the stairs. Milea spots Leon as her daughter spies the table where their companions are sitting. The sorceress acknowledges her friends then heads to the bar to sit and talk to the innkeeper. A petite glass of wine is placed in front of her as Leon greets the woman. Milea accepts the glass and places it to the side as she requests more information about the incident that involved Maya.

Leon sits back as he recalls the events of that night, more than sixteen seasons ago. He explains that a baby was born to the then-new queen of Selcros, Dysis. Maya was there to assist in the birth of the princess. That night, she stole the child from her crib as her parents slept. The captain of the guards at that time confronted Maya and a small skirmish ensued, which ended in an eruption of black flame. A week later, the captain returned half-starved and near death to report that the child was sacrificed. Presuming by Maya. The city the baby died in is now cursed by the same dark sorceress.

"The name of the city escapes me now," Leon admits. "I do remember the long mourning time and a yearly memorial to honor the child's birth and death."

"Has there been a memorial this year?" Milea inquires.

"The weather has been playing havoc with it this time around," Leon replies. "I don't know if there will be a memorial but Dwayne, the glassmaker, will be more informed about that event."

"I will seek him out, thank you Leon," Milea acknowledges and stands up.

"My pleasure," Leon said. "I'll have Colleen bring your breakfast out in a minute."

The table of Alnis that had greeted the Dresden siblings finally get up to leave the tavern. Large belts of laughter echo in the place as they still talk about the concert and meeting their new favorite entertainers in person. Milea avoids the towering men and sits down with her companions to go over plans on reaching the Temple of Nag'teragiea. Colleen brings over Milea's breakfast and at Neil's request, takes away the two large sacks on the table behind Vicki.

About an hour later, the group wraps up their meal and heads out to the harbor to board the ship. The scene, however, is something they least expected. From stem to stern and all the way up the mast, the ship is covered in a massive cocoon of ice. As far as the eye could see, there is a large, thick, sheet of ice instead of water, and it appears to be strangling the keel of the ship.

Sonja walks out onto the ice shelf and jumps a few times. She could not even dent it. Neil goes over to the ship and uses the butt of his dagger to break into the ice, noting that he has to go in about three to five inches before he hits wood. Vicki taps on the rope to loosen it and knock off a few icicles that formed overnight.

"Spring weather?" Vicki reiterates.

"I know," Brion grumbles. "The ice won't melt for at least a week."

"We don't have that much time," Zaria shakes her head.

"No, we don't," Milea agrees and walks the ice shelf until she is in front of the ship.

A thin flame shimmies to life around Milea, melting a little of the ice as she walks to her destination. Steam rises as the flames roar into a full bonfire around the sorceress, melting the ice and revealing the ocean underneath her. Milea looks down, then focuses on the path ahead as she gathers the flames and sends them down the way. The fire roars as it tackles the frozen ocean, melting the ice a few hundred feet. Milea releases her spell and calms her abilities as she stares at her handywork. Water laps at the edges of the ice as Brion bends down to examine it. Further along the path, the ice becomes progressively thicker. Milea moves back a little further from her original position and studies the ice.

"Good news is, you can melt the ice," Zaria said.

"Probable, yes," Milea agrees. "Practical, hardly. The spell I used to do that small section should have cleared it at least a mile down."

"Selcros's icebreaker can go through ice even if it is a mile deep," Brion said as he approaches his employer. "I can talk to the king, Koro, and request the assistance of the icebreaker. He is the owner of the ship."

"Going to see Koro will be tricky," Milea frowns. "I love my sister dearly but her legacy will be a tough obstacle for both of us to over-come."

"Then let me be the liaison," Brion offers. "When Eryn and I were here, we assisted the royal family with a multitude of issues, including a little disruption during one of Koro's state dinners."

"Disruption?" Neil inquires.

"At least the queen was entertained," Brion says cryptically as he starts towards the castle. "Shall we?"

"Before we reach the palace, Brion. I need to find the glass-maker, Dwayne," Milea requests.

"Of course, I need to visit him anyway," Brion agrees.

The streets are covered with packed snow. Some of the lighter weight people can walk on top without disturbing it. Sonja engages in a small game with a handful of children. The girl quickens her pace to catch up with her group when her mother calls her name. Bulky oxen groan while pulling a heavy cart of iron in the direction of a large, overbearing tower. Their hooves and the wheels of the cart cut deep grooves in the snow. Many of the houses that Milea and her companions walk by double as both residence and busi-ness. The owners calling out to those passing by.

An occasional dark alleyway breaks the monotony of the rowhomes. A blacksmith works diligently at his forge and is the only person without a shirt on. Sweat pours off his body as he pulls the metal he is working on out of the fire and hammers it again. Sonja hesitates a little, then is encouraged to follow the others by Brion, no need to get into more trouble. The group rounds the corner and the girl stops in her tracks.

The town square houses a multitude of tall buildings and colorful homes, to include a giant clock tower. A monotone jail house, just as tall as the clock, sitting off to the side. A large group of girls walk in single file behind a tall and proud headmistress. Each wears the same identical clothing; a black cape and a white fur hat. Milea meets the headmistress's gaze in passing and nods with respect to the woman.

The greeting is reciprocated as the head mistress continues to usher her charges to their destination. The clock tower strikes the hour as the visitors approach, bringing their attention to it. Several small sculptures dance around, moving in and out of designated doors to entertain both residents and visitors alike. Vicki smiles a little then starts to hum a song in time to the bonging of the bell as they near one of a multitude of shops lining the square.

"This is our first destination," Brion nods to the glassmaker's shop, "and it gives us a chance to warm up."

"I'm all for warming up," Zaria presses towards the door of the building.

"I don't think I've ever gone into a building to shop before," Sonja admits.

"There are not many nations that have them," Milea explains. "They exist mostly in colder climates such as this, or wealthier countries."

"Cholbek and L'ybrenthia's main city has a multitude of them on the main streets," Vicki adds. "Tenze has a few but I don't think we were there long enough to see them."

"Probably won't go back there for a little while," Neil said as he follows his friends to the shop.

The door to the shop opens and closes to the sound of a tiny bell located in the corner of the frame. The warmth of the fireplace replaces the cold winds that had followed them into the establishment. Sonja makes a beeline for the crackling embers, hopping over a large pile of fur that she assumes is a stack of rugs. The room is light and airy, illuminated by the rays of the sun that enter the large number of windows. Everything inside the shop is made of glass, from the merchandise for sale to the shelves that they sit on. Soft, soothing, music entertains the group as Milea picks up a glass dragon to study the intricate details. The ornament is perfection down to the individual scales.

"This is not a place to sing an opera," Vicki says, as she picks up a vase to check a price. She uses great care to put it back down.

"Not at all," Neil agrees and studies a large humanoid figure standing on a thin stem of glass. "Don't even sneeze."

The music stops and shifting is heard from the back as the owner of the establishment prepares to meet his customers. The merchant enters the room, smiling at his visitors. He is an elf, the same height and build as Brion, but with lighter color hair and eyes. He wears a flamboyant vest and long-sleeved shirt to keep warm against the winter chill. Milea catches his attention as she watches him enter the room. She notices the merchant's eyes drift to the fireplace, then back to her.

"What's the latest word in Selcros, Dwayne?" Brion inquires catching the merchant's attention.

"Lord Brion, when did you return to town?" Dwayne, the merchant, said with enthusiasm. "Still keeping company with the ladies, I see."

"Actually, traveling with legends, my friend," Brion says as he shakes the glassmaker's hand in friendship.

"Legends?" Dwayne asks, confused.

"The flames of your fireplace are very welcoming, Sir Dwayne," Milea says, as she pulls her hood down and smooths back her hair. "Thank you for keeping them burning."

"I...wait a minute," Dwayne stares at the woman intensely. "You seem familiar."

"Let me introduce Milea Sirus, Sorceress of Selvast Forest," Brion formally introduces. "Among the travelers is Zaria Shiadokat, Neil and Vicki Dresden and Milea's daughter, Sonja."

"Ok, wait, wait," Dwayne sits down on the floor. "Brion, you do realize that yesterday was Princess Chastity's birth and unfortunate death day?"

"The innkeeper, Leon, informed me of the unfortunate tragedy that befell Selcros when Maya visited many seasons ago," Milea said. "I can guarantee that the woman that came to Selcros that day is no longer around."

"In light of the tragedy, we stopped here to see if you've heard of any events marking the anniversary," Brion said. "Leon did not know and pointed us to you for the information."

"I didn't hear about anything," Dwayne said as his eyes once again drift over to the fireplace. "Uh oh," he mumbles, and gets to his feet.

Milea turns to see Sonja standing next to the pile of rugs as she examines it. The girl thought that she heard it snoring at one point and now it is not making any noise. Sonja uses caution as she reaches out to touch the fur, it does not move. The girl shrugs, thinking it is her imagination as she turns her attention back to the flames. Sonja is caught off guard as a large wet tongue licks her across the cheek. The girl turns to see that the pile of rugs is now standing up and just about equal to her in height. The rug opens his mouth and pants happily, showing off a set of sharp teeth as well as a bounty of bad breath. The large beast sits down with a whine and lifts his large paw, a tail wags playfully on the other end.

"What are you?" Sonja asks.

"Looks like either a shaggy horse or dog," Neil observes.

"As big as he is, he could be both," Dwayne admits. "Oliver, an-seo."

The large dog stretches as he stands up and trots over to Dwayne. He pauses by Zaria and faces her, nose wiggling as he catches her scent. Zaria takes a step back when the large dog barks loudly causing her to jump. The dog wags his tail as Zaria hisses at him in warning, then growls. Dwayne calls to the dog again and Oliver ignores the shiadokat as he bounces over to the glassmaker. The animal lays down on his belly, his tail beating the wood floor as if it is a drum.

"Sorry I could not give you more information," Dwayne said as he pat his dog's head.

"Eh, that's ok. It is good to see you again. I'll tell Eryn that you are still alive, despite your fascination with rock climbing," Brion offers and opens the door.

"Just... be careful during your stay here, Lady Milea," Dwayne stresses.

"I will do my best," Milea offers as she pulls her hood back up. She leaves the glassmaker's shop, followed by the rest of her companions.

A strong wind comes off the harbor and bites into those brave enough to come out on this otherwise sunny day. Milea pulls her hood closer to keep warm and prevent the wind from blowing it back. The group crosses through the two large towers leading to the road that takes them straight to the king's front door. A small group of soldiers march past them with at least one pausing to look at the strangers entering the castle grounds. The soldier turns around in haste and steps lively as he heads back to the castle. Milea takes note of his departure and pauses in her walk a moment to stare up at a window just above the entrance of the castle.

The snow melts from the very top of the castle, running in a stream down the large windows where Dysis surveys the grounds. She glances at the small group of visitors making their way to the castle then trains her eyes on the horizon. A soldier runs into the room and approaches the queen, bowing as he slides to a stop. Dysis listens to the man as he informs her that an old foe has returned to Selcros. She recoils in surprise at first, shock overcoming her features.

The Queen scowls and turns to the window once again to watch the small group approaching the door. Dysis leaves the soldier and seeks out her husband at once. She locates him in the throne room with his children, going over the lay of the land and the battle fronts. The queen contemplates disturbing the group and decides against it. Instead, she turns and walks out of the castle to meet the approaching visitors.

Boisterous laughter coupled with a host of foul language fills the air. Milea glance around at the practicing soldiers, studying their techniques. They appear not to be serious about the training until a senior officer comes around a chew them out for slacking off. A few of the men seem content with staring at the group, especially Vicki, as they pass.

Milea centers her focus on the woman walking towards them. She appears not to be in a hurry as she nods a greeting to those that recognize her. She is wearing lavish clothing; thus, Milea concludes that the woman is nobility. Brion acknowledges that the approaching woman is the queen, and the news causes a slight frown to cross the sorceress's face. The sorceress decides to minimize any confrontation by letting her companions do most of the talking.

"It has been a long time since we last saw you here, Lord Brion," Dysis nods to the elf. "Welcome back. Who are your companions and what brings you to Selcros?"

"Queen Dysis," Brion bows his head a little. "My company are Neil and Vicki Dresden, Zaria Shiadokat, and Lady Milea as well as her daughter, Sonja."

"My sister and I volunteered to assist Lady Milea on an important crusade, your majesty," Neil said with a slight bow to the queen.

"Lord Brion decided to tag along with us," Vicki also bows. "Something about legends, your majesty."

"I'm mostly here for the entertainment," Zaria informs the queen.

"Legends and entertainment," Dysis smiles and crosses her arms. "Has Brion told you about his stay in Selcros? I'm surprised that Eryn is not with you, I had been looking forward to a second visit."

"Unfortunately, we will not be staying as long as my first visit," Brion said. "We are on our way to talk to King Koro about borrowing his icebreaker to go north."

"Hmm, interesting. I'm sure that he will be ecstatic to see you, Brion," Dysis said, then faces the hooded woman. "Lady Milea, are you well? You have not said a word since I've been here."

Milea stares at the queen as she contemplates her next move. She feels that until she says something, they will not get past the queen to get the icebreaker. Time is plentiful yet their window of opportunity is starting to narrow down. Milea draws in a deep breath and slowly lets it out as she bows to the queen in respect and turns away.

"Brion, I will be on the ship," Milea says as soft as she can. Unfortunately, it is loud enough for the queen to hear her.

"Neither my hearing nor my memory has dulled over the years, cur," Dysis sneers as the temperature in the area drops dramatically.

The winds around Milea pick up, causing her to gasp ins surprise. The element grabs her cape and rips it from her. The material freezes in an instant and falls to the ground, shattering on contact. Milea feels the climate around her body take a nosedive. Ice crystals sting her skin and start to stick to her. A flame ignites in Milea's eyes as she glares over her shoulder at the queen, the source of the attack.

The wind changes direction and warms up considerably as Milea turns and faces her challenger. Sonja pulls Brion out the way. Zaria holds Vicki and Neil at bay. Dysis commands a large wave of snow to tower above her then directs it towards Milea with an angry yell. Milea counters with a column of flames rushing towards the queen. The elements collide and push skywards for several feet. The elements his and crackle then creates a warm rain as it falls back down to the ground, melting much of the snow around the courtyard. Flames wrap around Milea's body as she changes her stance in preparation for the next attack.

"It looks like you've learned some new tricks since we last met, witch," Dysis sneers as she too changes her stance. "Very well, let's dance."

Clouds gather above and darken as the wind once again switches to freezing. Dysis glows bright blue as she makes a scooping motion with her left arm. She points her palm towards her opponent with a single command. A column of ice gathers up and explodes from behind the queen and heads towards Milea with an angry sound. Steam rises from Milea as she changes the ice to fire and causes it to circle around her form twice before sending it back to Dysis. The queen takes a step back as the head of a dragon forms on the large pillar of flames. Dysis gathers ice and snow to form a shield around herself as the element nears her. Milea pulls the flames back towards her, the little bit that did reach the queen melts the shield away with frightening ease.

"Queen Dysis, you need to stand down," Milea said a little forceful. "I am not Maya Sirus. I am Milea Sirus. The creature that drove my sister to this frozen land is dead."

"You still practice the same lies and deceit you tricked us with years ago," Dysis responds in rage. "I will not be fooled again!"

The queen raises both of her arms, commanding whatever snow is left in the courtyard to rise and circle around her form. Dysis then expands the snow to encase both she and Milea, bringing the temperature down as low as she can stand it. The flames around Milea, however, did not stutter or die out as they do in the fireplace. Snow begins to fall, creating a localized blizzard. Milea makes note that she can no longer see her companions or daughter. The sorceress takes a deep breath in and speaks a few words of calm as she lets it out. She straightens her stance and cancels all but a small part of her flame magic.

Ice tries to encase Milea but is repealed, becoming rain every time, it squeezes in on her. Milea looks around once again at the winds then back to the queen. Their eyes meet as she raises her hand and pushing it out to the side. The wind blows out into a gentle breeze, ruffling the hair and clothing of all those witnessing the battle in the courtyard. A few birds camping on the rooftops call out in alarm as the winds push them off their perch, forcing them to take flight. Dysis straightens in surprise as she watches her strongest spell dissipate without her dismissing it.

"I am not here to deceive you, Queen Dysis," Milea assures in a calm manner. "Look at me, I do not resemble the woman that was here all those years ago. I can attest that neither does my sister, Maya."

"What you are saying does not make sense," Dysis said with anger.

"Then ask me a question only the Maya of your past would know," Milea challenges.

"I see," Dysis focuses on the woman. "What is the name of the city where my daughter will never awaken or leave?"

Milea contemplates the question, bringing a finger to her chin as she furrows her brow. She hears Brion explain to his companions, in a whisper, about the ruins where the baby princess died. Milea turns her eyes up to meet those of the waiting queen. Dysis feels her body freezing in place as Milea starts to approach her. The queen mentally swears, did she just fall for a trap? Milea stops about a foot from the queen and focuses on her.

"I do not know," Milea answers and cancels her incantation holding the queen in place.

"There is no malice in your eyes," Dysis whispers as she focuses on her former opponent.

"Rarely do I deceive anyone, Dysis," Milea said.

"What business do you have in the wilderness north of Selcros?" Dysis presses.

"My own," Milea answers. "A consolation for assisting us in our journey is that I will soon be out of your sight and nothing more than a memory."

Dysis looks her opponent over once then turns and walks back to the castle entrance without glancing back to see if they follow. Milea watches the queen leave and considers whether she should indeed trail after the woman. Her instincts tell her to leave and find a way to the north, perhaps through the forest, on her own. Yet her logic tells her that the fastest means to getting to the temple in this climate is by way of boat.

Milea grumbles to herself as she recalls the warning received by Chaehi about timing. Sonja touches the sorceress's arm, catching her attention. Milea turns her attention to her daughter, touching the girl on her head gently with a smile to match. She looks back up when she sees the soldiers move about, blocking the way back to the city as they continue their drills.

"We could get through the guard," Neil said, noting his client's line of sight. "Take a few lives and get to the ship."

"Easy enough on the way up," Vicki acknowledges. "Unfortunately, we must come back this way to get back to the open sea. If we leave with violence, we can expect it on the return."

"Is there another way to the ocean from up north?" Sonja inquires.

"Potentially. But it is highly uncharted," Brion answers.

"The last thing we need to do is get lost in frigid temperatures," Neil reasons as Sonja frowns from the words.

"After that battle, I agree with Neil," Zaria said. "Although Keela did tell us to take our time. We could sail out and come back in a few months during summer."

"The ice is thicker going out to sea," Vicki reminds her companions. "We still have need for an icebreaker to provide safe passage."

"Also, our ship, Lady of the Night, is not designed to break ice and the trip either up north or out to sea would be painfully slow," Neil points out. "Especially if we rely solely on Milea's fire magic."

"I do not know how far up the temple is," Milea muses. "Constant repeat of the spell I used to melt the ice would be very taxing. Dangerously so, particularly going into unknown territory." She pauses and stares at the castle. "I hope the king is more rational than his wife."

"I make no guarantees," Brion admits and leads the way to the castle entrance.

The temperature in the throne room falls significantly as Dysis walks through the door. The king barely glances up from his war table at his wife as she sits down upon her throne. Wyntre shifts with nervous energy, unsure what has unsettled her mother. Qwest says something to his father, to which Koro grunts and moves a few figures around on his map. The sound of footsteps coming down the hall catches Dysis's attention and the climate in the room becomes frostier, with ice forming on the inside of the windows. The queen turns her attention to the hall as the group that follows her nears the room.

"Dysis, what's wrong?" Koro inquires, tired of the cold in the room.

"You have company, I want them gone by dawn," Dysis informs with bitterness to her voice.

Koro gives his wife a strange look until he turns to the hall and sees Brion walk in the door first. The elf hesitates when he sees the entire royal family present. Brion manages to keep a straight face, bowing to the court as Vicki and Neil arrive behind him. Sonja comes into the room and gawks at the environment. She takes a few extra steps while studying the blue stone with wonderment in her features. The throne room is gigantic, rounded at the corners and full of flags from various ports around the world.

The chairs for the king and queen of Selcros sit up on a pedestal with the king's chair several steps higher than the queen. The positioning of the thrones strikes Sonja as odd. Zaria scolds the girl to stay behind Brion for right now. Sonja is quick to obey the request, apologizing as she moves backward. Milea takes her time as she walks into the room last and stands next to Brion. The sorceress notices that the king's features turn from curiosity to anger and crosses behind the elf to get closer to the windows.

"You!" Koro growls at the sorceress.

"Do not jump to conclusions, your majesty," Milea warns.

"Be silent, witch. I will not be smitten by your false words this time," Koro snaps. "Instead, I shall have your head!"

Dysis stands from her seat as Koro pulls his sword and charges towards Milea with intentions of fulfilling his promise. A sword appears between Milea and the king, blocking Koro's swing. Metal rings in the room and jars the body of the attacker. Koro takes a step back to see that the sword does not have an owner. Milea remains on guard as the sword flips in front of her and returns to Brion's outstretched hand.

Qwest reaches for his own blade, then hesitates as Dysis places a hand upon his forearm to stop his draw. The queen notices that

Neil's focus upon the prince, his hand poised to unsheathe his sword at the slightest hint of Qwest baring his weapon. Vicki keeps an eye on Wyntre but the young woman did not seem a threat right now.

"Brion, why are you interfering?" Koro demands.

"Because, your majesty, I am preventing you from making a grave mistake," Brion explains in short. "Lady Milea and her entourage, I among them, are not to be trifled with."

"Milea?" Koro scans the red-haired woman in front of him. "As in Milea Sirus, Sorceress of Selvast Forest?"

"Yes, among other titles," Milea acknowledges.

"I've heard a few, all of them I will not repeat here since there are children present," Koro says and sheathes his sword. "There are also a lot of sorceresses who claim to be Milea, how do I know you are the original?"

"Lady Milea and I had a discussion in the courtyard," Dysis says as she approaches her husband. "There is no doubt in my mind that you are the original." She directs those words to the guests.

"This is because I am," Milea assures.

"I hardly believe any sorceress that blows into the harbor, love," Koro said and walks away. "Brion, what do you think?"

"I've never doubted the claim, your majesty," Brion answers.

"I lost a little bit of my hair when I doubted it," Neil speaks up. "I have since come to the conclusion that Milea Sirus is truly the original Sorceress of Selvast Forest."

"Interesting," Koro turns and walks away from the sorceress. "Who else is traveling with you, Brion? And why are you here?"

"My company are Neil and Vicki Dresden, Zaria Shiadokar, and Lady Milea's daughter Sonja." Brion repeats for the third time today, annoyance evident in his voice and body language. "We are on an urgent crusade that takes us north into the wilderness. I've come here to see if we might have assistance from your icebreaker, your majesty."

"That's fine, nothing much up there but rough country," Koro agrees. "However, it will have to wait till tomorrow. The icebreaker is being repaired right now after running into a whale-seal. It is unfortunate for the seal and the blubber did some nasty damage to the rig."

"There are also some dangers that you need to be aware of, Brion, since the majority of your company consists of women," Qwest speaks up. "The diplomatic study is the most comfortable room here for guests."

"Excellent idea, son," Koro comments. "Dysis." He holds up a hand for his wife.

Dysis scans her husband once then glances over her shoulder to shoot a cold look at Milea before heading to her destination. She takes her husband's hand and he pulls her closer to him, taking her by her elbow. The king and queen then walk out of the room and down a smaller hall to the left of the thrones. Wyntre, who has been watching the antics of the guests in silence, smiles at Brion before following her parents. Both Brion and Milea do little to hide their expressions of disapproval at the behavior of the royals so far.

"He's lucky that Milea can't cast a spell to send him straight to Oswind's front door," Zaria snorts. "Unlike Maya, who would have sent both king and queen to meet the old man."

"I can still send them, the old-fashioned way," Milea offers. "Less trouble for me."

"If you need any assistance, I will be happy to volunteer my services," Vicki speaks up. The group quiets as the Selcros prince approaches them.

"Come with me, I don't want any of you to get lost," Qwest offers, not hearing the previous conversation.

The secondary hall is not as grand as the one that leads to the throne room. The walls are light gray with pictures of scenery gracing them on both sides of the hall. Between each picture is a fancy vase from one of many countries that Selcros engages in trade with. Milea recognizes a few countries represented in the artwork, including Cyenzie Island. Sonja identifies the strange bird on the vase and inquiries about it. Milea acknowledges the item and Zaria simply frowns at it; not happy it is here. Servants bow as the royal couple continue to their destination and stare at Milea outright when she passes.

Open doors in the hall allow the guests to steal glimpses of the contents of each room, including an enormous library with equally large fireplace. The windows they pass in the hall are smaller and have the added protection of iron bars imbedded within the glass. The lighting and mood make this hall more like a prison than a palace. Milea listens as Brion observes that the halls have been redecorated since he last saw them. Koro explains the reason for this, commenting that he had grown tired of seeing all his animal trophy heads hanging on the wall. Milea notices the queen's discomfort from the small conversation and concludes that Dysis is Koro's new trophy.

Koro enters his lavish diplomatic room and escorts his wife to the head of the table. Wyntre follows her parents as Qwest escorts the guests into the room. The diplomatic meeting room is full of images of past rulers and naval battles won by the great nation of Selcros. Plush blue carpet highlighted with gold and purple accents the room.

The walls are ice blue with a mural of the country painted on the ceiling above. Milea pauses to look around, then squares her shoulders and proceeds to the other side of the table, sitting down in one of the large, plush chairs. Brion sits next to his employer as Zaria flanks the sorceress on her other side.

"Lady Milea, how did your sister die?" Dysis inquires.

"She's not dead," Milea answers in a calm way.

"You told me that she is dead," Dysis said, upset, as the temperature in the room plummets.

"I informed you that the creature you thought is Maya is dead," Milea reiterates. "However, the past, no matter how painful, is not why I am here."

"You will not survive the wilderness of Selcros," Koro remarks. "It has more than just bears, large cats, and wolves. There are dragons, giants, and wild men also in the northern wilderness."

"Got to watch out for those wild men," Zaria quips.

"You are joking, but I am quite serious," Koro informs. "Brion and Neil cannot protect all of you at one time. The wild men will be able to steal a few of you away, especially the little one, during one of their blitz attacks."

"Trust me, Koro, these ladies can take care of themselves during any attack," Brion defends. "Specifically, the little one."

"Is there anything else that is cause for concern in the north, your majesty?" Milea inquires.

"So, you are still willing to go into the unknown," Koro notes. "Very well, in order to give Brion some support, I will send a group of my soldiers with you to assist in your protection."

"Do not take this the wrong way, your majesty," Milea said. "We do not need the assistance of your soldiers."

"What kind of heathen are you to refuse the assistance of Selcros' finest warriors?" Wyntre inquires, flabbergasted by the refusal.

"The woods are not a frightening place for those who know its secrets," Milea answers after taking a moment to breathe deeply.

"Eh, that's irrelevant," Qwest dismisses the comment. "Brion, you remember my sister, Wyntre?"

"I do. Your sensibility has not changed, your highness," Brion acknowledges the young lady.

"You look the same as well, Lord Brion," Wyntre said with a grin.

"It's my genetics," Brion offers.

"Are there any other worries or concerns up north, your majesties?" Milea inquires again.

"Do you happen to know where Maya Sirus is located?" Dysis inquires. "I wish to see this miracle you speak of in person."

"No, you wish to 'deal with her' in a negative way," Milea corrects as she stands. "I will not disclose her location. I do not want to be responsible for your fate should you greet her with the same zealousness as you did me. Since this conversation is over, I shall depart to prepare for tomorrow morning's voyage."

"That will depend on when the icebreaker is ready. The repairs may not be done until the afternoon or even the following day," Koro shrugs, uncaring. "Perhaps you can walk the forest that you do not fear."

"Perhaps we should," Milea reacts then heads to the door.

"Brion, I need to speak to you on world matters," Koro informs the elf, as the rest of the guests follow the sorceress.

Brion pauses along with Vicki and Neil as the trio turns back to the room. Milea, Zaria and Sonja continue down the hall without hearing the king's request. Vicki exchanges glances with both men before nodding and continuing down the hall after Milea. Brion watches her leave, then turns back to the table to notice Wyntre standing and watching them from her position at the table. Her expression goes from worry to relief as she meets the gaze of the elf. Brion and Neil exchange glances, then head back into the room and return to the table. Neil slaps Brion on the shoulder as the two sit back down.

"Brion, I hear things are not so well in Solis," Koro states. "Are you here to request the assistance from the might of Selcros?"

"No, Koro, I am not here for that," Brion answers in short. "I would not submit the armada of Selcros against a legion of undead ships that you will never win against. You would end up becoming part of the undead fleet that haunt the seas near the island of Solis."

"I've not met an enemy that can defeat the might of the Selcros armada," Koro laughs. He pauses when a servant approaches and whispers something to him. "So, it appears that I have yet another sorceress awaiting an audience with me in the throne room. Qwest, get details on Solis and I will meet with you after this entertainment."

Qwest acknowledges his father as the king stands and takes the hand of the queen. Dysis frowns a little as she stands and goes with her husband. On their way out the door, the queen overhears Wyntre and Qwest ask Brion a few inappropriate questions about the women in his group. Dysis makes a mental note of the situation as well as her reaction to the visiting sorceress, Milea. She scowls as she tries to figure out who could be waiting for them in the throne room.

The queen's brooding thoughts soon disappear as soon as she steps foot into the throne room. The woman stands up from the king's throne and saunters to the main floor. Koro frowns at the woman's disrespect for his authority but brightens when she bows to the royal couple. She is shorter than the women of this country, her skin tone indicating that she is from the sunnier side of the globe.

The woman's black hair shifts at her movements as she straightens her form and places a hand upon her hip. Mystical blue eyes dance with humor as she notices the royal couple's initial reaction. Dysis notices that the visitor is a L'vane, similar to the majority of Brion's party. A strong metaphysical aura emits from the visitor as she focuses on the king.

"Greetings King Koro Fone," the woman addresses. "And also, to you, Queen Dysis Fone."

"And you are?" Koro inquires as he releases Dysis's hand.

"I am Dee of Tandon," the woman answers. "I have come to you with a proposal."

"Are you headed north as well?" Koro interrupts. "Perhaps you and this Milea Sirus can join parties and venture north together."

"Milea Sirus? Sorceress of Selvast Forest?" Dee asks, taken aback by the information. "Why is she here? What does she want in the frozen North?"

"You mean you don't know?" Koro said, a little sarcastically. "I thought all of you magic types could sense what is going on with each other. Or even know where your mystical sisters are at all times."

"Hmm..." Dee decides not to answer the king but instead turns to the queen. "What say you to this revelation, Queen Dysis? From my understanding, you are, after all, a user of the mystical arts as well."

"I do not know where Koro gets his information or wild ideas," Dysis informs. "I did, however, deduce that you are not a part of Milea's party. What proposal do you have for us?"

"Ah yes, my proposal. I had forgotten with the news of Milea's presence." Dee admits. "King Fone, Tandon is offering assistance in dealing with your longtime enemies, the Northern Wildman, and the ice dragons. In exchange, we expect Selcros to pledge loyalty to Tandon."

"Excuse me, what?" Koro questions, laughing unapologetically.

"You are not seeking an alliance, are you?" Dysis inquires, unhumored at the events.

"You are astute, Dysis," Dee agrees. "What I seek in exchange is your inequitable surrender to Tandon. I will get it either by such negotiation as this or by force."

"First of all," Koro chuckles as he wipes tears of humor from his cheek. "You are a woman and cannot comprehend making such deals with me. And as a woman, I do not see any way you can get rid of my enemy except perhaps by offering their chieftain a little alone time. That will not work long, just so you know."

"You are sorely misunderstanding your predicament, Koro Fone," Dee interrupts, testily. "I do not need the assistance of anyone to take your country by force."

"Do me a favor and go back to your husband, lover, or whatever," Koro dismisses. "I do not fear the fits of women nor the threats of men. If Tandon wishes to discuss trade or treaty, then send your leader, Xandous, to see me instead."

"The level of your ignorance is astounding, Koro Fone," Dee observes. "Shadowed only by your arrogance. However, my leadership did tell me to give you a twenty-four-hour grace period before I crush you. And you shall have this, unless I grow tired of your nonsense."

The lighting in the room remains the same as Dee fades from sight. Dysis looks around in order to see if she could track her but senses the woman is gone. Koro starts to laugh again and make fun of the many threats that Dee had issued forth. He goes over to his throne and sits down. The queen looks out the window to see that the Selcros marketplace is in full swing, crowded due to the sunshine. She mumbles a little before approaching her husband. Dysis could see that he is still very humored by Dee's ultimatum and wonders if he had heard her conversation with the visitor.

"Koro, what are the plans against Tandon's impending raid?" Dysis inquires.

"What raid?" Koro asks, humored. "I doubt if there will be one, love. She is only trying to intimidate me into submission. That is not easy and as I told her, I would rather talk to her leader about treaties and trade agreements anyway."

"She is not offering a trade or treaty. She wants us to surrender," Dysis informs. "You didn't hear that, did you?"

"Eh, she's using scare tactics. Inefficiently, too, I should say," Koro dismisses. "Any lesser man would crumble upon hearing the name of Tandon. I, my dear, am no lesser man."

CHAPTER FOUR

The Plan

The doors to the inn open and close at a quick pace as Milea enter the space. She is alone, having decided that Sonja is in good hands with Vicki and Zaria. The conversation at the bar does not pause as she approaches the innkeeper's daughter. Colleen escorts Milea up to one of the empty rooms that houses a large dresser and mirror. The sorceress thanks the young woman and closes the door behind the innkeeper's daughter. The mirror on the dresser starts to waver as Milea approaches and settles down in front of it. The mirror falls away and starts to show the interior of a beautiful, manicured forest. The sound of a waterfall fills the air, along with a few birds whistling in the trees. Milea waits as Keela sits down in front of her with a kind smile upon her features. Milea tilts her head to the woman in the mirror.

"I have not heard from you in many days, Milea. I considered sending a search party for you," Keela says as she crosses her legs. "Did you make it to Selcros?"

"Yes, we made it but not without troubles," Milea answers. "I have also located Maya. She and Amadahy had a spat which has left Maya without her mystical gifts."

"Oh? Should I intervene?" Keela inquires as she arches an eyebrow.

"I've already had a discussion with Amadahy," Milea offers. "As soon as we retrieve the book, we will be heading to Dorma and I will deal with her precariousness."

"How much longer will you be?" Keela requests.

"We leave for the temple tomorrow since the Lady of the Night is encased in a large ice sheet," Milea relaxes, leaning back. "Zaria, Vicki and Sonja are gathering the necessary items needed to set sail first thing in the morning."

"Why not this afternoon?" Keela also sits back.

"The ice sheet is unusually thick and my mystical flame will not melt it far enough without multiple repeats of my most powerful incantation," Milea said. "Brion has gotten the king's icebreaker to help us. According to the king, it is in repair right now after colliding with a whaleseal."

"Hmm, and my helpers are not that far north," Keela places a finger on her chin. "Your brother, Tadious, lived up there at one point in time. Perhaps he has followers that can help break the ice to speed your way."

"I have not seen a Temple of Light in Selcros yet. However, I did run into the Queen. She has the powers to manipulate ice and snow," Milea said. "Unfortunately, I do not think she is willing to assist us, since it is the anniversary of her child's death. Allegedly, Maya came up to Selcros and sacrificed her newborn princess."

"She did what?" Keela sits up.

"I've gotten little information but will tell you what I know," Milea offers. "Then I will go see if I can find the girls before they get into too much trouble."

The sun kisses the snow, melting it at an unusual speed as a strong wind blows in off the harbor. Zaria shivers from the cold air then turns to the harbor when her sensitive hearing detects thunder in the distance. A storm is blowing in, promising to be a very bad blizzard. Vicki wraps her cloak closer to her body as she watches Sonja run from vendor to vendor. The girl is trying to find the best deal for their impending trip north. Her focus is on general items for any method of travel. The people of the city greet the visitors heartily, a few recognizing Vicki as one of the entertainers from the previous night.

Sonja runs past a group of shady-looking men on her way to another street vendor and captures their attention. Vicki notices the group and jogs to catch up to the preteen as Zaria hangs back a little. The harsh winds kick in, blowing up several inches of loose snow and temporarily blinding everyone in the area. Once it dies down, Vicki swears and looks about. Sonja is nowhere in sight. Frowning, Vicki turns and signals to Zaria before going in search of the girl. The shiadokat frowns as well and ducks down an alleyway to track the girl.

An hour later, the Alnis baker beams a smile down at Sonja as she hands the girl an apple tart. Larger than most tarts, it takes both hands for Sonja to accept the treat. The girl does a small jig and thanks the baker for the treat. A loud rumble of thunder echoes overhead shaking the buildings of the city. Sonja jumps from the sound and looks up to see the sky darkening. The impending storm is choking out the sunlight. The baker looks up at the sky with a scowl at the sudden change in the weather. Sonja turns to see that she has lost her two companions during her galivant through the marketplace. The young lady thanks the baker once more then runs back down the street in the direction she came so that she can reunite with her party. A large bald man blocks her path, prompting Sonja to swear and slide to a stop. She almost collides with him due to the slipperiness of the snow under her feet. She hops back several times just in time to avoid being grabbed by the strange man.

"You are not an Alnis, what are you?" Sonja inquires, then takes another step back as the man moves forward. "Don't come any closer."

"Pretty girl," the man says with a slurring sound.

Several men holler as they charge forward from all directions toward the young girl. Sonja drops her treat as she avoids the first attacker. She grabs and tosses a second one then punches a third square in the nose, sending him to the ground. A second wave of men rush forward from various directions to replace their injured companions.

Two of them fall to the ground with daggers sticking out of their knees. The harsh sound of a whip is unheard until it snaps around the neck of the man who blocked Sonja's path. His cry of pain causes the other men to pause in their attack. The winds blow in a gust, then die down as both Sonja's as well as her attackers turn their attention to the bearer of the whip. Vicki glares at the attacking group of men. Zaria stands next to her poised to release another dagger.

"Let the girl go, and I will release your friend," Vicki announces, "as well as let the rest of you live to see another sunrise."

The men hesitate a few seconds before taking a step back from Sonja. Seeing an opening, the girl rushes over to the shelter of her companions. Zaria quietly scolds the girl as she starts walking away with her. Vicki glances over her shoulder then yanks on her whip to free it from the neck of her victim. The whip twists tight into the man's neck and he fall to the ground, lifeless. The weapon then goes lax, allowing Vicki to coil her whip and places it on her hip as she turns to follow her companions.

The group of men creep over to evaluate their companion and notice that he is dead. Vicki catches up to her companions at the same time the men she left behind begins to yell angry obscenities in their direction. The trio turns, and each drops an unkind word or two as they see that the large group of men now charging towards them has at least tripled in number. Zaria turns her two companions and shoves them forward. All three start to run in order to outdistance the angry mob.

Townsfolk move in quick fashion to finish their business and get to shelter. The storm announces its closeness with a flash of lightning coupled with a clap of deafening thunder. The headmistress of the girls' school leads her troupe back to the institution after a fun day of walking the market. Vicki and Sonja round the corner and enter the town square first, setting course for the inn. Zaria is not far behind them, catching up to them once they are out in the open. Unfortunately, the men prove to be just as athletic and start to shorten the gap once they too reach the square.

Sonja pulls ahead as the procession of girls blocks her path. Instead of slowing down, Sonja increases her speed then jumps up and over the heads of the girls, landing on the other side to continue her way. Vicki follows the example of her young friend and lands a distance further than Sonja, catching up to the girl in a few rapid turns of her feet.

Zaria is last to make the great leap, landing briefly on all fours. She glances behind to see the men disrupt the troupe formation by weaving through the girls, knocking a few of them down as they continue to pursue their targets. Zaria swears, stands, and hurries after Sonja and Vicki. Neither she nor her pursuers notice the headmistress of the girls' school disappear.

Sonja and Vicki are three blocks from the inn when a figure appears in front of them. Vicki swears and leans back, sliding to her backside in the snow in order to stop. Sonja manages to stay on her feet, yet she too slides on the snow and ice. Zaria succeeds in stopping before she collides with either companion. She whips around with dagger in hand to face the oncoming threat. The men chasing them have also halted in their tracks.

The mob discusses their options among themselves before disbursing, heading in all directions to get away from the new threat. Vicki gets to her feet, arming herself with her whip to face the new threat. Zaria glances over her shoulder then swears and face the elder Alnis. Sonja takes a weary step back but kept her focus in front. The woman crosses her arms across her chest and peers at the trio with coal black eyes down her hawk like nose. She is dressed in a light blue fur coat with matching hat proudly protecting her head. She is thin built, yet there is an obvious air of authority about her.

"What kind of mischief do we have here?" the old woman demands, her words sounding clipped and harsh. "Are you out here causing trouble?"

"We are not the troublemakers," Vicki answers, her words a bit defensive. "The men that fled behind us are the ones that deserve that label."

"They are not Alnis," Sonja observes.

"This is true," the old woman said with a smile. "They have a few names, some a bit foul. To keep things simple, the entire kingdom knows them as the Noturi, or Wild Men of the North."

"You are the woman that leads the procession of girls," Zaria recognizes. "Are you a sorceress?"

"I know a few tricks, yes," the old woman admits, humored. "I am the Dean of the girls' school. Folks here call me Madame Hawthorne."

"You're the second magic user that we have met since we've arrived in Selcros," Zaria says. "The first we know about is Queen Dysis."

"Ah, you mean King Koro's trophy," Hawthorne nods in understanding. "I saw earlier this morning that you had three others with you. Lord Brion, a second man and a visiting sorceress."

"The second man is my brother, Neil," Vicki admits. "Both of them are at the castle entertaining King Koro. Our mystical companion is at the inn."

"Lord Brion is at the castle?" Hawthorne stares at the trio. "Well, neither man is in any danger, yet whatever mission brought you up here will be. Especially if Princess Wyntre spies him."

"She is among the group that greeted us at the castle earlier today," Sonja informs her.

"Really?" Hawthorne frowns. The sound of thunder echoes once again, reminding all that a storm is at hand. "Your mystical companion will be fine at the inn. I will go with you to see if we can get your male companions out the castle and I will escort all of you back to the inn if you desire."

"Why are you being so solicitous?" Zaria inquires, a hint of suspicion in her body language.

"Because this storm is neither an act of Nature nor is it Dysis's doing," Hawthorne says, bluntly. "Wyntre has the same abilities as the queen yet I am not entirely sure how she got them, and no one but Koro knows where she came from. But I am not sure if it is entirely her doing either. Let me tell you some history as we travel to the castle."

The winds moan in warning as the square finishes clearing out, even the traveling vendors having found shelter by now. Hawthorne walks at a quick pace as she explains to her guests the history of the current ruling family of Selcros. Koro is not the original heir to the throne; it should have been his brother, Liev. Another interesting fact is that Liev is the one that discovered Dysis wandering the deep woods of the North. At the time she claimed not to be lost and it was obvious that she had very little knowledge of the world outside of the pine forests she calls home. Liev had brought Dysis to Selcros and the two fell in love.

Koro returned from a naval campaign south of Selcros and was immediately smitten by the beautiful Dysis. However, the woodland beauty did not return his affections, stating that she had promised herself only to the King of Selcros. Not only this, but Koro was already married to the daughter of an ally and she had borne him a son. The day before the wedding, Liev went with his brother, Koro, on a hunting trip to bring down an artic bull. The hunt should have lasted a few hours, yet Koro did not return until noon the next day.

To Dysis's dismay, he was alone - Liev, and the entire hunting party with him, were missing. Koro announced to all Selcros that Liev and the others with him had all perished in an attack by Wild Men. Dysis was understandably upset at this news and returned to the forest to grieve in peace.

"Koro ascended to the throne and continued to pursue Dysis," Hawthorne continues. "She kept reminding him that he was already married at the time and had a young son to look after."

"What happened to the original queen?" Vicki inquires.

"If you believe Koro, she returned to her family willingly and died in route to her homeland," Hawthorne answers as snow begins to fall. "However, my sources tell me that Koro's first wife, Tiffany, was executed for treason. Three weeks later, Koro returned to Dysis's home and reminded her of the vow she made. That she will only marry the King of Selcros. Two years later, she relents."

"Why? First impressions of Koro are that he is a bit of an ass," Sonja interjects.

"Koro either threatened her or promised her something," Hawthorne hinges a guess. "The one who knows why she relented is Dysis herself."

A clap of thunder alerts Milea, interrupting her mystical search for her sibling. The conversation with Keela lasted a little longer than she had planned. Once done with that discussion, Milea decided to check on Maya or Amadahy once more but could not find either right away. The mirror returns to normal as Milea stands and moves to the window. The sunny day has now turned for the worst. Several people hurrying to get out of the surprise storm. Milea watches the chaotic rambling of the people then keys in on a small group heading to the castle. She recognizes three of the people, including her daughter, but the fourth is unknown. Milea can tell that the mysterious person with them is a residence of Selcros due to the height of the individual.

The winds slam against the window and the snow thickens as it falls from the overheavy clouds. Milea frowns, sensing that it is a spell but from an unknown source. She wonders if it is the same antagonist that had tried to stop her from a previous voyage. The recent battle with Dysis rules out the queen's abilities as the creator of the storms. Milea makes a curious sound as she retrieves her cape, wraps it around her form and disappear from the room.

The castle guards do not bother the group as they hurry to the front door. The snow increases, blinding the travelers. The door to the foyer blasts open from the force of the winds. Sonja pushes the door close once everyone is inside. Vicki shakes off her cloak and listens, hearing her brother's laughter down the hall. Zaria lets out a little growl as she shakes the snow from her entire body.

The group takes a few steps from the door then all turn to face it when it opens again. A hooded figure walks into the foyer a few steps, the door closing behind. Sonja tilts her head to one side then makes a whoop of joy as she runs over and hugs the woman. Milea chuckles a little as she lowers her hood and wrap her arms around her child to return the affection.

"You just about gave me a fright, milady," Madame Hawthorne addresses the latecomer. "If I had not hesitated to look twice, I would say you are Maya Sirus."

"I've given many of Selcros residents a fright since this morning," Milea admits. "I am Milea."

"Ah, Lady Milea. I have heard so much about you over the years," Madame Hawthorne nods. "It is your ship that is caught in the sea ice?"

"It is," Milea acknowledges. "My understanding is that Tadious frequented this area of the world. Is there a Temple of Light that houses his followers?"

"Sadly, the only Temple of Light is located in the remote North and destroyed seventy years ago," Madame Hawthorne says. "Whoever survived would not have the ability to break the ice that encases your ship. You need the icebreaker or the Queen's abilities to do that. With the blizzard outside, I would dare say both."

"I see. Thank you, Lady..." Milea says.

"Hawthorne," the old woman answers with a smile. "The original plan is to retrieve Lords Brion and Neil from the castle and escort everyone back to the inn without disturbing you, milady."

"I saw you heading to the castle from the window. Which reminds me," Milea turns to her silent-observing companions. "Ladies, what happened in the marketplace?"

"A bit of a disagreement with some Wild Men," Vicki summarizes.

"Apparently they tried to snatch Sonja, and we respectfully requested they leave her alone." Zaria adds. "They did not see it our way."

"The Noturi do not negotiate when they decide upon a target," Hawthorne interjects. "I am surprised the girl survived the initial attack; they call it a blitz. Doubly surprised to know they are inside the city walls."

"I lost my apple tart defending myself," Sonja grumbles a little.

"I pass the baker on the way back to the girls' school. I will let her know and I am sure she will replace it with twice what you lost," Hawthorne assures the girl, then focuses back on the leader. "Lady

Milea, do you want me to escort you and your party back to the inn today?"

"We will get to the inn after we gather up the last two. I do not think it necessary to keep you any longer than we have," Milea assures. "Thank you for your assistance, Madame Hawthorne."

"It is my pleasure." Hawthorne said, then turns and leaves via the door. The winds howl like a raging animal, then are silenced when the door shuts once again.

Milea watches the door a few seconds, then turns back to look down the hall. Vicki volunteers to go retrieve her brother and his unlucky traveling companion so they can get to the inn. Sonja peeks out the window next to the door, noting the speed which the snow covers the spot cleared out by the battle between Milea and the queen earlier in the day.

"Is this how a blizzard is supposed to behave?" Sonja asks. "Our path is now completely gone."

"I'm more experienced with sea storms and hurricanes," Zaria admits.

"When it comes to snow storms, the ones here are possibly the worst I've experienced," Milea said and look outside.

Lightning screams across the sky and strikes a building behind the clocktower. Thunder rumbles outside, and is barely heard in the diplomatic meeting room above the echoes of Qwest's laughter. He seems well humored by something one of his guests had said. Brion waits as the Alnis prince regains his composure. The elf is taken aback when Wyntre wraps her arm around his and leans against his shoulder. Brion pulls his arm away and stands up to move out of her reach. Neil witnesses the incident and frowns as he considers his friend's reaction. Vicki walks into as Qwest finally finishes his laughing fit.

"Sis, done with preparations?" Neil inquires, standing to greet his sibling.

"A storm came in before we could complete them, brother," Vicki explains. "I came to get you and Brion so we can head back to the inn before it really starts blowing out there."

"They are safe here," Qwest dismisses the woman. "Besides, Brion still has not told me what's going on in Solis."

"I have already made arrangements to take care of it, Qwest. Koro does not need to worry about it," Brion informs. "Knowing your father, there is a healthy price to pay for such assistance."

"But there is no price large enough to deter you from freeing your homeland, right?" Wyntre beams a smile at Brion.

"Yes, princess, there is," Brion responds, meeting her gaze. "I do not think the price is worth the headache."

"Well, since we are done, let's get going," Neil stands. "Is everyone here in the castle?" He directs his question to his sister.

"Yep, we are all waiting in the foyer," Vicki informs him. "We ran into another mage named Madame Hawthorne. She feels the storm is of mystical origin. I think Milea agrees with her."

"Madame Hawthorne is a kooky old woman whose information you should take with a grain of salt," Qwest dismisses. "If the redhead believes what the old bat said, then that says a lot about her as well."

"It also says a lot about you and your father for the treatment of your guests," Vicki observes, then focuses back on her companions. "Ready, Lord Brion? Lady Milea and crew gave me a limited time before they come in to rescue the royals."

"Lord Brion, you don't have to go with her," Wyntre beseeches. "Father would be happy to have you as a guest here at the palace."

"Can my friends stay as well?" Brion asks. He nods at the silence. "I thought not."

Brion walks away from Wyntre and into the hall leading to the foyer. He is followed by the Dresden siblings. Thunder roars outside, shaking the building as they make their way down the corridor. Neil uses a hush tone to mentions to his sibling that the royals are following them. Brion to grumble unfavorably about the heirs of Selcros. Milea stands from her perch when the trio enter the foyer. The winds whistle through the doors, causing the hair on Sonja's neck to rise from the sound. Zaria takes a deep breath and looks heavenward when Wyntre and Qwest come into the room after Brion and the Dresden siblings.

"To what do we owe the presence of Your Highnesses?" Milea inquires.

"Came to see Brion off," Qwest answers. "And try to talk him out of your foolish journey up north. If you want to go, that is fine, but don't take reluctant and innocent people with you."

"Wait," Vicki shakes her head. "Didn't we tell them we volunteered to go?"

"We all volunteered for this journey," Brion reiterates. "Qwest, I trust that the icebreaker will clear our way tomorrow morning. I look forward to it."

"The blizzard increased in ferocity a few seconds ago," Zaria informs.

"That means that you have to stay," Wyntre says, a smile in her eyes.

"Not for long," Brion quips. "We will be going to the inn as soon as the storm passes."

A small clock chimes the hour, one of several that have passed, and the storm continues raging even into the night. Milea sits in silence inside of one of the smaller studies upon a cushioned couch, indulging in one of the many books on the giant shelves. The room is as large as the diplomatic conference room, yet more tastefully decorated. The walls are painted with a mural of the mountains in the distance, including the strange dark one. The known northern constellations decorate the ceiling and seemed to glow in the firelight. Along with bookcases on the walls, four enormous ones stand in the floor like sentries. The couch that Milea occupies is in the middle of the room and positioned in front of the fireplace. She counts at least four more couches in the room at various locations.

A strong wind slams into the window, pelting it with bits of ice to draw the sorceress's attention. Milea glances at the glass just as lightning arcs across the sky, followed by deep and angry thunder. Milea stands up to look out the window, noting that it is still snowing relentlessly.

"Spring, he says," Milea scoffs a little. "Either Brion has miscalculated the seasons or our storm antagonist has resurfaced."

"My opinion is the storm antagonist, but not the original," Zaria hypothesizes as she appears out of the shadows. "A talk with Madame Hawthorne earlier today points to two suspects of royal origin."

"I think there is only one suspect," Sonja interjects, placing the book she is reading next to her on the floor. "I noticed the storm increase in intensity when Brion said that we would be going to the inn as soon as the storm passed."

"Yeah, Wyntre did not appear very amused with that announcement," Zaria recalls.

"Very curious," Milea muses as she sits back down on the couch.

The thunder outside does little to cover the footsteps in the hall as Milea once again returns to her book and continues reading. She figures to invoke a search for the rest of her party once she has finished the story. Vicki, Neil, and Brion, are wandering the halls of the castle, no doubt out of boredom. Zaria stretches then decides to sit down next to Sonja. The girl shifts a little to allow the shiadokat to look over her shoulder at the book in her lap. A set of footsteps draws ever closer, capturing the attention of Zaria and Sonja. Dysis continues her slow walk as she enters the room and pauses in front of Milea. A tense minute passes before Milea turns the page and places a leaf in the spine of the book to mark her place, then closes it and looks up at the queen.

"Good evening, Queen Dysis," Milea greets in calm, "How are you doing, is all well?"

"No," Dysis answers, her words sharp and hostile. "We had a visit from Dee of Tandon. She appears to know you. Are you responsible for her appearance and her ridiculous demand?"

"I do not know what you are talking about," Milea informs the queen.

"I am not in the mood for games," Dysis says with a hint of anger.

"Then stop holding us captive with this blizzard," Milea accuses. "It is plainly obvious that you are responsible for it, since these are your mystical capabilities."

The storm's rage shakes the entire castle as the queen stares dumbfoundedly at her reluctant guest. Milea leans back against the cushions of the couch and watches as Dysis' shoulders lower in defeat. The words, though sarcastic, appear to sink in as the queen realizes her capabilities. The queen lowers her gaze then moves to stand in front of the window and peers out at the weather. Milea hears Dysis as she claims that she is not responsible for the storm, and discloses that her powers have diminished since she took the throne as queen of

Selcros. Sonja moves from the floor to sit next to her mother on the couch. Zaria leans against the wall in the shadows.

"Dysis, how does Dee know that I am here?" Milea inquires.

"Koro foolishly assumed that you two are following each other and on the same mission," Dysis answers and turns back to the room. "He made a lot of assumptions during that brief encounter."

"I can imagine what His Majesty may have said to this very dangerous foe," Milea says with a slight scowl. "Out of curiosity, what is it that Dee wants from Selcros?"

"The short of it is that she wants us to either surrender or be conquered," Dysis summarizes. "She is generous enough to give us until tomorrow to make up our minds. My husband believes it is a non-issue due to the simple fact that Dee is a woman."

"That's no surprise there," Zaria quips. "Does Dee know about me?"

"Koro did not mention anyone but Milea," Dysis admits as she sits on the arm of the couch. "And before you ask, Koro has not made any plan or preparation for the impending attack."

Milea stares at the queen for a few silent seconds before she closes her eyes and rubs her temples as if to relieve a headache. With the impending attack from Tandon looming there is the potential for further delay of her mission. Milea knows Dee well enough to deduce that no solid timeframe would be given for the attack. It could happen any time after midnight.

Milea gazes into the flames as she weighs her decision. She could either assist Selcros with the threat coming against it or ignore it and go straight to her destination up north. She knows that no matter which choice she makes there will be consequences. She must figure out which consequence she can live with.

"I need to find Brion and the Dresden siblings," Milea concludes as she rises to her feet, along with her daughter.

"Last I saw them, they were going into the dining hall," Dysis informs, also standing up. "Do you know the likelihood of Tandon's attack?"

"My experience is that Dee does not make idle threats," Milea advises. "She is coming but on her own time. My concern is that I will have to help deal with her either before I leave or upon my return, since the harbor is the only safe way back to sea."

"So, deal with the threat now instead of later?" Zaria inquires as she follows the woman into the hall.

"Exactly," Milea answers. "I just hope she does not bring her estranged son with her. That would be a whole new crisis."

"How so?" Dysis asks. She is escorting the group to the dining hall.

"Tandon has an arsenal of ancient weapons at their disposal," Milea summarizes. "Dee's son, Brandon, has at his beckoned call one of the most powerful. Should he show up, I will provide more details."

The sounds of kitchen servants preparing the king's meal echo in the castle halls. A few of them expressing indignancies upon realizing they will have to prepare more food than normal. The dining hall itself emits the soft sounds of a mellow flute filling the void as Vicki plays a melody to stave off boredom. Neil taps out a beat on the table to his sister's song as he listens and watches Wyntre attempt to play with her new pet, Snowpuff. The snow leopard cub flips on his back to bat at the toy mouse that the princess is dangling over him. Snowpuff yawns and rubs his eyes with his right paw. Afterwards he starts to lick the same paw as he ignores the toy.

Brion sits back and observes the activity in the room. An idea strikes one or both men at the same time resulting in Brion and Neil discuss the toy mouse. Vicki stops playing her instrument and listens to the mischievous plan that her companions are hatching. She chuckles a little as she brings the flute back to her lips and patiently awaits the unveiling. Brion focuses on the toy mouse; his dark hair stirs ever so slightly. Neil bounces in his seat in anticipation of the event as Qwest and Koro walk into the room.

The toy leaps from Wyntre's hand so suddenly that it causes the young woman to shriek and jump back in surprise. Vicki plays a fast-paced song on her flute as the toy mouse dashes around the room. Snowpuff hops to his feet, eyes wide, as he follows the movement of the once inanimate object. The snow leopard cub lets out a sound of glee as he dashes after the mouse.

The toy keeps its distance and turns to go in the opposite direction when he gets too close. Snowpuff slides, putting his backside down, as he turns and skids to an abrupt stop, bumping into Qwest's boot. The Alnis prince curses as Koro himself laughs at the spectacle. Undaunted, the cub scrambles back to his feet and tries to get a foothold on the slippery floor as he goes after the toy once again. His claws tap loud against the stone floor as he fights for traction while trying to turn. Neil cheers "ole!" every time the cub pounces, just misses his mark when the mouse turns and darts off in a different direction. The toy scuttles between Koro's legs and is followed faithfully by Snowpuff.

Wyntre gasps in surprise and ducks as the toy goes over her head. Snowpuff leaps into the air and clear over the princess as he tries to grab his mark, just missing it. The cub lands on the floor and slides to a halt. Vicki pauses her melody to take a sip of water as the young animal sniffs around to track the toy. Wyntre notices Vicki placing the flute back to her lips to play a few long and low notes the princess watches as the toy appears to respond to the notes by moving left and right, peeping out from under the tapestry. Snowpuff sees the toy and wiggles his rear end as he stalks towards it.

At the same time, the queen and her guests enter the throne room with Zaria spotting the animated toy. With a catlike smile, she moves to one side and waits in silence. The toy mouse takes off across the queen's path, causing Dysis to jump and swear despite herself. Milea takes a step back along with her daughter as the snow leopard cub plows past them. Vicki increases the tempo of the melody as the toy mouse whips around the room and heads in a different direction. The toy comes within ten feet of Zaria and seems to disappear. Snowpuff makes a sound of surprise and slides to a halt, stopping short of bumping into Zaria. The shiadokat is standing, victorious, with the toy mouse in her hand. Neil and Brion both laugh heartily and applaud the cub's efforts. Snowpuff yowls in surprise or frustration.

"Well done, Vicki," Neil applauds his sister, "That was flawless."

"So, you're the one that brought the toy to life," Wyntre accuses the flutist. "Are you some sort of siren?"

"I only provide the music, Your Highness," Vicki defends herself. "The toy, itself, is brought to life by someone else."

"That would be me," Brion admits. "I didn't expect it to end when the big cat came into the room."

"You need to be a little quicker than that," Zaria concludes with a wink. She looks down when Snowpuff makes a strange meow sound at her. "Nope, it is mine now. You will have to find another one to play with." She walks away and is followed by a chuffing Snowpuff.

"You frightened me, Brion! I should turn you into a snowman," Wyntre said as she stomps her foot and placed her hands on her hips.

"Excuse?" Brion arches an eyebrow. "I doubt if you would be able to complete that incantation."

"Oh really?" Wyntre snorts at the challenge.

Thunder echoes outside as the temperature in the room cools down. Dysis turns to the young woman an is about to issue a warning but it is too late. Wyntre casts her spell directly towards Brion in the form of a frosty light. The elf sits back comfortably as his sword lifts from his scabbard at his metal command and hovers directly in front of him with the blade facing down. the light bounces off the blade and speeds right back at Wyntre . The girl gasps and dodges out of the way then seems horrified at the destination. Koro cusses and ducks as the spell explodes into harmless flurries of snow and cold rain.

"Wyntre," Dysis said with little emotion as she lowers her hand. "We will talk about your little transgressions after dinner."

"But I didn't do anything wrong," Wyntre said as innocently as possible.

"Do my eyes deceive me? So good of you to join us, Lady Milea," Koro announces as he sits down in his chair at the head of the table. "Have you finished your temper tantrum from this morning?"

"I am the one that invited Lady Milea to dinner," Dysis informs. "Since there is a potential delay of her departure tomorrow morning."

"Are you referring to the Tandon woman?" Koro inquires. "She is such a minor issue and a non-threat that I have forgotten her name. I would not worry so much about her."

"Her name is Dee, Your Majesty," Milea reminds. "She is not only a threat, but a major one. Do you have a plan to defend against her?"

"Of course. My plan is to put the two of you on a ship and send you north per your request," Koro answers sarcastically. "I do not bow to the feeble fits of women, remember that for future reference, Lady Milea."

"Your Majesty, as painful as it may be to you, Lady Milea is correct," Brion speaks up as he leans forward. "I'm sure you realize that Tandon is a city of wizards, with its ruling class among the most powerful."

"Dee is at the top of this chain. Her powers even dwarf those of their leader, Xandous," Milea offers an explanation. "I am sure she's told you this, but Dee does not need anyone to help her take over any country by force. She is more than capable of doing it herself."

"She was keen to let me know this," Dysis says. "I think Koro was too busy laughing to hear that."

"And I still laugh about it," Koro scoffs. "There is no way that a wizard, especially a woman, can defeat a warrior. Brion, do you believe that it can happen, or any of this nonsense that is being said?"

"I do believe it," Brion answers as honestly as he can. "Because the information, no matter how you view it, is coming from a very reliable source. I also know that the source is highly capable of defeating both warrior and mage."

"We've seen that in action, along with a few mages that are also warriors," Neil interjects.

"And vice-versa." Vicki defends.

"Is there a such thing?" Qwest inquires.

"You need to get out more, Your Highness," Brion answers. "So, Koro, what is your hypothetical plan for this very probable battle?"

"Well, first, I will assume that Dee is not going to be leading this theoretical army," Koro says, in a dismissive tone. "So, let me tell you my plan for the man who will be leading the charge of this punitive invader."

Vicki puts her flute away as dinner is served and the king begins his plans. He starts by informing his guests about Selcros and its many advantages due to its northern location, pointing out that during the present transition of seasons, the weather is unpredictable. Koro continues explaining, as he starts eating, that three of the four borders of the main city are surrounded by the northern ocean. The fourth consists of a vicious mountain range. Neil listens as he indulges in the meal presented to him. Sonja asks him a question about sea navigation.

"The Northern Sea, though dangerous, is not impossible to navigate. Especially if the ship's captain knows his vessel" Neil replies, in a hush tone

"I'm sure that Tandon did their homework before coming here," Vicki adds just as quietly. "To assume the opposite spells a lot about Koro."

"There is a thick fog that forms over the harbor every morning in the spring and lasts for hours at a time. If the invaders come by sea, they would be hopelessly lost." Qwest boasts loudly, interrupting his father briefly.

Koro once again laughs at the notion that Dee will lead her army, again stating that since she is a woman, she would be behind the lines. Snowpuff climbs into Wyntre's lap and proceeds to take a turkey leg from her plate and run away with it.

"You are woefully underestimating Dee, Koro," Milea warns. "Dee will not sit behind anyone, no matter if it is man or woman. She will be front and center to the entire thing. And she will enjoy watching your army fall to her might."

"You obviously do not have a clue about warfare, Lady Milea," Koro observes. "I suggest that you sit down, keep your negative words to yourself and let the men handle this." The king takes a swig from his tankard as he looks about the room. "Brion. You and Qwest will lead the army. One hundred men each."

"I do not recall volunteering for this bloodbath, Koro," Brion remarks.

"Do you want the use of my icebreaker?" Koro responds. "Then you have volunteered."

"I do not think it is fair to hold Brion for the use of the icebreaker," Milea speaks up. "This mission is mine; therefore, I should be the one on the field of battle."

"I would, with glee, place you on the battlefield, but I don't think I have anyone that is willing to protect you from this imaginary army you believe in," Koro dismisses. "Good night, Lady Milea. Perhaps once you have rested you will come to your senses. I will not, however, count on it."

"Very well," Milea stands up and pushes in the chair. "Are there any designated bedrooms since the blizzard is still raging outside? Or shall we continue to camp in the library?"

"I feel generous enough to give you a choice," Koro said and places his tankard down. "You can continue your encampment, or I can have the guards escort the entire lot of you down to the dungeon for your constant insubordination."

"Insubordination, Koro, is the least of your problems," Milea warns, then turns and leaves the room.

Sonja grabs a few rolls before she gets to her feet and trails after her mother. She almost drops one of them but is relieved when Vicki catches it. She helps the girl carry her load out of the room. Zaria stands and offers to speak to Milea about confronting Dee, to which Koro once again laughs and give his known opinion about the possibility of Dee's arrival. The king even proposes that his wife, Dysis, could handle Dee should she have the audacity to appear. The queen stares at her husband as if he has lost his mind and does not notice the shiadokat leave the room. Neil shakes his head and places a hand upon Brion's shoulder, pledging support in the upcoming battle, before leaving. The silence of the room is broken by the growls and snarls of Snowpuff as he wrestles with the turkey leg bone.

"Koro, have you lost your mind?" Dysis demands, her voice and features oozing with agitation. "Did you even listen to anything said about Dee and the attack she is mounting against Selcros?"

"Careful, love, you are treading on thin ice," Koro warns his wife.

"I am the ice!" Dysis corrects.

The temperature in the room plummets, forming ice crystals on the walls and frosting the tankards immediately. Snowpuff squeaks in surprise and hurries over to Wyntre to warm up as the cold penetrates his double coat of fur. The princess shrinks back from her parents, unaccustomed to such boldness from her stepmother. Apparently, neither is Koro as he seems taken aback by the bold move of the queen. Koro smiles at his wife, liking the danger that fills her eyes. He reaches to touch her and Dysis slap his hand away.

"Do not come near me tonight," Dysis warns as she leaves the table, and ultimately, the room.

"Come, Brion, we have to at least inspect the troops for this imaginary battle coming our way," Qwest stands up. "If anything, it will give them exercise."

"The battle is not imaginary, Qwest," Brion corrects. "It is very real. You and your father will find out just how real it is when it slaps you in the face." He stands and pushes up his chair. "I'm going to go check on my friends first. Then I will be down...eventually."

"Wait for me," Wyntre speaks up as she hurries after Brion. Snow-puff bounces after the young woman.

Koro scowls as the room empties out and warms up due to Dysis's departure. He picks up his drink and takes a sip. A grunt escapes him, as it tastes considerably more bitter than usual this night.

CHAPTER FIVE

Reviewing the Troops

The halls bustle with castle staff as they hustle from one chore to another, pausing long enough to acknowledge the princess and her handsome escort as they walk the corridor. Brion ignores his hostess as he processes the meeting in his mind. He concludes that Koro's underestimation of his attacker will one day cause Selcros to fall. Wyntre overlooks the elf's troubled frown and focuses on his other features, especially his hair and the unique color of his eyes. She allows her eyes to wander over his tall, lean, and obviously well-built frame, admiring the way he walks. Brion acknowledges a few of the staff as they continue their way, prompting a question to come to the princess's mind.

"Brion, are you a king?" Wyntre asks, a bit of hope in her words.

"Why do you want to know?" Brion responds with his own question.

"Because if you are not one, I think you would make a great one," Wyntre explains. "You would be a wonderful king of Selcros. I also saw you arguing with father earlier. No one but another king can do that."

"Koro needs to open his eyes and ears so he can hear the voices of reason," Brion pauses in his walk, much to his hostess's delight. He focuses his attention on her.

"He is not an unreasonable man," Wyntre says. "Your uncouth traveling companions just need to learn how to respect a man of great power. Particularly that sullen Milea."

"My companions are not responsible for Koro's behavior nor his treatment of them, specifically Lady Milea," Brion retorts. "As far as the offer to rule Selcros, no thanks."

"You are very protective of Milea, is she your love interest?" Wyntre challenges. "Or is it, Vicki?"

"Why is it any of your business?" Brion rebuts the challenge.

"I'm just curious, I'm sorry," Wyntre responds, innocently.

"Then why not ask them?" Brion suggests. "I'm pretty sure that Vicki and Milea will talk to you if you make a friendly effort."

"No thanks, I do not associate with heathens," Wyntre says bluntly.

"Really?" Brion answers, perturbed. "Well, if you will excuse me, I will go find my uncouth heathen friends so that I can associate with them."

Brion walks away from Wyntre, the princess taken aback by his words. Snowpuff catches up with her and rubs the young woman's legs, gently. Undaunted, Wyntre trails after Brion, scolding herself for her blunt words. Snowpuff makes a grumbling sound as he follows the princess. Brion arrives at his destination, the small library, and looks around.

It is empty with exception of the tall bookcases standing sentry over the room. One of the couches is also missing from the room, its disappearance leaving a large gap in the space. Brion glances around a few times then decides to bend down to see if he can track where his friends disappeared to. He mutters a few words under his breath as he hopes that they did not leave the castle to head to the inn. They would run a terrible risk of freezing to death during this strange nighttime blizzard.

"Hi, what are we looking for?" Sonja asks as she crouches next to Brion.

"What?" Brion turns to the girl. "Well, you for one."

"Excellent work finding me," Sonja teases as they stand. "We relocated to a larger library. Neil took the comfortable couch for Mom to sleep on. He's also out looking for you."

"Glad that you found me first," Brion smiles and gently ruffles her hair. "So, this larger library. Is it behind a locked door?"

"Yep, but not anymore. I think that is the best surprise of Selcros, Mom was smiling when we walked in," Sonja explains.

"Th-That's father's library. No one goes in but the king," Wyntre stutters in disbelief. "How did you get in?"

"Zaria unlocked the door," Sonja shrugs, nonchalant. "Ready to go, Brion?"

"Lead the way," Brion nods to the door.

The walk to the king's library is short. Sonja skips most of the way. Snowpuff charges into the room with the girl when he smells the one that has his toy. Brion pauses when he walks into the room, noticing row upon row of books lining the walls from the floor to the twelve-foot ceiling above. Several shelves stand back-to-back with in the middle of the room and form three rows leading up to the door. The dark hardwood floors echo with the thumps of Snowpuff's bouncy steps and Sonja's skipping as they head to the center of the library.

Suits of armor decorate the walls between the bookcases and the windows. Each suit stands at attention with either a sword or axe in its grip. Between the rows of free-floating shelves are podiums hosting large open books of various topics. Several couches, large and small, dot the entire space to provide enough seating for many visitors to these hallowed halls of knowledge. The crackling of a flame draws Brion towards one side of the humongous library. His sensitive hearing alerts him that he is being followed, presumably by the princess.

The area that he is heading to is simple in its decoration with a large white bearskin rug stretching between a couch and two large chairs. The mantel is carved out of a single block of limestone with two large statues of nude ancient goddesses holding up the shelf between them. An antique mirror hangs above the mantel, large enough to reflect the entire room. Milea is sitting on the bearskin rug, staring into the flames to gather her thoughts. Vicki is sitting with Sonja on the couch that Neil borrowed from the queen's library. The two are holding a quiet conversation about a book that Vicki is reading.

Zaria is leaning against one of the walls, still in shadow as she studies the entire group. Her senses centered upon the sorceress the most. Lightning illuminates a window next to the shiadokat as the storm continues raging. Milea blinks out of her self-trance as she realizes that others are in the room. She turns in time to see Snowpuff as he exits the forest of bookcases. A couple of growls of happiness escape him as he bounces over to Zaria. The cub then flops upon his back with his belly exposed. Sonja sits down next to the cub and rubs his soft middle. Snowpuff chuffs in joy, much to Zaria's humor, as Vicki also scratches the snow leopard cub's chin. Brion enters soon after the cub and nods as Milea stands up.

"Welcome to the library encampment, Lord Brion Kaiser," Milea offers. "Neil is worried about you, so we sent out a small search party."

"It seems that Sonja found him first," Neil says as he walks out of the darkness. "Your Highness." He addresses the startled princess.

"That means you owe Sonja a dagger and a lesson on how to use it," Vicki reminds her sibling. "It's quite interesting, you'll have to pay close attention for that one, Sonja."

"If it's the same way he uses his sword, you are in for an intense lesson," Brion warns the girl.

"I'm ready for it," Sonja says, puffing out her chest in confidence.

"Regardless, it will have to wait until after the upcoming battle," Milea says. "I'm very sure that Dee has a few surprises for Koro."

"My father comes from a long line of strong Alnis kings," Wyntre says, coming further into the light. "In our long history, Selcros has never fallen to any power, foreign or domestic. We will not fall to this imaginary non-issue that you believe is real."

"How quaint, you are just like your father," Milea says, humored as she meets the princess's gaze. "The only illusion here is your country's invincibility. Slone, Son of Roathis, came within a hair's breadth of conquering your home. He would have done so if he had not been defeated by the blood rain."

"Blood rain?" Neil inquires.

"Indeed," Milea acknowledges her companion, then refocus upon the princess. "Let me further educate you, Your Highness, by informing you that the one who bought the rains almost wiped all Alnis off the face of Bri'al. If it were not for the quick thinking of a queen, Selcros would no longer exist."

"Y-you're lying," Wyntre accuses her.

"No, Wyntre, I am not," Milea informs the princess. "It says so in your own books of history."

Milea lifts her hand as if she is picking up a book. A rattling sound is heard from the depths of the library before a large ornate book floats into the space, stopping short of Wyntre. It is the same book that Milea read while in the queen's library a few hours before. Thunder rumbles, but not as loud as the book splits open and the pages turn to the subject in debate. Penned in the ancestral queen's own handwriting, it tells of a day when there had been nothing but pure destruction, brought on by Slone and his unusual warriors.

The writer describes the attackers as half dragon and half horse, grotesque beings that lived to kill and drink the blood of those they desecrated. A lone visiting warrior called out Slone, challenging him to blade combat to the death. The challenge was accepted and the battle was on. The entire village watched the combatants, which turned out to be a folly. Slone, sensing he was losing, ordered his army to slaughter all those witnessing the battle.

The beasts gleefully obliged and started off by killing someone meaningful to the visiting warrior. That's when the storm came, heralded in by the screams of a hundred thousand angry voices and it bathed the battlefield in a deluge of blood rain. The visitor has changed from savior to slaughterer. Slone barely escaped with his life, but his beasts suffered greatly. The warrior killed every last one of them, eliminating them from the face of Bri'al.

The king at that time was grateful to the warrior and went out to greet him, as the rains increased. Instead of greeting the king as he should, the warrior killed the man in cold blood. Horrified, the village army then attacked the warrior, only to fall to the glowing red blade. The queen did not take time to grieve her late husband but ordered all who were able to get out of the village to do so at all haste. As the panicked evacuations ensued, the warrior advanced towards the village, killing anyone in his path, including innocent lives.

By the time he arrived at the village, it was empty. A fit of rage overcame the warrior and he destroyed the center of town with a single explosive spell. The writer had witnessed this from her hiding spot, which she did not disclose in her written account. Wyntre takes a step away from the book when she reads that only about seven hundred people had survived the onslaught. Sonja becomes distracted from rubbing Snowpuff's belly when she notices the winds outside die down.

"The lone warrior you read about is the one who brought the blood rains. He is not a king, Eltis or immortal, but a Car'laden. He has numerous deeds to his name, some honorable but most are deplorable. If Dysis is angry at my sister over the death of her newborn, she would be exponentially so with this person, for he has killed more innocent lives than any army on the face of Bri'al," Milea informs Wyntre as she once again makes eye contact with the frightened princess.

"Who is he?" Wyntre asks, her voice barely a whisper in her fright. She jumps a little as the page turns to display the name.

"Justin of Lortis," Milea answers as the pages settle down.

A bolt of lightning rips across the sky, coupled with a deep roar of thunder, causing Wyntre to jump and shriek in fright. Seconds later, the storm itself dissipates as if it had never existed. Sonja watches the weather and arches an eyebrow at the sudden change. Neil takes hold of the book and feels it drop into his hands, released by Milea. He flips the pages back to read into the legend with a bit of a frown. Vicki stops rubbing the snow leopard cub's belly, much to Snowpuff's dismay. He squeaks and rolls back over to bump his head against Vicki's arm, demanding more attention. Brion is now reading over Neil's shoulder as the two study this new topic.

"I heard that Justin of Lortis is dead," Vicki says, breaking the silence. "If he is still alive, he would be a very old man by now."

"He did die," Zaria agrees. "He was middle aged when he did, tricked and trapped by a group of cunning Orijete led by one with surname of Sa'Jak."

"However, he has been returned to life in recent times, complements of Jasmine Underak," Milea informs the group.

"That's not surprising," Brion grumbles a little and sits in one of the chairs. "Is he under her control?"

"For a long time, he escaped that fate," Milea admits. "I've not seen or heard from him for some time and don't have a good feeling about his absence."

"He could be anywhere," Zaria assures.

The sound of heavy boots against the hardwood echoes in the room and directs the attention of all to a door hidden beyond the bookcases. Zaria smirks and leans back on the wall, able to see the person coming into the space. She is enjoying Wyntre's reaction, the princess turning pale as a ghost. She trembles and backs away from the sound as it draws ever nearer.

Brion stands up and moves away to avoid the princess as she backs into the chair he had occupied and huddles down into it. Snowpuff's ears twitch around as his nose samples the air to identify the person coming their way. Milea stretches, then moves over to allow her daughter to sit down on the couch with her. Sonja leans back on the cushions as she focuses on the approaching figure.

Neil ignores the mounting fear filling the room as he turns to the next page in the book. He closes it once he is done reading the last few words of the diary and his hearing detects an intruder. Vicki captures Snowpuff's attention again and make the cub sit up for a small pat on the head. Snowpuff obliges and purrs a little when he gets his reward. Wyntre starts to whimper as the owner of the footsteps finally come into the light.

"Here you are, Brion," Qwest says as he walks further into the space. "How the hell did you open the king's library? That lock was considered foolproof."

"I opened it," Zaria admits with a shrug.

"Really? I guess you are useful after all," Qwest remarks, then focuses on the person he is looking for. "Brion, time to go see the troops."

"Humph, I suppose," Brion grinds out as he shifts his sword belt. "I should see what I'm fighting with. I hope they have improved from the last time I was here."

"Can I go too? I don't want to stay here with them," Wyntre pleads with her brother as she gets to her feet.

"What did you do to my sister?" Qwest frowns at the young woman's trembling form, then turns to the others in the room.

"Just reviewing some history with her," Milea leans on the arm of the couch. "She is easily frightened; it is not all that scary."

"History? So, you are scared of ghosts?" Qwest teases his sister and makes a spooky sound as he pretends to be a spirit.

"Stop it!" Wyntre swats her sibling. "It's not funny."

"It is funny," Qwest corrects. "I guess you can accompany us. Brion will protect you from the spooks and the soldiers."

"I'll go too," Neil volunteers as he stands up. "I will be out there with my friend. I need to see Selcros' might myself."

"Let us know what you see," Milea waves as she gets more comfortable.

"What? You're not going with us?" Qwest asks, sarcastically.

"Is that an invitation?" Milea retorts in kind.

Qwest laughs at the words as he turns and leads the way out of the library. Brion takes a deep breath in and lets it out at a slow rate as he follows the Selcros Prince. Neil walks with his friend and swats him on the shoulder in solidarity. Both disappeared into the darkness before Wyntre snaps out of her stupor and hurries to catch up with the men.

Snowpuff grumbles as he bounces after the princess, calling to her as if requesting that she slowdown. Vicki chuckles a little as she stands up and dusts off her backside. The storm has passed yet there is still very cold air that seeps into the library from the windows. Milea turns to the fireplace and causes the flames to increase a little to battle the elements.

"I think I will go and see if we can commandeer some accommodations that are a little warmer than here," Vicki offers.

"Can I come with you?" Sonja inquires.

"Ah, no I'm fine by myself," Vicki assures. "I might even follow the guys to make sure Neil does not kill anyone for getting on his last nerve."

"Don't get in trouble," Milea warns. "Sonja, time to settle down for the night."

"Yes, ma'am," Sonja pouts a little as she sits on one of the couches and Vicki leaves the room.

The dark halls ae illuminated with candle light to guide the group down the halls to the barracks. Qwest boasts how difficult it is to defeat the might of Selcros on land and sea. Each sailor and soldier go through a rigorous amount of training for several months. The product is a well-tuned fighting machine. Brion ignores the information while contemplating the whereabouts of the ice breaker. It is not parked in the usual spot for repairs. Wyntre remains silent as she admires her quarry, smiling from her thoughts as they traverse the hall. Loud barking finally reaches the ears of the group as they open the door and enter the very cold barracks.

"What the...?" Neil frowns, forgetting the cold for a moment as he watches the action.

Men run around to fulfil the orders of the senior officer as quickly as possible. Many ran into each other or stumble and drop their cargo. The result is more insatiable barking from the officers. Neil takes one look at Brion and knew that his friend is also in shock. Wyntre looks around in awe, this is her first time visiting the barracks and the new area has her intrigued. Qwest frowns at some of the antics and storms over to the officer in charge.

"I think we should break and commander the icebreaker," Neil said as Qwest lights into the officer.

"We passed the dock that it's usually parked in. Not there," Brion retorts. He takes a breath in. "Qwest, are these the solders?"

"Yes," Qwest answers and walks away from the officer. The man is fast to retreat from the area. "A fine example of Alnis strength in here."

As soon as he finishes boasting, one of the men trips over a discarded staff. The soldier swears as he falls and rolls, inadvertently bowling over a few of his friends. The group of men cuss their companion out as they all get to their feet and start swinging at each other. Swords clatter onto the floor when one of them is pushed into a table. Snowpuff jumps and backs away from the noise, staring in awe at the antics. An officer rushes over and put an end to the brawl, ushering the men out of the area before the prince could turn around.

"Yes, a fine example indeed," Neil said a little bit sarcastically. "So, where are the real ones?" Snowpuff looks up, curiously, as if asking the same question.

"These are the real ones," Qwest reiterates. "They have been run ragged since the news of my impending arrival. You will see how efficient they are in the morning during this drill called a battle."

"I hope so...," Neil frowns. He takes note of a few of the soldiers boldly gawking at Wyntre . The princess is blissfully unaware of the stares.

"Where are the ones I'm going to command," Brion asks, ready to get this over with.

"They are this way," Qwest thumbs behind him. "Wyntre , go wait in the hall with your pet."

"I want to hear Brion talk to the men," Wyntre counters. "Please?" she asks with a childlike voice, her eyes wide and pleading to match.

"I suggest you do as your brother says," Brion retorts.

"I've never heard anyone but father address the troops and never in the barracks," Wyntre counters. "I want to hear your words because I think you're great."

"The feelings are not mutual," Brion said.

"Awe, she has a little crush on you," Qwest teases. "Ok. She can stay."

The Alnis prince chuckles as he walks deeper into the barracks. Brion takes a deep breath in and follows his host into the freezing area. Wyntre grins and skips merrily behind her obsession. Neil and Snowpuff look to each other. The cub squeaks and tilts his head in question.

"Do not give me that. You are the one who has to live with her," Neil reminds the cub. He then trails after his friend. Snowpuff grumble as he waddles after them.

Strong male voices cuss and swear from the doorway as the visitors approach. A few hardy laughs follow the words as the men inside enjoy the game they are playing. Brion pauses and closes his eyes, wishing to be somewhere else. Neil cups his friend's shoulder to show solidarity. Wyntre reaches to hold Brion's hand then frowns as she misses her mark when the elf follows Qwest into the room. The soldiers inside look over their shoulder and briefly ignore the guests. They take a second look and stand as fast as they can when they realize the visitor is their prince.

"Men, this is Lord Brion Kaiser, I'm sure a few of you remember him," Qwest introduces. "He will be your commander during the practice drills tomorrow. Line up for inspection"

Wyntre watches and smiles as Brion walks away from her and go down the line. Neil stands patiently near the entrance and frowns at what he is seeing. Brion pulls the blade from one of the men's scabbard, looks it over, then puts it back without a word or any obvious body language. Qwest folds his arms across his chest, a cocky grin spreading across his face, confident in his soldiers. Neil notes Brion pauses a little longer at a few of the soldiers than others. Snowpuff yawns then sneezes from boredom.

"Hmm...." Brion muses as he stops and backtracks to the front of the line. He could smell the strong presence of ale upon the Alnis men. Satisfied with his curiosity, he returns to stand next to Neil.

"What do you think?" Neil inquires in hush tone.

"We are in trouble." Brion answers the same way then focus upon the man. "Soldiers of Selcros. Tomorrow you will face a mighty foe. The army which Tandon brings will, no doubt, strike with an awesome force. However, I believe that Selcros can match that force with one of their own and overcome this invader. Only if you fight with tremendous determination that the Alnis are legendary for that you will have victory."

"Sir, yes sir!" the solders answer in unison. Qwest beams with pride.

"Till tomorrow and victory," Brion announces. "Dismissed. You may resume your games but I want you to be sober in the morning."

Brion and Neil leave the room to the stunned looks of the soldiers. Qwest seemed shocked at first then frowns and marches over toward the men. Wyntre duck out of the room to follow Brion at the same time her brother light into the men. Snowpuff bounces after the princess dutifully. A strong wind whistle through the barracks, encouraging Neil to press faster to the warmth of the hall. Brion increases his step and enter the castle just as a second breeze trickles through the area.

Wyntre is last to enter with her pet and the door shuts itself behind them.

"Lord Brion, that was a great speech," Wyntre said with admiration. "I truly believe that, if that war tomorrow was real, you would bring us victory."

"The battle tomorrow is very real, princess," Brion reiterated. "The war is ongoing."

"Really? Then with victory tomorrow, you will be a Hero of Selcros instead of a lowly knight. Then you will qualify to be King." Wyntre chimes

"As I said before, I do not want or have any desire to rule Selcros," Brion said, agitation in his words.

"I'm sure I can change your mind," Wyntre hints with a seductive tone.

"Highly doubtful," Neil interjects. "Once Brion has made up his mind, it takes a little bit to change it. Either way, we should focus on the battle tomorrow."

"You can continue to be the disciple of the forest witch. Brion does not have to, he has a choice," Wyntre said to Neil and walks down the hall. Snowpuff follows her.

"She wears the patience doesn't she," Neil said.

"Oh, indeed," Brion agrees. "Let's get back to the library, I want to talk to Milea. Maybe there is a way we can postpone the trip North and come back after Tandon is done with Selcros."

"I'm for that." Neil agrees.

As they travel down the hall, the transition from cold to warmth becomes very noticeable. Neil pauses and looks back at the barracks doors now a distance down the hall. He mentally notes that the men of Selcros's army have very little comforts if any as they train. He shakes his head and continues to trail after his friend. It would be a surprise if the men battled at all tomorrow.

Neil catches up with Brion and both keep quiet as they walk behind the talkative princess. They ignore her as they focus on the upcoming battle. Brion pauses when something catches his eye as they walk through the light of a candle. He slows down and watches the shadows on the wall as they walk through another one. The snow leopard cub's shadow did not resemble the creature that cast it. It, in fact, appear to be enormous and walks with a jerky gait as it lumbers after the princess. Neil pauses with Brion, also taking note of the shadows. They watch as the princess and her pet walk through another candle's light and see that the cub's shadow is now normal.

"Do you think A'drianis is playing tricks on us?" Neil asks.

"No. that was not shiadokat," Brion responds. "Wyntre, where did your father find Snowpuff?"

"I don't know where but he found Snowpuff during the blizzard about a day or so ago," Wyntre answers and turns to face the men. "He said others were found but already suffered the weather's wrath. Snowpuff hung in there because he is special."

"Perhaps a little too special," Neil offers.

"Agreed, I think Koro should have left him," Brion said.

"Oh, Stop it!" Wyntre scolds and stomps her foot. "Snowpuff is not dangerous." The cub rubs against her leg.

"The blindness of this family no longer amazes me," Brion grumbles as he rubs the bridge of his nose.

"I think we need to turn in for the night to be ready for tomorrow," Neil stretches.

"Brion. Your room is next to mine," Wyntre said with a grin.

"Very good, and my friends?" Brion asked.

"What about them?" Wyntre retorts. "They made themselves a camp in the library. The couches comfortable if that helps."

"I see. Well, until tomorrow then," Neil said and walks into the shadows of the hall towards the king's library.

"About time," Wyntre said under her breath as the L'vane man departs.

"Good night, princess," Brion said with very little enthusiasm.

"What?" Wyntre is taken aback when her quarry walks away from her. "Brion wait!"

"Now, what is the issue?" Brion pauses and turns.

"You have beautiful eyes, a lovely voice and well-built head to toe," Wyntre answers honestly as she focuses on his sea-blue orbs. "I am just wondering how well built is all."

"Are you serious?" Brion arches an eyebrow. "And I suppose I should take off my shirt to satisfy that curiosity." He retorts with sarcasm.

"That would be a great start. Do you want me to help you?" Wyntre said with a gleam of enthusiasm in her eyes. She reaches for his collar and is stunned when he grabs her arms to stop the progression. Snowpuff licks his paws as he watches the interaction.

"I am not interested, Wyntre . Go to your room," Brion said.

"Who is she?" Wyntre demands with a hiss in her words.

Brion does not answer as he releases her and walks away, heading to the library. Wyntre glares after the elf, seething with anger. Snowpuff looks from her to the departing elf and back. The cub then squeaks a question to the princess. Wyntre draws herself up and follows Brion down the hall, determined to capture her quarry once and for all. Snowpuff's tail whips a little bit then he gets up, stretches a little. His front paws pat the floor then jumps a good two feet in the air when Neil melts from the shadows of a doorway. The L'vane frowns and follows the couple. Snowpuff calms his pulse and waddles after the group.

CHAPTER SIX

A Bold
Snow Leopard

icki moves in silence as she returns to the library, taking care to avoid the boards that creak. The shadows in the room are darker than normal, alerting her senses that there is danger in every corner. Vicki pauses when she hears a faint sound of laughter from the darkness. Shaking her head to clear it, she continues her slow decent into the library, allowing her eyes to adjust to the half-light of the fireplace. Vicki arrives at the library encampment to find Milea asleep on the couch that Neil had moved in from the queen's library.

The sorceress is on her back, her red hair spread across her form and onto the nice warm blanket that came with the couch. Milea is in a deep sleep, the rhythm of her breathing slow and gentle. Sonja is asleep on an adjacent couch not far from her mother. The girl is on her stomach, half of her body somehow clinging to the couch while the other half dangles towards the floor. A hand and a leg brush the soft rug underneath her, yet she sleeps comfortably.

Vicki looks around and notices that there is no sign of Zaria among the couches that she can see. The darkness also appears to have lightened a little once she reached her sleeping companions. Vicki glances around before taking care to approach the sorceress. She pauses and turns around as her senses scream at her of an intruder. Vicki scowls, seeing nothing immediately out of place, and the men having yet to return from their review of the troops. Vicki shakes her head, concentrating on her target once more, moving forward another step.

In the deep shadows, A'drianis folds her arms and mentally counts Vicki's steps as the L'vane woman nears the most dangerous creature in the room. Vicki leans over to touch the sorceress. Milea's eyes to snap open. Vicki drops several unkind words then shouts out in surprise as she falls to her backside. To her further horror, she is unable to move as Milea's sword appears in a flash. The blade comes within inches of Vicki's throat as the woman looks up. She notices that although Milea's eyes are open, she is far from fully awake.

"Milea, wake up! It's Vicki!" she says loudly, then gasps when the blade comes within a hair's breadth of her skin. "Hello, I'm not here to kill you..."

"Vicki..." Milea acknowledges the voice as it finally breaks through her sleep. She pulls her blade away from Vicki's throat and rubs her eyes to finish waking up. "What happened? Is Dee attacking already?"

"If she comes by, I'll have her wake you up next time," Vicki says, and hops to her feet. "No, I wanted to warn you that someone tried to hire an assassin that goes by the moniker of Dagger to kill you. Safe to say that you should have no worries about that."

"I see, did Dagger say who tried to hire them?" Milea asks with a smile, her sword disappearing during the conversation.

"No, I did not pry," Vicki assures. "I can guarantee that she will not be coming anywhere near you."

"I'll bet," A'drianis says from somewhere in the shadows. She laughs when she catches Vicki's dagger and walks into the light as Zaria. "Like I said before, bards, HA!"

"Oh yeah? Well, if you're a simple thief then I'm the Princess of Old Mondue," Vicki counters and folds her arms.

"That makes for interesting company," Milea says, as a mischievous grin lights up on her face. "Let's hypothesize that Zaria is really an Eltis, Vicki is a highly successful assassin and I'm the undisputed Queen of Dorma."

"No fair!" Zaria frowns at the very truthful words.

"Ok, I'll bite," Vicki chuckles, then makes a sweeping bow towards Milea. "Your Majesty, fancy meeting you in such a cold and hostile environment. Although the steam of the tropics does have its own impediments."

"It does indeed, Your Highness," Milea teases back. "I am surprised to see you here as well. Mondue is a desert city. Lost, I'm afraid, to the sands of time itself. How do you fare in this brutal and cold environment?"

"By putting on lots of layers, Majesty," Vicki answers, honestly. "My question is, how does the Eltis of Darkness, Shiadokat, enjoy this weather?"

"I stay indoors," Zaria quips. "Nasty out there during this spring weather."

"Someone is coming into the library," Sonja announces, bringing the bantering to a temporary stop.

Milea turns her focus to the entrance when she hears the soft footsteps echoing in the darkness. The library warms up even more as the flames increase and the shadows die back into the corners of the room. Sonja sits up and stretches as Dysis enters the room and pauses. The queen has not visited this library since Liev showed it off years ago. She remembers all the couches and notices that many of them are now set up near the fireplace. Other than being relocated, the furniture looks practically untouched. Dysis clutches the pile of blankets she has in her arms tightly to her chest as memories fill her mind, bringing tears to her eyes. The queen shakes her head to clear it and brightens her body language a little.

"Apologies for disturbing you," Dysis addresses the room. "I brought blankets to help keep everyone warm for the night. There are more if needed, just let me know."

"Thank you, Dysis," Milea addresses and accepts the blankets. "You looked a little distraught when you walked in. Is everything ok?"

"I am just recalling a few precious memories," Dysis assures. "I'm also looking for Wyntre, have you seen her?"

"She went with Qwest to show Brion and Neil the troops," Vicki informs. "I think Brion is a little annoyed by her."

"I can imagine that he is more than just a little annoyed," Dysis says. "The staff tells me that she has not allowed Lord Brion to leave her sight since he arrived."

"She also has adopted her father's example in the way she addresses everyone, to include Brion," Milea adds.

"I think she is the responsible party for the storm that caught us here," Sonja says. "It died down as soon as she became frightened enough to lose concentration on it."

"That would explain this unusual winter weather we are having," Dysis muses. "Lady Milea, I apologize for my own reactions earlier today."

"My timing is not the greatest in visiting Selcros, Queen Dysis," Milea responds. "We share the responsibility for what occurred this morning. More importantly, have you recovered from the battle?"

"It takes me an overnight rest to regain my mystical strength," Dysis admits. "Longer if Koro has his way with me. So far, I have avoided him tonight."

A combination of heavy and light footsteps echoes in the room, coupled by bouncing on the wood floor. Brion joins the group and looks as if he is on the verge of losing his temper. Wyntre seems oblivious to the elf's mood and stays as close as she can to his every step. Snowpuff and Neil enter last, both pausing at the edge of the light to take in the scene. The snow leopard cub seems to grumble a little as if fussing about the princess's behavior. Wyntre is so focused upon Brion that she does not see her mother sitting on the couch.

"I see what you mean," Dysis comments and stands. "Wyntre, why did you follow the men to the barracks? According to your father, that is forbidden."

"Mother? I...what are you doing here?" Wyntre inquires, taken aback by the woman's presence.

"Looking for you," Dysis informs. "I am awaiting my answer."

"Qwest said I could go and I wanted to hear Brion talk to the men," Wyntre whines. "I'm so glad I did, he's amazing." She swoons and grabs Brion's arm, leaning on him.

Brion gives Wyntre a very displeased look then snatches his arm out of her grip. He moves away from the princess to stand and stare into the fire. Snowpuff flops down and gurgles as he waits for his mistress. Milea crosses her legs and sits back as she watches the scene unfold. Dysis shakes her head as Wyntre stares in disbelief at Brion. The princess's features turn to determination as she takes a few steps towards the elf again. Brion looks over his shoulder at the young woman, stopping her in her tracks.

"Wyntre, let's go," Dysis instructs her daughter. "Lords Brion and Neil, as well as Ladies Milea, Vicki, Zaria, and Sonja need their rest. We are all facing quite a day tomorrow."

"Can I stay a little longer?" Wyntre pleads, as if she is a child. "Please?"

"You are far too old to be using such tactics," Dysis calls out. "The answer is no. You are to come with me or you will be forced to leave."

"You cannot threaten me," Wyntre says, taken aback by the words.

Dysis gives her daughter a very icy look before she turns and, bit by bit, takes her leave of the library. Wyntre watches her mother go, satisfied by her departure, then turns back to Brion. She notices Vicki sitting in a chair near the elf cleaning her whip. Feeling eyes on her, Wyntre turns to see Milea watching her, yet the princess feels as if something dangerous is happening.

Instead of cowering in fear, Wyntre lifts her head in defiance, then turns and saunters out of the room. Snowpuff hops up and bounces happily after the princess. Milea muses casting an enchantment to change the young woman into something more cooperative but decides not to waste the mystical effort. Zaria watches the girl leave the room and uses the shadows to close the door behind her. Those in the room then turn their attention to Brion, who has remained silent since his return.

"I think he's still mystified by the condition of the troops," Neil observes.

"On contrary, I think the amazing Lord Brion needs a break from the annoying Princess Wyntre," Vicki remarks.

"Actually both," Brion admits and faces the room. "Lady Milea, how likely is Dee's arrival going to delay our trip north?"

"Since she knows I'm here, highly likely," Milea assures. "Your question brings concern to me, Lord Brion."

"As it should," Brion pulls an empty chair to sit in front of Milea. "The troops that Koro has assigned for tomorrow are not to my standards."

"From my assessment, they would barely fight their way out of a flour bag," Neil adds. "Qwest believe they are adequate for the battle tomorrow."

"Today's blizzard has guaranteed that we will be here for Dee tomorrow, regardless of our urge to get out as fast as we can," Milea says and rubs the bridge of her nose. "Bringing warriors into this cold climate is not a good option."

"Too bad that Temple of Light has been destroyed," Zaria frowns. "What's the plan for tomorrow?"

"That will be dictated by Dee's timing," Milea offers, "and the fact that she is yet unaware of your presence."

The halls become less crowded as those in the castle start to settle down for the night. Snowpuff chuffs as he waddles after the queen and princess, fighting to keep up with the two. Dysis takes her time going over the details of Wyntre's interaction in the library. She processes her thoughts, knowing that Wyntre is Koro's favorite child even though he claims she is adopted. If the princess is somehow unsettled by anyone, the perpetrator typically faces the wrath of the king.

Dysis has escaped this fate so far, however, with someone such as Brion now in the princess's sights, the queen knows that those days are likely numbered. Wyntre daydreams next to her mother, thoughts firmly fixed on the time she spent with Brion. She smiles, wishing it had lasted much longer and had been more intimate. Perhaps next time.

"Wyntre, why are you annoying Lord Brion?" Dysis inquires.

"I like to call it pursuing," Wyntre says, haughtily. "He's handsome and possibly the strong king I'm looking for."

"Ah yes, you are searching for a husband similar to your father," Dysis recollects. "A strong and powerful king. Koro is a king, but his strength and power came at a heavy price."

"Father often tells me that people were not happy when he became king, but they are now prospering under his rule," Wyntre dismisses her mother's words.

"Koro likes to twist history to his liking," Dysis observes. "I never told you how Koro and I married. It is a bit embarrassing to me but he forced my hand. A threat to take away more of what I loved shifted my stance. I should have called his bluff instead, but that is hindsight now."

"Tsk, mother. Father told me he wooed you and swept you off your feet," Wyntre scolds. "In fact, you were so in love with him that you could not bear to live without him. I will do the same to Brion before he leaves. He will never forget me and will want to be with me for the rest of his life."

"You are in for a very rude awakening, child," Dysis informs the love-struck girl. "I will give you fair warning. Brion is not as susceptible to threat tactics as I was long ago. He will not bend to you, no matter what. He has told you his wishes. My advice is that you leave him alone and when he leaves let him go. There are plenty of strong kings just like your father in this enormous world of ours." She walks away, leaving the princess in the hall.

The night wears on and eventually all the castle residents and guests are asleep. A'drianis perks up when she senses a Tragin approaching and the door to the library opens a crack. The shiadokat growls and folds the shadows around her form. Snowpuff stalks into the library carefully and heads straight to the sleeping guests. The fire has gone out, placing the entire room into darkness. The cub sniffs the air and growls to himself, smelling something faint and unusual on the air. The fur on his feet further muffles his footsteps, yet he is seen clear as day by the one that is stalking him.

A'drianis allows the cub to pass within inches of her before she changes form and jumps to the top of the bookcases to follow the cub, in silence. She warps the shadows in front of the cub to fool him into believing that he had arrived at the library encampment. Snowpuff pauses when he locates a figure which he perceives, to be Brion.

A'drianis jumps down from the bookcase and lands on the floor as Snowpuff crouches down, wiggles his backside, then jumps with his claws exposed, intending to rip the elf apart. He sails straight through the image and lands on the floor, causing a look of surprise to cross his features. Snowpuff then lets out a squeak of shock when something swats him, harshly. The blow sends him clear across the room, back toward the door he had entered. A figure melts out of the shadows, causing the cub to hold back a scream in fright.

"Boo..." A'drianis growls.

Snowpuff backs up when he sees the large panther. She is the size of a tiger with fur dark as the night. The whites of her eyes are shining a pristine blue color, the pupils just as dark as her fur. Enormous black dragon wings unfold as she draws herself up to glare down at the cub. Snowpuff squeaks again and shuffles backwards a few more steps as the Eltis stalks toward him. A long mane of black hair flows down over the panther's shoulders as she bends down to focus upon her quarry. Her wings fold down against her body as a low, dangerous, growl emits from her throat. Snowpuff turns around and hightails it out of the library, pursued closely by A'drianis.

The snow leopard cub runs down the hall and slides around the corner. He manages to get his feet back under him and bounces into the throne room. He turns to face his pursuer, but sees no one following him. He looks around and frowns at the lighting of the room. It is much darker than normal. A'drianis continues to walk silently overhead from one beam to the next within the rafters. She studies the cub and realizes that she has to draw out the Tragin or kill both it and the cub to eliminate the threat. A'drianis' senses alert her to someone approaching that seems more than mortal. Perhaps another Tragin? Hesitantly, she lifts the shadows on the throne room but takes great care to keep herself hidden.

"There you are Snowpuff," Wyntre says as she enters the room. "Did you get lost? Just remember those mice that you are chasing are not toys, so do not bring one to my bed. Come on, let's go to my room." She picks up the whining cub and carries him out of the room. Once she is gone, A'drianis drops down to the floor, landing lightly on her feet.

"Damn," A'drianis frowns, then uses the shadows to return to the library.

The door to the bedroom opens and closes as Wyntre takes her pet into her room and places him on her bed. Snowpuff stops whimpering once he is safe in the princess's room. Wyntre opens her window and peers out onto the cold, dark, landscape with a little bit of a grin. The cub squeaks and stares at the young woman when cold air wafts into the room. Wyntre does not feel the change in temperature as she sits down in front of her mirrored dresser and opens a well-used book. She turns the page to a mirror spell and reads it over before looking at her reflection. She waves her hand and the image in the mirror falls away, revealing a reflection of the library from the large antique mirror above the fireplace.

Wyntre observes that most of the guests are asleep, yet she does not see Milea. The princess decides that she will deal with the sorceress later and test her new skills first. The princess focuses on Vicki, sleeping on a couch closest to the fireplace, and grins evilly. The winds outside her window pick up the snow and swirl it into an icy cyclone before it streaks into the mirror and quietly surrounds Vicki.

In the library, Milea stares out the window toward the mountain, now clearly seen on the horizon. She does not pay much attention to her sleeping companions as she focuses on her mission. The moons are approaching the time that she needs to locate the Temple of Nag'teragiea. Milea mutters a few words of hope that Dee attacks early in the day so that she can be out of Selcros before nightfall.

A soft blue light to her right barely catches Milea's attention at first, but its constant pulsing soon becomes annoying enough for the sorceress to turn and investigate. She is expecting a spirit or restless soul in the old library, but what she sees shocks her. A cold light is streaming from the mirror and surrounding Vicki. The L'vane woman seems to be having trouble breathing the cold air as it invades her lungs. Milea utters an expletive as she uses her telekinetic abilities to push the couch out of the cold blue light. The light spreads out over the wooden floor, freezing the wood and turning any moisture upon it to solid ice. Milea moves the other couches out of reach of the spell as she goes to check on Vicki. The woman is now breathing normally and groans a little in her sleep.

"Who in Ublivion…?" Milea quietly asks as she turns to the mirror.

The spell is still spilling from the looking glass and seems to be seeking its victim. A flame flashes in Milea's eyes as she purposefully moves to stand in front of the mystical predator. The fireplace roars to life, melting the ice as well as stopping the spell from spilling to the floor. It evaporates as soon as it hits the heat. Milea glares into the mirror and waves her hand once to reveal the perpetrator. In her room, Wyntre gasps as the mirror's image changes from the library to a pair of enchanting brown eyes. The mirror cracks as the princess stands up then shatters as a force crash into the young woman. Wyntre screams in surprise and pain as she sails back and slams into the wall just above her bed. She falls face forward onto the feather comforter, unconscious.

CHAPTER SEVEN

Tandon Attack

The king's boisterous laughter as well as his blatant insults fade as he and his men exit the castle. Brion and Neil are retrieved by Qwest to join ranks with the soldiers on the fields outside of town. The Alnis prince is surprised to see that the men are unaccompanied. Brion dismisses Qwest's tunnel vision regarding his friends as he grudgingly exits the room. Down the hall and into the throne room, Milea is greeted by the light of the dawn. She watches as Koro and his inexperienced army walk onto the field as if they are going on a picnic. Zaria stretches in the shadows as the queen enters the room. Dysis approaches her guests, bidding all a good morning.

"Koro seems eager this morning," Dysis says as she notes the battlefield.

"He is eager to discredit the things that I warned him of," Milea responds. "In truth I am surprised that he is outside. Perhaps he listened a little last night."

"I think we have to thank Brion for that," Dysis credits. "I looked out back before I came down. All his forces are concentrated on the harbor. Luckily, I did not see any movement associated with an attack at the back gate. I did inform the guards there to stay on high alert since there will be a total eclipse today."

"That is good to hear, now we are in a waiting game," Milea said.

A thick fog rolls in from the harbor, hiding the entire city in a blanket of low clouds. Milea concentrates on the phenomena and frowns a little, thinking that it is too thick to be formed by nature. Snowpuff roars in joy as he bounces into the room preceding the arrival of the Princess. Wyntre uses caution as she approaches the Queen, giving Milea a wide berth in the process. Dysis cocks her head to the side in curiosity when she notices slight bruising about the young woman's features. Seeing the look on her mother's face, the princess tries to explain by saying that an unknown assailant attacked her. Milea listens to her story, then decides to confront the girl about the actual event that led to Wyntre's condition.

"Wyntre, why did you attack Vicki last night through the library mirror?" Milea inquires in a calm manner.

"I..." Wyntre stutters, then draws herself up to stand taller. "How dare you accuse me of this nonsense!"

"She did what?" Dysis focuses on her guest. "What kind of spell?"

"From what I can tell, it freezes the victim to death, starting at the lungs," Milea deduces. "I know Wyntre cast the spell. I saw her weaving it through the mirror."

"You have no proof of that," Wyntre defends herself.

"Is Vicki all right?" Dysis inquires.

"Still asleep when I left the library. Sonja is keeping an eye on her as well to assure that she wakes up," Milea explains.

"I will pray that she recovers," Dysis offers then turns her attention towards her daughter. "Wyntre, you still need to explain your reasoning to Lady Milea."

"I owe her nothing," Wyntre corrects.

"Very well, Wyntre," Milea said. "I will not be so lenient the next time you attack."

"How dare you threaten me," Wyntre sulks. "Mother, I don't think she should get away with this."

"What is she getting away with?" Dysis inquires. "There is no issue unless you are foolish enough to attack. I would take heed if I were you because I do not see Lady Milea making idle threats."

"Indeed," Milea agrees.

Laughter coming from down the hall brings a bit of relief to Milea as Vicki and Sonja enter the room. Wyntre takes a couple steps back as Vicki approaches Milea and glances out the window. The fog is still intense, yet she can see a few fires that have been started on the field.

Sonja decides to play with Snowpuff as the two bounce around the throne room, careful to avoid both furniture and people. The snow leopard cub locks eyes with his playmate, a strange gleam cutting across his pupils. Sonja sees it and arches an eyebrow before she dodges, with lightning speed, out of the animal's way and once again faces him.

Vicki turns from the window then calls for the snow leopard cub's attention. She moves away from Milea so that she has room to runs the young animal through several tricks. Snowpuff sits up and chuffs happily when he gets a pat on the head as a reward. Vicki snaps her fingers and points with a command to roll over. The cub obeys the commands. Wyntre huffs in agitation as she watches the shenanigans. Vicki tosses Snowpuff a stick of jerky and walks away. The cub jumps up and catches the treat then wrestles with it as he chews.

Zaria watches the snow leopard cub as she determines whether killing the creature is worth the headache. She recalls the quick change in Snowpuff just before attacking Sonja. The training display that Vicki put the cub through, however, leads the shiadokat to conclude that the hidden Tragin is a nonissue at this time. Zaria turns her attention back to the window as she recalls the brief news of a total eclipse.

The event will cast the odds in their favor, particularly since Dee is not aware of her presence. Vicki returns to her post next to Milea to report that there is still no activity in the back and the fog is thin in the trees. She reports that the other vulnerable sides of the castle and city are also void of any signs of attack. The news leads Milea to only one deduction.

"She's already here," Milea quietly concludes.

"I am thinking the same," Dysis agrees. "How do we flush her out?"

"Hmmm..." Milea folds her arms across her chest.

"I'm going to go down and talk to Neil, see if he has noticed anything," Vicki volunteers. "I'll stop by the bakery on the way out to the troops."

"May I go as well?" Sonja asks.

"Just stay alert," Milea warns.

"I will go with them," Dysis offers. "The baker has a cupcake she makes from pine nut flour. It's quite good."

Dysis ignores Wyntre as she walks out of the room with Vicki and Sonja. The youngest one bouncing a little as they depart. The princess glares after her stepmother, then turns her attention to the unwanted guest. Wyntre's attitude changes when Milea glances at the nervous princess then focuses back on the forest as Zaria steps to the window. Wyntre decides to distance herself from the sorceress by leaving the room via a side door. Snowpuff follows his mistress, not wanting to be in the same room with Zaria by himself. Milea glances over her shoulder for a moment when she notices the departing pair as she continues to scan the area.

The fog has all but lifted by now, providing a beautiful sight of the bay sparkling in the sun and several men sitting on the snow around campfires. One of the trees in the forest begins to sway in an unusual way, as if a large creature is stretching itself against it. Once it is noticed, the tree stops moving as fast as it started. Milea arches an eyebrow at the movement. She watches the tree for a few more minutes before she turns and quietly leaves the room. Zaria focuses on the forest, where glints of metal catch her eye. She calculates the height and size of the creature carrying it and concludes that this invader is not made of all Alnis or Noturi .

Several furhens decide to start their walk for the day, parading in the street, leaving their roost to journey to the backyard of the baker's home. Sonja comments that the hens are the furriest chickens she's ever saw in her life. Vicki notes the size, each hen being equivalent to a great horned owl or larger. Dysis smiles at the antics of the two as she greets the townsfolk. More than a few of them are stunned to see the queen walking around with such freedom. Once they arrive at the baker's shop, Dysis leaves her guests to head to the grounds beyond the gates. The guards look confused as the queen walks onto the field and approaches two of the commanders. Brion notices the queen coming toward them first and alerts his friend.

"Brion, Neil, how are things going out here?" Dysis inquires as she stands in front of the seated men.

"Cold but anticipative," Neil admits, getting to his feet. "His Majesty is having a good time slinging insults about Lady Milea. Brion and I found it tiresome and isolated ourselves over here."

"Koro and his men have also taken to drinking a few strong spirits as we wait," Brion adds. "I've been focused on the trees; I think something is hiding within them."

"Milea has a hunch that Dee is already here. I agree with her," Dysis admits. "The assumption is that Dee is waiting for something."

"If it's for Koro and the men to get drunk, then she's late," Brion offers. "We need a new plan and new troops."

"Hmm..." Dysis turns to watch the king and his men. She takes a deep breath. "Ok, let me see what I can do."

"Be careful, milady," Neil warns.

The smell of the sea drifts upon the breeze toward the camp from the harbor. The slight draft also brings the aroma of liquor in Dysis's direction as she meanders towards her husband. She pauses and shakes her head from the pungent odor to clear her watering eyes. Shifting her path, she makes sure to keep from being downwind from the troops as she continues her approach.

Koro is sitting on a makeshift throne as he mocks the words of Milea while his men and son laugh at his antics. A large flask of wine is being passed among the men, filling them with good spirits. Koro looks up and laughs, causing his men to turn and see why their leader is so humored. Dysis pauses and places her hand on her hip as she takes in all the merrymaking around her.

"Koro, this is no laughing matter, nor is it a joke," Dysis informs. "Dee is here, you need to flush her out before she gains the upper hand."

"She's here, you say?" Koro laughs loud enough to drown out his troop's bantering. "Don't tell me that you also believe in invisible goblins, Dysis."

"I assure you, Koro, that this gremlin is very real," Dysis advises.

Koro laughs once again, failing to notice Brion getting to his feet. Neil swears as he draws his blade along with his friend. Both are facing the forest as several blackbirds call in alarm and take to the skies. A thundering battle cry from hundreds of men and animals roar from the woods as the Noturi attack.

The Wild Men are painted in various colors and designs for protection as they ride on the backs of giant horned mountain bruins. A few even have artic wolves as mounts as they cross the space between the woodland and Koro's men with great speed. The king stares, dumbfounded, before he swears and runs for his horse, yelling at the men to prepare for battle. Koro then orders his wife off the field as he yanks on the reins, turning his stallion to meet the enemy head-on. Dysis ignores her husband as she looks up. A great deal of unkind words escapes her while she raises a shield of snow and ice. The quick protection is taken down by a single blow of flame as Dee levitates down to the ground.

"Why, Queen Dysis, where is your red-haired guest?" Dee asks with a bit of sarcasm. "I expected her to be here instead of you."

"Lady Milea is where she wishes to be," Dysis answers.

"I have you!" Qwest yells as he attacks, swinging his broad sword to take the Tandon woman's head.

Dee whips around and blocks Qwest with her sword. She backhands him, sending the Alnis prince to the ground. She blocks the ice spell that Dysis had cast to her and, with a flick of her wrist, sends the queen sailing back until she hits the wall surrounding the city. Koro attacks next and is knocked off his horse, flying back several feet.

The stallion whinnies as he goes to the side of the king in order to protect him. Dee chuckles as she places a hand upon her hip and causes her sword to disappear. She saunters over towards Dysis, being mindful to avoiding a battle between a mountain bruin and unfortunate Alnis soldier. The beast roars with victory as Dee passes.

Brion disposes of his latest opponent, then looks up to see Dee stalking after Dysis. The queen is struggling to get to her feet. He looks around to see that Koro is off his horse. The king cusses and swears as he finally gains his feet and is fighting to remount his steed. Qwest is on his feet but facing an onslaught from a mountain bruin and its rider. Neil curses as Brion turns attention to him.

The trees are moving as several Noturi climb into the branches, most of them appear to be women. At the same time, several more warriors emerge from the woodlands, charging straight towards the men already under siege. A group of dragon-like creatures waiting at the edge of the trees also catches Brion's attention. The creatures have metal armor and deadly-looking weapons. Most of the creatures are various shades of darker brown or green, but two of them are colored bright yellow and blue. Brion mutters a few unkind words as he looks about.

"Where are the archers?" Brion calls to the field.

"None assigned, sir. They were deemed unnecessary," a soldier answers as he fends off his opponent.

"Of all the hairbrained ideas," Brion growls, then once again raises his sword to defend himself against yet another adversary.

Koro calms his stallion enough to remount him and draws his sword as he calls to rally the men. The stallion rears up as the king digs in his spurs. The horse jumps forward and charge towards the enemy. Koro manages to take the head of one of the mounted Wild Men. His horse uses sharpened hooves to wound the beast the opponent once rode upon.

The giant wolf howls as it falls to the ground and then expires, joining it's master. The Alnis men start to gain the upper hand against the enemy even though they are outnumbered seven to one. That is, until the arrows start to rain down from the trees. Koro swears and brings up his shield to protect himself; his horse is not as lucky and is cut down by the bolts. Several of his men also fall to their death from the arrows.

A second wave of arrows flies from the walls and into the trees, surprising all on the battlefield. Neil turns and cheers when he sees Vicki rallying the city archers to attack the enemy from above. Half of the Alnis archers focus upon the trees while the other half aim at the beasts on the field. Another volley mows down many attackers, giving the soldiers a fighting chance against the Noturi.

An additional wave of soldiers pours out of the city to provide support for their fellows, many of them well-versed in dealing with the enemy. The wall seems to shake as Dysis hits it once more, cursing as she continues trying to block Dee's spell instead of dodging it. She brings up an ice dome around herself in order to find some protection. It is short lived as dark flames melt the ice, taking a good section of the snow with it. Dysis tries to get to her feet as Dee dusts her hands, smirking in confidence.

"So, Your Majesty, do you surrender? Or must I continue to persuade you?" Dee offers.

"You are requesting that from the wrong person, Dee," Dysis says. "I will guarantee that Koro will not surrender to any woman, no matter how bad he is beaten on the battlefield."

"You have great admiration for your husband, Dysis," Dee complements.

"I know his habits," Dysis corrects her.

The sound of rushing feet catches Dee's attention in enough time for her to block the first blow. She dodges the second but does not see the third coming at her until the attacker lands a fist right to her midsection. Dee swears as she hits the ground, land on her backside, and slides back a few feet. The Tandon mage turns over and stands up, focusing her attention on her attacker. Sonja meets her adversary's gaze briefly then charges straight towards her.

The girl picks up speed at an unheard-of rate and is halfway to her destination when a bright blue blaze roars to life around Dee. Seconds before the Tandon mage launches a column of purple flames toward the charging teenager. Sonja slides to a stop and crosses her arms to shield herself from the mystical blow. Her silver scales shimmer in the approaching light.

An explosion of snow, dirt, and water blinds both the queen and her rescuer. Many nearby warriors halt their combat in order to shield themselves from the heat and light. Animals panic and head back to the forest, a handful dying from shock. A second wave of heat blasts from the epicenter of the explosion, stretching out to melt even more of the snow and ice, reaching into the bay itself. The same flames suddenly retract back to the center and die down, allowing Dysis and Sonja to focus on the figure now standing in front of them.

"Sonja! Why are you out here?" Milea scolds.

"I saw the queen in danger, so I came out to help her," Sonja explains.

"Such a noble deed. How can you be mad at her, Milea?" Dee says, placing a hand upon her hip. "She is a rarity when it comes to youth these days."

"You're not helping..." Sonja whispers, melodically, under her breath.

"Sonja, get Dysis back to the castle," Milea instructs as she concentrates on Dee.

"Yes ma'am," Sonja hurries over towards the queen. "Can you walk?"

"I've a feeling that if I do not, I will be in more trouble than you are," Dysis says as she grits her teeth and struggle to her feet.

The queen uses the wall to help pull herself along to the gate as Milea rolls her neck a little to limber up. The shadows on the field start to double as one of the moons begin blocking the sunlight. Soon these shadows also have shadows as the strange effects of the eclipse combine with the powers of the Shadow Eltis. Milea glances around, noticing the strange lighting now filling the area. She is quick to focus back on her opponent when the air crackles. Dee sends a strong lightning bolt towards her.

Milea slaps the bolt back to its originator. Dee moves out of the way, but the mountain bruin and its rider behind her are not so lucky and are struck by the spell. Both mount and rider are instantly turned to ashes. Milea dodges a physical blow but fails to see the second as Dee lands a solid punch. Milea hits the ground, rolls out of the way, and returns to her feet in time to grab Dee by the arm. With speed too quick to follow, Milea flips Dee onto the ground.

"I sorely detest you," Dee growls.

"The feeling is mutual," Milea responds in kind.

Dee vanishes unexpectedly, causing her captor to stumble in surprise. Milea disappears as well, to get out of range of her enemy. Both reappear a few feet away, with Dee slamming into the wall before a red flame careen towards her. She crosses her arms and dissipates it so that it does not burn her alive. Dee sends another lightning bolt towards her rival, combining it with a spell of green flame. Milea grabs hold of the incantation, spins around, and sends it back to Dee. The woman disappears before it can hit her, and the incantation destroys a section of the wall instead.

Milea curses, looks up, and falls backwards into a rain of golden dust as Dee reappears above her. The Tandon mage lands on the ground, fist connecting with the soggy soil instead of her intended target. Milea reappears, kicking Dee's legs from under her to slam the Tandon mage to the ground. An invisible force shoves Milea away from Dee, sending her towards the wall. She manages to stop before she goes through it, landing on the ground. Dee sneers at Milea then turns towards the forest as the eclipse progresses further. The day becoming twilight. The spectacle is ignored as several of Selcros civilians begin a hasty repair of the walls.

"Grawl! Finish them off!" Dee calls to the strange creatures at the forest edge.

Milea's attention goes straight to the tree line when she hears a bloodcurdling roar from the pack of thirty dragon-like warriors. They form a line and charge into battle. The first few Alnis soldiers they encounter are slaughtered without mercy. Archers from the wall take aim and fire upon the charging horde. Their arrows bounce off the armor covering the beasts.

On the field, Brion shouts to those around him, orders to defeat the nearly-impenetrable beasts. He instructs his fighters to aim for the eyes or, if the soldiers could get close enough, under the arm. Brion explicitly tells his companions to avoid the brightly colored ones, as they are poisonous as well as venomous.

Neil relays the message to Vicki using hand motions and physical cues. She signals that she understands, turning to those on the wall with her. Vicki shouts orders to the archers and the information is passed down the line. Many of the sharpshooters step forward and take aim at the charging dragons. The arrows fly and hit their mark, sending five of the thirty dragons to the ground, dead.

The light of the sun continues to dim, throwing off the archers and a few of the warriors from their marks. The moon is now blocking the sun complete in a total eclipse. The temperature drops as a 'ring of fire' forms a halo around the darkened circle. The total eclipse surprises the attackers. Surprise turns to outright terror when twilight plummet into full-on darkness. Dee slides to a stop halfway to her opponent when the light disappears.

"What...?" Dee looks around then snarls, "A'drianis..."

"Of course," A'drianis answers from the darkness.

A large claw swings out at Dee's head and is blocked, but the blow sends her to the ground. Dee is quick to gain her feet only to be shoved from behind and sent back to the ground. She rolls to avoid invisible claws and teeth, regaining her feet seconds later. Dee blocks another blow then curses as she disappears from the battlefield.

A'drianis appears briefly, snapping her fingers then disappearing back into the darkness. The Noturi yell and scream as they run back into the forest, terrified by the sudden disappearance of all light. The strange dragon creatures all stand still as they allow all the Noturi to run around them. Brion notices the stillness of the dragonmen and calls to the soldiers to retreat to the city. The Alnis men start to trickle back to the gate, confused.

"Shiadokitty," Brion calls out to the darkness. "Take care of the Sierge before they gain their night vision."

"The what?" A'drianis asks, standing next to the elf.

"The dragon creatures," Brion answers in haste. "I'll explain later."

"I'll be sure to take you up on that," A'drianis retorts.

The defending soldiers are rallied by the king and charge towards the unmoving Sierge. A'drianis swears as she folds the shadows back around herself and chases after the charging men. The Alnis soldiers are within a few feet of the attackers when the Sierge look up from their apparent trance. The first wave of defenders is cut down effortlessly as the dragonmen renew their charge. Those elite soldiers defending the king are plowed through by a bright green and yellow attacker. Koro yells obscenities at the beast as it nears him and prepares to defend himself against the much larger creature.

Shadows fall around the king without warning. The deep growl of a jungle cat echoes in the field. A shrill of surprise and annoyance follows the growl, then the shadows lift as fast as they fell. Koro takes a step back when he sees, in the twilight, that his former opponent now lay among the dead.

The king uses his sword to poke at the body and swears when the tail slaps him. A barb on the tip of the appendage gives him a deep scratch on his arm. Koro, angry from the slap, stabs the body just to make sure it is dead, and proceeds to go to the aid of his son. Elsewhere on the battlefield, Milea moves out of range of one of the larger Sierge. Undeterred, he is quick to spin around then swing down his double-bladed battle axe. The weapon connects with the ground, burying deep within it. Milea's sword appears in her hand in a flash, and she uses it to sever the arm of her opponent before he can remove his axe.

The dragonman roars in anger as he strikes the sorceress with his bloody stub. Milea hits the ground, then springs right back to her feet as her opponent yanks his battle-axe out of the ground with his other hand. Foam and drool exit his steaming mouth as he stalks toward her again. Shadows fall upon the wounded creature followed by a loud cracking sound. When the shadows lift, the large beast is dead, his head separated from his body. Milea follows the trail of blood and bone and note that the head is being held by a taller woman with long black hair.

"Thank you for the assist, A'drianis," Milea says as she approaches. "What are those things?"

"Brion calls them the Sierge. He promised to tell us more after this battle," A'drianis answers and drops the head. "The eclipse is almost over, can you drop a few? I can handle the rest."

"I will do my best," Milea offers.

The Alnis soldiers are ill-equipped to deal with the Sierge, the invaders toying with them prior to dealing a death blow. Brion is defending himself against the second multicolored creature as Neil helps the townsfolk repair the wall. Vicki is watching the sky, patiently awaiting the sun's return.

The shiadokat disappears back into shadows as thunder echoes in the space. Milea straightens her stance, facing the battlefield. A green glow surrounds the sorceress's hands as the winds pick up around her Lightning crashes down onto her as she spreads her arms out toward the field. Milea lets out a mighty yell as she unleashes a powerful thunderbolt. It branches out and slams into ten of the Sierge, sending them to the ground.

Darkness falls onto the field once again as the moon begins to release the sun from its grip. Several Sierge shriek in rage, training their attention on Milea and those still alive. Soldiers start to retreat despite Koro's orders to stand and fight. They are cut down by the raging enemy as they flee. The shadow rolls along, killing any Sierge that it falls upon, until it fades away as the sun returns to the sky. As soon as the shadows vanish, Vicki once again orders the archers to fire. The last of the Siege, as well as any stray Noturi, are dispatched of in a hail of arrows.

Once the last Sierge falls to the might of the archers, Koro lifts his sword and shouts in victory. Milea ignores the man, her sights trained on the scene surrounding her upon the battlefield. The snow is stained dark red with the blood of both friend and foe. Most of the bodies that lie upon the field are Alnis soldiers, unrecognizable from the mutilation dealt to them. Milea kneels next to a soldier just as he is gasping his last breaths. She shakes her head and closes the young man's eyes, wishing his soul well on its journey. A shadow falls over Milea, catching her attention. She looks up to see Koro grinning down at her. Milea stands and takes a step back from the king to give herself room from his overbearing presence.

"Finally decide to show up when all the work is done, eh?" Koro laughs sarcastically.

"Actually, Koro, I arrived on the battlefield soon after Dee's entrance," Milea corrects him, placing a hand on her hip. "It seems the wound on your arm is a little infected."

"You mean this scratch?" Koro scoffs. "I'm surprised you did not pass out from the sight of blood; you are very coddled."

"You know nothing about me, Koro, which is your undoing," Milea chastises. "If you had but listened, you would not have the immense loss of life at your feet."

"Their deaths are entirely your fault," Koro accuses, pointing his finger at the woman. "You need to get used to living with the ghosts of the fallen, woman. I hear they can drive a grown man insane. I can only imagine what they could do to a fragile woman such as yourself."

Milea decides to remain quiet as the king, satisfied with her silence, walks away. Koro approaches his son while he bends down to get a closer look at one of the Sierge struck by lightning during the battle. The beast appears to be still alive, although its breath is shallow. Qwest reports his findings to his father as the king bends and checks the pulse. Koro then stands up and shouts orders to those men still on the battlefield to check on the various Sierge on the field and gather them up. Brion stares at the king when the soldiers are told to take the living invaders to the dungeon of the castle.

"Koro, that is an absurd idea," Brion speaks up. "It's best to put them down now. Do not put them in the same space as you and your family. You are purposefully putting your life in danger."

"I have my reasons for locking them in the dungeon, Brion," Koro said with a slight hint of anger. "I think you should mind your own business. If you feel like questioning someone's judgment, you might want to look at yourself. Only a fool would follow the lead of a woman."

"The skills of at least three women kept your city from falling, Koro," Brion reminds him. "You have seen it with your own eyes. Are you going to question that?"

"The battle was long, Brion. I suggest you rest up before your doomed trip north," Koro advises and turns to his son. "Qwest, make sure to tie these dragon things up before they are tossed in the dungeon."

"Yes, sir," Qwest bows to his father and waits until the king walks away. "Brion, I think you need to leave the red whore to her mad pursuit. You do not need her help nor do you owe her anything."

"Oh really?" Brion crosses his arms, remaining as calm as he could. "What do you suggest?"

"Stay here in Selcros and leave that woman to her fate," Qwest answers frankly. "Father would be pleased and more than happy to help you with Solis. No one has defeated the mighty armada of Selcros. Besides, Wyntre has taking a liking to you."

"If this battle is an example of Selcros might, I will pass on the offer," Brion dismisses. "I do not share Wyntre's fascination. I would rather she leaves me alone." He puts his sword away and leaves the Alnis prince standing in the field.

Scavenger crows caw as they circle the battlefield and swoop down to feast upon the dead. Soldiers grunt while tying up the living Sierge and transporting them, via a team of horses, to the castle as ordered. Milea scans the horizon to see that the snow and blood have transformed the fields into mud. She is relieved to see that the harbor ice is melting in spots. Unfortunately, the path north is still frozen over.

Milea turns when she feels a hand upon her shoulder and nods to Brion as they head towards the city.

The sorceress calls to Zaria when she sees the shiadokat sifting through discarded belongings from the attackers. Zaria picks something up and jogs to catch up with her companions as they cross into the city. The short walk to the castle is made memorable as Vicki and Neil join the trio on their stroll. Once there, Milea breaks from the group and heads to the queen's quarters to retrieve her daughter. Neil promises to pack up their belongings for departure to either the ship or the inn within the hour.

The bells of the clock tower toll victory, vibrating the walls and windows of every structure in the city. Dysis looks down upon the square from her window to see Koro parading with his soldiers and son down the main street and into the square. A small crowd of grateful citizens shower the king and his men with accolades as they continue their march. Dysis turns her eyes from the spectacle in order to search for Milea and her small band. She frowns when she is unable to find them among the crowd.

The queen turns to the door when a loud knock echoes through the chamber. Sonja stands up and is bold as she goes over and opens the door. Snowpuff growls and bristles at it from a distance. Milea takes her time as she enters the room and touches Sonja on the head. She speaks quietly to her daughter then steps past her to address the monarch in the room.

"Greetings, Your Majesty," Milea says with a slight nod of her head. "I've come to check on you and retrieve my daughter so we can get ready for our trip north."

"I am bruised up and a little bit exhausted from my encounter with Dee," Dysis says. "I saw portions of the battle. How are you?"

"I too am a little sore and tired," Milea admits. "Dee is a very tough opponent and so are the creatures she brought with her."

"I saw them, what are those things?" Dysis frowns.

"I'm told they are called Sierge, an extremely dangerous race of dragon I've not heard of until now," Milea answers. "I am going to talk to Brion about them once we settle down for the day. He appears to have extensive knowledge about them."

"If you are able to fight them, I'm sure they are not that bad," Wyntre quips.

"Humph," Milea scoffs at the words. "I cut the arm off a Sierge warrior. He swatted me with the stub before grabbing his weapon with the other hand. To kill the beast, his head was ripped from his shoulders."

"Wow..." Sonja whispers, eyes wide with surprise.

"I would say more than just, wow," Dysis agrees with the girl. "If you do not mind, I would like to sit in on the conversation, just in case they come back."

"Koro has taken a group to the dungeon, I think you need to sit in," Milea agrees and turns to take her leave. "Brion's in the library with the Dresdens and Zaria. If Your Majesty pleases."

Milea walks past the threshold into the hall with Sonja at her side. Dysis stands up from her seat and wobbles a little before following her guest. Wyntre picks up her pet and hurries after her mother. Snowpuff grunts and gurgles a little as he struggles to free himself from the princess's grip.

The main hall buzzes with excitement as servants rush around to fulfill the king's orders. The castle is being decorated in grand fashion inside and out to celebrate the king's victory over the invasion from Tandon. Milea, Dysis and Sonja mosey past a dark hall as they make their way to the king's library. Wyntre lags behind them and jumps a little when a hand gently grabs her shoulder.

"Qwest! Don't scare me like that!" Wyntre scolds and drops her pet.

"You'll be fine. Come with me, Father wishes to plan a celebration for our victory today," Qwest said.

"What kind of celebration?" Wyntre asks as she follows her brother.

"Whatever you want I assume," Qwest said. Wyntre smiles as she rounds the corner into a room. The door closes behind the royal siblings.

Milea and Dysis enter the king's library, followed by Sonja. The trio pause when they reach the encampment. Though it is neat and tidy, it is still there. Brion and the Dresden siblings are nowhere to be found. Milea glances around. with a slight frown. Zaria is also missing. The sounds of a soprano warming up her vocal cords echo from down the hall, distracting those in the room. The rich tones are gentle as it vibrates a few fragile pieces of artwork that decorate the library.

"Who is that?" Dysis asks, amazed at the sound.

"That is Vicki," Milea answers as she gently pinches the bridge of her nose. "Now, what demands have been made?"

"Knowing Koro, something pertaining to his impromptu parade," Dysis said. She takes the lead to follow the sounds back down the hall.

The dining room is decked out in the finest silks and dishes to commemorate the king's victory. An orchestra warms up in the background. Neil uses a borrowed mandolin to play random notes upon the musical scale. Vicki responds by singing the same note but an octave higher. Sonja sits down at the table next to Brion to listen to the practice and observe her surroundings. Every time Vicki hits a certain note, the glasses vibrate on the table.

Brion picks up his glass as he and Sonja both study the item. The metalwork of the base is impeccable, depicting a legendary ice serpent coiled around itself. The jaws of the serpent open to a delicately thin glass that has a ring of gold at the rim. The liquid inside vibrates with the glass and a low hum comes from the metal when Vicki sings. Brion places the wineglass back down and pushes it away. Zaria, sitting on the opposite side of Brion. She whispers a few complements about the musicians then cringes whenever the metal vibrates. Milea takes in the situation then heads over to Neil, followed by Dysis.

"Neil," Milea addresses her friend. "What madness has invoked this?"

"His Majesty heard from Qwest that Vicki and I are entertainers. The prince, in turn, learned this through one of our new fans from the inn," Neil explains and plays a few notes. "So, the king demanded a victory song. Vicki and I mulled over his request and the consequences he outlined if we refused. We decided not to add to the body count."

"I still might add to it," Milea said.

"What consequences did he toss at you?" Dysis asks.

"Well, one is the use of the icebreaker. He also threatened to behead us," Neil answers. "I believe he purposefully waited until Lady Milea was not near to approach us."

"I see," Dysis pauses as she collects her thoughts. "Lady Milea, I assure you that the icebreaker will assist you and your friends on your journey north."

A bad rendition of the country's anthem echoes in the hall. Koro, singing his heart out, marches into the room with his soldiers, son, and daughter in tow. Wyntre hesitates when she sees Brion sitting with Sonja on one side and Zaria on the other. All three ignore her as they listen to Vicki sing a few notes while listening to one of the violinists. Qwest escorts his sister to the head of the table, purposefully taking her to pass through the line of sight of the guests.

Brion's attention goes from Vicki to the princess causing a bit of a frown to come to his features. The princess is dressed in what appears to be bridal attire the evening. Qwest has changed into his full-dress uniform, proudly displaying his rank and status. Koro has changed out of his battle armor into his most stately outfit, complete with large golden crown upon his brow. The king cuts his song short as his eyes fall upon the room. He offers his guests a harsh laugh.

"Well, well. So good of you go join us, Lady Milea," Koro says sarcastically as he sits down in the largest chair at the head of the table. "Neil, are you ready with that song?"

"That depends, Your Majesty, on my sister. She will be singing the song tonight," Neil answers.

"I'm ready to get this over with," Vicki retorts.

"I hope you are good. The last woman who tried to sing was executed. I guess I made her nervous," Koro sipped his wine. "Maestro, play the country's anthem, that should provide a fitting backdrop to the song."

The conductor bows to the king, then turns to the orchestra and raises his hands to signal the ready. A deep, brooding song emerges from the instruments in harmony as the song starts to play. Neil tickles the strings on the mandolin to inject a little playfulness into the otherwise heavy melody.

Milea scowls as she walks to the table with Dysis and Vicki begins to sing a powerful song in an ancient language. Milea pauses and glances over her shoulder when she hears the song and the sarcastic words Vicki is crooning. The sorceress focuses on the songstress and smiles a little when Vicki gives a little wink. Milea sits down at the table as the wineglasses vibrate from one of the higher notes. Vicki walks around the room as she sings, pausing behind Neil for a moment. She makes him laugh at the words she bestows upon him through song. She then comes to stand behind Zaria, Brion and Sonja, each in turn, as she continues her melody. Vicki gently touches Brion's shoulders then gives him a gentle embrace.

Wyntre glares at the songstress as she takes a step back, claps, and goes into a second verse of the song. Vicki marches past the soldiers to stands, dangerously, behind Koro. Once at her destination, the songstress raises her song an octave. Zaria winces a little as the vibrating glasses cause her ears to ring in response. Milea leans to one side and watches as Vicki places a hand upon the king's shoulder. She continues to sing, in a complementary way, about his leadership skills on the battlefield.

The melody still in the strange language she had begun with. Koro draws himself up and appears pleased at the words, although he does not understand them. Dysis quietly asks her guest what Vicki is singing. Milea considers the questioner then explains, in hushed tones, that Vicki is singing complements to those who had fought but is chastising Koro about his handling of the battle. Dysis listens to some of the words interpreted by Milea and nods.

"I hope he is satisfied," Dysis muses.

"I hope Vicki is not going to be foolish," Zaria comments.

Vicki brushes her hands across the king's shoulders as she leaves him and walks past Qwest. She pauses behind Wyntre and continues to sing, stepping within the young woman's comfort zone. The princess shifts nervously at the woman's proximity. Vicki paces back and forth a little behind the princess then lingers a little longer.

After a few bars of the song, Vicki heads back to where she started from, standing next to her brother. Moments later, the song concludes She faces her listeners and hits a final, triumphant note that echoes through the hall. The audience in the room applauds as Koro sips on his glass, pleased with the melody of his triumph. Vicki and Neil take a bow, then invite the orchestra to do the same. The maestro is stunned but motions for the instrumentalists to stand and take a bow.

"Not bad," Koro admits. "But you did not break glass."

"I kept it under glass-shattering level, Your Majesty," Vicki admits.

"Koro, you got your victory song," Milea said. "Now it is time for us to depart."

"I don't think she can break glass," Koro ignores Milea as he challenges the soprano.

"Your challenge, Your Majesty, is accepted," Vicki said curtly. "Neil, play the Lark and the Nightingale."

"Ok," Neil takes a seat and picks up the instrument.

Koro sits back when the music starts to play again. The king smiling to himself, pleased with the result of his meddling. Dysis notices the smug look and frowns; she knows that the king will continue his challenges to keep them longer. The queen takes one look at Milea and recognizes that the game Koro is playing will lead to deadly consequences. Brion picks up the wineglass in front of him and calls over a servant. The room lights up with Vicki singing in a high octave. The glass vibrates in his hand as Brion gives it to the man and dismisses him.

Vicki moves a few steps back until she finds the point in the room that will produce the best acoustics, in front of the amphitheater that houses the orchestra. The wineglasses start to sing as they vibrate. Zaria to hold her ears as she retreats from the room. Undaunted, Koro picks up his glass as Vicki hits her last and final high note. The glass in the king's hand shatters, along with the others on the table. Koro pauses, stunned at the display, his hand now cut and bleeding from shards of glass. The silence in the room seems to last forever, broken when Milea pushes her seat back so she can stand.

"Your challenge has been met, Koro," Milea says. "We are no longer going to entertain you or your court. My company and I are leaving at first light to give us time to rest up before our daunting journey north."

"You will not leave unless I permit." Koro growls out.

Milea scans the king once then turns and walks toward the door of the dining room. The soldiers in the room are unable to move from their posts. Dysis also stands and departs, going after her guest. Neil, Vicki and Sonja follow after her, with Brion standing to take up the rear. Wyntre gasps as the elf turns his back on her, jumping up out of her seat. The princess runs over and stops Brion in his tracks, grabbing hold of his arm. Brion looks down at the young woman and yanks free, turning to face her.

"What do you want?" Brion asks, his tone intentionally snappish.

"I know you are not one of them, Brion. I want you to stay with me," Wyntre beseeches. "I can offer so much more than a cold and lonely death in the northern wilderness. We can be happy together."

"I am going with my company," Brion said firmly and starts walking again. "I'd rather face the wilderness than your ideas of a happy life in Selcros."

"Brion, you don't mean that," Wyntre scolds and once again blocks his way. "Please, Brion. Please stay."

"No." Brion answers, in a stern and final way.

Brion continues down the hall as Wyntre watches him go, clutching her chest. Tears well up in her eyes as she turns and runs down a separate hall towards her room. She just about collides with her brother, Qwest, in her hurried departure. The Alnis prince watches his sister then decides to confront Brion about the scene.

The library rings with laughter and good-humored chatter. Dysis assists her guests in packing up their belongings in order to move back to the inn. Vicki accepts the accolades bestowed upon her by the queen for not only breaking the glasses, but also shocking Koro with the feat. The flames of the library fireplace are all but embers as Milea puts them out. Neil makes sure he has his cape on in a correct way, then helps Sonja with her vest. The night is clear but is still cold, evidenced by the wind creeping through the stone walls.

Zaria leans against the wall and watches the interaction of the group. Her mind turns to wonder as she tries to figure out where Snowpuff has disappeared to. Dysis offers to help escort the group to the inn once Brion arrives to secure his cape and belongings. Heavy boots upon the wood floor catch the attention of those in the room. The library begins to echo with Qwest's barking as he and Brion enter. The Alnis prince is treating the elf as a subordinate and demanding answers. Brion stops suddenly and faces Qwest.

"Be silent," Brion snaps angrily, stunning his agitator with the aggression. "I did nothing to your spoiled sister but tell her the one word she refuses to hear. No. I do not want or need her in my life. I refuse to be collared into any relationship with her, despite her belief of the opposite. In a nutshell, Wyntre has issues dealing with rejection."

"Hogwash," Qwest snaps back. "Wyntre is only a girl. The least you could do is entertain her fantasies."

"I'd rather not," Brion retorts.

"Brion, do you need assistance?" Milea inquires, interrupting the argument.

"Stay out of this, witch!" Qwest snaps at the woman.

"You need to watch your manners, boy," Milea warns, her features darkening as anger overtakes her.

"I am not easily enchanted by you," Qwest snarls back. "In fact, I've had just about enough of you..."

It takes the Alnis prince three large steps to cross the room towards the sorceress. Milea does not budge from her position as Qwest grabs hold of her arm. Her features go from shock to pure rage. The flames in the fireplace explode back to full life and reflect in the depths of the sorceress's eyes. Milea snatches her arm away from Qwest and makes a simple motion with her hand. The Alnis prince lets out a sharp sound as he is lifted by a strong and unseen force. Milea then performs a careless throwing motion with the same hand.

The library echoes with Qwest's bellow of surprise. Dysis watches her stepson sail across the room. Neil dodges to one side as the Alnis prince flies over and slams into one of the free-standing bookcases. The wood groans from the impact. The bookcase tilts backwards and falls over. The top of the falling case clips its neighbor and soon the entire collection of freestanding bookcases are falling like dominoes.

Milea glares at Qwest as the Alnis prince struggles to get back to his feet. The fireplace is now roaring with flames licking over the top and destroy the antique mirror above it.

Brion goes over to the couch he had slept on the night before and retrieves his cape. He easily puts the large, heavy, cloak around his shoulders and fasten it at the top. Brion secures his weapon then walks over to the agitated sorceress and bows, catching her attention. The flames start to die down as Brion presents a friendly arm to the sorceress. Milea smiles a little as she accepts the gesture, placing both hands upon Brion's extended elbow. He escorts the sorceress out of the room and toward the entrance.

Neil playfully escorts his sister in the same manner, bestowing gentlemanly complements upon his sibling as they exit the room. Sonja jogs to catch up with her mother. Zaria walks out next to last, chuckling about Qwest's impromptu flight across the library. She calls to Milea to wait for her and increases her pace. Dysis approaches Qwest and pauses just a few feet from him.

"For the record, Qwest. Wyntre is very much a full-grown woman," Dysis says. "More than capable of understanding exactly what she is doing."

With those words, Dysis leaves the library and the mess created by the toppled bookcases. Outside the castle, the night winds pick up and die back down as the main entrance is opened. The night watchmen salute the queen as she exits surrounded by her guests. Dysis nods to the guards and heads down the path without looking back. Milea walks next to her as the group makes a beeline straight for the inn at the harbor.

In the castle, Wyntre bursts into her room, still in tears as she collapses on the bench in front of her dresser. The spell book on top of the furniture falls into her lap Her tears wet the dark tome she covets. The book starts to glow with menacing words whispering from the pages. Wyntre stops crying then, bit by bit, sits up. Her eyes staring straight ahead as if in tranced. The mirror image shifts to show the town square and the small group of people making their way towards it.

The princess's body start to glow and pulsate with a strange blue light. Her breathing increases when the wind blows open the window and an artic chill fills the space. The glow wraps around the wind and flow into the mirror. On the bed behind Wyntre, Snowpuff sits up and concentrates, focusing his and Wyntre's energy on the scene in the mirror.

Nothing stirs in the night with exception of the crunching snow from the hurried footsteps of the travelers. They increase their speed once they reach the town square. The clock tower strikes the hour of early evening with the sun barely hanging on during this spring day. The light winds explode into a full-on gale, catching all by surprise. The sky clouds up with streaks of lightning arching through the void and striking the ground near the group. The winds pick up the lightest member of the group with ease as it spins around like a madden top.

Sonja cries out in surprise when her feet leave the ground. The crack of a whip is heard before it wraps around the girl's ankle. Vicki holds tight as Milea pulls Sonja back down to the ground. Neil swears and take a step back as the swirling clouds start to move inward towards them. Brion echoes his friend's words when his back meet's that of Zaria's. Dysis keys in on the blizzard and reverses the winds to spin around her form. The storm explodes out of her grip and continues to whip around the square. The falling temperatures soon start to rise again as Milea seizes control of the wind.

"Dysis, let's see if we can make a way out of this thing," Milea suggests, feeling her grip on the element slipping.

"Get ready to run as soon as we create the crack," Dysis said to her friends as she stands with her back against Milea's.

The two concentrates, creating a strong wind that swirls around in the opposite direction to the storm that is determined to suffocate them. A bolt of lightning screams down and strike the two sorceresses. The energy is absorbed and used to slam into the clouds. The blizzard stutters a little, creating an opening to the left of the clocktower. Zaria leads the charge towards it. She dives out of the raging clouds and lands in a feline like crouch. Neil and Vicki are next to exit, followed by Brion then Sonja.

"Come on Milea, get out of there," Zaria said to the winds.

The storm emits a leopard like roar as it increases in ferocity. Zaria perks up when she hears it and frowns. Inside of the square, Milea and Dysis both focus on the blizzard as the winds press against them. Soon the clouds are so close to the two that they can reach out and touch them. Dysis closes her eyes and physically push her arms out, pushing the winter storm away from them. It inches back, yielding to the queen's will.

Milea pulls her concentration from the counterwind and casts a strong flame spell. It explodes, sending both she and the queen rocketing into the clouds. They fly right through the icy wall and land, not so gracefully, upon the ground. The two slide back a few feet then finally stop just before colliding with the rest of the group. The strong winds and clouds continue to blanket the town square, preventing reentry.

"What kind of storm is that?" Vicki asks, flabbergasted by the attack. "That's almost as bad as the storm we had at sea."

"I think it's worse since the cold takes your breath away," Neil said and looks around. "The sky is clear here."

"The storm is a super concentrated blizzard," Dysis explains as she stands up. "It's not very strong, but being very cold it is efficient enough to kill even those prepared for the weather."

"It has Wyntre's signature, but she is being assisted," Milea said as she also gets to her feet.

"She is being assisted by the Tragin," Zaria says with a slight growl of disapproval. "I knew I should have taken care of that annoying ball of fluff."

"I think we should get out of the weather before they shift focus," Brion suggests.

"The girls' school is behind us. We should be able to seek shelter there. As I recall, the foyer has a very large and well-constructed fireplace," Dysis says as she leads the way to the building.

"I'm all for that," Sonja chimes in. She jogs to the door.

Milea watches as her traveling companions head to the building, then face the mystical storm still brewing. The clouds have thickened, the snow now mixing with the winds in the confined area. Milea crosses her arms then walks away from the blizzard to follow her friends. The winds howl in the background as Dysis knocks on the door to the girls' school. The thick wood edifice shudders a little before it is opened by an old woman. Her hawkish features reflect her displeasure at being disturbed. However, her anger disappears when she sees who is outside the door. The old woman pulls her robe closer to her form and bows to the group.

"Your Majesty, I did not expect such a visit this evening. Especially after the battle," Madame Hawthorne addresses the queen. "Is everything alright?"

"We were on our way to the inn when we ran into a little storm," Dysis explains. "May we come in to shelter here for the night?"

"Storm?" Hawthorne glances beyond the group to the square, noting the swirling wind and clouds still occupying the space. She steps to one side. "Please, all are welcome at the school."

"Thank you," Milea said and enters the building last.

The heavy door closes with a thump and the flames of the fireplace once again heat up the area. The smell of fresh-baked cookies drifts into the room, accompanied by the chatter of excited girls. Madame Hawthorne locks the door again as her last guest crosses the threshold. Sonja goes straight over to the fireplace to warm up. The hostess takes all their coats, leaving her guests in the large parlor to relax while she prepares sleeping arrangements for the night. Milea sits down in one of the many comfortable chairs in the great room. Dysis relaxes on a couch and stares out the window at the persistent winds in the square.

"Brion, you promised to tell me about the Sierge after the battle," Zaria sits down on the couch next to the queen. "Let me add that those things are hard to kill."

"Hard to kill and extremely mean," Brion agrees and pulls up a chair. "A Sierge has all the spit and venom of a full-size elder breed mountain dragon in a small package. And always ready to explode."

"Can you elaborate? Do you know where those things come from?" Dysis inquires.

"Of course," Brion sits up to focus on his companions.

Brion starts by informing his friends that the Sierge are from the same continent that his home, Cathalian, resides. They are nomadic, usually sticking with the plains. The Sierge are warlike, each member of their society must literally fight to gain rank and status. The female Sierge are the most dangerous, they are venomous as well as poisonous.

"I remember you told me to avoid the ones that are brightly colored," Neil also pulls a chair. "You are telling me those were the girls."

"Yes. They are poisonous from tip to tail. They have a venomous bite as well as a barb in their tail. For a short time, even their blood is a potent poison." Brion explains "Lots of historical figures in Cathalian have used it, if they were lucky to have a way to get it. The girls usually lose their coloring and potency as they mature to adults.,"

"That could be a dream or a nightmare. I know a lot of folks back home that would love to be on friendly terms with one of those," Vicki said as she sits on the couch with Dysis and Zaria.

"Koro has an angry wound upon his forearm," Milea recalls.

"He may have been hit by the green and blue Sierge he fought." Dysis returns her attention to the room.

"My advice for that is to watch out for unusual behavior from the king," Brion offers. "As far as those he put in the dungeon, death is the only option for them. They will surely kill you once they wake up."

"Why in the world would he take them to the dungeon in the first place?" Dysis asks.

"Koro is the one who would know that answer," Brion said. "I advised against it."

"Another reason to destroy them is this," Zaria produces a large medallion. "It has the Seal of Tandon on one side and the Arms of Sorshana on the other. As tough as the Sierge are to kill, this could spell bad news for all Bri'al."

Dysis picks up the medallion to study the two sides. It is made from silver with various small gems encircling the edges. The amulet is about a half inch thick with an attached ring hinting that the item hung from a heavy chain. The queen takes in the dragon's claw crushing a heart with strange symbols around it. She flips it over to see the head of the dragon with a wizard's staff in its mouth and ruins for the eyes.

Milea sits back and stares at the flame, in deep thought over the situation facing Selcros. Her thoughts turn to the trip north to the Temple of Nag'teragiea. She stares out of the window in a single conclusion. She must leave the country of Selcros to its fate and complete her mission. Milea looks at the queen and decides to at least advise her on the wisest course of action. Madame Hawthorne returns holding a candle. The group stands and follows their hostess.

The door to the last room on the upper floor opens to allow Madame Hawthorne and two guests entrance. The large room holds an oversized king bed with posts that almost reach the ceiling. The mattress is dressed in the colors of the royal family with a large flag of the country hanging on the wall. Dysis glances around the room with a look of concern, not sure why the room would be decorated like the royal bedrooms of Selcros. Only a select few have even ventured into the queen's private chambers. To her knowledge the school headmistress has never been among that group.

Milea looks around once then goes over to the window to continue her thoughts. Madame Hawthorne assures the queen is comfortable then takes her leave. The blizzard has stopped raging in the middle of the square, leaving behind a pile of fresh snow. Moon rays bounce off the white blanket of frozen precipitation. A small fog wafts off the field indicating that the air is warming.

A trickle of water cascade from the eaves of the school's roof, promising that spring has not forgotten Selcros. Milea looks past the haunted battlefield toward her distant northern destination. The frozen sea is slow to giving way to warmer waters. Large chunks of ice break off and bump into the small ship sitting in the harbor Milea glimpses to her left when Dysis stands next to her, also looking out the window. Several silent moments pass.

"Lady Milea, why are you going north?" Dysis inquires.

"Hmm," Milea glances at the queen then back out the window. "There is a dark storm about to overtake all Bri'al. Its origins lie with Tandon and has grown to those whom they coerce into their web as well as those they force into it. They have at their disposal a very ancient weapon and the knowledge to use it. My sister and I have been charged to find and awaken the last remaining Eltis children of Keela to form a resistance against this imposing threat."

"Your sister, Maya?" Dysis frowns as she restrains from an outburst.

"Yes," Milea said. "Maya has been freed from the creature that drove her to Selcros those years ago. She does not remember the encounter with you and your family else I am sure she would have told me when I spoke to her."

"What creature had possessed her and compelled her to murder?" Dysis demands.

"A Tragin," Milea answers simply. "According to Shiadokat, here is one in your court that is influencing Wyntre. The one that Maya is freed from coexisted in the same body as my sister."

"I've never heard of a Tragin that would possess a person's body. How did she become free?" Dysis frowns.

"It was an autumn day in the forest of Greson just outside of a small city called Breas," Milea recalls, staring into the distance. "A battle between two very powerful sorceresses ripped through the peaceful silence of the woodland. It was a battle that I will never forget as long as I live. I was in a life-or-death struggle with my twin sister, Maya. The last spell I cast in that battle hit my sister directly, she did not block it. There was an explosion followed by a mountain of debris raining down, nearly burying her."

"Yet and still, you say she lives, how?" Dysis presses.

"I heard her call to me," Milea said. "When I moved the debris, I did not see the woman who attacked me. I saw one who needed assistance. She was dying and her one wish was to see home again. Home is Selvast Forest. So, I took her..."

"Home is a forest," Dysis whispers as her attention focus upon the pinewoods just beyond the gates. Milea glances at the queen once again.

"It appears that we have more in common than we first realized, Dysis," Milea offers as she turns and nods. "Good night, Your Majesty."

"Very pleasant dreams to you as well, Your Majesty," Dysis offers as she bows her head in respect to her guest.

Milea pauses at the door and glances over her shoulder at Dysis. With a smile the sorceress leaves the room and closes the door behind her. The halls of the girls' school are lit by candlelight to keep the shadows at bay. Milea makes her way down to the other rooms so that she can check on her companions. The giggling of the schoolgirls brings a smile to her face with memories of home floating through her mind. She can imagine the girls being just as mischievous as the fae of Selvast Forest.

Milea pauses by the room that housed the men and knocks upon the door. After being acknowledged, she opens the door to let herself inside. The room consists of two large beds on one side with a large nightstand in between. A small fireplace crackles and sputters, producing enough heat to keep the space toasty. A motif of purple and blue dragons with various instruments in their talons dances across the walls. Brion sits on the bed closest to the window cleaning both his sword and scabbard. Neil is sprawled out on the bed closest to the door, staring up at the stars painted on the ceiling.

"Gentlemen," Milea addresses the room. "I came to check on you and wish you good night."

"Neil and I are just discussing the timeline for our trip north," Brion said as the sorceress sits on the arm of one of the chairs.

"I'm not sure if we will get to our destination in the required timeframe," Neil offers as he sits up. "The surprise battle with Tandon as well as Koro's purposeful delays have cost us time."

"I know," Milea acknowledges. "I thought about travel through the forest, but that would be pointless. We do not know where we are going. There is also the warning from the Fáidh of Desitana. She told us to follow a sea course."

"Is the Temple of Nag'teragiea a Temple of Light?" Neil inquires.

"I am told it held that title some time ago, yes," Milea nods.

"Then I think I know the way to get there," Neil said and once again sprawls onto the bed, looking up. "They have a map on the ceiling. There is also some Elvish up there. I'm a little rusty on that."

"He can read ancient D'haradune but not Elvish," Brion quips with a smile as he lays back and looks up. "It says, 'Never forget the way home'."

Curiosity takes hold of Milea as she sits on the bed next to Neil. She exhales a little, lays back and look at the ceiling. She notes the stylistic map drawn using the cracks in the ceiling. A few miniature dragons march to a great mountain range. A large cave is painted in the middle of the triangle and appears to swallow up the dragons.

A blue line of water wiggles along a path connecting the mountain to a picture of a castle that is drawn over the door to the room. Various stars and constellations on either side of the cave mark the path to the destination. Behind the mountain is a large drawing of a temple, complete with columns. A band of dragons sits upon the top of the roof with their heads raised in greeting. They are playing and singing to those marching to the cave. Milea studies the picture in earnest, then makes a sound of understanding.

"So, it looks like we are seeking a mountain or cliff at the end of a channel," Milea notes. "Does that castle represent Selcros?"

"That's what I think," Neil agrees. "If we follow that channel to the left, we should be able to get to the Temple of Nag'teragiea quickly. That, of course, depends on whether we can get through the ice."

"If it's thick enough, we can walk to that cave," Brion offers.

"If it has snow on top, walking is easy," Milea sits up, then stands. "If it is pure ice, we would be doing more skating than walking."

"Didn't Dysis say she is going to commandeer the icebreaker tomorrow morning?" Brion recalls as he sits up.

"If she needs assistance, Vicki and I will be more than glad to lend our expertise on the subject of commandeering," Neil offers. "Especially Vicki."

"If I knew where it is located, I'd have done so already," Milea remarks. "We shall see, Neil. Until the morning, gentlemen. Good night."

"For the record, it is not parked in its usual hold for repairs," Brion said. "Fair dreams to you, milady."

"We can always go ask Wyntre where it's at," Neil jokes in his suggestion.

Milea smiles as she closes the door to the room, drowning out Brion's honest, very obscene answer to his friend's suggestion. She continues down the hall, greeting a few of the residents along the way. Milea stops at the last door at the end of the hall just before the stairs leading down to the lower levels. She listens and hears laughter from the room. It seems that her roommates are entertaining themselves. With a smile, Milea knocks on the door then enters the space.

The room is narrow and long with two sets of enormous double bunk beds pressed against the walls, leaving a narrow path to the back. Milea closes the door as she watches Sonja jump from one top bunk to the other with very little effort. Zaria is sitting on the lower bunk closest to the door, combing out her hair with her fingers. Vicki is sitting on the upper bunk next to the wall, the one Sonja had just jumped from.

"I think this one is the most comfortable," Sonja proclaims of the bed she is sitting on.

"Are you sure? You only tried all four beds seven times," Zaria teases.

"They are all comfortable to me," Vicki assures as she flops backward onto the bed. She sinks into the material. "Yeah, I'm here until we leave tomorrow morning."

"I just spoke to Neil and Brion," Milea says as she climbs to the top bunk to sit next to her daughter. "There is a mural on the ceiling that maps the way to the Temple of Nag'teragiea. Our arrival time, however, will be cutting it very close."

"Are you sure you don't want to come back next year, when the weather is warmer?" Zaria inquires.

"By then, Selcros will be Tandon territory," Milea predicts. "The little skirmish with Dee did not discourage her. I am sure she is waiting for us to leave."

"Could Tandon take over while we are at Nag'teragiea?" Sonja inquires.

"They could," Milea pauses as she ponders the situation.

"Did that mural show another way out?" Zaria inquires

"It did show different paths leading to our destination. I am not sure how accurate it is or if it is just an illustration showing a pilgrimage," Milea answers.

"I can take a look at it in the morning," Vicki said, sitting up on her elbows. "We are still getting the icebreaker, right?"

"We will get it, one way or another," Milea assures her, then turns to her daughter. "Sonja, I think you should sleep on the lower bunk. I think it is safest with your sleeping habits."

"I...ok," Sonja says as she hops down and scoots onto the bunk below Vicki.

Milea smiles and flops back onto the mattress. The cushion sinks to hug the sorceress in comfort. The conversations of her roommates as well as the giggles of the residents of the halls soon fade as Milea falls into a deep and restful sleep.

CHAPTER EIGHT

The Icebreaker

The peaceful night soon gives way to daylight once again. The sun blesses the region with warmth and light, melting much of the new snow. The call of the young residents of the school shouting a floor below stirs the visitors to awareness. Dysis stretches as she sits up to start the day. She smiles at the light, finally able to get a relaxing night of sleep without disturbance from Koro. The queen sits up and reaches for the ceiling and stands to look out the window. She smiles at the day then looks at the clock.

With a frown she turns from the window in search of something to wear. She pauses in her search when she sees the civilian outfit hanging on a peg just outside the closet. It is forest green and looks both warm and comfortable. A light green cape had been laid across the foot of the bed to keep her warm overnight. Dysis looks at her royal attire that she had worn the previous night. The material is light and airy as well as thin and very expensive. The queen contemplates the two garments then reaches for the warmer clothing.

The large foyer of the girl's school echo with squeals of glee as three young members run as fast as they can. Sonja lope behind them, playing game of tag with the younger girls. She keeps her pace purposefully slower than the girls to extend the game just a little longer. Vicki and Neil are approached by a group of teenagers that happen to be at the event the siblings took over a few nights ago. Neil agreed to listen to them as they sing the musical scale. Vicki gives the teenagers a few lessons on how to hit the notes they are straining to reach. Milea speaks candidly to Madame Hawthorne about the dangers they face going north. The headmistress describes the various creatures including ice dragons and mountain bears.

The elder mention a legendary guardian protecting an old temple, but she has no further details. Brion listens to the various conversations going on around him, taking comfort on the large couch. Zaria is sitting on the opposite side of the couch, cleaning her daggers as she listens. Dysis enters the space and pauses to take in the activities. The toll of the clock tower is echoes softly inside the school as she counts the bells. The queen frowns a little; it is seven o'clock and Koro will be getting out of bed in about an hour if they are lucky.

"Good morning, Dysis. I did not recognize you without your usual attire," Brion greets the queen as he sits up.

"I decided on something warmer than court apparel," Dysis responds. "I'm going to need it aboard the icebreaker."

"First we have to find it," Zaria said and put her weapons away. "Any ideas? Is there another dock somewhere under the castle?"

"Actually, no. but there is one in a very inconspicuous place within the city," Dysis assures her. "For that, I need a favor."

"If it involves the icebreaker, I'm in," Brion offers.

"Me too," Zaria agrees.

"Good morning, Dysis," Milea greets as she and Madam Hawthorne make their way over.

"I hope you slept well, Your Majesty," Madame Hawthorne said. "I will have someone bring you breakfast."

"I slept wonderfully, Madame Hawthorne. I would like breakfast to go. I wish to get the icebreaker before Koro wakes up," Dysis assures. "Lady Milea, how was your night?"

"I had an excellent night's rest," Milea answers with a nod. "I see you are wearing appropriate attire to seize an icebreaker. Do you require assistance?"

"I do," Dysis admits. "My idea is to borrow Brion and the Dresdens, if possible. The crew of the icebreaker comprised a large part of the inn's audience the night you landed, and Brion is a leader among them."

"That will make it easier to get closer to our goal," Milea contemplates "I know Neil mentioned a possibility of commandeering the ship last night. He also said that Vicki would be more eager than him."

"I've already volunteered," Brion said and stands. "I'll go get Neil and Vicki."

"Let me go with you," Dysis says. Both walk over towards the Dresden siblings.

"While the icebreaker is being retrieved, I think it behooves you to get your own ship ready for a speedy departure," Madame Hawthorne suggests to her guest. "I'm sure once it's on the move, the large ship will draw the attention of the palace."

"Hmm," Milea looks out the window towards the docks.

The sun bounces off the pristine snow as Dysis leads the way to the jailhouse. A stone's throw from the main docks near the inn, the imposing tower has bars on the windows to add to its unfriendly look. Dysis takes a slight right into an alleyway between several buildings to circle around behind the jailhouse. The group runs into a wall where there should be another road. A large canal channels just under the oddly placed building. Dysis continues over to an ordinary door and knocks on it twice.

After a minute she repeats the knock, and the door is opened by two rough-looking men. Their sour look turns to complete surprise when they see the queen and her guest. Dysis smiles at the men then pushes her way inside with very little effort. Neil and Vicki follow behind, with Brion taking up the rear to close the door securely.

"What the hell's going on?" a gruff male voice yell angrily. "Who is interrupting training? I ought to skin you alive and feed you to the...." The man hesitates upon seeing his impromptu guests.

"Good morning, Captain," Dysis says with a smile. "I've come to borrow the icebreaker. Is she ready?"

"Queen Dysis," the captain sputters a little then bows repeatedly. "Sorry about me manners. It's been a rough night."

"I'm sure," Dysis agrees. "Now, the icebreaker."

"She's ready and fully stocked," the captain assures. "But I need to get permission from the king..."

"I assure you that Koro already knows, why else would I have Brion with me?" Dysis nods.

"My friends and I have need to go north," Brion said. "We will be using the icebreaker."

"Yes sir, of course," the captain agrees and focuses on the silent siblings. "Wait a minute, I know you."

"I do not remember making your acquaintance," Vicki answers in kind.

"I remember you," Neil admits. "You're the patron that paid for the last two songs of the night. How do you feel now that your head is a little clearer?"

"It feels fine and I'd rather keep it," the captain started.

"Good deal, then we should depart before you accidently lose more than your clothes," Neil reminds him.

"I..." the captain glances around the room to see his men appear to take the side of the entertainers. "Since the king knows, we depart immediately. Prepare the Iron Horse."

Seagulls sit upon the mast of the Lady of the Night, huddling close in order to keep warm. Sunlight bounces off the white landscape, brightening the mood and the day of those living in the northern climate. The ship sways gently as the passengers finally board after nearly a week of absence. The boards creak from the cold, sounding as if the ship itself is yawning as she stretches.

Sonja treads carefully upon the layer of ice, making sure to properly place her feet. She inches her way to the main mast of the ship. She loses her footing but manages to grab a frozen rope to maintain her haphazard balance. Thick, bumpy, ice covers the entire vessel from tip to stern, camouflaging it against the ice laden ocean just beyond the docks.

Zaria treads carefully around the deck, inspecting the ship to the best of her abilities. She steps down and swears as she loses her footing, grasping the knob to the cabin door in vain to maintain her upright position. Her legs slip from under her and she ends up on her rear end anyway. Zaria curses as she holds the offended body part and rubs it gently to ease the pain. The sound of rushing wind on the port side of the ship captures Zaria's attention.

A warm breeze caresses the ship, turning ice into liquid. Sonja turns in the direction of the original sound. Red and orange hues alarm the girl at first. Sonja takes a couple of steps back as her mother slowly boards the ship with flames wrapped around her form. The ice hisses as it melts away under Milea's footsteps, the water evaporating into steam.

The flames around the sorceress make a whooshing sound as they rush out to surround the entire ship. Mystical fire speeds past Sonja and Zaria, hitting them with the heat but not causing any pain. Snow and ice turn into steam as the water is boiled off the ship. Milea closes her eyes to increase the intensity briefly, then pulls the flames back to surround her and ultimately snuffs them out. Steam wafts from the ship as the sorceress casually strolls to the helm.

"How long do we wait for Dysis to return with the icebreaker?" Zaria inquires as her gaze falls on the castle. "I think the guards are stirring now."

"I will give them an hour," Milea answers simply.

"What does the icebreaker look like?" Sonja asks.

"I'm not sure. It may have some sort of metal affixed to it," Milea scans the cityscape closest to the docks.

Birds fly away from the ship as Milea's eyes fall upon the jail tower. Barely a block from it she notices an unusual cloud of steam rising into the air. The sound of metal grinding against metal sets Zaria's teeth on edge.as the cranking of a chain replaces the grinding, opening an unusually large gate to allow a great beast to exit.

Sonja climbs up to the crow's nest to watch to get a better look. One of the massive buildings start to move toward the sea.

The cracking of thick ice echoes in the air ahead of a ship made from iron creeps into the bay. The hulk of a vessel has the figurehead of a stallion rearing up. A deep red glow flickers in the statue's eyes and flared nostrils. Attached to the lower part of the horse is the thick and imposing hull of the ship. Blades spin around on the sides and in front of the icebreaker, effectively chopping anything in the path. The great vessel stops once it is pointing north and a lone figure levitates down to the iceshelf behind it.

"That's Dysis," Zaria observes. She turns her head when she hears an alert go off at the castle.

The winds carry the sound of the trumpeter to the bay. Dysis glances at the castle then mutters a few unkind words under her breath. She turns her attention back to the icepack and stomps her foot on the surface, causing it to crack. Sonja cringes when she hears it, the sound reminiscent of breaking a very thick bone.

Dysis lifts her hand and pushes it to one side. The thick ice following the motion, creating an opening for the smaller ship to sail through. Milea takes the wheel guides the Lady of the Night into the small area, barely missing the jagged edges. Dysis commands the ice to spread a little more to provide room for the thicker part of the ship.

The queen yells at the captain of the icebreaker to start the journey north. Steam erupts from the Iron Horse as it once again trudges forward. The thick ice is no match for the heavy blades as they slice and crush the frozen water to slush. Once the Lady of the Night passes Dysis, she refreezes the bay to prevent Koro's warships from following More alarms sound and raised voices are heard from the distant palace. Dysis uses her abilities to lift herself up and onto the deck of the Lady of the Night.

"The guards are more alert than I thought," Dysis comments as she watches the men hurrying towards the bay.

"Mayhap Koro did not sleep as deeply as predicted," Milea offers.

"That is a possibility. He is either irritated, suffering from his wound or comforting Wyntre," Dysis presumes.

"It looks like they are trying to get the attention of the Iron Horse," Zaria notes the men on shore waving and shouting, franticly.

"He knows better than to stop," Dysis smiles and leans on a rail. "Neil is using a very gentle persuasion to keep the icebreaker moving."

The Iron Horse picks up speed, creating a slightly larger gap between it and the Lady of the Night. Vicki sees this and picks up a rope, walking to the stern of the icebreaker. She ties one end of the rope to the rail of her current vessel then calls down to Sonja. The girl looks up in time to catch the other end of the rope and tilts her head upward to hear her mentor. Sonja acknowledges her understanding and ties the rope to the rails at the bow of the Lady of the Night.

The small vessel lowers the sails then jerk a little when the speed increased to match the icebreaker's clip. Milea keeps the ship in the calmest part of the Iron Horse's wake. Momentum picks up as Dysis goes to the stern of the Lady of the Night. She watches the guards and sailors use pickaxes as well as other tools to dig out a warship to pursue them.

The queen simply waves her hand again, freezing the channel behind the vessel she travels on. She casually raises the ice up to form a large hill of ice and snow. The sound of the men swearing soon fade to nothing but a whisper on the breeze as the two ships continue to sail north.

"The ship seems more cooperative," Zaria points out. "I remember when you tried to steer earlier and she was unhappy with you."

"I think the Lady of the Night is just as eager as we are to get this northern trip over with," Milea admits.

The day continues to pass with the sounds of ice crushing under the force of the Iron Horse. The landscape changes from city to deep and dark pine forest. Small songbirds sing to the passing group to welcome them to the woodlands. Curious squirrels chat up a storm as they follow the boats up the fjord.

Zaria is now manning the helm as Milea watches the trees off to one side of the ship. Dysis stares at the woodlands, feeling drawn to them. The queen takes a deep breath in and slowly releases it. She is feeling homesick for her past. Milea listens to the trees rustle in the breeze and relaxes, until she notices something stalking them.

"Dysis, does this forest have a guardian?" Milea asks.

"There is a great bear that lived in the forest," Dysis admits. "I have not seen her since I married Koro. He promised me that he would not kill her."

"Koro's track record on promises do not bode well for the bear," Milea said.

"I know," Dysis whispers, sadly.

Milea watches the woods for a few more minutes, listening to the winds. She goes over to her daughter and speaks to her in a hush tone. Sonja nods in understanding then quickly heads to the bow of the ship.

She climbs the rope that teethers the vessels together, landing on the bridge of the Iron Horse in record time.

The men of the Iron Horse continue to turn the cranks used to spin the blades below. Many are sweating so much that they form pools of it on the floor under them. A handful of sailors walk around to make sure their mates are well-hydrated. Vicki stands to one side of the ship, watching the woods go by. A golden light flash in the trees, catching her attention. Vicki stares at the last spot that she saw the light, able to distinguish the shape of a giant bear. Sonja notices Vicki's strong focus on the woods and decides it is best not to interrupt the woman, especially since Vicki has her weapons on her hip.

Sonja searches for Neil, finding him standing next to the captain of the Iron Horse. The L'vane man has his eyes facing forward to watch the progress they are making. Brion is leaning on the rail at the bow of the ship, observing the blades as they whirl around. The sound of ice being crushed is not as frequent now. The edges are simply whipping water for the most part. Much of the frozen stuff gone or melting in the sun.

"Neil," Sonja calls as she approaches.

"Hey, how did you get onboard, short stuff?" Neil teases as he turns to face the girl.

"I used the rope as a ladder," Sonja explains with a grin. "Mom sent me to ask if we can dock near the woods. She thinks that our ship may be able to handle the rest of the journey."

"I think she's right; it is warmer since we escaped the Selcros zone," Neil agrees. "Captain, how close can you get to shore?"

"With the blades, we don't want to get too close. The mud and rocks will dull them," the captain explains.

"A man concerned for his vessel, I like that," Neil complements. "Do you have a disembark ramp long enough to reach the shoreline?"

"Aye, we do. Give me a moment to steer her to the side," the captain relents.

The captain calls to his men to stop the blades and prepare to dock. Several of the sailors abandon their cranks and go over towards the starboard side of the ship. They line up and each bends down to untie an oddly placed knot. The Iron Horse slows down and glides over towards the shore, dropping anchor several feet from the shallows.

Zaria guides the Lady of the Night to stop a little closer to the shoreline. Sonja is about to shimmy back down the rope to her ship. She pauses when the sailors pick up a piece of the Iron Horse's deck and carry it over to the side closest to the shore. The men place the long plank on the rail, then slide it out until it hits the shore. Vicki tears her gaze from the woods to the oddly long ramp then to her brother as Neil approaches her.

"Why are we stopping?" Vicki inquires.

"Request by Milea," Neil answers. "Looks like we are untethering the Iron Horse and continuing up on the Lady."

"I think we should keep the Horse," Vicki frowns. "Just in case we run into some ice along the way."

"I think she has a reason for this," Neil said. "Brion, time to go ashore."

"Not a moment too soon," Brion mutters as he pushes himself up and makes his way to the ramp.

"Are you seasick again?" Vicki shakes her head as she follows him down. "I thought you had it under control."

"So did I," Brion admits.

"I think the enchantment on our ship keeps him from getting sick," Sonja said, standing next to Neil. "The stop has something to do with Dysis."

"That only creates more questions in my mind," Neil admits, walking with Sonja down the ramp.

Dysis seems in a slight trance as she walks off the Lady of the Night and onto the shoreline. The queen continues to the edge of the woodland and simply stares into the distance. Milea disembarks next and pauses to watch Dysis. Something seems to be calling to the queen from the forest. Milea looks past her hostess and notes nothing out of the ordinary.

The forest itself is not hiding anything malicious that she can detect. Sonja stands next to her mother and tilts her head from one side to the other as she searches for the fuzzy light she saw while on the ship. It is no longer there. Vicki crosses her arms as she stares at the specter watching the queen. It is no longer a bear but a tall, middle-aged, slightly heavyset woman. The ghost looks as if she is happy to see the queen, overwhelmed with joy but not actually wanting to get too close.

"Vicki, are you ok?" Neil touches his sister. "You are spacing out on me."

"I'm watching a ghost," Vicki answers simply. "She does not seem unfriendly but I don't think she's alone. I saw the ghost of a bear trailing us through the woods while on the ship."

"How big of a bear?" Brion inquires.

"Possibly half the size of our ship," Vicki answers. "Maybe bigger? Hard to tell but I do not want it to introduce itself."

"I agree with that," Neil nods. "Let's go talk to Milea."

The wind rustles a little as Milea notes the approach of her three companions. She looks to the sky to see that time is getting away from them. The sorceress watches the queen a little longer then turns and reboards her vessel.

Neil hesitates a little but follows her onto the Lady of the Night. Sonja jogs up the ramp and heads straight to the crow's nest. Brion goes over to Dysis and bids her farewell. He barely gets a response, and thus decides to leave her and follow Neil. Vicki catches one last glance of the ghost in the woods to see that she has not moved. Frowning with concern, Vicki boards the Lady of the Night.

The small vessel lifts anchor and moves away from the shallows and back into deeper water. The sails unfurl and tie into place by themselves as the ship points north and picks up the winds to speed away. Dysis turns in time to see the Lady of the Night disappear around a large bend and behind a group of tall pine trees. The queen then faces the icebreaker awaiting her in the fjord.

"Captain, take the Iron Horse and return to Selcros. Our mission is complete," Dysis calls to the man onboard.

"Of course, milady. As soon as you board, we will be on our way," the captain acknowledges.

"I will not be riding back on the ship, captain. I will meet you all in Selcros by traveling through the woods," Dysis informs. "There are old friends that I must pay homage to while I am here."

"Wait, what?" the captain sputters. "What do I tell the king?"

"That I made the decision and I will take up our differences about it when I return. I should be back in a week's time," Dysis said.

With that, the queen turns and takes steps into the woods. She ignores the calls of the captain and relaxes in the shade of the pines. The warm feeling of welcome radiate through her body. Dysis takes another breath then travels deeper into the forest. The captain of the Iron Horse watches her disappear behind some large trees with a worried expression upon his features. He reluctantly tells his men to turn the icebreaker around and head back to Selcros. If they arrive at night, they can return the Iron Horse to her berth and pretend the queen left after they arrived.

CHAPTER NINE

The Ice Dragon

The relatively calm waters of the fjord make for smooth sailing for the Lady of the Night and her crew. The narrow channel soon opens into a larger space like a bay or natural harbor. Three large mountains jut out of the water with the roar of a waterfall nearby. Sonja calls from the crow's nest to alert Neil of the location of the falls, much closer than is comfortable. He steers the ship clear of the danger and makes sure to make a note to mark his map of the location.

Milea steps to the front of the ship to study the three large landmasses that could lead them to their destination. The sun is starting to slip beyond the horizon as the moons begin to rise. Twilight changes the sky into an array of beautiful colors as the auroras begin to shimmer to life. A pair of blue eyes suddenly appear in front of one of the peaks. Milea to swear softly as she takes a few steps back. The eyes flash once then disappear.

"I knew you were not done with us," Milea sneers at the empty space.

"What's wrong?" Zaria inquires.

"Prepare for an attack," Milea calls out for all to hear.

"Where?" Neil says as he scans the immediate area.

The ocean in front of the ship explodes straight up into the air, blinding the crew. A large beast emerges with a howl of anger bursting from its lungs. Brion swears and falls to his backside as his footing is lost due to the rapid rise of the deck. Sonja is left speechless as she grabs the nearest rope. Neil is barely able to hang on to the wheel to keep his balance. Vicki's back presses against the wall of the cabin as she struggles find a grip to avoid being tossed overboard. Milea is able to maintain her balance as she glares at the creature attacking them.

The sea monster has the torso, head, front legs and paws of a male lion. From the waist down it is an enormous fish. Secretions ooze from under the creature's scales as tentacles shoot out. The beast grabs the ship in several places and pick up members of the crew Curses and shouts of surprise fill the evening air as the sun sinks on the western horizon and the shadows become long. Sunset turns to pitch black and a very different feline roar echoes across the water. The smell of blood fills the air as everyone, including the ship, is abruptly dropped. Sonja is carefully lowered to main deck much to her surprise. The shadows move, revealing only the shredded remains of the attacking sea monster. Zaria stands at the bow of the ship, glaring into the dead beast's eyes as the waves drag the head under.

"Those things are not supposed to be in these waters. Why did that sea monster travel this far north?" Neil questions. "Is he the legendary Guardian?"

"That would explain why he appeared here," Vicki responds. "No match against the cranky shiadokat."

"Let's get out of the carnage to someplace we can easily see the moons," Milea suggests. "Zaria, go find a space to warm up."

"I'll warm up when we leave this frigid hell," Zaria growls.

"I'm right there with you, shiadokat," Brion acknowledges.

"I think we all are," Milea said.

The wind fills the sails allowing Neil to steer the ship away from the bloodied remains of the sea creature. Large fish move in to clean up the grizzly mess quickly. After a few minutes, Neil finds an ideal spot to catch the moonrise. Milea takes a deep breath and watches as the moons, one full and the other half as much, rise over the waterfall. She pulls the book half and bracelet out of a sack and places them on the deck. The sorceress then takes a few steps back for the items to get as much moonlight as possible.

The moonbeam hits the bracelet, causing it to glow brightly in an array of colors. The red jewels sparkle as the item flies upwards at least ten feet into the air. The book slides under the bracelet on its own and flips pages all the way to the end. A pentagram with several ancient symbols surrounds it and lights up the deck underneath the book.

A beam shoots up from the book to the bracelet and then from there to the second largest mound of snow. The outline of the cave entrance is seen briefly before the bracelet simply falls to the deck; all energy lost. Milea stares at the mound, then grows perturbed at it. The space around the ship warms up considerably as the sorceress slowly moves to the bow of the vessel.

Flames run up around Milea, circle her form a few times, then she directs them toward the snow mound. Fire streaks across the sky and slams into the snow triggering an eruption of water, steam and fog. Once the air clears the entire snow mound is thawed and an entrance is clearly seen. The ship starts sailing towards the cavern at a fast rate. They reach the gaping maw and it becomes evident that they are docking inside a Temple of Light. Dragon statues sitting at attention adorn the sides with a sign above it.

"It says 'welcome home'," Brion interprets.

"It might say it, but I'm not feeling it," Zaria admits.

The Lady of the Night tips into the cave effortlessly, gliding on the cool, crisp water. A strong yet gentle current takes over, allowing the sails to fold down and tuck in place. Vicki looks up and notices that the ceiling is a thick block of ice. It glows a soft blue, thanks to the moonbeams above. The lapping of the water in the quietness of the cave serves as a lullaby to those aboard the craft. Sonja leans back onto a coil of rope and relaxes as she listens to it. Milea places a blanket on her daughter then heads to the helm to stand next to Neil. Brion and Vicki are studying the wall of the cavern. They all agree that the entire place is not made by Nature.

"She said this had once been a Temple of Light," Vicki recalls what Milea told them.

"This looks like a hall," Brion slowly takes in his surroundings. "Did it sink?

"Neil, there is a fork up ahead," Zaria calls back.

"I see it," Neil acknowledges. "I'll steer her right." He grunts as he tries to turn the wheel.

"What's wrong?" Milea asks.

"I think the rudder is frozen," Neil said. "Looks like we are at the current's mercy. We are going left."

The ship gently bumps the walls as it drifts down the left passageway. The entire crew is awed by the cavernous hall with its ice-blue light. They begin drifting past representations of the various Eltis who once were studied in the temple. The picture of Kaidar has deep claw marks across his chest. Keela's likeness as well as A'drianis' both have similar claw marks across the face, their alternate forms destroyed.

"I'm not liking this," Zaria says cautiously.

The picture of Armels has claw marks covering her entire body. The random strikes cause the observers to draw the conclusion that the vandal has vented a great hatred on the image. Only the top half of the depiction of Tadious remains, the rest of it completely clawed out. Milea crosses her arms, lowering her head a little as she contemplates the images. There are many around the world that would desecrate a Temple of Light, yet the temples themselves are usually protected by strong warriors and wizards. They are never an easy target since many of them are in locations far too challenging to reach. That is, until recently.

The ship rounds the corner to a depiction of an Eltis that is in pristine condition. The picture is of a powerful woman with the muscular definition of a warrior. Behind her are two animals. One is an enormous white tiger with dragon wings and the other is an even larger dragon like creature with tiger stripes. Milea stares at the picture and is hardly surprised when the picture glares back at her, the eyes appearing to follow her movements.

"Who is she?" Neil inquires.

"I don't know," Vicki answers. "I don't recognize that one."

"Grimalkin," Zaria informs the group. "We definitely need to tread carefully."

The ship bumps around another corner and through a double door that is held open by the waters they glide upon. Neil whistles at the artwork on the wall as they pass through the doorway. Brion takes a couple steps back in order to take in the entire canvas. The depiction is of a giant ice dragon complete with a crown of horns. The life-size portrait is about ninety to one hundred feet long from nose to tail. Large wings envelop the ceiling and a portion of the wall across from the main portrait. At the front of the picture and at the feet of the dragon are several figures, presumably frozen in ice.

"How big did Madame Hawthorne say ice dragons could get?" Neil asks.

"She didn't," Milea recalls.

The ship makes an abrupt and hard stop. Wood groans from the impact of the vessel colliding against a hidden object. Milea stumbles forward and catches herself with a rope to prevent her from tumbling down the stairs. Vicki slides forward but maintains her balance and stays on her feet. Sonja is tossed from the coil of rope where she had been reclining and quickly gets to her feet, ready to fight. Zaria nearly crashes into the bow of the ship, swearing and taking several steps back. Brion holds onto the mast, suddenly becoming entirely too familiar with it. Neil grunts and curses as the wheel dig into his torso. Attention goes to the front of the ship as Zaria swears again and takes another dozen steps backward until she is in the middle of the deck.

Ice crackles and creaks as it builds upward in front of the ship, reaching for the ceiling. The ship buckles skyward from the sudden rise of water. A small portion of the deck freezes over from the drop in temperature. Once the ice reaches a height of ninety feet it stops growing. A cold wind whistles around the area shortly before a zigzag crack cascade down the iceberg erratically. The sound of the ice shattering is accompanied by the angry roar of a giant dragon. Shards of ice explode outward, forcing everyone to shield themselves. Milea lowers her arm and gawks in complete shock at the new threat to her mission.

An ice dragon, just as large as the picture on the wall stands between them and their destination. He is covered in thick, dark-blue fur that only accentuates his muscular physique. A set of large horns fold back and curl under, with a second set sticking straight up, curling forward slightly at the tips. Large ears resembling those of a deer press back, revealing his agitation.

A long, white beard covers his entire chin, along with a thick mane of the same color around his head and long neck. He lifts his left claw and digs it into the wall, displaying both his talons and a group of lighter blue scales between his toes. Huge blue wings stretch out to block any light that may be pouring in from the moon above. Blue steam exits his nostrils as he lowers his muzzle and glares at the intruders. His eyes are yellow with dark-blue pupils, a light blue flame flickering in their depths.

"Whoa, big ice dragon," Sonja comments.

"Who do I have here? Visitors? Why are you in my home?" The Dragon inquires, his voice echoing the into the temple.

"I am Milea Sirus. I am from Selvast Forest," Milea answers. "I come to the Temple of Nag'teragiea to retrieve a relic. I ask that you let us pass."

"I am the guardian of the temple," the dragon said. "To get past me, you must defeat me through combat. Be warned, the last group that tried met a frozen and watery grave."

"He's kidding, right?" Vicki muses aloud.

"Afraid not," Brion answers.

"If my mission means that I must go through you, then so be it," Milea says as her staff appears in hand and hums to life.

A deep sound rumbles from the large dragon as flames erupt around Milea's body. Neil and Brion pull their weapons in support of their friend. Vicki studies the dragon's head as his wings start to encircle the ship. The shadows around the ship start darken slightly, barely noticeable, as Zaria crouches down. She studies the dragon's entire anatomy above water, keying in on his vulnerable spots.

A growl–click sound catches the attention of the crew and the great dragon. Milea loses her focus as the ship starts tilting and moving. The flames around the sorceress snuff out as she concentrates her attention on her balance. Sonja carefully approaches the port side of the ship to see who is boarding. The invader has her hopping back to make room for the smaller version of the great dragon as he pulls himself onto the ship with an audible grunt.

The smaller dragon is about the size of a pony and just as shaggy. He is chubby and possesses the same characteristics as the large dragon, except for the horns, which he has yet to grow. His ears seem larger than the rest of him and turn in every direction as he takes in the situation. The little dragon starts to heave a few times with his mouth open and eyes shut. Sonja takes the hint and drops to the deck just in time to avoid the little dragon's sneeze.

A column of blue flames rockets from the little guy's nose and mouth, the force of which scoots him back a good distance. The flames slam into the wall on the other side of the ship and freeze it. The little dragon shakes off a small bit of snow and ice from his fur. A squeak of excitement escapes him as he bounces over towards Sonja to sniff her little bit.

"Um, hello little ice dragon," Sonja says with a smile as she touches his nose.

The small dragon makes happy clicks then decide to lean on his new friend. Milea boldly turns her back on the giant dragon to watch the interaction between her daughter and the baby. Sonja pats the neck of the baby dragon then gasps as she loses her balance and falls to the deck. The baby squeaks in joy as he lays down next to her and places his head on her lap. A low rumbling purr escapes his throat as he closes his eyes. The giant dragon's ears droop down as if in defeat.

"Okay, what do we do?" Vicki said as she takes in the situation.

"I don't know but it looks like the guardian is just as perplexed as we are," Neil admits.

"Listen to that purr," Zaria comments. "That is one oversized kitten."

"For the love of ice and snow," the giant dragon mutters and rubs the bridge of his nose. "Bryce, what are you doing? Let the young lady stand and help her up, gently."

The little dragon's head pops up as he makes a couple of squeaks and stands up. He trots until he is behind Sonja and uses his nose to gently push. Sonja gets to her feet as more clicking is heard off to the side. Bryce starts clacking and runs around in a circle as his excitement builds. He hurries to the port side of the ship and places his front talons on the rail and leans over. His tail wags enthusiastically as he makes sounds of encouragement to those below.

The giant dragon frowns as several more of his hatchlings board the ship. The Lady of the Night sways as the new passengers bounce onto the deck. The coloring of the new invaders ranges from a midnight blue to pure white and all are as chubby as their brother. The biggest hatchling is the exception, being the size of a well-fed warhorse. Bryce clicks and dances around before he charges towards Sonja once more. His siblings follow his lead as they surround the girl, each chirping and sniffing.

"So, it seems our battle is forgotten, Sir..." Milea says as she turns to the former opponent.

"Dover," the giant dragon finally introduces himself. "And yes, no battle. Their mother would kill me if something happened to them."

"She has cause to worry. They are fearless," Milea complements him as one of the babies approaches her. "Hello, little one."

"I told them to stay with her," Dover said exhaustively. "Why did all of you decide not to listen?"

Dover's question falls on deaf ears as the hatchlings decide to spread out and explore the ship and crew. Vicki is coerced into petting two of the purring dragons when they approach and rub against her arm. Zaria chuckles a little as she scratches behind the ears of a midnight blue baby. Neil is taken aback when a medium blue hatchling decides to lay on its belly next to him and leans against his leg Neil lightly strokes little dragon's back and is rewarded with a few musical chirps as the dragon purrs and closes his eyes. Brion finds himself charmed while rubbing the belly of the biggest hatchling.

"They are all nothing more than giant kittens," Zaria said with a smile.

"And all boys," Neil observes.

"Yes, all twelve of them," Dover boasts. "And since they are here, I have no choice but to tow you to the center. Whatever you are looking for is awaiting you behind an enchanted door."

"Thank you, Sir Dover," Milea nods in respect.

Dover pushes back away from the ship and then drops out of sight into the water. The resulting wave gently rocks the ship, much to the delight of the twelve hatchlings. Dover reappears several feet away and shakes a little to clear the water out of his ears. He begins to walk through the water, towing the ship behind him. His footsteps thump loudly, echoing throughout the cave as he hums to himself. Milea remains alert, feeling that someone is hunting her.

Zaria watches the shadows, occasionally catching a glimpse of a feline head here and there. The sight makes her think about the different abilities of her clan, the Shiadokat. A few minutes later, Dover is pulling himself out of the river as he continues to tow the ship a few more feet. Once he is fully on the ground, the great ice dragon briskly shakes himself dry. He then takes a deep breath in and fluffs out his fur, the motion accompanied by a loud whoosh. With all his fur on end, Dover has the appearance of a colossal hairball with legs. Milea and her companions laugh a little at the sight of him.

Squeals of delight from the hatchlings capture Milea's attention as she faces the main deck. One by one each the little dragons imitate their father and fluffs up. Soon the ship is full of dragon furballs. Vicki lets out a sound of surprise, then giggles when the dragon next to her puffs up. He seems fluffier than his brothers. Dover relaxes his fur as he turns to face the ship. A smile graces his features when he sees his sons imitating his behavior.

"The doors to the Temple of Nag'teragiea are there," Dover takes a few steps to the side and nods to the ornate doors. "You will be the first adventurers in nearly seventy years to cross that threshold. The others did not pass me."

"I think we have a curious and fearless Bryce to thank for that," Milea said. "Regardless of the final outcome of our battle it would not have benefitted at least one party."

"Agreed. I bid you good luck in whatever you are searching for," Dover nods.

Dover turns and walks into a different part of the cave, a deep rumbling sound emitting from his chest. Six of the hatchlings mew in response as they jump off the ship and follow their father. Neil goes to the side of the ship and pulls out the disembark ramp as the remaining baby dragons watch curiously. Brion takes the other side and they carefully lower the ramp until it hits the shore.

Vicki tosses a rope after the ramp, then hops ashore to tie up the ship. With nothing to secure the rope to, she stabs one of her daggers into the ice and ties it to the handle. Sonja jumps off the side of the ship, landing dangerously close to the water's edge. Bryce and his brothers squeal in delight as they also jump off ship, each landing at various distances from the vessel. Milea walks off the boat with Neil and Brion and goes straight to the door, studying it closely. Zaria lingers behind as she stares at the door intensely.

"Why do I have a bad feeling about this," Zaria mumbles to herself.

A set of double doors, they are at least fifty feet tall, yet only about half that wide. They are carved out of a strange blue wood with various ornate symbols etched into its surface. Some of the symbols are clawed out in the same manner as the pictures down the corridor. Milea approaches the door and touches it, feeling a powerful spell upon the wood. She takes out the bracelet and book half, placing them on the floor in front of the entrance.

The moonbeams from above drift down and strike the two items. The bracelet starts to rise, reaching a height of about five feet before it suddenly drops, lifeless. Milea watches the action and waits patiently for a few moments, then goes over to the door and touches it again. Her features turn to despair when she notices that the doors remain firmly shut.

"Damn it," Milea punches the door. She places her head against it, feeling defeated.

"Are we too late?" Neil inquires and goes to touch the door himself.

"Maybe we should have left right after the battle with Dee," Vicki said.

"I do not think it's our timing. Something else is keeping the doors shut," Zaria says, and places a hand on Milea's shoulder.

"Can you unlock the door?" Sonja asks the shiadokat.

"No," Zaria admits. "My instinct is telling me that my interference is expected and there is something in place to make sure I never do it again."

"What is the plan?" Brion asks. "Do we break it down?"

Bryce tilts his head a few times before he trots over to the door and sniffs it. He rears up onto his hindlegs and presses against the edifice. His brothers come over and push against the door in similar fashion. All six are grunting and trying their best to push the door open, to no avail. Bryce makes a disappointed sound, sitting down and looking up at the door. Milea gently pats the baby on his head, complementing them all on a valiant effort. The sorceress then walks away from the door as she thinks about how to get into the temple. Bryce watches the woman leave, then looks over at his larger brother. He gets to his feet as an idea seems to dawn on him. Milea turns when she hears the dragon chatter and squeak as if he is trying to communicate as he approaches her.

"I do not understand you, little one," Milea says, touching Bryce's head again. "Go follow your father. My friends and I must make ready to camp for tonight as we contemplate our next move."

"It's going to be a cold night aboard the ship," Neil said.

"I know," Vicki agrees as he pats one of the hatchlings. "Follow your papa, fella."

The baby dragon made a series of clicks as he circles Vicki rapidly, wrapping his furry body around her briefly before laying down. Vicki gasps in surprise as she falls backwards and lands on the dragon. His soft downy fur cushions her fall and wraps her in warmth. The hatchling then tucks one wing under his chin as he lays his head down, the other wing carefully covering the I'vane woman. Vicki blinks in surprise as she tries to recall what just happened to her. To her eyes, it is all a blur.

"Vicki," Neil calls. "Are you alright?"

"I..." Vicki gently pushes down the dragon's wing to focus on her sibling. "I think so. Although this little guy is surprisingly quite warm and comfortable."

"Baby dragon bunks?" Sonja asks. A short time later, she finds herself falling backwards onto Bryce.

Brion pats the head of the biggest boy and sends him over to Milea. The sorceress gently scratches the nervous hatchling on the chin and neck then gently instructs him to lay down. The dragon squeaks a little, then lowers his body to the ground carefully. Milea rubs the hatchling's neck as she gently sits down, leaning back comfortably. The dragon curls his tail under Milea's feet as she rubs his back a little. Deep purrs emit from the big boy as he lays his head down on one wing and covers his charge with the other.

Milea gently lowers the wing to glare at the double doors as the rest of her party settles down for the night. Unbeknownst to her, Bryce and A'drianis also study the ornate doors as they contemplate how to open them. Sleep soon takes over the entire group as the six hatchlings that had departed return to cuddle up with their brothers and guests. A much larger host, on silent wings, soon joins the slumber party in order to keep it guarded.

CHAPTER TEN

Temple of Nag'teragiea

A vicious lightning bolt interrupts the low rumble of thunder, temporarily blinding Milea. She makes a sharp sound of surprise as flashes of lightning strike beside her. Milea captures the next bolt, then sends it back in the direction it came from. The lightning stops in midair and spins itself into a disk. Milea says some very un-ladylike words as the disk speeds back in her direction. She erects an arcane shield just in time for the disk to connect to it. The sorceress yells angrily as the shield shatters.

Milea jumps to her feet and looks about in a slight panic. She slowly realizes that she is still inside the ice cave with their little hosts. The sorceress shakes her head to awaken fully and scans the area, noting that it is still dark. They are now surrounded by all twelve of the baby dragons. The brothers are cuddling together to keep themselves and their guests warm and dry.

The hatchling that Milea had rested upon lifts his head and blinks sleepily as he squeaks a question. Milea pats his head as he yawns and lays back down to return to slumber. A smile graces the sorceress's features until she detects movement above her and daylight filtering in. She slowly looks up in time to see the previously undetected dome fold away. It takes her a moment to realize it is an enormous dragon wing. Following the movement, Milea soon lays eyes on a second adult ice dragon.

"Mother of Light..." Milea utters softly as she takes a hesitant step back.

Milea stares in awe at the seventy-foot female dragon glaring back at her. The dragon is a lighter shade of blue than the guardian who appeared the day before. Her head is also slightly smaller, and her body built more for speed than strength. Her fur is a mixture of different lengths and varying shades of blue throughout her coat, giving her a silvery appearance. Deep sapphire-blue eyes seem to hold a slight glow as the dragoness briefly turns her gaze from Milea to scan the room before returning her focus to the sorceress.

"You appear to have frightened yourself awake, wanderer," the dragon addresses the sorceress.

"Milady," Milea acknowledges the female behemoth. "I experienced an unexpected nightmare, perhaps fueled by my exhausting trip."

"Is your exhaustion the reason why you are using my son, Tor, as a bed?" the dragoness asks, her tone of voice leaning towards irritability.

"I meant no disrespect nor did I in any way harm Tor," Milea said. "The idea of resting upon the hatchlings is collaboration between young Bryce and his brothers."

"Really?" the dragoness said. She turns her attention from Milea to her brood and makes a couple of musical chirps.

Milea keeps her eyes on the dragoness as the hatchling, Tor, chirps in response and stands up. He shakes out his fur and gently nuzzles Milea's cheek in morning greeting. The sorceress pats the baby dragon without turning from his mother. Tor, confused, looks in the direction of Milea's attention then makes a happy sound as he trots over to the dragoness. Several other hatchlings start to awaken and respond to their mother, albeit groggily.

Neil stretches as he stands up; his dragon buddy follows his example before shaking his fur into a poof. He then starts to lick it down as if a giant cat. Brion offers to help Vicki to her feet. He chuckles when the woman and baby dragon both ask for five more minutes. Brion simply takes Vicki's hand and pulls her to her feet. Zaria yawns as she approaches Milea and stands next to her. She tilts her head quizzically when the sorceress does not acknowledge her. The shiadokat turns to see what has her friend's attention then swears and takes a step back.

"Whoa," Zaria said. "Angry momma dragon."

"Very observant, Shiadokat," Milea complements.

The dragoness once again utters a musical call with a hint of annoyance. Instead of responding, Bryce decides to ignore it as he snuggles down and starts to snore again. Sonja also turns over a little and relax back into slumber. Both unaware of the situation beyond the dragon's wings. Milea briefly glances over her shoulder and notices that everyone else is awake but her daughter. She turns back to face the female dragon.

"Sonja," Milea speaks her child's name gently. "Time to get up."

Under Bryce's wing, Sonja stretches and yawns as she turns over again. She hears her mother's voice once more, still gentle yet urgent. The girl opens her eyes and sits up, reaching for the ceiling a little. Sonja snickers a little when she hears Bryce snoring as she moves his wing out of the way. Sonja stands up and limbers up her muscles a little, focusing on her mother's back. Her attention goes from the sorceress to the large, angry-looking ice dragon staring intensely at her.

"Oh shoot," Sonja says, all vestiges of sleep leaving her as she turns. "Bryce, time to get up buddy."

The little ice dragon simply flips his wing over his eyes and settles back into sleep. His snoring is much deeper as he digs in. Sonja lifts the wing and rubs Bryce's nose a little. He twitches it once and settles down. Sonja repeats the irritation then moves to one side as the baby ice dragon sneezes. A small column of ice-flame shoots out of his nostrils, followed by a rumbling growl as he gives Sonja a disgruntled glare.

The dragoness makes another sound, this time with a distinctive warning about it. Bryce's eyes widen as his head pops up and turns toward the direction of the noise. He makes a shrill sound as he jumps to his feet, steadying himself. He quickly approaches his mother, nearly tripping over his own feet in the process.

"Bryce, tell me how you came to host these wanderers," the dragoness demands.

Bryce unleashes a series of clicks, chirps and mews to explain his actions to his mother. As he is speaking, Dover lifts his head to look over the dragoness to his son. The guardian has a look of surprise upon his features when he hears his name is brought up during the explanation. Milea keeps her attention on the dragoness as the hatchling explains. The sorceress's hearing detects the approach of her companions. She does a quick glance over her shoulder at the person next to her.

Zaria nods in understanding then takes a few steps back. She places her hand behind and motions to signal the others to keep their distance. Neil pauses when he notices the shiadokat's careful retreat along with her hand signals. He tells Brion and Vicki to stop and follow Zaria's example of a very slow and cautious withdrawal. Sonja keeps her distance, anticipating the next events.

"It seems you speak truthful, wanderer," the dragoness concedes to Milea.

"I would not purposefully deceive you, milady," Milea responds.

"How did you defeat Dover?" the dragoness inquires.

"I, urr..." Dover clears his throat. "The boys interrupted the intended battle. Specifically, Bryce. Apparently, he wanted to meet the little dragon girl on the ship."

"Dragon girl?" the dragoness asks.

Several of the hatchlings gather around Sonja, chattering away. They user their foreheads to gently nudge her to push her forward. The girl resists a little then just gives in to their combined persistence. She keeps at least a half step ahead of the hatchlings they approach the dragoness. Sonja stands next to Milea and looks up to her. The sorceress places a reassuring arm around her daughter's shoulder. Bryce gently puts his nose under Sonja's left arm and lifts it up, showing off her silver scales.

"Fascinating, I've never seen a child like this," the dragoness admits.

"There are three L'vanes on board that boat," Dover boasts. "She's the girl, there are also two adults."

Neil, Vicki, and Brion's slow retreat is cut short when the brood of ice dragon babies charge towards them, with enthusiasm. Vicki places a hand on her whip, unsure of the unprovoked charge. She hesitates in pulling it as Neil gently grabs her arm. The dragons surround them, full of chatter. The large balls of fluff begin to gently bump the l'vane siblings from behind to herd them towards the mother dragon. The hatchlings persuade Brion and Zaria forward as well.

"Be gentle boys," Dover instructs the excited hatchlings. "Don't hurt your new friends."

"I'm sure if they could pick us up and carry us over, they would," Neil admits as he stands next to Milea. "Not an ideal situation."

"No, it is not," Milea agrees.

"We are surrounded," Brion announces as the dragons line up on the side and behind the group.

"When I first encountered them, Lady Milea had been unwavering in her determination to get into the temple and go through me in the process," Dover recalls. "I found that admirable, especially since her companions seem to share her courage."

"I still am determined, Sir Dover," Milea said. "Unfortunately, the doors to the temple did not open for us last night."

"What?" Dover frowns. "You do have the key, right?" "We do," Milea assures and holds up her hand.

A spark appears above Milea's hand, brightening a little as the bracelet and book appear. The items levitate just a few inches above her palm, rotating slowly and surrounded by a mystical glow. Dover stands up and leans over his mate to examine the items, determining that they are authentic. He sits up and places one hand upon his knee while stroking his beard with the other. He strokes his beard a little as he ponders the situation. A low sound of curiosity rumbles from the dragon as he lumbers over to the tall doors. The tip of his tail taps the ground while he studies the symbols. He frowns as he notices that several of them are scratched out.

"It should have worked," Dover muses. "Sapphire, why are some of these symbols scratched out?"

"Could it be due to the phenomena we experienced a few weeks ago?" the dragoness asks as she stands to look over Dover's shoulder.

Milea listens to her companions as they talk amongst themselves. Zaria informs her, in a hush tone, that the symbols and the pictures they passed had been clawed in a similar fashion. The shiadokat admits that she has a bad feeling about this part of their journey. Bryce trots over to the door and once again tries to force it open by pushing upon it. He looks up at his parents with doe eyes and a slight whine. Sapphire shakes her head and walks away, causing the little dragon to whimper a little. Dover looks down at his son and rubs his beard again. He turns to walk away and his tail 'accidently' slams into the door, knocking it open. Bryce perks up and jumps in excitement.

"Oops," Dover cranes his neck to look behind. "It looks like the doors may have just been stuck."

"Dover, why did you do that?" Sapphire scolds.

"I'm a big dragon, sometimes I run into things while turning around," Dover grins sheepishly. Bryce gently bumps his head against his father's leg and makes happy sounds.

"That door was locked, and for good reason," Sapphire retorts.

"Eh, it's just the ice holding it," Dover insists. "Milea, your way is open but only two of you can go in."

"I..." Milea starts, but thinks better of it. "Thank you, Sir Dover, for the assist with the ice. Zaria, you and I should be the ones that go."

"I think you're right on that," Zaria agrees. "That door was locked." She whispers to Milea.

"I know," Milea whispers back.

"Milea, you have four hours to find the book," Neil warns. "If you're not back, we are going to come after you."

"Give us a day," Milea requests. "I'm not entirely sure what we are running into down there."

"My old drake didn't tell me what exactly is sealed behind the door but he said it is not to be taken lightly," Dover lay down next to the door and coils his tail around. "I will sit here to make sure it does not escape while you are inside."

Milea takes a few steps toward the yawning entranceway leading into the depths of the underwater temple. A wave of warm air washes over her, much to her surprise. Zaria crosses her arms when a sweet, yet musky odor hit her senses. The darkness inside the doorway yields only a little bit to the light of the ice windows above. Zaria takes the first steps in and hears a very faint growl. Both of her eyebrows rise slightly when she hears it. Undeterred, she goes deeper, disappearing into the shadows. Milea enters the temple next and take a few steps before total darkness surrounds her. She stops and turns to see a pinpoint of light reflecting the spot where she had entered the space and barely hears Vicki talking to the adult dragons.

A cold wind blows down the hall, moaning as it rounds one of many corners of the darkened passage. Milea slows down and keeps her hand on the wall in order to guide herself through the unnatural shadows. She pauses when she nearly collides with her companion. A'drianis glances behind, then peers through the shadows in front of her. The shiadokat continues forward a few more feet and pauses again. She frowns when she does not sense Milea right behind her. A'drianis turns around and goes back the way she came. A bit of surprise masks her features when she notes that she had gone down the middle tunnel of a three-way split. Uttering a few unfiltered words, A'drianis shifts her form to that of a winged panther and sniffs around. She finds Milea's scent as well as that of another, larger, shiadokat. Muttering under her breath, she hurries after the sorceress.

The sounds of creaks and moans keep her company as she continues to traverse the darkened hallways. Milea finds herself wondering if the sounds are from the stones holding back the ocean or the ghosts that haunt the temple. She barely makes out the shape of an elaborate door inches from her nose Reaching out to touch it, her fingertips trace out ancient writing carved in the wooden edifice. Taking a step back, she casts a light spell in order to give her some illumination. The first thing she notices is that she no longer has the company of the Shadow Eltis.

Milea looks around with a slight frown and faces the door once again. The name, Tadious, is carved where her hand has touch. There are a few words below that are illegible but seems intended as a term of caution. Milea takes heed of the warning and turns around to retrace her steps. A slight groan echoes in the hall as the doors open by themselves. The wall collapses down the pathway she once traversed, filling the corridor with ice and snow. The pile of debris block retreat. Milea takes a deep breath as she faces her only option and walks through the door.

The Hall of Tadious has elaborate decorations of symbols and carvings of singing dragons lining the entire room. The giant statue itself looks to be of a man of Elvish descent. His actual height unknown due to the size of the monolith yet his stature reminds Milea of her friend, Brion. The statute's right hand is extended in friendship while his left hand is holding the neck of a mandolin. At the feet are several weapons, musical instruments, and harvest vegetables symbolizing Tadious' love of festivities.

Milea approaches the statute with caution as she studies it in earnest. There are strange runes painted in bright red on the edifice's chest. Milea goes through her mental catalog of various languages. She makes a curious sound when she is unable to interpret the dialect on the statue. The sorceress trains her eyes on the carving of a book next to the mandolin. She takes care to place her feet solidly as she approaches the item. Using the same caution, she reaches out to touch it, noting that it feels different than any stone she has felt before.

"I wonder," Milea voices her curiosity aloud.

The sorceress raises her hand and causes the bracelet that she obtained from the Fáidh of Desitana to appear above it. The jewelry pulsates with a strange green light as it seems to synchronize with something in the room. Milea, focused on the book, does not see the runes on the chest of the statue beginning to oscillate in the same color as the bracelet. The statue's eyes start to glow an angry red as it moves its head side to side. The sound of cracking stone causes Milea to look up as the statue glares down at her. She quickly grabs hold of the bracelet then dives to one side as the statue brings down its extended arm, attempting to capture her.

Milea tucks the bracelet in her coat pocket as her eyes dart about the room to find a way out. The statue steps off the podium, causing the room to shake as it stomps towards the intruder. Milea spies her way out between the legs of the golem in the shape of a door leading to another corridor. The animated statue raises its foot in order to step on Milea. She seizes the opportunity and makes a break for the exit. The golem tries to turn and follow her but ends up tilting over and crashing to the ground. Milea dodges some of the debris as she escapes the room.

The doors to the Hall of Tadious close as the sorceress catch her breath. Her new surroundings are just as dark as the corridor she had passed through. Milea revives her light spell as she continues to creep down the new passageway. She comes across another set of double doors, but this time they are open with at least one of them torn off its top hinge. Deep claw marks and several scorched spots hide the identity of the resident of this part of the temple. Milea pauses at the threshold and sends her light ball into the room first. The scene that it reveals disturbs the sorceress deeply.

From floor to ceiling, the entire room is caked in dried blood, with a few bones marking where the stricken had fallen. The statue in the middle of the room is headless and armless yet Milea recognizes that it once paid homage to Keela, the Eltis Guardian of Selvast Forest. The sorceress carefully steps into the room to take a closer look at the statue. Scrawled across the statue's torso are several angry slurs and a few unsettling curses written with the blood of the victims in the room. Milea notices that there is another book carved at the feet of the statue, yet it has been destroyed by the same claws that ripped through the door.

"Whatever did this or whoever did this does not care for Keela in the least bit," Milea quietly observes as she leaves the room. "I've got to find A'drianis and the book then get the hell out of here."

The hall goes to the left then turns right as Milea makes her way to an unknown destination. She calls to the shiadokat in a hush tone and does not get a response. The temperature starts to drop, prompting her to pull her cape closer for warmth. The small orb she uses for light sputters as she concentrates on keeping warm. The glowing orb's reach is now a few feet before darkness overwhelms it. A light dusting of snow is all the traction she has over the black ice that cakes the floor. Milea pauses when she sees the large cat prints in the snow and bends down to study them. She counts a missing digit in the left back paw and knows that A'drianis still has all her toes.

"Hmm," Milea muses as she looks around. "The Shiadokat clan is disjointed but not completely dead. But what Eltis from the tropics would willingly stay in cold and ice?"

Milea stands and eases down her path. Her slow pace allows her small light to guide the way. The light hovers over a portion of the floor that drops steeply beyond the light. The sorceress stops at the very edge of the incline and peers into the darkness. A deep growl behind her causes Milea to whip around to face the owner of the paw prints. The light orb is smacked by a large paw, knocking it to the wall and snuffing it out.

Milea does not have time to voice her surprise as she blocks the same paw coming from the darkness, aimed at her head. She edges dangerously close to the slope that is now invisible to her. Milea takes another step back to avoid unseen claws and her foot leaves solid ground. She manages to pivot on the toes that are still firmly on the floor. Something smacks her in the back. Milea reaches out to grab the wall; it is not there, and she slides down the unseen incline. It takes her down a few feet before stopping at a slight hump.

"Ok," Milea breathes, "That did not seem so bad."

Milea turns over and digs her nails into the ice to try and climb back up. Her hand touches something that is thick and furry. Milea pulls back and casts a small light spell. Instead of the expected black panther, she gets a glimpse of a large white tiger with one eye gouged out. The beast roars angrily and crushes the light, knocking it out. Milea hops back and slides but manages to keep above the small hump she stopped at. She turns around when she hears the beast behind her. It swats her with a large claw, sending her over the hump. Milea leans back, her hands seeking something to hold on to, her fingertips finding only ice.

"No!" Milea cries out in surprise as she goes down the slide.

Milea feels the slide she is on tilt sharply to near vertical as she goes into an unknown depth. A thin red flame wraps around her body but is snuffed out when the paw smacks her again, increasing her speed to a mysterious destination. The slide twists rapidly to the left then right, then drops straight down. A small light that signals the end of the tunnel starts to grow as she nears it. A ghostly image of the white tiger covers the exit and opens its mouth.

Milea swears in a few different languages as she slides right into the creature's mouth and out of the tunnel. She sails, at rapid pace, toward a wall opposite the tunnel. Milea quickly erects an arcane shield as she impacts the wall. She holds onto the wall and looks down to see that she is at least twenty feet from the ground. The sorceress takes a deep breath and slowly descends to the floor. She cancels her shield and looks around.

The room is light by a mystical glow. It is cavernous and decorated in various pictures and languages. Various stains have soaked into the stone floor, marking an epic and bloody event. A warm wind stirs her hair as she approaches a set of windows and touches one of them. A thick layer of ice covers the glass and cracks a little from the heat of her fingertips. She peers out of the portal to see that it is very dark out. The sorceress frowns and leans forward to get a better look. She takes a step back when she is greeted by the jaws of a large shark.

"So, it is sunken, but how and by who?" Milea wonders out loud.

"You have come to a sacred grave site, mortal," an unfriendly woman growl at her.

Milea faces the owner of the voice and hesitates. Her mouth drops open as she looks upon the statue of a warrior woman. The edifice is depicted as strong and is proudly raising an arm to the ceiling in the middle of the room. Larger than life, she is clad in just enough armor to keep her modest. Milea focuses on the face and notices that one eye is blinded by a claw while the other is glaring at her angrily. Milea scans the statue once or twice to fully study the item. She then turns her attention to the various depictions around the room. She recognizes a picture of Keela but the white tiger-like dragon she battled remains a mystery to her.

"Why are you here, mortal?" the woman demands.

Milea's attention goes back to the statue then to the woman standing at its feet. She takes a single step back when she notices that the woman is a miniature version of the much larger edifice. The woman's skin has similar markings to the white tiger that Milea had encountered on the slide. Black leather wings stretch out to either side of the woman as she sizes the intruder up. Milea keeps her distance while searching the room for a clue to the identification of the creature in front of her. The only clue she has is that the woman has a claw mark over an eye that is blinded.

"I am here on a sacred mission," Milea answers cryptically. "I know you are an Eltis. However, you are unfamiliar to me."

"I would be surprised if you did know me, mortal. I will give you a clue," the woman said smugly. "I am the one who dragged the first gods down from their mountain and beat them at their own game. I destroyed countless Tragins when they foolishly attacked the Katriatic in a lame fit of rage. In fact, I ruled the Katriatic until my own son toppled me in a game of war."

"The Katriatic," Milea said and pauses before taking a deep breath. "I know the answer to your riddle, milady. You are Grimalkin, Mother Eltis of the Shiadokat clan."

"Impressive, you are not as naïve as I first thought," Grimalkin comments. "Not many mortals can answer that riddle."

"My education included becoming familiar with the founding mothers of all the Eltis houses," Milea said with a bow of her head.

"So, you are a pilgrim," Grimalkin identifies. "You are too late for this place. Those here left seventy years ago. I arrived not too long ago in search of a book. Care to help me find it, mortal?"

"What book do you seek here, Lady Grimalkin?" Milea asks.

"It is a half book right now, called the Book of the Eltis," Grimalkin explains as if she is talking to a child. "I did not find the first half at the Boiling Sea's temple. Which, by the way, is as ruined as this place."

"I am aware, I have visited the Boiling Seas in recent times," Milea admits. "Unfortunately, Lady Grimalkin, I must decline assisting in the search for the book."

"I do not see you having a choice, mortal," Grimalkin said as she takes a step forward.

The light in the room dims as Grimalkin charges. She reaches out towards Milea's throat to grab her. The sorceress does a hasty retreat, then fades from view as Grimalkin hand nears her throat. A green flame erupts on the Eltis' arm, then travels down to her hand to form a sword. Milea reappears near the statue and blocks the blade with her own, a look of shock on her features. Grimalkin sneers as her sword changes to chains. Milea does not have time to move as the chains encircle her, tightening. The sorceress tries to free herself from the chains. She receives a shock for her efforts. Milea grits her teeth to prevent a cry of pain.

"You amaze me, mortal. I did not expect you to wield a sword," Grimalkin said, happily.

"I did not expect you to attack me," Milea counters. "Why are you toying with me?"

"How do you know I toy?" Grimalkin inquires, coyly.

"I have experience with shiadokats, Lady Grimalkin, I know," Milea admits. The shadows in the room darken a little more.

"Oh, really? Who from the Katriatic are you familiar with, mortal?" Grimalkin asks.

The room goes pitch black as a large black paw swats Grimalkin, sending her sailing backward and away from the sorceress. The chains around Milea shatter, freeing her as the room lightens to twilight. The sorceress quickly gets to her feet as a winged panther the size of a mountain bear melts out of the shadows. A'drianis roars as she spreads her wings to intimidate the woman that attacked her cousin.

"I am truly glad to see you, A'drianis. However, it's not very wise to challenge Grimalkin like that," Milea offers.

"Grimalkin? Are you serious?" A'drianis asks.

"Very," Milea answers.

Grimalkin stares at the panther as she gets to her feet. With a snort, she stalks toward the two intruders at a purposeful slow rate. A'drianis holds her ground as a gleam flash across Grimalkin's eyes. The warrior Eltis charges with quick speed, then changes forms to that of a winged white tiger. There is no time to react as Grimalkin pounces at the panther. A'drianis drops a few vulgar words as she dodges out of the way of the attacking cat's claws and teeth.

Milea drops to the floor and rolls out of the way to avoid the beast's tail. The impact from Grimalkin's tail leaves a large hole in the floor where the sorceress once stood. The panther moves again then squeals when her tail is snagged by the tigress and she is dragged to the floor. The tigress roars in triumph as she steps on her prey and pins the smaller cat to the floor

A'drianis yowls in pain then splits into shadows as Grimalkin brings her teeth down. The tigress snarls in anger when her jaws clamp shut, finding only air. A powerful lightning bolt slams into Grimalkin, sending her into the statue that bears her likeness. The tigress roars as she gathers the lightning and falls to the ground, landing on her feet. Electricity courses around her entire body as she focuses on the creator of the spell. Milea mutters words unbefitting a lady as Grimalkin returns the powerful bolt of lightning back in her direction.

Milea takes a couple of steps back to reposition her footing. The air sizzles as the sorceress catches the head of the lightning bolt, spins around, and sends it towards the giant statue that the tigress is standing in front of. The bolt slams into the statue, destroying the legs. Grimalkin turns and yells in rage as the rest of the statue collapses on top of her. Dust and debris rise as the tigress is buried. Milea uses a soft wind to clear the air and focuses on the rubble

A'drianis fades back into the room, out of the shadow, in the form of a woman.

"That's not going to keep her down for long," A'drianis said. "We have to find a way out before she wakes up."

"We have to find the book first," Milea reminds her. "She is looking for it as well."

"Did she tell you why?" A'drianis asks.

The rubble starts to rise, sounding as if bone is breaking against stone. The room vibrates with the sound of a very angry beast. Milea retreats away from the pile while looking around the room for way out, or possibly a place to hide. A'drianis spies another set of double doors with the word sauna scrawled across it. She heads straight for it as the rubble steadily grows taller. Milea follows her lead and both discover that the doors are locked.

A'drianis swears in three separate languages as she quickly navigates the lock and it springs open just as the pile of debris explodes outward. Both enter the room as fast as they can and slam the door shut to avoid any missiles heading their way. Milea draws a quick seal onto the door. It is just in the nick of time as Grimalkin crashes into it. A'drianis exhales in relief when the only thing penetrating through the door is the angry curses of the warrior Eltis.

"That was too close," A'drianis said. "I knew someone was here, I saw the evidence. But I had no idea it would be Grimalkin herself."

"She did not reveal how long she had been here. However, she did mention that she has visited the Temple of Light in the Boiling Seas not too long ago," Milea explains. "She is trying to recruit me for some reason."

"Perhaps for a game of sorts," A'drianis hypothesizes. "Grimalkin is a great fan of games, especially those that involve strategy."

"That is good to know. Maybe we can use that as a means of escaping this place," Milea acknowledges.

The sorceress turns to the room and takes in the scene. The walls are decorated with a floral design that is repeated on the floor. There is a huge, deep pool in the middle of the room that is now void of water. A large statue of a maiden lounging on a chase with nothing but her hair covering her nudity stares at them from across the room. Behind her is the statue of a winged panther with its head up and a feline grin across its lips. A similar grin is reflected on the face of the statue of the woman and slowly trickles down to A'drianis herself.

"So, this is once either a bathing hall or a recreation area," Milea observers. "It also seems to have served as a place to pay homage to you, A'drianis."

"I see that, but I can guarantee you that the pool did not serve as a place of bathing or recreation. It is possibly part of a trap," A'drianis said. "I'm surprised at the detail in that statue, I only posed for it once."

Both jump in surprise when Grimalkin slams into the door once again. Milea glances back to make sure her seal is still in place, then takes a step forward in order to resume her search for the book. Taking a second look around the room, the sorceress keys in on the carving of an open book sitting under the hand of A'drianis's statue. In previous versions of the same statue, she remembers that there is supposed to be a dagger.

A'drianis gently takes hold of the sorceress's arm to prevent her from going any closer to the pool. The shadow Eltis shakes her head in warning and pulls her friend back a couple of steps away from the center. Since this hall is dedicated to A'drianis, she knows that it is ripe with all kinds of booby-traps. Milea nods in understanding as she takes out the bracelet from her pocket and holds it up. The jewelry once again begins to glow with a pulsating green light. The book underneath the statue's hand also pulsates with the same glow before it cracks open to reveal the book half. The items stop glowing at the same time as Milea lowers her arm and puts the bracelet back in her pocket.

"Let me see here," A'drianis muses as she takes a few careful steps towards the pool.

The shiadokat notices strange symbols in the floral design that lines the rim of the pool. She places her foot on a certain tile and then leans forward to investigate the abyss. There is still water inside the pool but it is not very deep and the color is completely odd. A'drianis slowly trains her eye back up to the book. She takes in the size of the obstacle as well as the landing pad on the other side. The shiadokat crouches down, carefully placing her hands on either side of her body, and extends her legs back to the same tiles that she stepped on previously. Shadows wrap around her swiftly as she changes form, back into the winged black panther. A'drianis leaps into the air and uses her wings to suspend her over the pool as she studies the statute and the book.

"Oh, ho, ho, that's a nasty trap," A'drianis says of the hidden danger within the statue. "These guys were ruthless."

The winged panther ascends until she just above the statue. She takes care to place her front paws on the head of the woman statue and the back paws on the head of the panther statue. A'drianis reverts her form back to that of a woman and crouches down to maintain her balance. She nimbly climbs down the statue until she is balancing on the arm of the panther, within reach of the book. A dagger appears in her right hand as she leans forward with the left towards her prize.

Milea watches with baited breath as A'drianis continues her slow movements toward the object they had come for. In one swift move, the shiadokat takes the book and replaces it with the dagger. The statue's hand closes on the handle of the dagger. Both women hold their breath for a few seconds. The two ladies slowly release it at the same time when the statute does not move any further. A'drianis once again wraps herself in shadow as she changes form to return to Milea's side. The shiadokat lifts the shadows and holds of the book in triumph with a grin of confidence plastered on her face.

"I had no doubt in your abilities, Shiadokat," Milea nods her head respectfully. "Now we have to figure out a way to get past Grimalkin."

"Challenging her to any type of dual is suicide," A'drianis said as she hands the book half to the sorceress. "We're going to have to think outside of the box for this one."

"She likes games," Milea muses as she places the book and bracelet in a bag. It disappears soon after she is done. "How about challenging her to a foot race?"

"She's a bigger cat than I am and she's been here longer than we have," A'drianis informs. "She would know these halls better than we would. I see evidence of her destruction in every one of the sacred spaces within this temple."

"I know, I saw what she did to Keela's statue," Milea agrees. "But we do have a chance of getting out of here by way of trickery. Do you remember the trick on the ship that mother showed us against the Dragodu?"

"I do," A'drianis said almost hesitantly. "But that's not going to help us against her keen sense of smell."

"I will keep the wind from giving us away if you can keep the shadow just out of her reach long enough for us to get close to the exit," Milea offers. "We will be seeking the Hall of Tadious as our finish line. From there it is a straight passage out."

"I don't like the odds but it's better than putting our friends in danger," A'drianis says as she turns to the door. "Well, let's get this started."

The door creaks as it cracks opens. Grimalkin, now once again a woman, stands from her seated position and glares at the entrance. She emits a deep, angry, sound when she sees the two women peek out of the room, then pull back. A'drianis takes a deep breath in and closes her eyes to concentrate. Outside the safety of the room, Grimalkin frowns as both women casually walk out and stop a short distance from her. The wind in the room picks up a little and blows from behind the warrior Eltis towards the sauna. Grimalkin scans both ladies twice and frowns. The mortal does not have her sword and that the Eltis with her is a descendent.

"What is this? You, girl, what is your name?" Grimalkin demands.

"We will get to that in a minute, old woman," A'drianis answers.

"It seems to me, Lady Grimalkin, that you will not let me go freely," Milea said to capture the older Eltis's attention. "May I inquire as to why you wish to recruit me into your service?"

"It's very simple, mortal," Grimalkin said. "You are both mage and warrior. I have need for such a well-rounded mortal in my plans, especially after I find Kaidar."

"Elder son of Keela and Oswind? He's a warrior Eltis such as yourself. Why..." A'drianis says out loud then hesitates as she thinks about the possibilities. "Oh..."

"It is no stretch of the imagination, child," Grimalkin informs her with a sly grin. "So mortal, what do you say? Do you wish to be my second in command?"

"My answer remains the same, Lady Grimalkin," Milea answers. "However, I do realize that you will not let me leave this temple unless I either agree or I perish. Since I wish for neither to happen, I propose a game."

"Oh really? What type of game do you propose, mortal?" Grimalkin inquires, her interest piqued.

"My companion and I wish to challenge you to a foot race. The finish line is the Hall of Tadious." Milea answers.

"Interesting. What is the prize when I win?" Grimalkin asks.

"Should you win then I will join you in your plans," Milea explains. "When we win, you will drop your relentless recruitment of me and allow us to leave this temple, free of any obligations. Understand that by accepting this challenge you are taking the oath of a Mother Eltis that you will abide by these rules under penalty of punishment, to include death."

"I will agree. However, it does not matter because you will not win," Grimalkin insists as she places a hand upon her hip. "When does this race began?"

"When?" A'drianis laughs harshly. "Old Mother, it already has."

As the last word presses her lips, A'drianis and Milea fade from sight. Grimalkin takes a few steps back in surprise then growls as she shifts form to become the winged tigress. With a roar of anger, she charges out of the room using a hidden passageway. A few seconds later, A'drianis and Milea peek out of the door then enter the space. The shiadokat changes into a winged black panther and crouches to allow Milea to climb onto her back. A slight grunt escapes the panther as she follows the white tigress through the hidden passageway.

The shadows of the hall appear to shift and move in a mocking way. Grimalkin increases her speed in order to catch up with the tricky Shadow Eltis. The stones of the sunken temple creak and moan, disguising the footsteps of the pursuer. A'drianis finally catches up to the white tigress. The racers are only a tail length away from the leader. In front of Grimalkin is an exact image of them running into the shadows. The white tigress presses forward slightly and sees the rear end of the winged panther.

The warrior Eltis sees the passenger sit up and look behind her with a cocky grin highlighting her features. Moments later the shadows fold onto the leader, effectively hiding them from the white tigress. Grimalkin unleashes a flurry of angry words when she realizes that she has not mastered the shadows as well as her descendent. With a snarl of determination, the tigress whips to her left in order to take a shortcut to her destination. Behind her, A'drianis does the same as she continues to follow Grimalkin turn for turn.

They run through several twists and turns, navigating a multitude of split tunnels in their pursuit. Grimalkin increases her pace in order to get in front of her racing opponent. She comes to the edge of a large ravine and takes a flying leap over it without slowing down. Grimalkin lands on the other side with a grunt. Digging her claws in, she explodes into the tunnel beyond the obstacle. Behind her, A'drianis also takes the leap but uses her wings to fly over, landing in silence. She folds her wings against her body once on the other side. Milea holds onto the Shadow Eltis as her speed accelerates with the aid of the darkness around them.

They temporarily lose sight of Grimalkin but soon find her trail and cut the same corner as the warrior Eltis. A few more paces and they are once again behind the white tigress. Grimalkin starts to glow suddenly as she unleashes a strong lightning spell to destroy a fallen column that blocks her way. She then bounces off a wall to avoid a pitfall as she rounds the corner and hones in on the passageway that leads to the Hall of Tadious. A'drianis follows the tigress's lead and remains hot on her heels.

"Our destination is right ahead," Milea said.

"All right, hold on," A'drianis answers.

The shadows darken considerably within the corridor, surprising Grimalkin. The white tigress slows down in order to allow her eyes to adjust to the new dark. Once they do, she sees A'drianis melt out of the shadows, galloping full speed toward the finish line. Milea glances over her shoulder when she hears the warrior Eltis roar and her speed increases. The sorceress turns the wind, causing it to pass over her and her panther companion to slam into their pursuer.

The force slows the white tigress but does not stop her. A'drianis passes through the doorway leading to the Hall of Tadious a leg ahead of her competition. Milea notices that the statue of the Storm Eltis is once again standing, his position unchanged from the first time she saw it. The panther slides to a stop seconds before she hits a wall and turns to face the larger feline as Grimalkin enters the room. Milea climbs off A'drianis's back and bows in respect to Grimalkin.

"Lady Grimalkin," Milea addresses. "We have won and now we shall take our leave."

"You cannot expect me to accept defeat," Grimalkin snarls as her form reverts to that of a woman. "Both of you cheated."

"We did not cheat. We did use our combined talents to achieve our goal," Milea corrects her adversary. "That goal was to be the first to enter the Hall of Tadious."

"I see," Grimalkin said. "You are a clever mortal. To be able to enlist the help of a shiadokat, you must have some clout about you. What are your names, so that I may forever remember the mortal and younger shiadokat who outfoxed me?"

"I am the daughter of Armals," A'drianis said. "I've been known by many names over the years, but you will know me only as Zaria."

"You are my direct descendent, Zaria," Grimalkin observes and focuses on the panther. "I did not care much for your mother, but you can redeem yourself by joining me as I retake what is mine."

"No, I will pass. I do not have any desire to return to the Katriatic at this moment," A'drianis responds, rejecting the offer.

"I will let you think about it," Grimalkin said, ignoring the refusal. "What about you, mortal?"

"My birth mother was lost to me as a babe. However, that did not affect my development in the least," Milea said. "I am a mortal daughter of the Guardian of Selvast Forest, Keela."

"What!!?" Grimalkin interrupts.

A bright white glow overtakes Grimalkin, instantly, her features reflect immediate rage. Milea swears then is quick to climb onto A'drianis's back as the entire temple starts to vibrate. The two exit the hall towards the entrance at top speed, diving into the darkened passageway. Grimalkin tilts her head back and lets out a mighty yell of pure, unbridled, rage. The glow spreads from her body and pursues the perpetrators as Grimalkin herself initiates a chase.

The vibrating walls catch up with Milea and A'drianis as the shiadokat leaps up and over the obstacle blocking the way out. The light is next to catch them, brightening up the hall and causing the panther to utter a few unkind words as she changes back to Zaria. The transformation immediately causes both women to fall to the ground. Milea looks behind her and gets to her feet in haste. She reaches down to drag Zaria after her when she sees the giant tigress crash through the barrier that they had leapt over. The two intensify their pace substantially, making a beeline straight for the entrance.

The vibrating walls start to give as water breaks through the barrier to fill the passageways and rooms. Deep booming sounds reverberate throughout the space, steadily sinking the rest of the temple into the depths of the ocean. A brief run through shallow water and the two are back on solid ground. Milea and Zaria can hear the cries of alarm from the baby dragons as they near their destination.

Milea exits the temple first then slides as she turns around to face the oncoming threat. Zaria is next to leave the space, a dagger jumping into her hand as she too faces the temple. Brion, Neil and Vicki ask no questions as they prepare for battle with an unknown attacker. The entire cave starts to vibrate with the angry roars of a giant feline. Dover snorts as the fur on his neck expands and he roars in answer to the hidden challenger. The baby dragons all stay with their mother as Sonja goes to Milea's side.

"Sonja, get to Sapphire. Do not argue," Milea instructs.

"What are we facing?" Brion inquires.

"Grimalkin," Milea and Zaria answer at the same time.

Sonja tries to hide her confusion as she retreats to Sapphire and the group of baby dragons. The female dragon stands up and over her brood as the walls surrounding the temple door collapse. The rubble soon explodes when the head of a large dragon emerges. She is white with black tiger stripes. One eye is blinded but the other sees very clearly.

Milea shakes her head; this is Grimalkin's third and most powerful form. A large shadow covers the group as Dover stands directly over them. His nose is flared and eyes glowing red with fury. Cold steam wafts from his mouth as he roars at the intruding dragon. Grimalkin focuses on him and growls as she frees herself from the ruins, revealing a dragon nearly the same size as Dover.

"Oswind's beard," Neil mutters under his breath as he takes in the size of the emerging creature.

"Out of the way, Guardian. I am after the mortal," Grimalkin demands.

"I am defending the mortals, old wyrm," Dover responds with the insult. "You want them, you have to go through me."

"That is easy enough," Grimalkin said.

Milea and her companions move back to a position just beyond Dover's tail. Grimalkin leaps into the air to pounce upon the guardian. Dover unleashes a powerful ice spell and combines it with his cold breath weapon, hitting the challenger head-on. The guardian then spreads his wings and stands up on his hind legs to catch the falling frozen adversary while he lifts off towards the ceiling a mile up. He surges forward, using Grimalkin as a battering ram to crash through the thick ice, shards raining down on the witnesses below. Dover reaches optimal height before he tosses Grimalkin away from him.

Seconds later, she frees herself from the ice with a bellow of rage and green fire.

"You are dead!" Grimalkin yells, furious.

Grimalkin lets out a loud bellow as a column of green flame exits her mouth. She charges Dover at the same time, creating the illusion of a giant green fireball. The guardian does a barrel roll to get out of the way of the jet of flames, then unleashes his frosty reply. Grimalkin ducks under the pillar of ice and is quick to change directions to charge her opponent once again. She reaches him and immediately sinks her teeth into his hind flank.

Dover barely flinches as he whips around and bites into the base of Grimalkin's tail. The Eltis shrieks in pain and disappears from the guardian's grip. She reappears several feet away, changing once again to a winged white tigress. Grimalkin makes an angry sound as green flames erupt around her. When they dissipate, she is gone. Dover lands on top of the cliff that hides his home and roars in triumph.

Milea pause her conversation with her companions when she hears the thunderous roar of the male dragon. She notices Sapphire relax as she sits down and the brood of hatchlings jump around, play-wrestling with excitement. Sonja takes her mother's hand and gently leans against her arm. Milea places her arm around her daughter and holds her close. Neil smiles at the touching scene, then turns when he hears the water sloshing erratically. Dover emerges from the water and shakes his head before he gives a sheepish grin toward his guests.

Hours later, the sun is once again setting upon the frozen tundra. Milea is standing outside the cave, staring off into the distance south of their location. She knows they will have to somehow get past Selcros in order to reach the open seas so that they can journey back to Dorma. Milea holds up her hand and causes a small flame to light up in her palm. It ignites, though it is not as strong as her usual fire. Milea cancels the flame as she brings her hand back down to her side, once again staring into the distance.

"It's going to take at least two days to get back to Selcros," Neil mentions as he stands next to the sorceress. "We've got enough supplies to camp here for a couple of days as well if you need to recover."

"My goal is to get us out of the cold sooner rather than later," Milea said. "But this entire trip has taken its toll on me."

"It has been a challenge. Especially with the surprise attack from Tandon. However, I don't think it would've mattered, especially with Koro's actions," Neil observes. "My goal when we sail out of here is to try and creep past the city at night."

"That would be ideal, especially since we have the help of a Shadow Eltis in our midst," Milea muses. "I think we should take at least a day and then head back South. Sonja, Zaria, and I have a destination of Dorma. You, Vicki, and Brion are invited to come along."

"Dorma, eh?" Neil scratches his chin and rubs his neck as he debates. "I think you convinced Vicki that a legend she idolizes is still alive and is currently residing in Dorma. But everything I know tells me that Ra'jil is dead. I guess one way to find out is to go to Dorma and see for myself."

"Did you put a wager on whether or not Ra'jil is alive?" Milea asks with some humor in her tone.

"I may have placed a small bet with Brion about the chances," Neil admits. "Nothing too dramatic. Just a flask of his favorite beverage when we reach Cathalian."

"Just make sure that you have enough coin to purchase a drink for Ra'jil as well," Milea offers advice. She turns and walks back into the cave as the sunset gives way to twilight.

Queen's Return

The red hues of the sky stretch out to paint the leftover snow in various shades to reflect the sunset. Dysis nods to the guards at the gates as she enters the city. The men cannot hide their shock at her presence, staring openly with slack-jawed expressions as the woman walks past. The queen ignores the strange looks as she continues into the city and to the square. The townsfolk endure their daily errands, although there appears to be a heavy sense of anxiety in the air. Dysis takes note of the atmosphere and the stares she is receiving. It is as if some of the people have seen a ghost. The queen pauses in front of the bakery then decides to go in to get a snack prior to her journey to the castle.

A tiny bell sounds as the door to the establishment opens and the queen walks into the establishment. Dysis pauses and draws a deep breath, enjoying the smell of fresh baked bread. She moves to the counter to take in the wares as her stomach growls a little bit. She then realizes that she has not had fresh baked goods in nearly a week. The door opens again yet Dysis does not pay attention to the new customers until she hears an exclamation of surprise. The queen turns and makes a friendly nod to the innkeeper's daughter and the dean of the girls' school. Dysis then turns back and greets the baker, who has just come out from the kitchen.

"Your Majesty, when did you return?" Madame Hawthorne asks, her words ripe with disbelief. "We heard that you died."

"I helped a guest and her entourage, then decided to go visit old friends since I was already out," the queen said with a shrug. "I have noticed that the town has a dreadful feeling about it. What has happened while I was away?"

"Milady," Colleen bows her head in respect, "the captain of the Iron Horse has been executed by the king. He had been charged with treason. The crew is all locked up in the jail tower awaiting a similar fate."

"Wait, what? No...what?" Dysis shakes her head, trying to comprehend what she had just heard.

"King Koro had the captain arrested because he thought that the man having an affair with you, Your Majesty," Madame Hawthorne informs. "My sources tell me that the captain steadfastly denied the affair. In fact, he informed the king of the trip up north involving Lady Milea and her companions. He claimed he had no choice."

"Prior to the battle with Tandon, the king made an agreement to assist Lady Milea up north because of her association with Lord Brion." Dysis frowns. "I will talk to him. This is madness."

"Do be careful confronting His Majesty, milady," the baker said. "My daughter is one of the cooks in the kitchen and she has informed me that the king is starting to display some very disturbing traits."

"I witnessed myself that he yells at invisible people, perhaps ghosts," Colleen informs. "He also has a festering wound on his arm. That may be the cause of his sudden madness."

"Thank you all for your information," Dysis nods to the three women. "Lady Baker, may I please have something to snack upon before I venture into the castle? I am famished."

"Of course, Queen Dysis," the baker bows her head. "You may have whatever you desire. I just hope it is not your last meal."

The evening turns to twilight by the time Dysis enters the castle. Should the guards try to stop her, they will be pushed aside by an icy wind. The queen marches purposefully into the throne room but pauses when she notices that the king has company. Qwest is standing by his father, while Wyntre seems content to sit in the queen's throne. Koro is focusing upon the two men that are standing in front of him. One is a short man; he is bald and appears to have a hunch in his back. A small black tail protrudes under his equally black robe. Every time he speaks, his deep voice resonates with malicious intent. Because of his robe, it is hard to identify him, yet Dysis knows at least he is not from anywhere near Selcros.

The tall man that is standing next to the spokesperson. He is a Car'laden-this much the queen knows due to the frequent visits of the southern cousins of the Alnis. He is wearing a dark outfit with his arms exposed to the elements. Dysis could see that the man is a warrior, yet he did not appear to carry any weapons. He has shoulder length brown hair that has a tint of grey mixed throughout. He stands in one place as the shorter man continues to speak. The queen scans the tall stranger and centers her attention on the circle of gold that graces his forehead. There is a malevolent enchantment emitting from the crown.

"I come to you in desperation, King Koro," the short man implores. "For you see, I have run into one of Bri'al's most wicked of beings. Perhaps you are familiar with her, she is Maya Sirus."

"I am very familiar with both her and her twin sister," Koro informs. "The one, Milea Sirus, was most recently here, and hopefully she has perished in the wilderness of the North. She has brought nothing but disdain to this court."

"Indeed, the twin sisters tend to do that my lord," the short man agrees. "Forgive me for being so rude my lord and allow me to introduce myself. I am Nul, Master Mage of Sentical."

"I see," Koro sits back. "You are a powerful user of magic, yet you were defeated by a woman. What happened? Did she catch you by surprise?"

"How else would I be defeated, Your Majesty?" Nul reacts with a bow. "Upon my defeat, I went to a fellow mage in Tandon, and he pointed me to the cure for my current predicament. I need the Orb of Mostorfist that is located within the ruins of Yedis."

"Mostorfist was an elder breed ice dragon," Dysis says as she walks past the guests in the room towards her throne. "He had at his disposal some of the most wicked magic. Why would he be a cure for whatever ails you, Nul?"

"You dare to come into my court and spout such nonsense to my visitors?" Koro demands, showing obvious displeasure with the queen's presence.

"My Tandon friend will have the answer to that question, Your Majesty," Nul answers cryptically.

"What of your companion with you? Why does he wear a crown?" Dysis inquires, purposefully ignoring her husband. "Is he a king? If so, why doesn't he speak up, as is proper for a king?"

"He is a borrowed warrior, milady," Nul said. "He is acting as my bodyguard, though he might be a king of something. I would have to ask my friend."

"With your bodyguard, why didn't you go straight to the ruins? You really do not need permission to do so," Dysis presses.

"Your absence from my court has not only slowed your thinking but has made you absolutely ignorant, woman," Koro snaps. "You will stay out of my business."

"My Lord, does this mean that I am able to request an escort to the ruins of Yedis?" Nul asks hopefully. "Although my bodyguard is capable, neither he nor I have knowledge of where the ruins are located. That, my lady, is why we are here."

"And I say to you and your escort, leave at once and do not return. You will not have help here," Dysis said.

"You do not have any authority in this court, Dysis. Your absence from my sight for so long is both troubling and treasonous," Koro said angrily. "Nul, you will have your escort. I will send three of my best men with you as well as my son, Qwest. You will leave once your escort has prepared to go."

"Your Majesty is generous," Nul bows his head. "My bodyguard and I shall be waiting at the inn."

"Give us time to prepare and I will come and get you," Qwest announces.

Nul bows to the court then turns and limps out of the throne room. The crowned warrior does not move at first. He shakes his head and looks at the queen briefly. Dysis could see that his eyes are a sage green color. As she stares into them, they change to a mustard yellow as the crown upon his brow pulsates. The warrior seems to stiffen before he turns and walks out of the room. From the slight jerk of his movements, Dysis could tell that it is not willingly. The queen crosses her arms as she stares into the now-empty space in contemplation.

"Mother, where did you go over the past week?" Wyntre inquires, catching the queen's attention. "Is it something to do with Brion?"

"No. I just visited some old friends," Dysis said. "Koro, why are you entertaining the Sentical Mage?"

"I will deal with you shortly, heathen," Koro addresses her sharply, then turns to his son. "Qwest, I want you to escort this mage. Once you get to the ruins, I want you to take the orb and bring it back here."

"I see no problem with the mage since he is able to be defeated by a forest witch," Qwest said. "What about his bodyguard?"

"If you use your eyes, my son, you would have noticed that his so-called bodyguard did not have any weapons upon him," Koro said. "I'm sure that neither one of them will pose any kind of problem, but I will give you my three best elite guards. The orb must remain intact so that it can be used against any more mystical invaders. You can kill both the mage and his bodyguard."

"I will do as you ask, father," Qwest bows to the king. "Will you require evidence of their demise?"

"I trust you to do the right thing, my son," Koro said. "Unlike a certain woman that has recently returned to my court."

Dysis meets the king's gaze as Koro turns and faces her. The prince bows and departs the room via a second door. The queen holds her ground as her husband approaches and stands with in an arm's length of her. She scans his physique and notices that he may not have bathed since she left. She also takes note of the wound that he had suffered during the battle with the Tandon mage, Dee. The queen raises her eyes to meet the maddened gaze of the king. Behind her, Wyntre shifts slightly, nervous at the impending altercation.

"Koro, why are you aiding an ally of Tandon?" Dysis inquires. "You do realize that Tandon is the one that attacked us last week."

"It astounds me how quickly you have become a slave of the forest witch. I thought you possessed a stronger will than that, Dysis." Koro snaps. "You do not see that Milea has made up lies about Tandon and in fact hired and controlled the woman who attacked us. I would say that it is planned, and the only reason Milea won is because she orchestrated it that way."

"Do you realize how foolish that sounds?" Dysis demands.

"Where is your mistress, witch?" Koro counters with his own demand. "I know that she is not far. You cannot possibly function without her."

"You honestly believe the lies that you keep telling yourself," Dysis observes. "I can assure you that I am not being manipulated. The battle with Tandon was very real and we lost a substantial number of men because of it."

"The lives of those men rest squarely upon the shoulders of the Red Devil herself," Koro summarizes. "You were gone for a week, woman, what did you do in that timeframe? What pact did you form with this demon? Did you sell your own soul? Did you sell those of the entire city?"

"I did nothing that you accuse me of, you jackass," Dysis retorts.

"Where is she?" Koro insists as he takes another step forward.

"Gone. Milea Sirus and her traveling companions are all gone. Never to be seen again," Dysis said forcefully, interrupting her husband.

"Even Brion?" Wyntre asks, meekly.

"Yes, even him," Dysis assures without facing the young woman.

All color within Wyntre's features drain as the queen's words sink into her soul. Tears well up as she clutches her bosom. The princess flees from the throne room. Neither the king nor the queen takes pursuit of the highly upset young woman. Koro sizes up Dysis, as a satisfied grin creeps across his aging face. The queen reads her husband's expression and body language, deciding not to correct him at this time. She needs to figure out what has happened since her departure.

"So, you took the haughty so-called sorceress to the forest and eliminated her, along with those that traveled with her," Koro misinterprets her. "It's too bad for Brion, but I did warn him to get away from that creature. We will blame his death on Milea, as it should be. I will send word to Queen Eryn in the morning."

"You may believe what you want. I truly have no time to argue with you," Dysis said. "Tell me this, why did you execute the captain of the Iron Horse?"

"The captain's death is partly his fault and partly yours," Koro says matter-of-factly. "However, I am willing to shift all blame to the now-deceased forest witch if you come serve your King in your queenly duties, which you have neglected since the she-devil's arrival. If I am satisfied with you, I will even free the icebreaker's crew prior to their termination."

"No," Dysis says.

Koro watches in disbelief as Dysis turns and walks away from him. The king sneers and takes a few steps towards the queen. Dysis pauses and glances over her shoulder at her husband. Koro stops in his tracks, taking in the situation. An icy wind whips around the throne room briefly as Dysis turns and leaves the room. The queen takes a few steps down the hall when she hears Koro begin yelling at someone. Curious, she heads back to the throne room and peeks inside, keeping to the shadows.

"I am your King! You will leave me be at once!" Koro shouts to thin air. "You were a soldier of Selcros, not the minion of a dead woman."

Dysis looks around and then stares at the spot her husband is focused on. She sees nothing in front of him nor does she sense anything. She jumps a little when Koro pulls out his sword and swings it in the air, yelling at the top of his lungs for the dead to leave him be. Apparently, it works, as the king watches the door leading to the entrance for a few moments then grunts as he marches back to his throne and sits down. His eyes shift from side to side as he rubs his wounded arm and mutters incoherently to himself. Dysis shakes her head as she takes her leave, heading to her room.

"Guards! Send for the necromancer. I want to make sure Dysis did indeed kill the forest cur," Koro shouts, causing Dysis to pause again.

"There is no necromancer in Selcros," Dysis said to herself. "I'm going to get more comfortable, then I will see what in Ublivion is going on."

The door to the room slams open and then shut, frightening the sleeping snow leopard cub. Wyntre runs over to her bed and flings herself across it. Snowpuff watches as the princess proceeds to bawl, tears soaking into the sheets. The cub chuffs a little and rubs against the crying young woman in order to comfort her. He uses his nose to nudge her on the forehead and instantly regrets it. Wyntre sits up and pulls the snow leopard into a vice-like hug. Snowpuff grumbles as his fur becomes damp with tears. A slight tapping on the window finally reaches her ears. Wyntre looks up in time to see a few pebbles being tossed and striking the glass gently. The princess dries her eyes as she goes over to the window and opens it. Snowpuff squeaks a little and tucks his paws under his body to keep them warm against the winds that enter the space.

"Wyntre, are you there?" a deep male voice calls from under the window.

"B-Brion?! Oh, my god, is that really you?" Wyntre blinks in surprise as she leans out to try and get a good look. "You escaped! Queen Dysis did not freeze you to death like she did the others. Are you alone?"

"Yes, I am alone and yes, I escaped. It was not easy," The voice assures.

"Is it true that Milea and the others are dead?" Wyntre presses. She hears shifting below but it quiets down. "Who is with you?"

"I would say it is true that she is dead, I saw the queen freeze her solid right before my very eyes," the voice claims. "I have with me a trusted friend. We must get out of Selcros before Dysis knows I still live. She is vindictive."

"She is probably with Father right now, so you have time," Wyntre assures.

"I do indeed. I stopped by because, well, I could think of no one else but you since I have broken the spell of the forest witch," the voice said. "I am asking if you will run away with me."

"I...I don't know," Wyntre hesitates a little.

"Please, Wyntre. I have a burning desire for you," the voice insists. "I want to hold you, kiss you.... Can you feel it, Wyntre?"

"Yes, yes I can!" Wyntre agrees, her voice trembling a little bit. Snowpuff licks his paws as he listens to the conversation, amused.

"Then come with me and we shall indulge in our desires this night and every night hereafter," the voice says with a firmness that Wyntre cannot resist.

"Just one moment, I will be back," Wyntre said as she stands up.

A girlish giggle escapes her as she runs into the dressing room. Snowpuff yawns and stretches as he waits. His nose tells him that the owner of the voice is not Brion. The snow leopard cub curls up again as the princess reappears wearing a very skimpy see-through gown with matching slippers and robe. Wyntre hurries over to her desk and picks up a black book, tucking it in her robe's pocket. The princess giggles again as she then sits on the windowsill and shifts until her feet are dangling in the gloom of the night. She looks down as a tingle of excitement goes through her body, oblivious to the cold weather that she is about to plunge into.

Dysis pauses in the hall next to the princess' bedroom door when she hears voices. The queen frowns as Wyntre continues a conversation with a deep male voice. She is about to continue to her room until she hears the name, Brion. Dysis listens a few more minutes, shaking her head when she hears Wyntre giggle and call out to the stranger, asking him to catch her. The queen tries to open the door but finds it locked. Swearing under her breath, she freezes the lock, then breaks it forcing her way into the room. Dysis clears the threshold just in time to see Wyntre drop from the windowsill into the frigid night. Her look of surprise shifts to Snowpuff, the cub watching from the bed. The queen hurries to the window and utters an unkind word or two when she looks out. It is completely black.

"What's going on? Where is Brion?" Wyntre demands, somewhere in the bleak below.

"Right here," Nul responds. "I must admit, princess, that you are very gullible."

"What?! No..." Wyntre says, then there is the sound of something cracking against her skull.

"So much for that, now to the Ruins of Yedis," Nul announces.

Dysis turns in haste from the window and heads out into the hall. She stops a group of guards to inform them of the situation. The men salute the queen and disburse to find and capture the impersonator. Dysis doubles back to the throne room to inform Koro of Wyntre's kidnapping. She pauses when she hears unfamiliar male voices talking to the king. Dysis uses caution to approach the room. She keeps to one side of the doorway as she peeks inside.

The first man that she sees is her husband seated upon the throne. Koro is talking to two additional guests. One is another Car'laden man just as tall and as built as the previous visitor. He is wearing a completely white sleeveless outfit. He yawns and stretches to the sky, then runs his fingers through his slightly disheveled, sand colored hair. The figure next to him is hunched over and covered in a black hooded cape. Unlike the previous wizard, this one tends to hide his features against those in the room. He leans upon a strange staff that has a human skull at the top and strangely glowing eyes. Dysis catches a glimpse of the hooded figure's hand and notes the large number of folds of his skin.

"I am pleased that you have met me at this hour as I have an emergency," Koro said. "My estranged wife has returned with the news that the forest witch, Milea, is gone. I assume she is dead but I wish to make sure. That is why I want to see you, Loca."

"Your wife has returned? My understanding is that you told us she perished in the forest," the Car'laden man perks up. "Where is the queen right now?"

"I assume she is in her room but don't count on it," Koro answers with a hint of annoyance. "You can have your way with her once we are done here. Right now, I wish to make sure that this nemesis is indeed dead."

"If she is truly dead then I will easily find her wandering spirit," Loca said, confidently.

A sickly green tint envelopes the room as the hooded figure sits down upon the floor. Dysis leans a little further into the room to see what is happening. Several nested circles spread out from underneath Loca. Feeling that she seen enough, Dysis slowly retreats so she is once again hidden by the wall and turns. She nearly jumps out of her skin when she notices a strange Car'laden woman observing her. Standing the same height as the queen, the stranger is covered in layers of clothing, yet a few strange tattoos can be seen around her neck.

"You seem awfully nosy about what's going on in that room," the stranger observes. "Are you the queen of this frozen wasteland?"

"I..." Dysis begins, then takes a deep breath in. "No, milady. I am simply a handmaid and only stopped when I heard strange voices talking to His Majesty."

"I see," the stranger grins. "Did you wish to study the proceedings a little closer?"

"That is not necessary, milady," Dysis bows her head in respect. "I have chores to complete before the king turns in for the night. If I see the queen, I will let her know that her presence is required in the throne room."

"Your excuse is really no reason why you should not accept my generous offer," the stranger informs her.

"Jasmine," the Car'laden man calls, spotting the woman in the doorway.

The stranger turns to face the room when her name is called, giving Dysis a brief opportunity to escape. The queen does so as speedily as she can down a narrow hall that leads to the barracks. The visitor turns back barely in time to see her departure. With a little frown, Jasmine walks into the throne room and bows to all those present.

"Who were you talking to in the hall?" The Car'laden man asks.

"Just some handmaiden, my Lord Slone," Jasmine answers. "She appeared interested in what is going on so I invited her in. She refused and escaped to the barracks."

"Too bad you did not get her," Slone said. "Once Loca is done you may have a new toy to play with, otherwise you definitely have a much warmer assignment."

"I have searched the furthest regions of the underworld and my informants tell me that there is no one named Milea Sirus among the dead," Loca informs as he stands up and cancels his spell. "Your nemesis, King Koro, is still alive."

"I knew that traitorous winter witch would betray me to protect her new mistress," Koro sneers angrily. "I do not know where she went and why she went there. However, she will not return to Selcros alive. I will send my armada in search of this red she-devil and hunt her to the ends of Bri'al."

"You do not send an armada to hunt a land-based sorceress," Slone advises. "However, we will discuss this shortly. Jasmine, you have a new assignment. Apparently, Tandon is unable to persuade the Queen of Dorma to surrender unconditionally. We must assist them in this matter."

"I would be happy to coax the jungle dwellers to comply," Jasmine said merrily as she bows to her master. "What method would you like me to use to influence them?"

"Any method that you deem appropriate which will obtain the desired results," Slone said. "You leave immediately."

Jasmine bows once again and then disappears in a rainbow of colors. Slone then turns his attention to Koro as the discussion shifts to Milea. The king sits back as he listens to a different plan than his original strategy, still involving the ships, but only a handful and not the full armada. Koro relaxes as he finds that he likes the plan.

Soldiers in the hall continue searching for Princess Wyntre. Dysis runs against their flow as she heads toward the castle exit. She reaches it and steps out into a cold spring night. The queen rubs her arms a little but does not go back for a coat or cape. Instead, she makes a straight line toward the back gates of the city. There are no guards to stop her as she exits into the forest. Dysis knows that she must reach Milea before her husband figures out that his nemesis is still alive.

CHAPTER TWELVE

The King's Attack

The birds of spring sing as they herald the morning sun. The sound of the boat gliding through the waters of the large river is somehow comforting to those on board. Milea and her company have spent a few days with the ice dragons forming unbreakable friendships. As a parting gift, Bryce had given Sonja a summoning stone. Once he is older, he should be able to answer her call anywhere in the world. Milea smiles as she reflects upon the time spent with their giant hosts, noting that she and Sapphire are now friends.

Neil and Vicki even assisted in naming the rest of the 12 boys. Brion and Dover had encouraged the hatchlings into much mischief. Zaria stands next to Milea and looks upon the path ahead. Neil has just informed them that at their current pace they should reach Selcros in the middle of the night. Milea relaxes her shoulders at the news, feeling that once they pass the city, they should be safe.

"Zaria, I've been meaning to ask this since we encountered Grimalkin," Milea turns toward her companion. "Why would she be seeking out Kaidar?"

"Because she can't get hold of Oswind," Zaria answers without taking her eye off the path. "Grimalkin is seeking a breeding partner."

"Really?" Milea's features reflect her slight confusion.

"Don't think too hard into this," Zaria assures. "Just realize that if Grimalkin finds Kaidar first, it will not be hard to convince him of the pairing. Kaidar is desperate for a son, and Grimalkin has a record of producing male children. In fact, I have twice as many uncles as I do aunts on my father's side."

"I think we should at least warn Keela considering the raw emotion Grimalkin showed in the temple," Milea said.

"I agree," Zaria nods.

The ship skips along the water as it rounds a bend in the river. Neil is the first one to curse loudly as he orders the anchors to drop as fast as possible. Milea braces herself as the ship hops a few times then stops, hard. Zaria reaches out and touches the giant ice wall that they had nearly collided with. Sonja shouts from above that the wall blocks the entire river, from bank to bank. It is also very thick, almost like a glacier. A flame flashes in Milea's eyes as she glares at the obstacle. The fire spreads to her body and erupts to life around her.

"I wouldn't do that right now," Dysis calls down from the top of the wall. "I seek permission to board your craft. I assure you it is with a friendly purpose."

"Blocking the way to the sea is not considered friendly, Dysis," Milea retorts.

"I am aware of how this appears, Lady Milea, but you must trust me. Koro has lost his mind, He has aligned himself with allies of Tandon," Dysis responds. "I will reveal more once I am aboard."

Milea studies the queen with a frown. Reluctantly, the sorceress coaxes the flames surrounding her into slumber and folds her arms. Neil, as captain of the ship, gives Dysis permission to board the craft. The queen conjures up an ice slide and uses it to skid down to the deck. The crew gathers around Dysis as she explains to them the details of the past two days. Brion turns toward the ice wall as he listens to the information.

The sound of horns in the distance catches the attention of those on the ship. Vicki jumps when there is a loud explosion from the other side of the glacier. The entire ice structure shudders from the impact of the unknown missile. A large iron ball sails over the wall, barely missing the stern of the ship. Milea notes where the object lands and is astonished when she hears the familiar whoosh of a powerful flame.

The top half of the wall melts away easily as the red flame licks at it from the side. Sonja gawks at the mechanical ship with a large flamethrower that is pointed in their direction. The flickering of the flames increases in agitation as it once again belches forth a long stream of fire. The girl slides down the pole in haste as the stream of flames flows over the wall and nearly strikes the top of the mast.

"There are about thirteen ships on the other side of the wall and one of them is shooting fire," Sonja reports as her feet touches the deck.

"We're going to have to abandon ship," Dysis suggests.

"I do not abandon my ship so easily," Neil reacts instinctively.

"Koro had two very interesting guests last night," Dysis says as another round of flames roars over their heads. "We must abandon ship before they break through. I know that the crew that mans those ships will not be anything like those that battled on the field. They are very ruthless."

"I hate to admit, she is right, brother," Vicki agrees.

"We better hurry before they get through that wall," Zaria points out.

Milea swears as another round of large metal balls flies overhead and comes dangerously close to destroying the ship. Dysis hurries over to the side of the vessel closest to the forest and conjures an ice ramp connecting the ship to the shore. The queen hustles everyone off the ship, with Milea being the most reluctant to leave. The sorceress is finally coerced to leave the ship just in the nick of time as the ice wall gives in to the pressure of the flame thrower. Several ships make their way through the deteriorating barrier. Milea watches from the safety of the tree line as several men board the ship.

The enchanted vessel suddenly locks all access to every portal on board, trapping the invaders. The men that had boarded the ship express various levels of surprise as the Lady of the Night unfurls her sails and starts to turn around to head back north. Milea retreats into the forest with her companions. She pauses when she hears the thunder of a cannon. The sorceress faces the river just in time to see an iron ball strike the enchanted ship. The Lady of the Night appears to explode from the impact, killing all the invaders on board.

"What the hell," Neil exclaims in anger.

"Our ship," Sonja mourns.

"We have to move away from the shore before they spot us," Brion reasons.

"How are we going to get out of here?" Zaria inquires.

"We will just have to replace our ship with one of Koro's," Vicki answers with a shrug.

"That is easier said than done," Dysis said. "I know of a place to rest and come up with a plan."

"Just remember that our ship, Lady of the Night, is an enchanted vessel," Milea reminds her companions. "She will be back."

"We must hurry," Dysis insists.

The queen leads the way down the forest path as she describes the events of three nights ago. Milea listens as she navigates the darkened trail. A quiet sound of curiosity escapes the sorceress when Dysis describes Nul. Brion asks a series of questions about Koro's behavior during the mage's visit. The queen recounts how the king had been hell-bent on assisting Nul reach his goal without even questioning his motives. As Dysis relates her experience, Vicki notices that they are being followed and gently nudges her sulking sibling to get his attention.

Neil cuts his sister a mean look then glances at the trees; several faces appear to fade in and out of the shadows. He frowns a little before pulling Sonja from the edge of the path to walk between himself and Vicki. The girl pouts a little at first then stretches and enjoys the peaceful views of the pine forest. Zaria glances over at the trees in response to the Dresden siblings' action. She hesitates slightly then smiles, mischievously, as she fades into the shadows of the woodlands.

"Nul looks as if he is being transformed into a dragon at a very slow rate," Dysis recalls. "He blames your twin, Maya, for his condition and insisted on traveling to Yedis. He also earnestly requested an escort for himself and his bodyguard."

"I can personally guarantee that Maya did not curse him to transform," Milea assures the queen. "My sister has a very strong fear of dragons. She would not change a person to that which she fears. What did Nul's bodyguard look like?"

"Why would he need one to begin with?" Brion adds.

"I asked the very same question; I will not repeat Koro's response. The bodyguard is a Car'laden, though I think he might be a little shorter than the average Car'laden man." Dysis places a finger on her chin as she continues her way around the corner. "He wears a sleeveless purple vest, which I thought odd for this climate. He has a crown upon his brow and is completely weaponless. Nul said that this strange Car'laden is borrowed from a friend."

"Nul's circle of friends includes some very dastardly folks," Milea frowns. "Anything else distinguishable that you noticed about this weaponless bodyguard?"

"His eyes," Dysis said immediately. "We locked gazes once before he left. I noticed they were a sage color. He appeared to physically flinch and fight something within. When he focused on me a second time, they had changed to a mustard yellow color."

"His eyes," Milea muses then stops in her tracks as she recognizes the description. "Justin."

"Is he friend or foe?" Vicki asks, slightly suspicious.

"He is currently a friend, but I don't know why he is under the control of Nul," Milea frowns. "Justin of Lortis is not easily controlled by anyone."

"Wait, you mean the Justin of Lortis?" Neil asks. "The one we read about in the library?"

"Seems like it. Another legend, my friend," Brion offers. "Dysis, who did Koro send with Nul as an escort?"

"A group of elite guards, including his son, Qwest. Nul is after the Orb of Mostorfist and Koro seems to think his son can wrestle it from the mage. I don't know what Koro thinks he can do with it." Dysis shakes her head, sadly. "Nul has also kidnapped Wyntre, for unknown reasons. I heard him; he is taking her to Yedis as well."

"What would he need her for?" Sonja inquires.

"I do not know," Dysis said. "I do know that Yedis is where my newborn daughter was sacrificed. At the feet of the mountain known as Oswind's Throne."

"Then most likely, it is cursed," Milea said and stare into the trees. "I do not know if Maya would remember what she did. I don't want to trigger any memories that would set her back. She has come so far."

"I would like to meet her one day, truly," Dysis says. "Perhaps the conversation will bring closure to the tragedy of that night for me."

"Do we make a trip to Yedis to recover Justin?" Neil inquires.

"Not all of us," Milea said. "Zaria, we have to take a northly trip."

"I listened from the shadows," Zaria agrees as she drops from a branch. "The Wild Men that are following us did so out of curiosity. They are gone now."

"The trip to Oswind's Throne is a three-day horse ride," Dysis informed. "Two if you are willing to kill the horse through exhaustion."

"Nul has at least two days head start," Vicki calculates. "Then we need to get to steppin'," Zaria announces.

"Neil, it may take more than a day for the ship to recover, but it will," Milea assures her friend.

"We will wait for two days before doing anything rash as long as we have a warm place to camp," Neil assures. He watches as Milea nods and heads down the path with Zaria.

"Wait for me," Sonja jogs to catch up with her mother.

"In the book, Justin of Lortis battled and won against Slone, Son of Roathis," Neil recalls as he watches Milea walk further into the woods away from the path.

"Slone is here, in Selcros, as we speak. I believe he may be responsible for the ice wall's destruction," Dysis said as she continues to walk to her destination. "He brought with him a strangely tattooed woman named Jasmine and a necromancer named Loca. We are going to the hunter's lounge, once there I will tell you more."

A short distance from the departing group, Zaria pauses when she hears Slone mentioned in the conversation behind them. Milea and Sonja hesitate, and along with the shiadokat they turn to face the direction from which they had come. Milea frowns slightly as she and Zaria briefly exchange glances. The shiadokat nods then goes after Dysis and their traveling companions. She calls to them to wait up as Milea and Sonja turn back to the woods in order to find a clearing. They now must call their new friends, the ice dragons, to transport them to their destination.

Several dark blue birds call out in song as mother and daughter continue their track through the woodlands. A light wind rustles a few of the pine needles, cascading the loose ones towards the forest floor. The tall pines of this northern forest cover the land for miles between the mountains and Selcros. The densely populated trees stretch out to soak up every ounce of sunlight, keeping the forest floor in shadow. Breaks in the otherwise thick foliage provide enough light for saplings

and other forest plants to grow. Hungry carabao nibble on the suc-
culent shoots and do not notice Milea and Sonja as they pass by.

A light sprinkle of melted snow showers the travelers, providing
gentle kisses of cool liquid upon their faces. Sonja bends down to
examine the ground for any signs of their quarry. There are multiple horse tracks leading to the northern edge of the forest. From
the looks of it, the beasts are all in full gallop. Sonja finishes taking
in the scene then stands and catches up with her mother. Milea
makes sure her daughter is with her then takes in the environment,
feeling at ease within the branches.

The sorceress keeps her wits about her while seeking a huge
clearing somewhere in the woods. A large owl hoots as it flies over
the heads of the tourists, landing on a tree not too far from them.
White as snow, it shakes out its wings then focuses on the mother
and daughter. The owl moves its head left, right, then up and down
as it watches them. Sonja grins and imitates the owl's head movements. The bird fluffs up as if insulted and turns its back, causing
a chuckle to escape from Milea.

"Mom, do you think Grandma would like it here?" Sonja asks
softly.

"I think it has to be warmer than it is now. Keela does not take
to the cold very well," Milea explains gently. "She simply does not
like it. Her son, Tadious, was here for a while but it is unclear why."

"Is he still here?" Sonja asks.

"Alive, yes. He is sleeping. Where he is sleeping, I do not know.
The answer is in the book," Milea said. "Once we get it stitched back
together, we will find all of the sleeping Eltis."

"Wasn't the book on the ship when it exploded?" Sonja frowns.

"It was..." Milea answers. She continues to walk in silence for a while.

Several of the carabao look up with nose flaring as they sample the air. They make grunting noises then cry out in alarm as they run deeper into the woodlands. Milea's sword appears in a flash as Sonja stands back-to-back with her mother. Both focus on the tree line for the slightest movement. Deep, guttural, growls accompanied by several reptile-like hisses fill the air as a handful of dragon-like creatures appear. Milea whispers several unladylike words, recognizing them as the same creatures she had battled when Tandon attacked Selcros.

The Sierge hesitate and begin to bang their weapons against their armor as the largest of their number continue forward. His head moving side to side as if to limber up for battle. A gleam cuts across Milea's eyes as she concentrates on her opponent. A whistling sound echoes from the trees, followed by a cry of surprise from one of the Sierge as he falls to the ground. An arrow twice as thick as a regular shaft, is embedded in the downed warrior's forehead. The color leaves his eyes as death claims him.

A volley of arrows shoots from the trees and plummets the Sierge, hitting them in places where their armor is nonexistent or weak. As sudden as the hail of arrows had begun, it ends. The only Sierge that remains standing is the leader. The large male roars in defiance and charges forward. Milea changes her stance to meet the opponent. A wild battle cry echoes in the forest as several men charge out of the shadows and attack the dragon-like beast. Wave after wave of men swoop in, attack, and then retreat until the Sierge is on his knees. A warrior with a strange tattoo is the last to attack the beast, beheading him.

"Mom, what's going on?" Sonja asks as a whisper.

"We will find out soon enough," Milea answers in similar fashion. "Stay vigilant."

The slayer lifts his sword and yells out in victory as he shakes his weapon above his head. His fellow Wild Men do the same before they start stripping the dead of their weapons and their armor. Milea focuses on the man that killed the leader as he turns and takes a couple steps towards her. Sonja glances around the tree line to see that the archers are still in place. The leader of the wild men stops only a few feet from the sorceress.

"You, woman, why are you in the woods along with your child?" The man asks with a gruff voice. "Did Koro send you in, then have these things pursuing you in a sick hunting game?"

"I do not cater to Koro and his games," Milea replies. "I am unclear why the Sierge are here, but it is not because of me."

"Then why are you here?" The man rephrases.

"I seek a clearing, the reason is none of your business," Milea answers.

"You are in our home, everything is our business," the leader informs her.

"Then I will make a clearing right here," Milea retorts.

Both the sorceress and the Wild Man turn their attention towards one of the looters when he makes an angry sound of recognition. Sonja takes a step back in surprise and then repositions herself in a defensive stance as the large man charges towards her. There is a look of pure murder in his eyes. Foam is coming out of his mouth from his instant rage. The leader puts his sword away, steps in front of the girl, and punches his fellow Wild Man squarely in the nose. The attacker fell backwards, hitting the ground and holding his offended appendage.

Taking advantage of the situation, Milea causes an explosion of wind to whip around the area. Loose pine needles fly up in a tornadic like fashion as the trees themselves whip back and forth violently. The debris thicken to a point where the archers in the lose sight of the sorceress and child. Sonja dodges around the Wild Men and heads into the forest under the cover impromptu storm. Milea disappears in a rain of golden dust as she releases the winds. The pine needles fall to the forest floor as the area returns to normal. The leader of the Wild Men looks around with a very displeased look upon his features.

"Find the sorceress and child, we have to take them to Liev," the leader orders. Several men head into the forest to hunt for the two escapees.

Animals keep a wide berth away from the travelers as they continue their way. The thirty-minute travel feels like hours as the darkness of the woodlands start to fade to daylight. They enter the clearing and seem to freeze in place. Milea's eyes take in the sheer destruction that lay before her. The thick tree line has transformed into a clear-cut plane that stretches as far as the eye can see. Low cut tree stumps dot the area where tall, proud, pines once stood. The sorceress shakes herself out of her stunned state and exhales a little. She leads her daughter into the clearing, walking until they are near the middle of it.

Milea remains vigilant as Sonja takes a small bluestone out of her pocket and holds it in both hands. She closes her eyes to concentrate. After a few minutes, the girl opens her eyes with a frown informing her mother that nothing is happening. Milea studies her daughter then holds out her hand. Sonja gives the stone to her mother and watches as the sorceress takes a good look at it.

Milea smiles explain to Sonja that the bluestone is activated by magic. With that, the sorceress holds the stone in the palm of her hand

and focus upon it. The stone levitates from her palm as it flashes a rainbow of colors and emits a musical sound. Once done, the blue-stone gently comes to rest on Milea's palm.

The winds around the area begin to pick up as soft thunder rumbles from above. The sounds of happy mews echo around the clearing as the baby ice dragon circles his friends before landing, not very gracefully, a short distance from them. Milea smiles when Bryce trots over and snuggles against Sonja, inadvertently knocking the girl to the ground.

The winds do not die down, but rather increase. Milea watches as Sapphire circles the clearing, her great wings causing small tornadoes as she uses them to maneuver. The dragoness lands a few feet away from her son, shakes off a little. She walks space between herself and those who had summoned them.

"Lady Sapphire, this is an honor to see you again, although also unexpected," Milea nods to the mother dragon.

"Dover and I happen to be in the middle of giving the boys flying lessons when Bryce decided to go off on his own," Sapphire said. "I decided to pursue him. You seem troubled, Lady Milea."

"There are many things troubling me, this is true. However, I currently need to get to the ruins of Yedis," Milea explains. "I must recover a companion whom I thought lost. This seems to be the only opportunity that I have in order to retrieve him."

"I'm glad I did follow Bryce," Sapphire says as she sits down. "There are many factors that would have been against you if I had let him alone. First, Bryce does not know the way to your destination, and second, Yedis is cursed."

"All the more reason I need to get to Justin," Milea agrees. "There is a mage that appears to be controlling him named Nul."

"Vicki told us about him. This Nul is partnered with one called Sorshana, a misguided dragon queen," Sapphire said, recognizing the name.

"She is no queen, milady. She has come across a mighty power and is using it to control many other dragons and their kin throughout Bri'al," Milea explains. A small silence settles between them. The wind rustles the trees a little as if in anticipation.

"I am your ride to Yedis, climb aboard," Sapphire says.

"I..." Milea starts, stunned by the dragoness's words. "Thank you, Sapphire." Milea bows to the dragoness then assists her daughter to her feet.

Bryce makes a few whistles and clicks as he gently bumps his head against Sonja. The girl pats the hatchling on the head then takes a step back when he stretches his wings and flaps them forcefully. Sapphire explains that Bryce wants Sonja to ride upon his back. Milea studies the smaller dragon a little then pats him on his nose as she nods to her daughter. Sonja takes a deep breath as she grabs the dragon's furry collar and pulls herself onto his back.

Bryce dances in place as he emits happy sounds, then bounces twice before his wings take over, lifting both dragon and passenger into the air. Milea climbs aboard Sapphire's back and holds on as the dragoness crouches, wings spread, then takes to the air in one strong leap. Sapphire calls out gently to her brood and mate as she circles about, then sets course for Yedis. Dover circles once to gather the boys and get all pointing in the right direction.

"Why are we going toward the mountain?" Dover inquires.

"I will tell you when we get there," Sapphire answers cryptically as she increases her speed. "Keep up, boys, we have at least an hour's flight ahead of us."

The red hues of the evening sun fill the small clearing as Dysis arrives at a hunter's retreat with the rest of her guests. Made of stone and timber, the lodge is overly large and built for a king. Huge windows reflect the sun's rays, and the entire structure is void of people. The door opens as the group enters the lodge.

A set of gigantic windows frame an equally large fireplace that is covered with cobwebs. The webbing attaches to a spear meant to be held by a titan, which is hanging like a trophy upon the wall leading upstairs. Gracing the middle of the room is a bearskin, its left paw reaching for the door. The fur is a mixture of dark brown and white and extremely thick, to keep the bear warm in the cold climate.

Neil and Zaria enter the space, with the shiadokat taking the stairs to explore the upper level. Neil lights a few torches to chase away some of the shadows as Vicki leads the way. She stops in her tracks when she sees the bearskin rug as well as the spirit of a middle-aged woman staring back at her. Dysis catches up with the pair, and her jaw drops as her eyes widen in surprise. Her breathing is nearly nonexistent as she wills her legs to get a little closer.

"No!" Dysis wails as she falls to her knees and hugs the giant head of the deceased bear.

"What's going on?" Brion enters with his sword in hand. He puts it away when he sees there is no threat.

"I'm not sure, but it seems we have spiritual company," Vicki answers as she watches the ghost approach Dysis and try to comfort her. "Friendly this time."

"There are four large bedrooms upstairs, the biggest looks like it's for the king," Zaria said as she walks back down stairs. "Is she alright?"

"I think we might have found someone meaningful to her," Neil offers.

"I did overhear her mentioning a bear while we sailed towards the temple," Zaria goes over to check on the queen. She shakes her head and leaves the woman alone.

"Let's plan a way back south," Neil offers. "Even if the ship does return, we still have to deal with Koro and his guests."

"Hmm..." Zaria crosses her arms.

"Dysis, can you tell us more about the partnership between Slone and Koro?" Vicki asks as she kneels next to the grieving queen. There is no answer.

"I'm going to Selcros to see what's going on," Zaria walks to the door.

"I'm going with you," Brion offers.

"Not this time," Zaria replies and disappears into the shadows.

CHAPTER THIRTEEN

Ruins of Yedis

Twilight replaces the beautiful colors of the evening sky as the dragons fly through a dark veil. Several of the hatchlings squeak in surprise as they hesitate at the border of the mountain. Sapphire calls to them to encourage the brood to follow. Dover gives a gentle nudge to those more cautious. Bryce follows his mother, bravely, without looking back to see if his brothers are with him.

Sonja glances behind to see that the sun is still shining, at least for now, yet it is much darker than the sky they had just left behind. The wind turns freezing cold as snow flurries fill the air. Steam rises from both Dover and Sapphire as the fast pace continues. A few of the hatchlings hitch a ride on their father's back, exhausted from the flight.

The ruins of Yedis loom into view at a very rapid pace. The light of the twin moons dances hauntingly upon the crumbling buildings. Milea recognizes the mountain; it is the same one that she saw though various windows in Selcros. Always dark, no matter what time of day she observed it. Sapphire locks her wings and starts to circle as she looks for a place to land outside of the ruins. Bryce follows his mother's example, making wide arcs around the city. The view provides Sonja an opportunity to study the layout of the broken town. She sees that the only structure still standing in one piece is a single tower toward the middle.

Sapphire slows down as she decides on a clearing large enough to accommodate her family one hundred yards from the entrance of Yedis. The wind bites into Milea as it rushes past during the dragoness final approach to landing. The wings beat in the opposite direction to take most of the speed away. Sapphire lands on the ground, sliding a few feet in the snow and stopping about thirty yards from where she started.

Dover roars overhead and lands in front of his mate, sliding until he crashes into the trees. Several of the towering structures give way to the dragon's ungraceful landing. Those hatchlings that are holding on to their father squeal in delight from the uncontrolled landing. Others follow his example but end up bumping into their father. Bryce lands and slides, placing his bottom down to stop before he hits his mother's tail. Milea climbs off the dragoness's back as Sapphire folds her wings down.

"Sapphire, I thank you for the assistance," Milea repeats. "Can I implore you to stay until we find Justin? We will need a ride back."

"I planned on staying, the boys need to rest after the speedy flight," Sapphire agrees. "We will be here, be careful in the ruins."

"Thank you," Milea said. "Sonja, be prepared for anything."

"I already am," Sonja assures. "Especially after that flight."

The snow crunches underfoot as Milea and Sonja jog though the trees to their destination. The dead tree trunks host a variety of unsettled souls that never found their way through the veil. Sonja keeps up with her mother as she studies the ground. There are several tracks, many seem to go in directions that are impossible or lead deeper in the woods. The end of the woods come into view and not a moment too soon.

Milea is first to exit the woodlands with Sonja a step behind. They are standing at the front gates of Yedis. The stars above them do not move or twinkle as they do a normal night. Both the moons are near the full stage and stuck in place. The mountain outside the ruined city is still several days away yet the wind coming down from it is as cold as it's namesake's gaze.

"Mom, we have company," Sonja said, gaining the sorceress' attention.

Milea tears her gaze from the distance and focuses on the man standing in front of the gates of the ruins. She squares her jaw a little when she notices it is Qwest. Milea decides to go toward him but hesitates when she notices that he has not moved in at least a day. Snow covers his shoulders and head yet he seems oblivious of the cold. Milea steps in front of the Alnis Prince and waves her hand, he does not blink but continues to stare straight ahead.

"I'll deal with him shortly," Milea muses and turns to the wall.

The thick gray stones of the ruins are held in place by ice and snow. Carved into the face of the stone are strange letters spelling out warnings about what is inside. The words are covered with fresh blood dripping from above. Milea looks up and frowns, three Alnis guards are pinned against the wall with sacrificial daggers. Their clothing is torn from their bodies, their hearts ripped from their chests. The faces of the men are forever frozen in pain yet the eyes appear to reflect extreme pleasure. Milea cautiously touches the stone. A powerful dark jolt coupled with a mask of evil fills her mind. She pulls back and turns away to go stand with her daughter once more.

"It is as I suspected, Maya cursed this place a long time ago," Milea informs.

"That was during the time of her being controlled by a Tragin, right?" Sonja asks.

"Yes," Milea agrees. "It looks like it requires three sacrifices for three people. We don't have to repeat what Nul has already done."

"Thank the old ones," Sonja said, relieved. "Are we going to leave Qwest here?"

"It looks like he has been standing here for a long time," Milea looks over the Alnis Prince. "I think he will be fine."

Milea and her daughter enter the city, their senses on alert. Sonja points out the similarities to Selcros, but the constant winter frost has taken its toll on the buildings. Everything is now covered in a thin sheet of blue ice, to include piles of rubble. The duo is walking past a once grand inn when, behind them, Qwest finally blinks and takes a deep breath in. The Alnis Prince groans as he shakes his head then holds it while he regains his balance. He looks up and is horrified by the bodies dangling on the wall. Qwest looks down the path and notices the back of Milea as she moves away from him.

"You brazen witch!" Qwest shouts angrily and pulls his sword.

Milea turns when she hears Qwest yell. The Alnis charges towards her, full speed, wildly out of control. Sonja also faces the threat then glances behind. She turns and jumps over a hidden obstacle. Milea notices her daughter's movements and follows her example, taking a couple more steps away from the threat. She causes her sword to appear and stands facing the raging Alnis. Milea glares at Qwest as he nears them. The Alnis Prince reaches a point in the road then suddenly disappear as he falls into a pit-trap. Milea looks over the edge to see that Qwest has fallen at least ten feet, his sword is now stuck in the wall of the pit.

"Welcome to Yedis, Qwest," Milea said. "I'm sure you don't remember how you got here."

"What did you do to my men, cur?" Qwest demands.

"Nothing," Milea said calmly. "Why did you agree to assist Nul?"

"None of your business," Qwest sneers. "Why are you here? Are you going to finish what your sister started?"

"If you mean sending Nul on a permanent vacation to Oswind's front door, then yes, I am," Milea informs. "Otherwise, it is none of your business."

Milea takes a step back and turns to walk away. Sonja glances at the angry Alnis then trails after her mother. They hone in on the tower that is still standing in the middle of the city. The road is covered with fresh-laid snow, covering up most tracks. Sonja bends over and identifies two different men walking in the same direction they are headed. One is a large set of prints while the other is smaller. Milea ignores the curses and threats that Qwest hurls at her as she trails after her daughter down the street.

"You are not going to get away with this," Qwest growls as he grabs his sword.

Black ice wraps around the sword immediately, causing him to swear. More of the dark ice appear around him. Qwest mutters an oath to his ancestors as he jumps up and grabs the top of the trap. He places his foot on the sword embedded in the wall of the pit and pushes himself all the way out. Qwest rolls away from the trap and gets to his feet in time to see the opening seal over with black ice. He gets to his feet and follows the sorceress.

A strong wind blows loosened snow up into the air, then ceases, allowing it to fall back down as flurries. Milea and Sonja pause when the ground shakes. The sorceress moves back and pulls her daughter with her. The house they are standing next to begins to collapse from the pressures of the eternal winter. The movement of the falling building is slow and methodical, each stone taking several seconds to reach the ground. The shaking slowly ebbs away as the last stone reaches its destination. Black ice ooze out and covers the pile of rubble.

"Get to the tower," Milea instructs her child.

Milea turns and runs toward her destination. Sonja jogs and catches up with her mother then quickly passes her. Behind them, Qwest also starts running to the edifice, if only to catch the one he believes murdered his men. Sonja suddenly jumps, flips, lands and keeps going. A moment later, the girl swears and slide to a stop when she nearly runs into a collapsed building. Milea stops within an inch of her daughter. Qwest bellows behind them, causing both to turn and dodge out of the Alnis' way as he attacks with his bare hands.

The air warms up as Qwest reaches for Milea's throat. She is quick to punch him in a very sensitive spot. The man's eyes widen and all the air to leave his lungs. Milea takes a single step back to allow the Alnis Prince to fall to his knees. He hisses out a few words as he holds his groin. The sorceress crosses her arms as she watches him grip the ground in an effort to breathe.

"Why are you following and attacking us, Qwest?" Milea demands.

"You will pay dearly for killing my men," Qwest manages to gasp.

"Again, I did not. However, the one who did could possibly still be here," Milea informs. "You are welcome to follow to ask Nul himself the same question. Else you can go home."

"Lies," Qwest sneers.

"The next time you attack, you will be face to face with the Eltis of the Underworld," Milea warns with little emotion.

The ruins quake again, this time the building blocking the way suddenly falls to rubble. A strange black liquid oozes out of the stone and creeps towards the trio a few inches then freeze solid. Milea frowns at the liquid, whatever curse has hold of this place is toying with them. Without a word, she turns and starts running to the tower once again, followed closely by Sonja. Both increase their speed and disappear down the street as Qwest wrestles to his feet and limps after them.

The tower of Yedis looms into view as flurries swirl about the edifice. Snow and ice cover the imposing structure, creating an ominous sight. Black ice forms stripes from top to bottom of the tower, absorbing the light of the moons. All the windows appear to have bars to keep prisoners inside.

The tower is connected to a second, once divine, building. That structure is half-collapsed from some unknown battle and neglect. Sonja takes in the strange lights that circle the structure. They are flying in and out of the windows. The girl's ears pick up the moans of pain emitting from the apparitions. She frowns as she is unable to distinguish if they are male or female.

Sonja shakes her head and concentrates as she increases her speed and jumps over a large wall, careful to avoid the black ice. Milea follows her daughter as Sonja hurries past the threshold of the tower. The girl slides in her attempt to stop. The slippery floor and her speed prevent her from stopping. She swears when she notices that she is heading straight into one of the walls. Sonja manages to balance herself long enough to jump, bounce off the barrier and land back to the floor in a crouch. Milea enters the space and slows her pace until she can stop.

Steam circles the sorceress's head as she takes a deep breath and calms her racing pulse while catching her breath. The entire room is barely intact, icicles hang from the ceiling with the points aiming to the center. Sonja approaches her mother as she while taking in the scene. The young woman is sensing a multitude of angry spirits in the area above their location. Milea focuses on the single living occupant that stands sentry in front of a large set of stairs. Qwest enters the room and focuses on the man guarding the stairs.

He is a seven-foot Car'laden man wearing a dark purple vest, his arms exposed to the weather. He is handsome, and resembles the description given to Milea by Dysis. His powerfully built chest moves slowly, indicating that he is still alive and perhaps meditating. The rest of his clothing is black and seems more suited for the cold weather. The man's long brown hair is held back by a golden crown.

The item pulsates with an unholy energy, shifting colors between yellow and deep red. Milea takes a step closer as she scans the guardian, noting that his eyes are still closed yet she can tell he is struggling with something, perhaps an internal battle. He holds in his hands a strange spear with a blade that looks more like a modified ax. A jewel in the middle of the weapon glows red with an audible growl emits from it.

"What the hell is Nul's bodyguard doing here?" Qwest inquires.

"You are still here?" Milea glances at him then focuses back on the guard. "Sonja, do you see Nul anywhere?"

"No, but his tracks suggest that he made a straight line down those stairs," Sonja said. "Justin does not look well."

"Physically, he is fine," Milea assures. "Do you remember when Vicki and Neil told us about the Crown of Hestor?"

"I do," Sonja nods as she watches the guardian. "Is that on his head? Do we knock it off?"

"It is, and it is not a simple task to knock off the crown," Milea said.

"What the hell are you talking about?" Qwest demands. "You! Where is Nul, I need to talk to him about this relic he is seeking." He directs his orders towards the guardian.

"He is just down the stairs," the guardian answers, his voice deep and a little raspy, as if he needed water. "All you have to do is get past me."

"Easy enough," Qwest snorts and takes a step forward. He finds his movements limited as he freezes in place.

"You don't know how tempting it is for me to leave you to your fate, Qwest," Milea said. "However, Justin of Lortis has enough blood on his hands, he does not need to add to it. Sonja, see if you can find and take care of Nul before he sacrifices Wyntre. We do not want him to add to this already-cursed place."

"Yes, ma'am," Sonja said.

"Wait, my sister is here?" Qwest finds that he can move and faces the sorceress once again. "How is that possible? She is at the castle."

"Ask Nul," Milea reiterates in short. "Sonja, I wish you good hunting but be very quick. We cannot stay any longer than we already have."

"Be careful, I don't want anything to happen to you," Sonja hugs her mother gently.

"I will be as careful as I can, my little silver wind," Milea gently kisses the top of Sonja's head. "Once I start the battle, you start your hunt."

"You? Battle him?" Qwest laughs harshly. "What could you possibly do to a warrior except be a distraction? And if he is truly Justin of Lortis, then you don't have a hope in Ublivorin in taking him down."

The air in the room heats up slightly as Sonja releases her mother in the silence that follows the prince's comments. The girl creeps to one side of the room as Milea turns, little by little, to face Qwest. A red flame flickers deep within her eyes as they meet those of the prince. Qwest takes an involuntarily steps back as Milea's sword appears in her hand with a flash. The light green and white blade glows brightly, synchronizing with the sorceress' energies. Milea turns from the Alnis without saying a word as she concentrates on the Car'laden.

Ice melts under her footsteps as she approaches him. Justin's eyes are slow to open when he senses his challenger. Milea concentrates on them and nods, noting that the pupils are a mustard yellow. He has slipped into the darker parts of his abilities. The sorceress knows that if he goes any deeper, the blood rain will start and there is nothing she will be able to do to get him back if that happens. Steam rises from Justin's body; the heat melts the icicles above. Sonja inches a little closer to the stairs then pauses in the shadows to await her opportunity.

"Justin, fight the crown. I know you are stronger than it," Milea addresses the Car'laden man.

"You know nothing, woman," Justin responds hypnotically.

"I know that you swore an oath to me," Milea reminds him. "I know you will never harm me and that you will protect those around me. Those words you spoke to me yourself. Where is my dark guardian? I need him."

"I do not know of any oath," Justin said.

"Justin, you know I speak truth," Milea said gently. "I have come to recover you, to get you away from Nul and his allies. I will not abandon you in this forsaken land of ice and snow. But you must help me. You must fight the effects of the crown, Justin. I know you can break its hold, my warrior."

Justin holds his head with his free hand, his eyes temporarily changing to sage green then is quick to return to mustard yellow as his body shudders. The jewel upon the spear brightens considerably at the same moment that Justin charges forward with unnerving speed. Milea takes a couple of steps back to gain her footing then dodges the spear he thrusts at her. She blocks the next three blows then disappears, reappearing a distance away from the staircase and too close to Qwest. The Alnis Prince drops a few unkind words as he moves out of the way when Justin disappears in a flash of light. Milea twists to block the attack when the man reappears behind her. The two blades meet, causing several red sparks to rain down over the floor.

Justin grabs Milea by her shirt and lifts her off the ground. Milea holds onto his arm as he turns to toss her into a far wall. Instead of leaving his grip, she lands upon her feet, still holding his arm. Justin bellows in surprise when he flies towards the wall instead. He flips and lands upon the ground, sliding back until his left heel hits the wall.

Milea uses a mage wind to push herself back several more feet away from the staircase. Justin hones in on her and uses speed to cross the gap between them. Milea blocks his blade, locking the two weapons together. Sonja sees her opportunity and sprints over to the stairs, heading down a flight in haste. Qwest follows her lead then hesitates when he hears Milea unleash a series of unkind words. He turns to see the battle is continuing.

The sorceress hits the floor, breaking her hold on the deadly weapon. Justin pulls back and plunges his weapon down just as Milea seems to turn into a rain of golden dust. Justin sneers at the spot, he has buried nearly half the blade of his spear into the stone floor with the blow. Milea reappears a distance away from Justin, her mystical abilities roaring to life around her body. With a mighty yell, Milea launches a strong fire spell at the man. Justin turns and takes several steps back, swearing as if he were on the high seas. He falls flat on the floor to allow the spell to pass right over him, unaware that there is a witness.

"Oswind's beard," Qwest exclaims as he dives into the staircase. The fire follows the Alnis as he rolls down the stairs, stopping on a landing not too far from Sonja's feet.

"Stay silent," Sonja hisses her words.

"I do not take orders from a child," Qwest says angrily.

"Then I suggest you go back upstairs to assist with Justin instead," Sonja recommends.

The girl is quiet as she descends the second set of stairs into the shadows of the basement. Her hearing has picked up the sounds of chanting and she figures to follow it to find her quarry. Qwest looks back when he hears one of the combatants upstairs curses bitterly. Soon after the words, thunder shakes the building. He decides to trail

Sonja, concluding that it would be easier to dispatch of the girl. Sonja resists the urge to punch the Alnis in his nose as he arrives in the shadows next to her. The girl calms her instincts and focus on the altar holding the princess.

Wyntre groans as she starts to awaken from her forced sleep. She tries to put her hand on her head, only to feel a restriction. All sleep disappears from her mind when she feels the rope holding her down. She tries to move her other arm and finds that it too is tied down. The wind whistles, causing a gasp to escape followed by a few very colorful words as she remembers the clothing she chose to elope in. She barely remembers the handsome Car'laden man that kidnapped her. She remembers that he is the 'bodyguard' that stood in the throne room a few hours earlier. She listens to the deep voice chanting next to her and wonders if it is the same man.

"Where am I?" Wyntre demands. The droning stops.

"Oh, you're awake," the deep voice that lured her said, humored. "I'm pleased to tell you that I did not need to sacrifice you."

"Who..." Wyntre turns her head and is startled. "You are the mage that visited father. The one that Maya cursed."

"Ah yes, I forgot I told your father that. Well, he seems to believe it anyway," Nul shrugs and leans on the altar a little.

"My family and I are also enemies of Maya Sirus and her horrible twin sister Milea," Wyntre assures him. "Why did you tie me to this filthy thing? I would help you find your artifact if that is what you want."

"Actually, I already found it," Nul says and holds up a watermelon-shaped black orb. "Behold the Orb of Mostorfist. As far as untying you, I will do that once I finish consuming this and partake in ravishing your pretty young body."

"What?" Wyntre blinks in surprise.

"Don't misunderstand me, it is all a part of the price to pay for consuming a dark dragon," Nul shrugs. "If you survive the experience, I will let you go. Simple as that."

"I don't want to participate in this," Wyntre struggles with her bonds.

"Ah, lovely princess. You do not have a choice," Nul said with mock sympathy.

Sonja shakes her head as she rises to her feet, even though she finds Wyntre annoying, the princess does need rescuing. Qwest stands up and rushes forward to help his sister. Nul sees him and simply raises his hand. The Alnis prince stops his charge and stands in place, his head slumps over and shoulders relax. Sonja limbers up and lets out a slight grunt as she moves forward swiftly. She accelerates in record time, streaming past Qwest and completely surprising Nul. A few seconds later, Sonja slams her fist into Nul's stomach. The blow knocks him backwards, sending the orb one way while he sails a different direction. Nul gets to his feet only to be slammed again. Sonja punches the mage several times then tosses him into a thick wall of ice. He hits the barrier, cracking it, then falls to the ground.

"Where in Ublivorin's Gates did you come from?" Nul grumbles as he stumbles to his feet.

"That blow should have broken your back," Sonja responds.

"It might have if I did not have the Orb of Ikedo already consumed," Nul admits. "I'm no warrior, so I guess he'll have to take care of you."

Sonja faces Qwest as he attacks her, swinging his fist. The girl captures the appendage and twists it rapidly. Qwest bellows in pain as he flips and falls to the ground on his back. Sonja brings down an open hand and knocks the Alnis prince's head against the floor, rendering him unconscious. She looks up from her opponent when the lighting of the room changes to a strange orange color.

Lightning wraps around Nul's body as he gathers it to his hands. Sonja gets to her feet and charges towards the mage. Nul cackles as he casts the spell towards the attacking girl. The orange lightning caresses Sonja's body as she charges, yet does not affect her. The charge of the spell collects on her fist as she slams it into Nul. The man loses all the air in his lungs and nearly coughs up the first orb he ingested. Sonja takes a couple of steps back as the mage collapses to the ground and does not move.

Sonja nods as she dusts her hands. She turns towards the princess and snaps the rope holding the young woman down. Wyntre sits up and immediately strikes out to slap the young girl. Sonja catches the hand and stares at Wyntre intensely. The princess tries to pull away but finds her arm held fast by her rescuer. Sonja clenches her jaw as she decides to release the young woman's arm and walk away.

"Why are you here?" Wyntre demands as she stands up.

"To retrieve a friend," Sonja answers, glancing over her shoulder. "I suggest you get out of here the best way you can."

"Are...are you going to leave me here?" Wyntre said, slightly panicked.

"You have him," Sonja gently kicks Qwest awake as she walks past him. "You two can find your way back home."

Qwest groans as he turns over then stands up to go check on his sister. Wyntre cries a little and is comforted by her older brother. Sonja places one foot on the stairs on the way up when the cry of a baby catches her attention. She turns and walks back over to the altar at the same time the Selcros royals face the artifact. The three

gawk in surprise as they lay eyes on a newborn girl wiggling and crying. She is laying on the altar in the same spot Wyntre had been tied
up. The baby is red and covered in blood, strange symbols decorate the
head and tiny body.

Sonja shakes her head, taking a step back. She notices that the
same symbols upon the child now illuminate the entire basement. The
ancient words pulsate with a slight hum emitting from them. Sonja's
attention goes back to the baby as Wyntre picks her up, rocking her a
little bit. The babe quiets enough to open her eyes. The light green
orbs shine briefly before they cloud back up and she starts to cry again.
Qwest examines the child and notes the black hair clinging to her
head. Sonja sees a black shadow engulf the baby then lighten back up
quickly.

"Put the baby down," Sonja warns.

"Who is she?" Wyntre ignores the warning. "How did she get here?"

"That blanket," Qwest frowns then blinks. "Chastity!!"

"This is the one that Maya sacrificed, the baby that Dysis lost,"
Wyntre said in awe. "But how is she still alive?"

"She's not," Sonja informs her. "I strongly suggest that you put her
down and walk away."

"You are a heartless heathen," Wyntre snaps. "If she is my sister,
then we are taking her home."

"Suit yourself," Sonja says.

With that, Sonja heads back to the stairs and increases her step to
ascends back to the top. At first, she did not notice Qwest and Wyntre
following her. The cry of the baby, however, makes her aware of their
ascent. Sonja exits into the upper room as it trembles from the mystical energy level of the combatants. The battle and power level have

both reach a critical high. Ice falls from the walls and the stone crumbles from the lack of frozen mortar.

Justin yells angrily as he tosses his opponent with all his might. Milea lands on the wall and moves quickly to avoid the spear he sends after her. She keeps her angry words to herself, dodging several more times as he tries to skewer her. Milea changes directions, going up the wall briefly then jumping off, landing behind Justin. She is about to move but hesitates when Justin suddenly appears in front of her. Milea unleashes the words she had been holding in as she raises an arcane shield. A rainbow of sparks fills the air as his blade collides with the barrier.

A yellow glow caresses Justin's body then consolidates on his hands as he punches the obstacle. The shield shatters at the same time Milea stands. She lands an uppercut on the man's chin. The blow sends Justin back, causing him to lose his balance and fall. Milea, panting a little, bears down and prepares for another attack. She briefly glances behind to see Sonja standing in the shadows of the staircase. Her attention returns to the danger at hand when Justin returns to his feet at a slow rate. He wipes blood from his lips.

"You know better than to show restraint," Justin said cheekily.

"I do not want to kill you, Justin," Milea responds. "I know you are still there. How are they controlling you?"

"When your other senses are fighting the elements, it is easy to manipulate the mind," Justin answers.

The crown upon Justin's head pulsates a few times as thunder rumbles outside. A loud clap of it is accompanied by the screams of a thousand voices. The baby in Wyntre's arms hushes as a stronger, darker, energy rises in the air. Sonja looks to the window as does

Qwest. The girl feels fear rush through her core when she sees red rain is now falling. The wind blows in and carries with it the smell of blood. Sonja mutters a few words and backs deeper into the shadows. The spear in Justin's hands appears to make a sound of glee. Justin reels back, shaking his head as he battles for control.

"No..." Justin manages, attempting to control his abilities.

"I'm sorry, my warrior," Milea said gently.

The flames around Milea roar to life and caresses her form. The entire room glows red from the light of the element and heats up rapidly. She goes through a range of motion before releasing the intense flame towards Justin with a mighty yell. Flames fill the entire space between the sorceress and her target, taking the form of an enormous red dragon. Justin looks up in time to get slammed by the blaze. He bellows as he flies back and into the solid wall next to the stairway. His head slams into the stone, hard, cracking the crown. Justin slides down to the floor unconscious. The offending item controlling him finishes breaking in half and drops to the floor, harmless.

Milea calms her mystical gifts as she closes her eyes and exhales. She approaches Justin, seeing that his brow is now clear of the menacing jewels. She gets to her knees and studies his body with a nod. Justin is still breathing; his features resemble a peaceful sleep. Milea brushes a stray hair from his masculine face and places a gentle kiss on his lips. Sonja kneels next to the Car'laden man as his eyes flicker open.

"Cold," Justin mumbles as he draws his arms closer to his body.

"Glad that you are awake, my warrior," Milea addresses.

"Milea," Justin looks at the woman, then to the girl. "Sonja...where am I?"

"You are in Yedis. A cursed ruin in the county of Selcros," Milea answers. "Do you remember anything?"

"Barely," Justin sits up. "We have to get out of here."

"I agree," Sonja nods and stands up. "Especially since Wyntre and Qwest are trying to take a cursed ghost baby out of here."

Milea looks up, then beyond her daughter to the royals that are watching in silence. Wyntre seems to snap out of her stupor when the sorceress stands up. Qwest lifts his chin high and takes Wyntre's arm to guide her out the staircase with the child. The baby in Wyntre's arms opens her eyes and focuses on Milea. The sorceress swears as Justin and Sonja both get to their feet. Instead of a baby, Milea sees a strange horned being with glowing blood-red eyes. Justin and Sonja both curse as the entire ruin starts to rumble violently and the baby fades away.

"What's happening?" Wyntre exclaims. She shrieks when black ooze belches from the wall behind them.

"Run!" Milea commands.

The walls groan and moan as the building collapses. The slow, methodical, movements imitate the ones in the village that Milea and Sonja witnessed upon their entrance. Sonja sidesteps then passes her mother as they head to the exit. Justin runs beside the sorceress. Both increase their pace to keep up with the Sonja, keeping the gap between them at a minimum. Qwest tows Wyntre along until she can run on her own. Village buildings begin to fall and are swallowed up as fire belches from the large cracks that rip open along the ground.

The black and red flames lick at the retreating group, nearly consuming the two that lag. Wyntre increases her speed and starts to narrow the gap between herself and those ahead, fear pumping her legs. Qwest, astonished, follows his sister's lead. Sonja avoids the falling buildings and hops over all the pit-traps in the road. Milea and Justin follow the girl's lead, performing similar maneuvers behind her. Wyntre shrieks as a hand made from black ice grabs hold of her robe. It tears as she pulls away, the book she held in her pocket falls to the ground. The item is immediately covered by the black ice. The tower behind them quakes again with the cry of an angry baby fills the air.

The ground trembles as the entire tower collapses upon itself. Milea glances back to see the dust and snow from the structure plume into the sky. She then focuses back on her daughter and increases her speed to catch up with her. Justin does the same, miraculously keeping up with them. The frozen victims of the ruin's curse melt into pools of black water as those fleeing stream past them.

The cry of a newborn baby amplifies into a roar as they pass yet another falling building. Milea, Justin, and Sonja are long gone as the first stone hits the ground. Wyntre and Qwest barely have time to squeeze through an opening before the building becomes an impenetrable barrier. The ground heaves as Sonja jumps over a small crack. Milea follows and the crack widens a little. Justin jumps over it next as it expands. Qwest tosses his sister over then jumps himself. He reaches and grabs the ground as it shoves skywards, tearing the frozen village in half. Qwest hauls himself over the edge and stands to see that Milea and those with her are near the exit. He also notices that Wyntre is pursuing them and utters an oath as he follows his sister.

Sonja is the first to exit the ruined city with Milea and Justin following close behind. The sorceress closes her eyes to concentrate but finds that any attempt to teleport has been blocked. Justin turns when he senses a rapid rise in dark energy coming from the ruins. Qwest and Wyntre exit as the symbols on the outer wall light up brilliantly.

The dead Alnis that are pinned to it melt into black water as the living watch. Wyntre shrieks when the ground they stand on rumbles and opens. Milea jumps back to avoid a hand created by the black flames. She blocks and counters the flame with a spell of her own. The hand snuffs out.

"How do we get out of here?" Qwest demands.

"Are we going to die?" Wyntre whines.

A great roar echoes in the sky causing all to look up. Above them circles two great dragons and a bunch of little ones. Five of the smaller dragons break off from the circle and dive towards the group. Bryce makes a sound as he lands, galloping. Sonja quickly runs after him, getting up to speed in no time as she catches up to him. The hatchling folds his wings down but continues to gallop. Sonja grab hold of his mane and pulls herself onto his back quickly. Bryce stretches his wings back out and take to the sky as fast as he can.

"And she does that effortlessly," Justin observes.

"She does," Milea agrees.

Milea then starts to run herself as another baby dragon lands and begins to gallop. The light blue hatchling sneezes a little as he runs next to the sorceress. Milea grabs his mane and tosses her leg over his back, taking care to keep his wings free. The hatchling makes a triumphant sound and takes to the sky as a third one, Tor, the biggest, lands and starts his gallop. Justin, taking the hint, runs a little then disappears. The dragon grunts when he feels the man's weight on his back. With a hoot, the large hatchling spreads his wings and takes off with little effort.

Cries echo into the sky as the smell of blood and sulfur fill the air. Two more hatchlings land and gallop but neither take back off with passengers as Qwest and Wyntre fail to keep up with them. Instead, they chatter to each other as the flames consume the forest. The two hatchlings circle back, one of them grabbing Qwest by the shoulders. The man curses when the little dragon's claws dig into his collarbone. The second dragon hatchling grabs Wyntre in the same way causing the young woman to cry out in pain.

"Put them on my back," Sapphire instructs the two hatchlings.

"Sapphire, thank you for being vigilant," Milea calls to the dragoness from the back of her mount.

"We figured you did something when the entire forest began to shake," Dover said. "Did you find Justin?"

"They did find me," Justin answers. "Thank you for assisting them."

"Good, I need to meet you properly when we land once again." Dover informs him.

A hand made from flames nearly singe Bryce, prompting the hatchling to maneuver in haste to get away. Sonja turns and gasps when she sees eyes and an open mouth resembling baby Chastity within the collapsing ruin. The red eyes sparkle with black water as it opens its mouth and belts out a cry of anger. The sky lights up briefly with a purple light as a comet screams from the ruin's mouth toward the mountains in the background. The two hatchlings carrying the Selcros royals deposit them on their mother's back as instructed. The princess gasps when she gets a good look at the ruins below.

"No!!" Wyntre shrieks in surprise. The ruins respond with a high pitch cry. Wyntre belts out another scream when black ice water belches from the ruins.

"Ublivorin Gates!" Qwest exclaims as he grabs Wyntre to prevent her from falling into the ruins below. "Wyntre, are you okay?"

There is no response as the princess continues to hyperventilate. Sapphire and her hatchlings use speed and skills to dodge to one side, allowing the water to spew towards the heavens. The stream turns toward Milea. The sorceress glows brightly as she casts a flame spell at the water. The two elements collide, creating steam and a very foul odor. All but a few of the hatchlings land on their father's back and grip tightly.

Dover dodges the black water and the hands made of dark flames. The steam condenses back into rain when it hits the cold air and falls onto the ruins. Instead of stalling the black flames below, it enhances them. The ruins once again reach out for the dragons, blocking any exit from the sky. Milea swears as her mount dodges and weaves around the various attacking elements.

"We need a blizzard!" Milea calls out.

"Wyntre, calm down. We need your help," Qwest speaks with a soft voice to his sister.

"If we wait on that, we will all die," Sapphire speaks her foremost thought and dodges again. "Dover, finish this quickly."

Dover climbs a little higher as he moves past another column of black ice water. Sapphire rolls out of the way of the element attacking her as she also climbs higher. The ruins wail in anger as Dover responds with a roar that deafens those around him. Lightning rips through the skies as the winds pick up to near-hurricane strength. The hatchling Justin rides upon squeaks as he lands upon his mother's back, behind the Selcros royals. Both Justin and his mount hang on tightly as Dover unleashes his abilities. Snow begins to dump in bucket loads from above as thunder resounds and the blizzard kicks in full speed.

Sapphire grunts as she rides the winds to sail above her mate's location. Milea's dragon mount follows his mother, gaining a little higher out of the blizzard winds. Bryce rides the winds a little more, then climbs above the storm. Dover roars as he directs the storm's lightning right at the ruins, striking hard and causing it to cry out in pain. The snow accumulates at a rapid pace, easily reaching the height of the walls within minutes. All the flames eventually go out as the combination of frozen precipitation and winds beat upon it mercilessly.

Sapphire lets out a call to her children as she makes a beeline straight for the entrance. The hatchlings call back and hurry after her while Dover continues his battle. The ruins let out one last yowl of anger and pain before going silent. Milea glances back as her mount continues his pursuit of Sapphire. The ruins are once again sleeping, returning to the way they looked prior to the attack. Dover circles around then follows his family as a deep cooing emerges from the sleeping structure. The guardian ice dragon lets out a whoop of triumph and it is echoed by his brood.

"That's what I like," Dover said, ecstatically.

Sapphire and her family bank left as the wind whistles in the ears of all the passengers. Clouds drift apart and dissipate as they once again fly through the veil. Behind them, the tower of the ruins stands tall in the center of Yedis with many of the buildings reconstructing themselves. The deep sound of a giant cooing baby echoes in the darkness but does not penetrate the veil. The light of the twin moons reflects from the horns and talons of all the dragons as they turn toward the field where they had picked up the passengers. Bryce decides to do a few barrel rolls, much to Sonja's delight, as they head to their destination.

The large clearing is now hosting an enormous herd of reindeer. The animals are feasting upon the fresh spring grass after a long winter fast. A buck lift his head, nostrils flaring. Bryce circles the clearing, causing the deer to cry out in panic and run into the forest. His brothers also circle as all of them slow down to land without harming their passengers. Sapphire is next to circle the clearing, then rears up and beats her wings until she is hovering above the clearing.

The trees around the clearing bend to the winds she creates as she slowly descends and lands without disturbing the passengers upon her back. Sapphire folds her wings as Milea climbs off the back of her dragon mount and Dover lands in a similar fashion as his mate. Sonja hops from Bryce's back and hugs the dragon. The hatchling's tail whips rapidly, showing his excitement for the embrace.

Qwest jumps down from Sapphire's back, landing on the packed snow on the opposite side from Milea. He encourages Wyntre to follow and catches his sister easily. Justin dismounts and pats the side of his dragon friend. Qwest notices him, then looks around to see Milea still busy talking to the dragons. The Alnis prince decides to approach Justin, perhaps to convince him to help take care of the red witch that plagues his country. Justin faces the approaching royals as the large hatchling walks away.

"Greetings, friend," Qwest says as he stops a short distance away with his sister by his side. "I'm glad we made it out of there in one piece. How long do you think it will take before she orders the dragons to eat us?"

"Considering that there are fourteen dragons total in the clearing. Twelve of them are possibly starving due to the quick flight back because they are hatchlings," Justin observes as he crosses his arms across his chest, "if we are to be a meal, I'm sure we would be one by now."

"A matter of time, I suppose." Qwest rubs his chin, then gets a little closer. "Before that happens, I need for you to help me rid Bri'al of the red witch."

"Excuse me?" Justin arches an eyebrow.

"Milea, the she-devil talking to the dragon," Qwest explains. "We will have to get rid of her daughter, too. I hate to do that to a child but it will be necessary. For your assistance, I will make sure you receive Selcros' highest honor. I will even tell your lord, Slone, to reward you accordingly as a hero of Bri'al."

"I'd rather see Slone's head on a pike than to receive any honor from him," Justin retorts. "Thus, the answer is a very hard no. I will not help you with your foolish plan. You are lucky that I do not take your head for suggesting such an imprudent thing."

"Are you under her spell?" Qwest demands. "Wake up man, you are a Car'laden."

"I am, and very proud of it." Justin agrees. "However, I am not, nor will I ever willingly be, Slone's servant. Your willingness to fraternize with him says very low things about your home."

"What I hear is that you are a slave of the witch, Milea," Wyntre observes.

"Really?" Justin said as he focuses on the young woman. "That is quite an accusation coming from a young woman that was fooled by a second-rate dark mage."

"Are you an idiot?" Qwest starts. He almost regrets it when Justin takes a step towards him.

"Perhaps you need to rephrase your words, boy," Justin responds in a calm manner.

"Justin, can you come over here please," Milea calls.

"Of course," Justin answers and walks away from the Selcros royals.

The sorceress nods as he arrives at her side. Wyntre shrieks in alarm, bringing attention to herself. The hatchling that sniffed her hand also lets out a high pitch sound and runs away from the frightened young woman. Qwest pulls his hunting knife as the baby dragon hides behind Sapphire. The dragoness turns her attention to the threat as Qwest commands his sister to run. Wyntre is quick to take flight into the woods and is followed by her brother a few seconds later. Dover tilts his head to one side and is mirrored by at least half of his brood.

"I do not know what is going through their minds nor am I curious to find out," Milea rubs her temples. "Justin, Sir Dover wanted an introduction prior to our departure."

"I remember," Justin nods and approaches the ninety-foot guardian, unafraid. "Sir Dover, it is an honor."

"You're the one causing all the trouble, eh?" Dover bends down to get a good look at the man. "These ladies went through a lot to recover you."

"They did, and I appreciate them to no end," Justin assures. "I owe Lady Milea my life and allegiance."

"How much longer are you staying in the north woods, Milea?" Sapphire inquires.

"As soon as we meet up with the rest of our companions, we will be leaving," Milea answers. "I am anxious to return to Dorma."

"I know very little about Dorma," Sapphire says as she lies upon her belly. "We will settle in this clearing for the night. I wish you good luck on your journey."

"Thank you," Milea nods. "I hope for pleasant dreams for the night and good winds for your departure tomorrow."

"Don't be sad, Bryce," Sonja gently pats the hatchling's head. "We will see each other again in the future."

Bryce lets out a warble as he whimpers a little bit. Sonja once again assures him. Milea pats him on the head with a little gentle talk. Justin provides a pep talk to the little dragon. A few minutes later, the trio heads into the woods. Sonja easily finds the tracks made by their friends and follows them deeper into the forest. Milea warns Justin to keep an eye out for both the Sierge and the Noturi. Justin frowns at the news of the Sierge, knowing that they are not usually found in cold areas.

CHAPTER FOURTEEN

The King's New Allies

The sound of an owl echoes outside of the hunter's lodge marking the late hour. Neil and Brion discuss their options in hush tones so not to disturb the rest of their companions. Dysis is sitting in front of the fire, staring into it as she makes several life-changing decisions. Vicki sits in one of the large chairs, cleaning her daggers. She looks up occasionally to keep an eye on the ghost standing next to the queen. All but Dysis turn when the door to the lounge opens. Sonja makes a beeline for the fire and exhales in relief as the warmth spreads through her.

Milea enters the room and hesitates when she sees the bearskin rug. Justin stands next to her and watches the three well-armed people observing them. Milea introduces Justin to the rest of the crew. Brion boldly goes to shake the Car'laden's hand in welcome.

Neil hesitates a little then also greets the taller man by grasping his forearm. Vicki simply waves from her seat on the stairs. Dysis has yet to acknowledge anything as she stares at the fire. Milea quietly speaks to Vicki about the situation and is surprised to learn of the ghost sitting next to the queen. The sorceress studies the queen's back before going over to sit on the opposite side of the woman.

"I see the unfortunate fate of the Great Bear," Milea said softly. "My condolences, Your Majesty."

"That title no longer applies to me," Dysis said. "Koro has broken his promise; thus, I am no longer obligated to keep mine."

"I see. That is your choice," Milea focuses on the flames. "Just remember, a queen is not just a consort to a king. She is the mother and protector of the country she reigns over."

Milea stands up and goes over to the large table her companions have gathered around. Neil informs her that Zaria had left earlier to spy upon the situation in Selcros. Vicki reports that the ship has yet to return from the ordeal earlier in the day. Justin listens as Sonja explains the enchanted vessel to him. The sorceress sits back and focuses on her companions one at a time. She concludes that if Zaria does not return a half hour after midnight, they would find a way out of Selcros without her. Brion perks up when he hears that Sapphire, Dover and the hatchlings are in a clearing not too far from them. Dysis shifts her attention when Milea mentions the books in the wreckage.

"Lady Milea," Dysis addresses as she stands and faces the group. "I humbly request passage upon your ship. In exchange, I will dredge the river for the treasure that you lost from the attack and destruction of your craft."

The door slams open before a response could be given. Brion takes a single look at the intruders and rolls his eyes. He sits back down and releases grip upon his sword handle. Justin turns to satisfy his curiosity. Once he notes them, he turns back around and continues his conversation with Neil. The L'vane man does not acknowledge the intruders, yet his sister does keep her eye on them. Wyntre complains about the dark woods as she enters the room. She pauses and takes a deep breath in when she sees the group. She cries out in fear, prompting Qwest to enter the building with his dagger drawn. He swears angrily as he stands between Wyntre and the perceived threat. Dysis takes a few steps forward to catch the Alnis prince's attention.

"What are you doing here?" Qwest demands.

"Keeping warm, why are you here?" Dysis turns the question around.

"What father says is true, you are in the service of the red devil," Qwest observes.

"I suppose it is an upgrade," Milea says as she stands from the table and walks until she is next to Dysis. "Being a devil instead of a simple witch."

"I've had enough of you," Qwest shouts angrily.

Sonja is quick as she takes hold of Justin's arm. At the same time, Qwest yells with his charge towards the sorceress with murderous intent. Milea arches an eyebrow then lifts her hand. The Alnis prince stops in his tracks as he is levitated slightly off the floor. Sonja releases the car'laden when the situation is under control. Justin leans back and watches the scene unfold. Dysis keeps an eye on Wyntre. The young woman appears to be frozen with fear. Milea takes her time as she walks to the prince, then around him as he struggles to free himself from her spell.

"You have always been an ass, Qwest," Milea informs him, pausing in front to look him in the eye. "So, an ass you will be."

A bright circle lights up just in front of Wyntre causing the young woman to shriek and run to one side of the room. Milea makes a slight motion with her wrist and Qwest is tossed into the circle. The Alnis prince swears as he is forced to stand on all fours. He yells at Milea only for his words to come out as the brays of a donkey. Milea simply turns her hand up and snaps her fingers. Golden dust sprinkles down onto Qwest, causing him to sneeze. The Alnis seems to drop away in a rain of dust and is replaced by a well-dressed donkey. The beast brays and kicks angrily then head straight out the door as the circle of light fades to nothing.

"That is a first for me, I never thought I'd see that," Dysis said. "How long will that last?"

"It's an enchantment and will last until I depart Selcros," Milea answers.

"You're not going to get away with this," Wyntre blurts out.

"Are you going to retaliate?" Milea crosses her arms.

"I..." Wyntre hesitates, then looks beyond the threat. "Mother, do something. She cannot get away with this heinous crime."

Dysis stares at the young woman as if she lost her mind. She then takes a deep breath and walks past Milea, pausing briefly to glance at her, then the table of witnesses. The former queen then crosses her arms and continues to walk, ignoring her guests for the moment. Dysis goes to the door and closes it, freezing the lock so that it will not open easily. Wyntre starts to relax when Dysis then strolls to the princess' side. Dysis meets the princess' gaze then walks around her, making a full circle before finally stopping next to her.

"May I make the suggestion of using Wyntre as a means to get past the barricade impeding our escape to the open sea?" Dysis inquires.

"What?" Wyntre shouts in shock as she looks up at the queen.

"I don't know," Brion frowns. "That will be a very uncomfortable few hours. Maybe we can use Dover instead."

"Since Slone is here, I can honestly tell you he brought his dragon-slaying experts with him," Justin said. "Slone himself would love to have Dover's head as a trophy on his mantle."

"I don't want to put the old dragon in any danger," Neil rubs his chin.

"His kids are too cute for following their old man into Ublivion," Vicki agrees.

"We have to consider the madness that you mentioned, Dysis," Milea said. "Will Koro be willing to negotiate, or will he simply blow all of us out of the water, including his beloved child?"

"He'd probably think she betrayed him somehow," Dysis agrees. "But it is worth a try."

"Mother, how could you? Why are you helping these people?" Wyntre cries. "Why are you betraying Selcros? You are even hurting father."

"Koro does not know the meaning of pain, yet," Dysis corrects. "Come with me, princess. I will show you your cot for the night."

"No, I refuse to cooperate with your insanity," Wyntre snaps.

"Suit yourself," Dysis places a hand upon her hip, then relaxes and meanders up the stairs for the night.

Milea sits down at the table and crosses her legs as Wyntre runs to the door. In a panic, she tries to open it. The princess speaks urgently to herself as she uses her abilities, attempting to break the frozen spell. It does not work; the results cause tears of fear to flood from Wyntre. The princess sinks to her knees as she pleads in desperation to any deity that is listening to open the door. Sonja stands up, the movement catches the captive's attention. Wyntre springs back to her feet and backs away from the approaching girl. She screams once and runs up the stairs after Dysis. Neil applauds Sonja's intimidating show as the girl simply shrugs. Milea shakes her head as she smiles, humored, by the event. Vicki announces the time, five hours until they depart.

"I think we should all go up and get some rest before we leave," Vicki adds and stands.

"I agree," Milea stands. "Sonja."

"Goodnight, all," Sonja wishes to the room.

"Pleasant dreams, Terror of the North," Neil teases.

Sonja beams then heads upstairs with her mother. Vicki trails after them, after making sure the ghost is no longer in the building. Neil and Brion talk with Justin for another half hour before they decide to rest for the night. Justin stays downstairs to keep watch over the lodge. He picks up a small piece of wood and studies it a little. Taking out his carving knife, he begins to whittle away at the block. He pauses in his task when he feels a gentle hand upon his shoulder.

"I am very happy I found you, my dark warrior," Milea said as he faces her.

"As am I," Justin takes her hand and kisses it. "Forever in your debt, my red queen."

"How did they capture you?" Milea inquires.

"I was handing a toy I carved to a little girl," Justin answers, a little embarrassed. "She was an orphan and provided the perfect distraction for Jasmine to activate the orb in my chest."

"You have such a giving heart," Milea touches his chest with her free hand. "I cannot remove the orb which is attached to it."

"I know," Justin brushes her cheek. "I heard there is now an Eltis of Healing?"

"Yes, her name is Frey," Milea seems to perk up a little. "She does not have a lot of experience, but Keela will be able to help her."

"That will be a great honor," Justin said as he stands. "Most importantly, it should put your mind at ease, my queen."

"It does," Milea smiles.

Justin once again kisses her hand as Milea takes a step back. The sorceress turns to the stairs and takes another step. She pauses, not wanting to move any further, neither appears to want to let the other go. Milea meets Justin's gaze briefly, then turns back to the stairs and begins to ascend. Justin follows her up the stairs, still holding her hand.

An owl hoots in the woodlands, calling out to the night creatures. A second story window on the side of the hunter's lodge opens in silence. Wyntre glances behind at her sleeping stepmother then peers out into the darkness. She slides onto the windowsill then launches into the bleak. Wyntre grunts as she lands in a large snowdrift. She scrambles out of the snow dune and runs headlong into the woodlands.

The princess stops a short distance from her prison and grabs onto a tree. A deep guttural growl startles her to stand and once again rush into the woods. The growling creatures pursues her prompting tears to flow from her eyes as she tries to keep silent. The princess trips and falls, face first, onto the ground. She turns over and gasps in horror when the creature pounces on her. Her shriek of terror is silenced when the creature licks her. The 'kiss' is followed by the familiar bellows of a snow leopard cub.

"Sn-Snowpuff?" Wyntre acknowledges. The cub licks her again. "Oh, I'm so glad it's you!"

Snowpuff grunts as the princess hugs him tightly. Tears of joy and terror wet down his perfectly groomed fur. The cub grumbles a little from the experience. He manages to wiggle himself free and start walking in a direction. When the princess did not follow, he went back, rubbed her legs, and once again started to walk.

"Are you showing me how to get home?" Wyntre asks.

The cub rolls his eyes as he repeats the motion, this time walking a further distance ahead. Taking the hint, Wyntre gets to her feet and follows the snow leopard cub into the woodlands.

The clock tower tolls the hour as a dark shadow cruise through the night sky. The entity's presence is only shown when the starlight dims slightly in her wake. A'drianis circles the tower a couple times then lands on its rooftop to observe the scene below. She notices that the streets are unusually quiet for the city. An air of tension replaces the winter chill. The Shadow Eltis flexes her wings and launches from her perch in the direction of the inn.

The smell of charred wood reaches her senses long before she lay eyes upon her destination. A quiet gasp of surprise escapes the shiadokat when she reaches the smoldering ashes where the inn once stood. She transforms from winged panther to her alter form of a taller elven woman as she lands to examine the damage. The shiadokat sensitive smell detects that the building had not been empty when the fire was set. A'drianis searches through the ashes for clues then hesitates when she hears approaching footsteps. She steps back into the deep shadow and folds it around herself as a patrol of three well-armed Car'laden men march by.

"What in the name of Ublivion are they doing here?" A'drianis said to herself.

The Shiadokat waits a few minutes to ensure that the men do not double back then heads up the street toward the town square. A'drianis ducks into the bakery to avoid a second patrol and notices that it is no longer occupied. Many of the baker's racks, pans, and cooking supplies are strewn all over the floor. She takes a quick look in the kitchen and sees that there is no more food on any of the shelves. Blood and feathers mark where the chickens had their last stand. A'drianis leaps out of the open window in the bakery kitchen and into the broken window of the butcher next door. She finds a similar scene of broken kitchen items and all the butcher's sharp instruments are gone.

A'drianis leaves the butcher shop through the front, which is already open. Continuing up the street, she reaches the glassmaker's shop. Her sense of smell immediately detects the pungent odor of blood and other bodily fluids. She pulls her dagger as she quietly stalks into the building. The floor is littered with broken glass. A'drianis tiptoes through the room as she looks about, noticing the large spots of blood and some remaining entrails scattered throughout the place. There is no sign of Dwayne or his dog, Oliver, anywhere in the building.

Frowning with concern, she leaves the glassmaker's shop and heads toward the girls' school. Along the way she realizes all the citizens of Selcros have barricaded themselves inside of their homes. On top of the tallest buildings are strange ballistic weapons designed to kill enormous dragons. She does not have to pass the jailhouse to know that it is occupied to full capacity as prisoners await their unfortunate date with death.

"This is madness," A'drianis says in disbelief as she looks around the city.

She avoids yet another patrol as she ducks into the shadows of an alleyway. When she finally reaches her destination, she drops words unbefitting a lady. The three-story structure is only half-standing. The left side is completely collapsed to the ground. The right side is barely hanging on, with bricks falling occasionally, when the wind strikes it just right. A'drianis searches the structure and is relieved to see that no one is trapped inside. She also discovers that no one has died inside, indicating that the school did not have any occupants when it collapsed. She goes back to the town square and pauses by the clock tower once again. This time there is a poster nailed to the side of the structure.

"Notice to all, there is a military curfew in effect until further notice. Anyone caught outside after sunset will be jailed and executed," A'drianis reads the words out loud. "By orders of King Koro, there is a bounty on the head of anyone who claims to be a follower of the Eltis, Tadious. Reward is 50,000 gold coins per head."

A nightingale calls out as several men rush toward the shiadokat. A'drianis turns, swears, then folds the shadows upon herself and those attacking. When the shade lifts, the men are dead and the shiadokat is no longer standing in front of the sign. A'drianis watches from the top of the tower as a second group of men arrives to check on their fellows. Upon seeing the carnage, they call an alert to search for the killer. A'drianis turns her attention from the streets below to the mouth of the river, the only way out to sea. A frown graces her features she sees the large blockade of metal clad ships stretching from one shore to the other with their weapons aimed upriver. Having seen enough of the city, A'drianis decides to go into the castle to spy upon the situation and perhaps find a means to escape.

Getting into the stronghold of the king proves to be a simpler task than she expects. Much of the staff is asleep in their assigned rooms. Those that are awake walk around carefully with nervous glances over their shoulders. The crackling fire draws the shiado-kat to the throne room. She uses caution and sticks to the shadows as she climbs the walls to camp in the rafters. From her perch, she sees Koro pacing in front of the fireplace, rubbing his good hand over his bandaged arm. The shiadokat leans forward when Koro sudden snap of anger at someone that only he can see. Apparently, the invisible person leaves him at his request, as he calms back down and once again focuses on the fireplace. A'drianis is about to explore the rest of the castle when she hears the unmistakable roar of a snow leopard cub.

"Father!" Wyntre shouts as she runs into the room. "Father, I have escaped their evil clutches. Oh, that horrible woman has done something terrible to Qwest."

Wyntre hurries over to the king for a comforting embrace. Snowpuff bounces behind her, then pauses as his nose detects an intruder. Wyntre is an arm's length away when Koro quickly turns and backhands her. The blow sends the young woman to the ground, and she holds her cheek, stunned. Koro turns to glare into the eyes of the now frightened princess. The king's eyes appear to glow, the fire highlighting the madness within. Wyntre draws her knees to her chest, cowering from his gaze. Snowpuff steps between the king and the princess, letting out a deep and mighty growl.

"Snowpuff, good boy," Koro said. "It looks like you have found and rescued the princess. You will be well rewarded."

"Father, why did you hit me?" Wyntre asks as tears tumble from her eyes.

"I..." Koro falls to his knees. "I am being haunted by the evil servants of that demon forest witch, Milea. They are everywhere and make me do horrible things. The only way I can be rid of them is to destroy the witch herself and all her subjects that travel with her."

"Even Brion?" Wyntre says softly.

"Once Milea is destroyed, I can see about saving him but there is no guarantee. He simply might have been under her influence far too long," Koro responds. "It seems that you escaped her servants. Where did they take you?"

"Nul took me to the ruins of Yedis by her command and would have sacrificed me if it were not for Qwest's interference. Then we both were captured but we escaped into the woods. Qwest and I sought shelter at the hunter's lodge but found that it is occupied by Milea and her vile company," Wyntre explains as she is helped to her feet by her father. "She changed Qwest into an ass and held me captive. I escaped out of a window and Snowpuff found me."

"Is Dysis with her?" Koro inquires.

"Yes, and it is as you said. She is in the service of the evil devil witch," Wyntre informs her father as Snowpuff rubs her legs.

"I knew she turned traitorous," Koro turns to the fire. "Go to your room, Wyntre. You will be safe there. I will send a strong warrior to check on you later."

"Okay," Wyntre says, and hugs her father briefly before leaving the room.

In the rafters, A'drianis watches as the princess and Snowpuff exit the room. The shiadokat is about to follow, but hesitates when Slone and Loca walk into the room from the other side of the room through a once-closed door. Koro gives a side glance to his guests then refocuses on the fireplace as he explains what he has heard. A'drianis shakes her head at the tense silence that mounts during the full minute that passes.

"Slone, you have my permission to do whatever you want to Wyntre," Koro informs. "Although she claims to be a victim, I do not believe that is the case. Her fascination with Brion has sealed her fate. She will be executed in the morning."

"The timeline of her execution will depend on whether or not I am done with her," Slone responds with a feral grin.

"Whatever you want. Her birth mother is one of the maids I used as a concubine. Be warned, she was blessed by a strange goddess as a mimic mage." Koro says and turns to the hooded figure. "I have a favor to ask of you, Loca."

"If my master permits it," Loca said.

"You have my approval," Slone says as he walks out of the room after his prey.

"I want you to send the strongest, most vile, and bloodthirsty fiends at your disposal to destroy Milea and everybody with her," Koro demands. "I do not want anything left of the devil, not even a hair, in this realm."

"Do not worry so much about your antagonists," Loca cackles. "They will not survive the night."

The old mage continues to cackle as he leaves the room, lifting a deep pressure from the one hidden in the shadows. A'drianis weighs her options as she watches him leave. Koro returned his gaze to the fireplace as the shiadokat creeps out of the throne room. A soundless trailer follows her on padded paws. Night scavengers squabble over the dead bodies still littering the fields where the battle with Tandon had occurred. The wind carries the pungent smell out to the ocean, sparing the city of the noxious fumes. A hooded figure walks with a long, strangely-carved staff, unaware of the shadow following him.

Loca stops in front of a large heap of decaying flesh and taps his staff three times. Dark-colored liquid oozes up from the earth, collecting to form a strange spiderweb along the ground. A'drianis cuts her swearing short as she rushes forward to stop the incantation. The shiadokat's instincts kick in and she dodges to the left as a streak of white fur pounces at her.

"What in Oswind's name are you doing here?" A'drianis questions the snow leopard cub.

Snowpuff does not answer but instead stands up on his hind legs as he starts to grow into a strange humanoid beast. His arm and torso muscles are grossly out of proportion with his smaller legs. His head is twice the size of an adult tiger, and his jaw stretches down towards the top of his massive chest. He flashes his claws and swipes at the shiadokat.

A'drianis jumps back and changes her form to a winged black jungle cat. The shadows fold around her as she moves and swats Snowpuff harshly, sending him halfway across the field. The ground where the dark liquid had collected starts to glow brightly as the spirits of those slain on the field rise from the pools.

"Oswind's beard," A'drianis exclaims when she sees the entities.

The shiadokat once again dodges her opponent as she wraps the shadows around her and hightails it into the woods. She barely hears the laughter behind her while dodging through the trees. The urgent need to get to the hunter's lodge increases her speed threefold. She needs to get there before Loca completely unleashes the spirits he had just summoned.

The forest noises hush into silence. The sudden change does not go unnoticed by those camping in the hunter's lodge. Milea wakes up and stretches as she rises and dresses herself. She frowns as she glances out the window, the lack of noises causing her some concern. She quietly voices her uneasiness as she focuses on the small fireplace in the room.

The sorceress crosses her arms, a small gleam shining in her eyes as she uses magic to cause a flame to ignite inside of the hearth without a log. Milea cancels her spell and smiles, pleased that her mystical gifts are now back to full strength after a good rest. She turns to see that Justin is still asleep. Approaching him carefully, Milea kisses him gently. The sorceress then decides to go check on Sonja and her traveling companions. Her hand touches the doorknob when the room suddenly goes dark. It lightens just as fast revealing A'drianis breathing heavily from her panicked run through the woodlands.

"Milea, glad that you are awake. We must get everybody up and out of this house before they get here," A'drianis said as she fights to catch her breath.

"What's going on?" Milea inquires.

"Loca is summoning and bringing under his control the ghosts of those who have fallen on the battlefield in front of the city," A'drianis explains. "He is sending them after you and everybody in this building. We have to find a way to defeat them but first we have to get out of here."

"I do not have much experience defeating ghosts. That gift belongs to Maya," Milea admits.

"My experience is limited. However, I do know that fleeing into the forest without at least trapping them in one spot is a bad idea," Justin remarks as he finishes dressing, pulling a shirt over his head.

"Whoa, where did you come from?" A'drianis asks.

"I found him in Yedis," Milea said. "I'm going to go wake Sonja and Vicki."

"I'll go downstairs and see what I can do to help prepare for the upcoming encounter," Justin says as he follows Milea out of the room.

A'drianis watches the two leave then shakes her head to clear it before she folds the shadows around her and disappears from the room. The night wind barely rustles the leaves of the surrounding trees. Neil looks out of his window and listens to the silent woodland with a look of worry about his features. Brion quietly verbalizes his uneasiness over the sudden cessation of nighttime foraging. It seems that every forest creature has fled the immediate area. Brion is first to notice the change in the shadows of the room.

"Shiadokitty, are you frightening the critters away?" Brion asks as he and Neil turn to face the room.

"Not me," Zaria admits. "Not a lot of time to explain. Gather your things and go downstairs immediately."

"Why? What is going on?" Neil inquires.

"Loca has summoned the ghosts of the battlefield," Zaria informs. "They are coming."

Brion and Neil stare at the shiadokat for several seconds, then quickly start gathering their weapons. Brion ditches his coat in favor of a cape he had found at the lodge. Neil does the same and ties his katana to his waist. Brion sheaths his sword and both men head out of the room. Zaria checks the room for any missed items before she follows them out. Neil goes downstairs as Brion decides to retrieve Dysis and Wyntre.

The wind moans as it blows into the open window. Dysis sneezes herself awake then expresses her surprise in an uncouth manner when she notices that Wyntre is gone. She jumps to her feet and pulls back the covers to make sure she is not dreaming. Her attention goes to the open window as she remembers the young woman's leap of faith out of her castle bedroom. Dysis swears again as she looks out and down, seeing the exact spot the princess landed. Apparently, she did not break anything as the queen sees no signs of blood or body. A solid knock on the door makes Dysis jump and turn as the wooden door opens.

"Dysis, gather your belongings. A situation has occurred and we need everyone downstairs," Brion said as he steps into the room. "Where is Wyntre?"

"She escaped while I slept," Dysis admits and pulls her cloak over her shoulders. "Why are we gathering?"

"My understanding is that the spirits from our battle with Tandon are not finished with us," Brion summarizes.

"What?" Dysis said then pauses as her mind recalls events at the castle. "The necromancer."

"Let's go," Brion insists as he leaves the room. Dysis trails after him.

Milea hesitates briefly outside of the room that Sonja and Vicki occupy. She knocks once then opens the door. To her surprise, both occupants of the room are wide awake and appear to be having a conversation with an invisible third party. Milea summarizes the need to gather in the great room. Vicki looks to the invisible companion when the sorceress mentions ghosts. Sonja explains to her mother that there is a ghost present at this time. The spirit assures her and those around her that she is not under anyone's spell.

"Who is she and why has she decided to contact us?" Milea inquires.

"She said her name is Eursali and she was once the guardian of this forest," Vicki informs. "She also said she will help us but I'm not too thrilled with the method which must be applied."

"Eursali... I do not recall that name," Milea said. "If the method that she implies makes you uncomfortable, Vicki, then I do not recommend it."

"Mom, Eursali said that she is the great bear whose pelt lines the floor downstairs," Sonja said. "I'll do it, Vicki, since you are uncomfortable."

Milea studies her daughter a little then goes to sit next to her on the bed. The sorceress places a hand on the girl's shoulder and closes her eyes briefly. When she opens them, she is slightly surprised to be able to see the ghost sitting on the stool between the two beds. The spirit woman shares many features with Dysis, including her height. She is slightly heavyset and her clothes are made of buckskin. The ghost woman's eyes are full of concern as she glances over her shoulder out the window and then back to Vicki.

"Eursali, how would you be able to assist us?" Milea inquires, capturing the spirit woman's attention.

"You can see and hear me now, it seems, this is good," Eursali says as she fully faces the sorceress. "I know you have seen the mountain in the distance. The one which sunlight never touches. It is a trap for the ghosts of fallen Tragins. I am the one that laid that trap. Mortals have foolishly built a city at the base of the mountain but that is a story for another time. In order to repeat the process, I need a host. Sonja, I am afraid, is too young and inexperienced."

"I do not want to subject Vicki to anything that she is uncomfortable with," Milea expresses her concern. "Is there anyone else currently residing in the lodge that will make a good host for you?"

"You are very powerful and will fight me even though you know it is for a greater good. The men are simply too stubborn. Dysis does not have nearly enough experience, the same as Sonja," Eursali said. "I'm only asking Vicki because she has experience and we are very short on time."

The winds outside increase slightly as moaning floats upon the breeze. The sound sends a shiver to crawl down Sonja's spine. Vicki stands up to look out the window and she mentally contemplates the situation facing them. She catches quick glimpses of blue lights meandering through the woodland, heading straight to the hunter's lodge.

"How long must I host you?" Vicki inquires of the spirit woman.

"Only long enough for me to trap the vengeful spirits headed this way and to get everyone to a spot that is safe within the forest," Eursali answers. "I promise you no longer than that and not a hair upon you will be harmed."

"Okay," Vicki relents. She takes off her necklace and approach Sonja. "Keep this safe for me."

"I will guarantee that you will not be harmed," Milea says to Vicki, then focuses on the ghost. "What long-term effects may she have after hosting an Eltis?"

"The only effect that will remain is a gift," Eursali assures. "Vicki can never be an unwilling host to lesser, unsavory spirits."

"I'll mull over that information once we are done," Vicki said as she lays down upon her bed.

"Relax Vicki, sleep," Eursali instructs gently.

Milea keeps her eyes on the spirit woman as Vicki falls into a deep restful state. Eursali waves a hand over the L'vane woman's body and fades from sight. A light pulsates around Vicki's body and then disappears. Milea makes sure that the woman is still breathing then instructs Sonja to gather all their possessions and head downstairs. The girl takes only a step out of the room when Eursali, in Vicki's body, sits up and stretches. She stands up and looks out the window with a frown before facing the room.

"You are Milea Sirus of Selvast Forest," Eursali addresses. "Vicki and Sonja told me a lot about you. Are you capable of drawing a dark seal?"

"Dark and black magics are more my twin's forte. My dabbling into it is not as deep," Milea admits. "I know only a few seals. I do have a dark lord waiting for us in the lobby. Perhaps he can be of greater assistance."

"That will have to do," Eursali said.

In the great room, Justin listens to Sonja as she explains what had occurred in the other room. Neil frowns at the report of his sister playing host to the spirit of a bear. Dysis and Zaria stares at the girl in shock when they hear the name of the spirit that Vicki is accommodating. The queen faces the staircase as Brion greets the last two to come down from the rooms above. Eursali walks over to the wall and yanks the spear from its tether, breaking some of the brick in the process.

"How many of you are able to see spirits?" Eursali inquires.

"Only Vicki and Sonja are able to see through the veil at this moment," Milea answers.

"I see," Eursali frowns and quickly draws a symbol on the wall. "This is the rune of my name. Draw it on your person, anywhere, and it will guide you to defend against this incoming horde."

"Don't argue with her," Zaria warns. "Eursali, maybe we can catch up after this is over."

"It will have to be very brief, Shiadokat, as I have promised to release my host as quickly as possible," Eursali said. "Which one is the dark lord?"

"That would be me," Justin admits.

"I need your help in drawing the seal of D'kevol. We will be trapping these ghosts inside of this lodge," Eursali explains. "Dysis, do you remember the spirit shield that I taught you when you were a child?"

"What?" Dysis asks. "I'm a little confused right now."

"I know the spell which you speak of," Milea admits. "How large of a space must I cover?"

"At least the back of the bear pelt. Everybody must stand on the back," Eursali instructs.

Sonja hurries over to the fireplace and picks up a piece of burnt wood. The girl looks up, swearing in a couple of different languages as she stumbles backwards. She draws her dagger and blocks the sword of the ghost soldier that comes through the fireplace. More ghosts melt through the wall as Sonja retreats to her companions. The girl quickly explains what is happening and draws the symbol provided to them by Eursali onto the back of Neil's and Brion's hand. The results are immediate as the two draw their weapons and defend themselves against the ghost soldiers.

Justin brings up his darker abilities as his spear appears in his hand in an eruption of purple flame. A dark red haze covers all the walls of the lodge then consolidate into long strands of spiderweb like shape. Where the web connects are small, barely visible, runes of various unsavory immortals. Dysis is next to receive the symbol on her hand then swears as she takes several steps back to avoid the large battle ax swung at her head by a ghostly Sierge. Milea sits down in the middle of the rug and concentrates, quickly bringing the spirit shield as Sonja finishes drawing on Zaria's forearm.

A handful of ghosts are trapped inside with the living but most of them are banging against the obstruction on the opposite side. Eursali taps the floor with her weapon and a large amount of blood erupts from underneath the bearskin. It swirls around and start to form different symbols upon all but one wall of the hunter's lounge.

Justin concentrates on the symbols, and wills them to catch fire in order to burn them into the stone. Dysis casts an ice spell and consolidates it into a blade which she uses to stab one of the ghosts in the forehead. To her surprise the ghost dissipates and does not return. Zaria repeats the action with the ghost that she is fighting, achieving the same result.

"Keep concentrating, Milea," Eursali encourages her as she sits down on the massive head of the bear skin. "Everybody else, hold on tight."

Neil finishes dispatching the last ghost inside of the shield as a pulse ripple through the bearskin. Brion drops a few unkind words as the rug starts to rise to its feet. He grabs hold of the side in order to keep from hitting the ground, several feet down. Neil echoes his friends curses as he too hangs on. He reaches out to catch Sonja as the girl tumbles from the back of the behemoth. Sonja finally grips the long hair of the bearskin as it takes a step toward the wall leading to the front door. Dysis and Justin are holding onto the bearskin on the other side while Zaria is standing on its back, keeping an eye on Milea.

Eursali closes her eyes and concentrates. The bearskin rears up slightly and pushes on the wall, breaking it down easily. The giant bruin lumbers out of the lodge. A large tree springs up as soon as the rear end of the rug crosses the threshold. The ghosts howl as they pursue the living. The ghouls hit a barrier that is formed by several branches twisting into various strong blockades.

Milea finally lowers her shield and stretches while looking about. The involuntary movement of the forest around her surprises the sorceress. She looks down to see the fur of the bearskin, the site of which causes her to stand. Milea nearly loses her balance and decides to kneel instead. She looks up when Zaria explains to her what is going on. Eursali opens her eyes and glances behind briefly.

"I know the travel accommodations are not ideal but the circumstances require more speed than comfort," Eursali said. "We will be reaching our destination within the hour."

"Eursali, how did you die? I've known you since childhood," Dysis said. "You were very strong and like a mother to me."

"That's good to know because I am your mother," Eursali informs. "I do not know what the Alnis used to cause memory loss in you, Dysis, but I am glad you finally returned to the forest."

"Oh, no way," Zaria said to herself.

"While you were giving birth to your daughter, Koro was busy killing me," Eursali said, continuing her conversation with Dysis. "He used my own weapon against me to do so. We are going by the mechanism he employed to launch it into my heart."

Neil and Sonja scramble to the back of the bear and lay across it in order to see the mechanism Eursali speaks of. Brion joins the two a short time later, finding it more comfortable to lay across the bear's back than hang onto the flank. Justin frowns at the device, recognizing it as a ballistic that dragon slayers use to bring down particularly large or powerful beasts. It resembles a crossbow yet is made entirely out of iron.

The string is braided metal, rusted from being exposed to the elements. Harnesses meant for either slaves or mules are tethered to the middle of the string and serve to pull back the mighty arms of the ballistic device. A slot has been carefully constructed to hold specific kinds of ammunition. Eursali points to the spot where she had stood, in the form of a bear, when the weapon's wrath was unleashed.

The clearing has yet to grow new foliage following her demise. Dysis turns her head and buries her face into the fur of the reanimated bearskin to hide her tears. Milea lowers her head as she contemplates the scene and the information while the bear continues its way. Sonja quietly discusses the weapon with Neil.

The L'vane man explains exactly how the ballistic device works. Justin adding that it can easily penetrate the tough hide of a full grown and armored mountain dragon. Brion informs that there are several similar devices on ships that sail from certain ports of the continent that he calls home. Zaria stays quiet during the rest of the trip.

The twin moons are still shimmering in the sky when the bear and her passengers arrive at a large cave overlooking the city. Once inside the bearskin starts to slowly sink, becoming inanimate. The passengers all manage to keep to their feet. Zaria gently touches one of the large paws of the bear. To her relief and dismay, it does not move.

Eursali stands from her position on the head. She grips her spear tightly while she approaches Dysis.

"Dysis, my child, our world Bri'al is withering in turmoil. Dark forces both ancient and modern are joining to see the demise of the planet's guardians. Though you have not fully reached your potential, you will be called upon to help protect Bri'al and whatever light is left," Eursali says gently. "I present to you this, the spear of your ancestors. May it help guard you and guide you during these tumultuous times."

Eursali holds out the spear with both hands as she smiles warmly at Dysis. The queen hesitates, unsure if she wants to touch the weapon that killed her mother. Eursali takes a half step closer to her daughter and once again presents the spear. This time, a distinctive gleam cuts across her eyes as she stares into those of Dysis. The queen takes note of the silent warning as she carefully touches the weapon. She ends up holding the entire weight of the item as Eursali lets it go. A bolt of electricity races through Dysis's body, giving her no time to cry out in pain as she passes out. Justin catches the Selcros queen, being the closest to her, and eases her down to the cave's floor. Eursali thanks the dark lord as she turns her attention to the rest of the group.

"Milea," Eursali addresses as she approaches. "I have a favor to ask of you, Daughter of Keela."

"I will do my best, depending on what the favor is," Milea answers hesitantly.

"I would not dare ask you to stay in Selcros. Dysis must find her own path to enlightenment," Eursali said with a smile. "I ask that you provide a proper funeral pyre for my skin. So that I may once again be whole in my afterlife."

"I can do that. It will be an honor," Milea nods her head, respectfully.

"Thank you," Eursali said.

Eursali starts to levitate off the ground slightly. She stretches the body out and crosses her arms over her chest as she closes her eyes. She lands, peacefully sleeping just behind the great bear's head. Sonja reports to her mother that Eursali has left Vicki's body and is sitting next to the woman, watching her. Vicki opens her eyes slowly, then yawns and stretches as she sits up and looks around. Neil helps his sister to her feet, asking her a ton of questions in the process. Vicki assures her sibling that she is unharmed, well rested, and curious about the cave. Milea approaches Vicki and offers her the whip she had nearly left behind. Vicki accepts her weapon back and cracks the whip once before coiling it up and putting it back on her hip. Dysis groans as she sits up and the giant spear disappears.

"Are you alright?" Milea asks the queen.

"Other than feeling like the Great Bear herself has sat upon me, I am fine," Dysis answers. "What... The spear...?"

"Eursali gave you the gift of awakening your mystical talents," Milea answers. "You have all the knowledge you need to use them wisely. Take it slow and easy to familiarize yourself with them."

"I..." Dysis looks at her hands and frowns. "Where do I start?"

"The best way I know is that you should not go with us, but return to your home, the pine forest. I am sure Eursali's spirit will be there to guide you," Milea answers. "My companions and I have to find a way out of Selcros before Koro knows that his ghastly horde missed their mark,"

"Let me tell you what I saw during my prowl of the city," Zaria offers.

Milea sits down on the cave floor with Zaria as the shiadokat starts to describe the obstacles they face to exit the country. Neil and Vicki take a seat next to the sorceress, listening to the information. Justin kneels and watches as Zaria draws a picture of the different obstacles and their locations. Brion asks a few questions about the castle defenses as Sonja leans against her mother. Dysis add her knowledge of the situation then asks about the guests that the king has as she too sits upon the floor.

"Slone and Loca are still there," Zaria reports. "Wyntre did show up and Koro sent her to her room. The king then gave Slone permission to do as he pleases with the princess"

"Knowing Slone, he did just that," Milea said with a frown.

The sorceress stares at the back of the cave as she contemplates the information. Zaria continues to answer questions and draw various diagrams to illustrate what she saw. Dysis looks outside as she too sinks into deep thought. The cry of strange birds barely reaches the ears of those occupying the cave. Neil looks out when he does hear them, pondering the species as the animals return.

"Our path out is to go through Slone and Koro," Milea voices her thoughts as she stands. "I will fulfill Eursali's last wishes then we will all sit down and come up with a strategy."

"We are going to need an army to get into Selcros," Dysis muses. "When I left, I noticed a lot of enhancements to the defense walls. From what you told us, Zaria, there are a whole lot more since my exit two days ago."

"Oh, we can get in. We just have to be cognizant of our mission," Vicki said confidently.

"Mission awareness means you do not add yourself to the body count," Neil adds. "We also need to commandeer a ship to escape once we are able to."

"The path that you wish to take is a difficult one, my red queen," Justin says as the sorceress walks past him.

"I am aware of it, but what other choice do I have, my dark warrior? I do not want to leave my friends and family behind," Milea answers, then continues her way out of the cave.

The red flames consume the bearskin hungrily, rising steadily higher into the sky. Milea finishes the chant to help guide the spirit of the bear into the afterlife. She leaves her post as Vicki and Neil sing a song to honor the dead. Milea travels to the edge of the cliff and looks out at the city of Selcros. She crosses her arms as a scowl takes over her features. Dysis stands next to her and takes in the view of the obstacle ahead of them.

Zaria stands up and looks down the path that they took to get to the cave. Barking is heard seconds before a large dog rush into the camp and tackles the shiadokat. The animal has shortened fur on his limbs, belly, and face with long, mop-like tresses on the back of his neck along the spine, traveling to the base of the wagging tail. Zaria manages to push the pooch off her and sits up while the dog continues to whine happily as he dances around.

"Ew, dog drool," Zaria complains as she uses her cape to wipe her face clean.

"Oliver, anseo," Dwayne calls as he crests the hill. The dog barks twice, then trots back to his master.

"Dwayne," Brion greets as he shakes his friend's hand. "What brings you out here?"

"Unfortunately, it is not hunting for squirrels," Dwayne says with some relief in his words. "Oliver and I are not alone."

The sounds of voices and various footsteps alert the group as they look past Dwayne to the path just beyond. A large crowd soon comes into view, led by Madame Hawthorne riding on the back of a mountain wolf. Among the crowd are several familiar faces, including the baker, butcher, the innkeeper Leon, and his family. The group includes all the girls from the school. The surprise for Milea, at least, is the group of Wild Folk that she had encountered while seeking a clearing among the crowd. The leader of the Noturi assists Madame Hawthorne to dismount the wolf and holds onto her as they approach Milea and Dysis.

"Majesties, I am very happy to see that both of you and all of your companions are still alive," Madame Hawthorne nods respectfully to the two women.

"Zaria has informed us of the destruction that befell you in the city," Dysis said. "I am very happy to see that all of you have survived."

"You are the last high priestess of the Temple of Nag'teragiea," Milea concludes.

"I inherited the title by outliving the survivors who escaped the temple's destruction over seventy years ago," Madame Hawthorne admits. "My training stopped in the hall of Tadious. I trained as a warrior; my magic, secondary. As I grew old, my mystical abilities became my primary form of defense."

"Grandmother Hawthorne is legendary in my home town," the Noturi leader said. "According to our chieftain, Liev, she trained many orphans in her discipline and they in turn trained us."

"Wait, did you just say Liev?" Dysis interrupts as she shakes her head. "Liev Fone?"

"Yes," The Noturi answers. "He is not with us right now. Our town is a three-week travel on foot to the northeast."

"Why did you come to this area? Are you a part of the group that attacked the city?" Milea inquires.

"I do not know about any attack," the young man admits. "My friends and I journeyed this far down in search of the legendary sorceress that our chieftain is pining for."

"What will you do when you find her?" Milea asks.

"Are you her?" the young man retorts.

"No, but you are in her presence," Milea answers as she turns to the elder. "Madame Hawthorne, I have a favor to ask of the Warriors of Tadious."

"Ah, I see," Madame Hawthorne carefully steps away from her crutch. "Come then, Lady Milea, we can talk while Faul is face to face with his father's true love."

Dysis and Faul stare at one another, each has a level of shock masking their features. Milea assists Madame Hawthorne over to a large stone, taking care to help her sit comfortably. Oliver sits next to Madame Hawthorne and places his head upon her lap. Milea explains the plight that they are facing to get out of Selcros. Dysis tears her gaze from Faul and leaves him to go and listen to Milea to hear a solution.

Instead of providing an answer right away, Madame Hawthorne decides to talk it over with the rest of her party. Milea nods and leaves the elder. Neil and Brion are curious enough to approach with the rest of the Warriors of Tadious as they gather around their leader. Vicki, Justin, and Sonja join the sorceress as she stands at the cliff's edge. They stare out at the city, each contemplating a scenario of their escape. Zaria sits down on the edge of the cliff, looking out past the horizon. Dysis joins the shiadokat, drawing her knees into her chest as she digests the information she has received over the last few hours.

The sun is rising and the fire is nothing but embers when Dwayne retrieves Milea to go and speak with the council of elder warriors. Leon strokes his beard as he attempts to look sternly at the sorceress. Milea calmly meets his gaze then turns her attention to Madame Hawthorne when the old woman addresses her.

"We have come to a decision," Madame Hawthorne says solemnly.

CHAPTER FIFTEEN

Queen's Revenge

Twilight of the following day stretches across the sky. Soldiers pace back and forth along the wall of the city, trying to contain their boredom. The empty streets are now the normal sight with many of the residents locking themselves behind sturdy doors. A strong wind blows through the streets, lifting anything that is loose and whirling it around playfully. Many of the Car'laden that Slone has brought with him audibly complain about the cold weather and tediousness of their duties.

A dragon's roar rips through the silence and causes all the soldiers to jump to their feet. The great beast flies overhead, the wind from its wings blowing off anything that is not properly tied down. The dragon roars again, banks, and flies tauntingly past the ballistics as the dragon slayers curse and swear. The men shout obscenities to each other as they arm the weapons and pull the strings back.

Arrows fly with deadly accuracy as the dragon once again banks to fly back over the walls. The objects go straight through the dragon, yet it continues to fly. The men are stunned. Thinking that they missed, they load the crossbows again and call out to their fellows to combine their efforts. As the dragon flies overhead, they release the arrows one at a time and each appears to miss the behemoth.

As the dragon slayers once again reload, they do not hear the death cries of a couple of their men. Neil and Vicki finish disposing a handful of guards watching the events. Dysis tries the back door and finds that it is unlocked. Milea looks around to ensure they are alone, then follows the Dresden siblings into the back courtyard of the castle. A short distance later, they are inside the castle via the kitchen door. The group walk through the room with Vicki picking up a few sharp knives to replace the ones she had lost.

"Where do we start?" Vicki inquires. "I don't want to waste time fumbling around a castle I am not very familiar with."

"I'm going to wait for Slone in the throne room," Milea said. "With all the commotion going on outside, he will go there to observe the events."

"I will go find Koro," Dysis volunteers. "I am familiar with the layout. If you go through those doors you will get to the throne room." She points to a set of plain-looking doors.

"I'll go with Dysis," Neil offers. "Vicki, do me proud, sister."

"Plan on it," Vicki nods.

Milea wishes Neil and Dysis good hunting as she and Vicki take the doors that lead to the throne room. The short, dark, hall they find themselves in has both on high alert. Milea casts a small light spell to chase away the shadows. Once they are gone, the feeling of being watched subsides. Milea assures Vicki that the shadows are not the result of the shiadokat's ruse. The sorceress speculates that these shadows are being manipulated by the Tragin.

Vicki glances around, seeing no signs of anything in the hall with exception herself and Milea. They quicken their pace, exiting into the throne room in time to hear the thunder of cannon fire. Milea looks out the window to see the dragon figure still flying around as twilight starts to give way to darkness. Vicki notices that the cannons on the barricade have joined the crossbows in trying to bring it down. Milea turns to the hall and frowns.

"Get into position, he is coming," Milea warns.

"Stay alert, I don't like what I've read about Slone in the library," Vicki said as she melts into the shadows just beyond the thrones.

"I want you to stay safe as well. Remember do not look him in the eye," Milea reminds her. She goes to Koro's throne and sits down. The sorceress then crosses her legs and waits.

In the hall of the royal bedrooms, Dysis is careful in traversing the space in wonder to see that no guards are present. Neil walks in stealth just behind the former queen. He holds his katana at the ready as he rounds corners and meets with empty silence. He frowns at the situation, sensing that it is not right. Angry shouting draws the attention of both as they near the king's bedroom. Dysis opens the door and looks inside to see Koro shouting to the empty space of his chambers.

The king looks as if he has not bathed for several days as sweat pours from every part of his body. His clothing is tattered into rags while his hair and beard appear to stand on end. His crown, however, still has its shine, evidenced by the gleam from the light of the fireplace. Dysis takes a deep breath and barges into the room.

"What is this?" Koro whips around. "You traitorous bitch, how did you survive?"

"Simple. You missed," Dysis answers.

Neil moves forward with quick speed only to duck, dodge, and block as he jumps back from an unexpected opponent. A large Car'laden soldier sneers at the L'vane man as he attacks. Neil blocks the man then turns his blade to slice at the midsection of his opponent. The Car'laden falls in half as Neil blocks another attacker. The room's temperature plummets as the flames go out in the fireplace. A cluster of guards hold rank, putting their shields in front of them as they banish their swords in front. Neil finds himself now standing next to Dysis and witnesses a second group of soldiers doing the same thing behind them. Dysis glances to the left and right before she crosses her arms as if daring the men to come forward.

The soldiers increase their pace, coming within a foot of Neil and Dysis, when a concentrated blizzard erupts in the room. The only safe place is right behind Dysis, which is where Neil thankfully finds himself. The Car'ladens' shouts are cut short as the winds die down and the blizzard ceases. Everyone, including Koro, is frozen into a solid block of ice.

Dysis casually steps over to the nearest Car'laden. He is like a perfect ice sculpture, down to the wrinkles upon his jaw as he yells out his last breath. Dysis lifts her left hand and taps the statue. The Car'laden explodes into new fallen snow. The effects ripple through the ranks on both sides of the room as each man is reduced to liquid. Neil approaches the ice statue of Koro and studies it. He frowns when he sees that the person is not the king but a body double. Slightly perturbed, Neil uses his blade to take off the head of the ice statue. It erupts into snow then melts as the room warms back up.

"It's the king's double," Neil says to Dysis as he returns to her side. "Do you think he is in this room?"

"I guarantee he is still here," Dysis assures and looks around. "But I have not visited his chambers enough to know where the secret room is at."

"Should I search the area?" Neil asks. He looks out the window in response to the sound of cannon fire. "What are they doing out there?"

"I will lock this room down. If he is in here, I will deal with him after we are done with Slone," Dysis offers. "I think we should check on our friends and see what the blazes is going on outside."

"Alright," Neil said hesitantly.

Neil leaves the room first, going down the hall a few yards to peek around the corner as Dysis follows him out. She closes the door and uses her mystical abilities to freeze the entire threshold. The ice emits a cold fog and crackles a little as it seizes the wood together. The former queen nods, satisfied with her spell, then turns to look outside as more noise from the cannons and other weapons fill the air. Neil decides to leave Dysis to go outside the castle and take care of some invaders in the courtyard. Dysis explores the castle before she goes to assist in the throne room.

The air in the throne room grows thick as the sound of heavy footsteps echo in the main hall. Milea relaxes and concentrates on her spell. She hears Vicki controlling each breath that is taken. Slone walks into the room and straight over to the window, oblivious to the women watching him. The dragon roars several more times as the men continue to try and bring it down. A stray cannonball accidentally strikes one of the crossbows sitting on top of the clock tower. The men and weapon go crashing to the ground, killing them instantly. The dragon finally disappears from the sky, as if it never existed. Many of the men outside appear confused. Slone, on the other hand, is highly annoyed.

"Shiadokat..." Slone growls angrily. He looks to the wall near the forest. "What do we have here?"

A powerful blast of ice freezes the wall solid seconds before a large ninety-foot ice dragon rams through it then takes straight to the air. An archer on his back take aim at the remaining ballistic operators and picks them off one at a time. The men on the ground shout obscenities at the dragon, they are out of ammunition. Dover responds with a blast of his ice breath, freezing everything it touches.

The dragon does a barrel roll, providing his passenger, Leon, opportunity to fire his weapon at a few more targets. At the same time, a mighty battle cry goes up just beyond the broken wall. The rest of the wall comes down as several smaller dragons ram through it followed by a horde of Noturi riding on various large forest animals. Slone's soldiers muster their defenses but find themselves facing a strong legion of warriors.

A large dog jumps on a Car'laden and rips his throat out while an archer riding on the back of a mountain wolf jumps over him and attacks as his passenger picks off several defenders. Sonja calls to the ice dragon hatchlings and leads them toward the jail tower. Brion leads those on foot into the city and heads straight to the harbor. Slone arches an eyebrow upon seeing the intentions of the invaders.

"Seriously?" Slone asks himself. "I guess I will have to take care of these vermin myself."

"I am surprised that you have ignored me this long, Slone," Milea says, capturing her prey's immediate attention.

"Well," Slone smiles brightly when he turns. "You look much better than Koro upon that throne. How is it that you got past my guards?"

"They were a minor nuisance," Milea answers. "You, on the other hand, are a far greater prize."

"I do consider myself a fine catch," Slone agrees. "You have a good eye. Why are you here?"

"Curiosity," Milea continues to cast her enchantment. She repositions her legs and leans to the side a little, resting her jaw upon her hand.

"Oh really? About what?" Slone takes another step closer to the woman.

"There are many legends about the Son of Roathis. The one that piques my curiosity is the story about his chest." Milea said. "It is said that you have permanent markings of a sea creature scarred across a most beautiful muscular torso. Is that true?"

"Yes, it is more than true. I will tell you the legend of how it happened, but you must be in my arms for me to do so," Slone coaxes.

"Before I surrender to your prowess, perhaps you can show me this scar?" Milea entices. "We are alone."

"Indeed, we are," Slone says as he carefully opens his vest, exposing his chest. "Well, what do you think?"

"Come a little closer," Milea beckons.

A feral grin spreads across Slone's face as he takes another step closer to Milea. He removes his vest, dropping the item onto the floor. Slone flexes his muscles a little and focuses on the redhead. Milea shields her mind as she meets his gaze. She notices that the closer Slone gets to her, the stronger his paralyzing gaze becomes. In the shadows, Vicki lines up with her target and pulls one of the larger knives she carries. She weighs it carefully and waits. Slone takes one more fatal step and Vicki lets her knife fly.

The knife soars true then hits an obstacle before it strikes its mark. The room seem to shatter as a spell is broken. Milea rises to her feet as Slone shakes his head and holds the bridge of his nose, taking multiple steps back. The clicking of wood on stone captures the attention of all in the room. The knife drops to the floor and Vicki feels a force grip her tightly as she levitates from her hiding place. Milea turns to the doorway as a hooded figure walks into the room, cackling. She whispers a few unclean words under her breath.

"So, you are the woman Koro speaks ill of," Loca boasts as he pauses just next to the window. "You are more a nuisance than anything threatening."

"Why are you interrupting?" Slone demands of his servant.

"Forgive my intrusion, master, but this cur had you under an enchantment," Loca answers with a bow. "And her minion nearly killed you."

"She did?" Slone seems taken aback. He glances at Vicki then once again seems to concentrate on Milea. "I would have happily traveled to the pits of Ublivion."

"Oh, indeed you would," Milea said as their gazes meet again. "Your servant is delusional, Slone. Dismiss him so we may continue our conversation."

"Loca, leave us," Slone commands.

"I will not obey that command, master," Loca refuses.

"What...did...you...say?" Slone slowly turns to the old man. "You dare to disobey me?"

Loca raises his staff and taps the floor. The sound echoes in the throne room as Slone takes a step back and once again holds his head. The sound of shattering glass fills the space as Milea takes a couple of steps back. She stands next to Vicki and quietly dispels the hold that Loca has on her. The L'vane woman pretends that she is still in the grasp of the old mage as she fingers her whip.

Slone shakes his head and focuses on Loca then once again looks over at Milea. Another feral grin plasters his face but soon fades as another person enters the room and stands calmly next to Loca. Justin crosses his arms as he takes in the situation. He meets Milea's gaze and grins a little. The small expression of sentiment enrages the Son of Roathis.

"What is he doing here?" Slone demands, jealousy ripe in his words and body language.

"My master is not of his right mind," Loca said sadly. "Justin, destroy the infidel."

Justin glances over at the old mage, a little surprised at the open-ended command that he is given. He then focuses completely on Milea as he takes a step forward, drawing his sword. The sorceress causes her blade to appear in her hand in an eruption of red flame. The fire continues to swirl around her form as she takes a few carefully placed steps towards the dark lord. The castle shakes violently when the great dragon roars and flies past the window. At the same time, Justin charges and attacks Slone.

The Son of Roathis stumbles back in surprise but manages to recover and pull his own blade to defend himself. Loca watches, his jaw slack, only to get slammed by a column of flames. Milea concentrates as she increases the intensity of the flames, burning much of Loca's clothing. The flames suddenly go out as Loca recovers from his stupor.

With this cloak destroyed, Loca is revealed as a very wrinkled man. It is hard to tell if he is Car'laden or something else. His eyes glow like coals as he glares at the sorceress.

"You will pay for this infraction, wench!" Loca shrieks.

Milea is quick to switch her footing and erects a solid shield. Loca sends a strange beam of dark energy towards her, exiting his mouth, and eyes. The spell hits the shield, pushing Milea back a couple of feet. Vicki feels a cold heat from the beam as it passes her. Milea manages to reverse the beam to send it back into Loca. It hits the old mage but does not affect him. Vicki decides to vacate the room by ducking into the secondary hall that they had traveled when they first entered the castle.

Thunder rumbles from the room as Vicki makes her way through another hall that leads to the barracks and ultimately outside. She rounds a corner and freezes when Snowpuff growls at her. Vicki gives a command and the snow leopard cub ignores it as he jumps at her, claws extended. Vicki pulls her whip and cracks it, knocking the animal from his trajectory. Snowpuff lands on the ground, turns and attacks again. This time he gets smacked by a large black paw, sending him spiraling down the hall. Snowpuff hisses as he then turns and hightails it away from Vicki. The shadows in the hall growl and follow the cub.

"Vicki," Madame Hawthorne calls to the woman. "Quick, over here."

Without a second thought, Vicki obeys, ducking behind one of the decorative walls in the castle. A group of Car'laden soldiers curse and swear as they jog down the hall toward the barracks, making their way outside to assist their companions. Vicki waits with bated breath until all two hundred of the invaders pass by. The

L'vane exhales in relief and turns to the elder. She is suddenly overcome with concern. Madame Hawthorne is sitting on the floor, clutching her chest as she grimaces a little. Her back is against the wall and she is clearly suffering pain. Vicki goes to her side and gets to her knees to check on the grandmotherly woman.

"Madame Hawthorne," Vicki addresses. "Were you attacked? I can help treat your wounds."

"Only attack I am suffering, Vicki, is the strength of my own heart," Madame Hawthorne answers gently. "My warrior days are over. I will be following my fellows into the afterlife very soon."

"Oh no," Vicki said, sadness in her features. "What can I do to ease your transition, Lady Hawthorne?"

"Just... keep me company until I am ready to pay homage to Oswind's court," Madame Hawthorne requests.

Vicki settles down to sit next to the elder, her attention on the old woman as she speaks of her past. The L'vane keeps an ear toward the hall to make sure that neither Snowpuff nor the Car'laden legion returns and finds them. Cannon fire is heard through the thick walls of the castle.

Outside the castle, Neil finishes off his last opponent while making his way down the hill to the docks of the city. He pauses and looks out to the bay to see a large galleon attacking the barricades with unmatched firepower. Neil frowns in curiosity as he continues down the hill. The ship fires a round from its port side then retreats faster than most vessels its size. The galleon turns around and attacks, this time turning its starboard cannons to the obstacles and firing with deadly accuracy.

Brion pauses in his press for the docks when he hears and notices the large vessel. The men on the barricades leap from their posts, preferring the wrath of the waves to that of the mysterious ship. Sonja, on Bryce's back, pauses by the elf and looks to the river. Dover roars overhead doing several barrel rolls, much to his passenger, Leon's, delight. The innkeeper has long run out of arrows from the initial attack and is simply hanging on to enjoy the ride.

Dover roars as he unleashes a strong blue flame at the barricade, freezing it along with whoever is left upon the structure. The galleon fires a round from all twenty of its port side cannons and shatters the barrier. The last of the blockade and its unfortunate crew are sent to a watery grave as it sinks to the bottom of the fjord. The galleon rams through whatever is left of the blockade and sails around the beach towards the docks.

"The hatchlings and I freed all the men in the jail tower," Sonja reports to Brion. "Did you need our assistance getting to the docks?"

"Who was in the tower?" Brion asks.

"The crew from the Iron Horse," Sonja answers.

Men bellow loudly as they rush past the dragons and Brion towards the wall blocking the way to the docks. The invading Car'laden momentarily hold their position as wild animals join the charge. Bryce and his brothers squeal in delight as they give chase after the men, joining the masses. The Car'ladens holding the wall break rank and start to retreat to their ships as clouds develop around the castle. Those that continue to hold the line are taken down by the wave of allies.

Bryce and his brothers take to the air to give chase to the retreating Car'laden through the square. Sonja spots the flame thrower before the dragons do and tugs on Bryce's mane, making the

hatchling pull up. He is followed by his brothers as the Car'ladens unleash a mighty flame towards the attackers. Many of the Noturi fight
for control of their wild steeds, a few of which are caught in the flames
and immediately incinerated.

Steam exits Bryce's mouth, as well as those of his brothers. All
twelve of the hatchlings unleash their icy breath upon the flame throw-
ers. The Car'ladens turn their weapon to the approaching ice and fire
it full blast, melting the ice into rain. The little dragons all dodge out
of the flame's path then regroup and once again unleash their weapons. This time, they are joined by their father. The flamethrower does
not stand a chance and is hit hard by the large column of blue ice. The
Car'laden men, however, survive the attack only to have to defend
against Brion and the Noturi.

Red lightning erupts through the clouds that surround the castle's
keep and breaks through the window of the throne room. Milea captures the bolt meant to hit her, spins, and releases it in Loca's direction.
The old man encases himself in a strange dark cocoon, allowing the
bolt to spider around him, hitting the wall behind the old man. Milea
mutters obscenities under her breath in frustration as Loca releases
his cocoon and cackles. No one in the room notices the temperature
dropping with every second of battle.

Justin locks blades with Slone and holds his ground as his opponent
growls angrily at him. They are evenly matched, a fact that has not
changed through the years. Justin smirks cockily as he tries to figure
out how to strike the killing blow to the Son of Roathis. Slone sneers
as a quick flash flicker across his eyes. Justin sees it and disengages,
disappearing right before a dark blade erupts from the floor where he
had been standing.

Slone yells furiously at his opponent. He did not notice that his breath is visible in the air. Light ice crystals form upon the walls and all the furniture in the room. The Son of Roathis looks up and moves out of the way as Justin nearly skewers him with the spear from above. The dark lord lands and automatically swings the spear. The weapon strikes Slone's metal brace. Sparks fly as the two items connect. Milea takes note of the temperature change and lights a flame around herself, keeping it close to stay warm.

Justin backs away from Slone to get a better swing to strike his opponent. Slone sees his opportunity and charges forward with a battle cry. He gets two steps in before the entire floor becomes covered with ice. Slone's foot hits the thin layer and he starts to slip and slide. A fierce wind slams into him, knocking the Son of Roathis into the distant wall. Justin seizes the moment, aiming for his opponent's exposed chest, and throws the spear with all his might. The weapon skewers Slone and buries itself into the stone behind him.

Loca's eyes widen when he hears his master's cry of pain. The old mage turns and falls to the floor as he slips upon the ice. He is unable to regain his balance as a force picks him up and slams him into the wall opposite his master and upside down. Milea calls her discarded blade back to her hand and wraps flame around it as she glares at the old man. Justin pulls his dark sword from its sheath once again as the ice on the floor melts.

"Justin, what are you doing?" Loca demands.

"I should have never agreed to bring you back from your hell," Slone adds angrily as he pulls on the spear. It does not budge.

"At least I am obeying orders," Justin said. "By destroying the infidel."

Milea and Justin charge at their individual opponents simultaneously. The sorceress gets to Loca quicker and is about to strike when a dark wind explodes from the old mage. She curses as the winds send her backward and into the throne. She crumbles to the ground from the blow. Justin swings, intending to take Slone's head. His sword bite through the stone wall instead. The long scar upon the brick and mortar are a testament to the force he used to fulfill his promise. Justin frowns when he sees that his mark is gone, leaving a pool of dark blood upon the floor. Justin grabs the butt of the spear and effortlessly pulls it out of the wall. The weapon disappears as the dark lord turns and sees that Loca is also gone. Dysis walks into the room as Justin assists Milea to her feet.

"What happened? Did Loca explode?" Dysis inquires.

"I don't think that was all Loca," Milea said.

"It may have been Roathis that aided them in their escape," Justin offers an explanation. "I was about to behead her favorite son.

"That could be it, but I am thinking someone much more powerful did it," Milea said.

The trio looks to the window when Dover roars past one final time, clearing the rest of the clouds from around the castle. The last of the invading Car'laden army retreats to their ships. The orders come from the admiral to pull anchor and leave with many of their fellows still running for their lives. Some manage to swim to their ship while others stop at the docks and watch as their only escape leaves them behind. The stragglers are rounded up by the crew of the Iron Horse and carted off to the jail tower. Dover does an aerial flip then lands in the middle of the square upon his hind legs. He lifts his head and roars in victory. His twelve hatchlings echo their father's roar in various parts of the city. Sonja covers her ears as Bryce bellows as loud as he can.

The bells of the clock tower ring jubilee but the sound barely breaks through the thick walls of the dungeon. A'drianis stalks Snowpuff, cornering him in one of the furthest and darkest cells within the castle. No one else is in the dungeon, which she takes note of but does not seem worried. Snowpuff cowers down, shaking with fear as the large black winged jungle cat comes ever nearer. A'drianis roars as she takes a swipe at the snow leopard cub only to go through the image. The shiadokat expresses her surprise as she turns. A bright light illuminates from just beyond the cell as the door slams shut. A'drianis hisses at it then jumps into the last of the shadows before they disappear. When the light reaches the corner, she is gone.

The sounds of victory barely reach through Vicki's thoughts as she gently places Madame Hawthorne's hands together across the chest. As soon as the bells tolled, the old woman had lost her battle with her failing heart. Her eyes had closed and a smile had tipped the elder's lips when the sound echoed throughout the castle.

Vicki lowers her head briefly as she recalls the few stories that the elder shared with her during her final hour. The sound of approaching people catches Vicki's attention and she stands. She hears the familiar voice of Dysis as the former queen explains that the front door is not an option due to the large amount to glass that litters the ground. She shows her friends the way out through the barracks. Vicki goes to the hall.

"Milea, we have a tragedy," Vicki calls to the backs of her companions.

"Vicki," Milea turns around and heads her way. "What...?" she pauses in her question when she rounds the corner.

"Madame Hawthorne passed away after she heard the clock tower," Vicki explains as Justin and Dysis also round the corner. "Her heart gave out on her."

"So passes the last High Priestess of Nag'teragiea," Justin says solemnly.

"Let's...take her to her family," Milea said.

Just a stone's throw to from the docks, Dwayne calls to his dog and is rewarded when Oliver, dirty from the battle, leaps into the glassmaker's arms. Both fall to the ground and Dwayne laughs at Oliver's enthusiasm as the canine insists on licking him to death. Brion smiles, humored at the sight of the overly-zealous animal.

Faul and the rest of the Noturi release their wild steeds and thank them before sending them back to their forest homes. Boisterous laughter echoes in the sky, stemming from the town square as Dover listens to Leon boast about fulfilling a childhood dream. Sonja climbs off Bryce's back once she has gathered all the hatchlings. She is immediately surrounded by all the little dragons as they chatter and chirp in excitement.

Milea approaches the group on the square. She has added Neil to her small party as they travel. The sorceress spots Brion with Dwayne and decides to go and speak to the glassmaker. Dwayne notices her and takes a step back, his eyes wide with surprise when he sees Justin carrying the body of Madame Hawthorne.

A large crowd gathers around Milea and her party as Vicki explains to Dwayne what has happened. Justin follows Dwayne to the glassmaker's shop so that the Warriors of Tadious could prepare their leader for burial. Milea seeks out and finds her daughter in the center of a mass of little dragons. Sonja is patting and complementing each one of the dragons as Milea places a hand upon her shoulder and smiles. The girl looks back and relaxes when she sees her mother. A roar followed by a high pitch whistle echoes from the distance. Dover lifts his head and looks to the forest to see Sapphire hovering over the trees. He trumpets an answer to his mate then turn to his children.

"Boys, it is time to go. Your mother is calling," Dover said to his brood. "Say your goodbyes."

Milea takes a step back as one by one; the little ice dragons gently head-butt Sonja's hand then turn to trot down the street. When they reach speed, they spread their wings and take to the air. Milea could not help but chuckle a little bit when Tor, the biggest, places his chin upon the girl's head. He follows his siblings down the street but has to kick up a little more speed in order to take to the skies. Soon, there is only one more little dragon left and he seems very sad to be going.

"It's ok, Bryce," Sonja pats his head gently. "You must go with your mom. She knows way better than we would when it comes to taking care of you. You are still a growing boy."

"She is right, Bryce," Milea also pats the dragon. "I'm sure you will run into Sonja once again during her travels."

"Bryce, we cannot tarry too long. Your mother wants to migrate to a cooler climate," Dover says gently. "Did you have something to say to Sonja?" he watches his son nod. "Then go on." Dover stands up as Bryce takes a deep breath in.

"Bye... bye... Sonja," Bryce says then gently taps her shoulder with his head.

"I..." Sonja places a hand over her mouth to compose herself. "Goodbye for now, Bryce." She pats the dragon on the head.

Milea hugs her emotional daughter as Bryce turns and trots down the street. He stretches his wings and takes to the skies, flying toward the large figure of Sapphire in the distance.

"Safe travels, Dover. To you and your very brave family," Milea says to the guardian dragon.

"You too, Milea." Dover said. "I don't want to hear about any more trouble from you, young lady."

"I will try," Milea smiles at the mock scolding.

Dover grins as he turns and walks down the street. He jumps over the galleon that is parked at the docks, landing with a mighty splash in the ocean. Seconds later he launches himself into the air, using his great wings to carry him into the skies quickly. Dover roars joyfully as he flies past the city and over the woodlands. Neil approaches the sorceress and her child as Milea hugs Sonja tightly then takes a step back.

"Is she ok?" Neil asks.

"Yes, saying goodbye to friends is never easy for this one," Milea said as she brushes Sonja's hair.

"I just wasn't prepared for him to talk," Sonja said, taking a deep breath.

"Oh, she's a tough one. She will be fine," Zaria said as she claps Sonja on the shoulder. "How did the battle go?"

"Koro of course is a no-show," Neil answers. "We got a taste of his bodyguards but he was not in the main room. Dysis froze the king's chamber door to lock him in. She has reason to believe that the king is hiding in one of many secret places within that area."

"Loca and Slone were aided by either Roathis or our antagonist in escaping with an explosion of dark wind," Milea reports. "I will give details on how that battle went once we are at sea. Did you come from the docks?"

"I did," Zaria said. "I escaped Snowpuff's clever trap and ended up on the ship that's docked there."

"Really?" Who is she?" Neil asks. "That vessel assisted with the blockade?"

"She flies the flag of a woman resting underneath the stars," Zaria answers cryptically.

Neil stares at the shiadokat for a few seconds before he starts to run for the docks. Zaria laughs at the man's enthusiasm and admits to Milea that the ship is the Lady of the Night. Sonja jogs to the ship as Milea goes to collect Vicki, Brion, and Justin. Zaria leads the way as they walk to the docks. Shiadokat explains to Milea that there is a gift for her in the treasure chest clutched to the stomach of the figurehead. The sorceress stops at the side of the ship and stares at Zaria. Her companions board the vessel and go exploring with Sonja and Neil.

They are in awe of the sheer size of the ship. This is a floating fortress complete with cannons to defend or attack and a metal battering ram to clear obstacles in her way. Milea focuses on the treasure chest and levitates up to it. As she nears it, the item opens to reveal the bracelet and both book halves, carefully preserved. Milea lets out a sound of joy and hugs the figurehead.

The town of Selcros eventually settles down for the night. The Noturi decide to start their journey back to their home. Dysis politely refuses to join them, stating that Faul is evidence that Liev has moved past her. Instead, the former queen has decided to spend time with Milea and A'drianis, asking questions about Eltis and the abilities that she has inherited.

The clock tower tolls a late hour as Wyntre finally exits her room. The hallways are clear of any living creature. No guards greet the princess after her long, brutal, attack. To her relief, she does not find evidence of Slone or his men in the castle either. Wyntre nearly jumps out of her skin when Snowpuff bumps up against her leg, rubbing it gently. The princess picks up the snow leopard cub by the scrub of his neck.

"Where were you when he came to my room, fleabag?" Wyntre snaps at the cub.

"Trying to take down a Shadow Eltis, you ungrateful cur," Snowpuff answers abruptly.

"Wait, did you just speak?" Wyntre blinks and drops the cub.

Snowpuff appears stunned at the question then let out a strange cub-roar in response. Wyntre watches the snow leopard a little before she walks down the hall to the throne room. She sees a mess from some unknown event. There are marks on the wall where Slone had been pinned as well as a pool of dark-colored liquid on the floor.

Wyntre clutches her robe to her breast as she turns and runs down the hall, straight toward her father's room, Snowpuff hot on her heels. The door to the king's chambers is frozen solid with a large mystical block of ice. Wyntre calms her pulse and dispels the ice block with a little effort. Her jaw drops in amazement when she does, ignoring the door opening.

"Wyntre," Koro said, causing his daughter to jump. "I am glad you survived the attempt to overthrow me."

The princess recoils at the man that appears from behind the door. He is Koro yet he has a very haggard appearance. His body odor is pungent, with a slight smell of decay about it. His eyes appear to shift left and right as he tries to concentrate on the girl yet something seems to distract him. His arm, usually carefully wrapped, is now exposed and black in color. Puss oozes from the arm and drips to the floor. It is evident that there is no more blood going to the appendage.

"Father?" Wyntre asks in disbelief. "My god, what has she done to you?"

"Her minions tried to kill me but I outsmarted them," Koro boasts. "It was not hard since the one leading them is the traitorous witch, Dysis. I will send out a reward of kingly proportion for any-one who brings me her head."

"What about the one that hurt me, father? Slone?" Wyntre demands.

"I apologize, I thought he more of a gentleman. He is the strong king that you spoke of so many times," Koro informs. "He is much more powerful than Brion and I suspect him to be a better husband as well."

"I didn't know," Wyntre said, stunned.

"I'm sure in his excitement he wanted to consummate your wedding before the actual date," Koro continues. "Is he still here?"

"No one else but you, me, and Snowpuff are in the entire castle," Wyntre explains. She takes a few steps back when several Sierge walk up behind the king. "F-f-f-ffather...." She points a shaky hand to the perceived threat.

"Grawl and his men are my personal bodyguards. If Dysis had found me, it would have been her end," Koro said simply. "We will set a trap for the traitorous whore and wait for her return to the castle."

The Departure

The city is bustling once again before Milea even considers leaving her room for the day. The enormous space on the ship has three chambers for her personal use. A sitting area, a sleeping area, and a place to enjoy a relaxing bath if she chooses. A smile touches her lips when she recalls the enthusiasm from Neil as he explored the entire vessel. The quarters below deck consist of several rooms, presumably for those wanting a private sleeping place. Below that is another floor containing a treasure room filled with gold, jewels, and other riches that the ship had returned with. Dysis had gifted the riches to Milea and her friends as a means of repayment but tells her that it is not nearly enough for what they did for Selcros.

Voices increase on the ship as the rest of the crew wakes up for the day. Milea stretches once more then gets up to start her day. She finishes tying back her hair and opens the door then recoils immediately from the brightness that invades her space. Milea is slow to uncovers her eyes, blinking multiple times as she tries to adjust to the bright light. She squints as she walks out onto the deck to join her companions. The sorceress takes off her heavy cape with a slight frown at the warmth of the weather. Milea hears Dysis swear a little in exasperation when she comes from below deck. The weather and the bright, sunny day are a surprise, if not a worry, for the former queen.

"Good morning, ladies," Neil offers a confident greeting. "It is a lovely first day aboard the Lady of the Night. Spring has finally come to the land of Selcros."

"This heat is more like summer weather," Dysis responds and uses her hands to fan herself.

"The temperature does not have me as worried as the sunlight," Milea said. "Zaria will basically be blind in this light."

"Ahoy! Permission to come aboard," Leon belts out from below.

"Permission granted, welcome aboard," Neil calls back.

Oliver is the first to jump onto the deck, being able to climb the boarding ramp at a rapid pace. He lets out a short bark and lumbers over toward Milea. He is completely shaven now, the long hair upon his back replaced with the short buzz cut. The sorceress laughs as she gently pats the canine's back and scratches just above the tail. Oliver moans and whines happily as Dwayne and Leon arrive on deck. Dysis casually pats the dog on his head as his tail wags fiercely. The whole dog shakes as he prances between the two women.

"Well, he's in his happy place," Dwayne said as he shakes Neil's hand in greeting. "Thank you, Captain, for allowing us to board."

"No problem, we were just about to venture out for a few supplies before we set sail," Neil says.

"I've a warehouse that escaped the fury of the battles," Leon volunteers. "All I need is some help getting the items here."

"How much help did you need, Leon?" Milea asks, overhearing the conversation.

"As many hands as you can spare, milady," Leon answers. "There are enough supplies in the warehouse for you to take on whatever journey is before you."

"Thank you, Leon, for your generosity," Milea says and takes a step away from the dog. "Sonja, time to get up. Justin, I need your assistance, my dark warrior."

Milea casually folds her arms and looks up when Sonja opens the door to the housing that serves as the crow's nest and shimmies down a ladder. The sorceress looks behind to the middle door next to her room as her daughter approaches. The door opens, allowing Justin out first then Brion right behind him. The Car'laden approaches Milea while the elf goes to speak to Dwayne, Neil, and Leon. Justin places his hand upon his heart and nods respectfully to the sorceress. Sonja stretches and yawns as she adjusts her sight to the extremely bright day.

"How can I assist you, my red queen?" Justin asks gently.

"Sir Leon has generously offered supplies for our voyage," Milea answers. "I need you and Sonja to assist him in bringing them from his warehouse."

"Consider it done," Justin says, then turns his attention to Sonja. "Ready to go, warrior chief?"

"Yep," Sonja yawns and follows him over toward the other men. "What's for breakfast?"

"I don't know," Justin answers. "Last night, I think Vicki volunteered to fix it."

"Luckily for us, there is no food onboard at this moment," Neil said. "I am going to beseech Leon to give us one last good meal before we head out to sea."

"I'd be honored," Leon laughs a little. "But it will have to wait until after Madame Hawthorne's funeral."

"We will be there," Brion offers. "I'll help with the supply run."

"I'm with you, many hands make light work," Neil agrees as he and the volunteers leave the ship with Leon.

An hour later, the party returns with the supplies for the ship. Oliver rushes aboard the ship once again, this time with a large saddlebag across his back. He sits as commanded to allow Dwayne to take the pack off and follow Neil down to the storage area on the ship. Milea goes to awaken both Vicki and Zaria as the men place the supplies inside the storage room.

As soon as she steps outside, Zaria hisses angrily then grumbles about the excessiveness of the bright daylight. Milea gently claps the shiadokat on her shoulder and leads the way off the ship and toward the ruins of the girls' school. The trip is a short walk and Zaria nearly runs into Milea when the sorceress stops at their destination. She grumbles an apology as Justin stands next to her, providing a little reprieve from the light with his own shadow.

"Are you alright, Zaria?" Neil inquires.

"Not really," Zaria answers and squints. "The light is playing havoc with my sight; I can barely see you."

"This daylight is giving me a headache," Brion agrees. "I don't remember the sun being this bright in Selcros."

"I'm not even going to talk about the headache," Zaria rubs her temples.

The crowd quiets down as the proceedings begin. A soft melody plays as pallbearers carry the coffin holding Madame Hawthorne's body walk through the crowd. Many start to weep and some throw fresh flowers on the ground in front of the men as they pass by. They carefully place the coffin on a funeral pyre and ceremoniously back away. The music fades and Dysis walks into view upon the makeshift stage. She takes a deep breath and starts her speech, the last official one as queen of Selcros. Her words are strong and complementary towards the late school dean. Zaria listens to them until her ears start to twitch. Her sense of smell picks up a faint scent, yet it brings her to full alert. Zaria looks around but the light makes it impossible for her to see much past her own nose. Milea notices the behavior as does Justin and Brion.

"What's the danger?" Milea asks.

"Snowpuff," Zaria answers.

"What direction?" Brion follows up the question.

"Still making that determination," Zaria said.

"Tragin?" Justin asks.

"Yes," Milea and Zaria answer together.

A cool wind trickles into the area, unnoticed by those listening to the queen's speech. Milea pulls her cape a little closer as her hearing detects a faint voice upon the breeze. She recognizes it immediately as Wyntre. On the stage, Dysis pauses in her speech when she also hears the soft words. Milea takes a deep breath then releases it in a cascade of unkind words as the winds explode all around, picking up any loose dirt or leftover snow and whipping it into a blinding fury. Justin senses something approaching and pulls his sword, prompting Neil and Brion to do the same.

The dark lord grunts then curses as he is hit by a creature hiding within the dense fog of debris, knocking him to the ground. Neil falls to the ground, harshly, his blade scattered a short distance from his hand. Vicki trips over him as people start to panic and run in every direction in order to escape the strange phenomena. Milea finally captures control over the winds and grits her teeth as something fights her. The sorceress lets out an angry sound as she disbands the winds. All the dust settles back down as Neil gets to his feet and retrieves his katana. Vicki is helped back up by Brion. Sonja stands from her crouch and looks around.

"Mom, Zaria is missing," Sonja informs.

"I felt something solid push me to the side," Brion frowns and bends down. "I'm not sure what it is, but I do see Zaria's tracks here. Then they disappear."

"The Tragin knocked me down," Justin also bends to examine the ground. "Both Tragins and Eltis, especially the shiadokats, can hide their tracks from even the most elite of trackers or hunters. To find them, you must be very familiar with their signature."

"So, you hunt Tragins?" Brion said, a little awed.

"Yes," Justin answers. "I cannot teach it. The skill is something you are either born with or are blessed with through various means."

Justin focuses on the area where he had been standing before being knocked down. He sees a green tint outlining paw prints of an oversized cat. There are at least two different sizes belonging to the Tragin. Justin frowns, then focuses on the spot where Zaria had stood. He notices that she had moved out of the Tragin's way before she fled into the square. Her tracks, outlined in purple, intermingle with the green ones indicating that her predator has pursued her.

Justin informs his waiting companions of what he has seen. The sound of people screaming in terror draws the attention of everyone in the group. Neil and Vicki are the first to jog toward the noise in order to start the evacuation of the area. Dwayne follows them with Oliver at his heels. Milea calls to Justin to stop him from joining the group as Leon prevents anyone else from going after the others.

"Before we go in there, we need a plan of action," Milea says to her remaining companions.

Zaria hits the ground while defending herself as Neil and Dwayne herd witnesses out of the square. Vicki's mouth drops open when she hears evil laughter escape the chest of a full-grown snow leopard. In fact, he is twice the normal size of any leopard with stronger legs in front than in back. His fur is thick and white, the perfect camouflage against the light-blinded shiadokat. Snowpuff stalks around Zaria and lashes out at her, clawing her back. The shiadokat swears angrily as she once again falls to the ground, this time she is bleeding. She rolls out of the way when he tries to pounce on her, returning to her feet with dagger in hand.

"Aw, what's the matter shiadokat?" Snowpuff mocks. "Feeling helplessly blind? Where are your friends? They have abandoned you it seems."

"I may be blind, but I am not helpless," Zaria snarls. "My friends are around; they will find me."

"If they are not frozen solid," Snowpuff says confidently. "The princess does have her uses."

"You are sorely underestimating my family, Tragin," Zaria informs. "It's fitting because your king did the same thing and you see what happened to him."

"Oh really?" Snowpuff laughs as Zaria turns to face him again. "This is easy, I should have thought of this earlier."

Zaria centers on the voice and readies her dagger. She pauses when her senses tell her that the target has moved. Seconds later, she is yelping in pain as she lands on her back with the weight of her predator on her chest. She tries to move her arm to stab the Tragin but finds that it is locked to the ground with a large paw upon her shoulder. Snowpuff opens his mouth wide and turns his head to the side in order to crush her cranium.

A loud hiss fills the air and is accompanied by a terrifyingly powerful crack. The sound frightens Snowpuff, causing him to jump off his prey. Vicki cracks the whip again, driving the big cat back and away from Zaria. Snowpuff roars and swipes his paws at the offending weapon while he keeps his distance from it. He continues to back away as Vicki moves forward. Sonja helps Zaria up; a look of concern crosses her features when the shiadokat yelps in pain and falls to her knees. Brion goes over to help Sonja and quickly explain the plan to Vicki. Snowpuff sees the interaction and growls as he crouches down to pounce. Instead of jumping forward, he ends up leaping straight into the air in fright as the whip cracks again, coming within inches of his nose.

"Snowpuff, sit up," Vicki commands.

"What?" Snowpuff questions, a look of confusion crosses his face.

"Sit up!" Vicki demands sternly and cracks the whip again.

The whip snaps again and Snowpuff roars in protest as he obeys the command. Vicki continues to give the stern commands she had taught him a little more than a week prior. Each time, she would crack the whip and the snow leopard would obey, though not without a lot of roaring. Milea watches the tricks with a little smile as she sits down in front of the clock tower. The sorceress closes her eyes to block out the noise and concentrate. She starts to levitate as several symbols are drawn on the ground in a circle. The lines that interconnect them pulsate between yellow and light blue. The binding circle comes to life with a slight whoosh as Milea settles into a meditative trance. Vicki takes note of the sorceress' position and cracks the whip twice.

"Snowpuff, roll over!" Vicki said and points. The leopard obeys. "Again!"

Snowpuff does the trick again as the whip snaps just above his head. He stops his roll only inches from the seal. Vicki snaps the whip again and makes the demand for him to roll once more. Instead of obeying the request, Snowpuff gets a look of annoyance upon his features, suddenly realizing that he is being made the fool.

Vicki unleashes the whip again and swears when the leopard dodges it and jumps right at her. She pulls the whip back at the same time she is tugging a dagger out of its holster. She takes aim at the beast as it bounces into the air then ducks when two halves Snowpuff fly over her head. She turns to witness the decapitated animal land a few feet away.

"You alright, sis?" Neil inquires and puts his katana away.

"I am, and a little concerned," Vicki answers. "There is no blood."

"I...Oh," Neil says as he looks at the creature he thought he had just killed.

Snowpuff raises his head and shakes it as if to clear it out. He turns and places his nose directly into his own posterior. His eyes widen at first then start to glow blood red as he whips his attention back towards Vicki. Snowpuff roars with rage as both of his halves start to pulsate with a sickly green light. Neil drops a few sailor oaths and is echoed by his sister as they look for a way out. Brion calls to his friends from the rooftop of the glassmaker's building. The two L'vanes see him and quickly make their way to the side wall. They climb the structure at record speed as Snowpuff finishes regenerating and repairing himself. The Tragin turns toward the glassmaker's building as Justin calmly steps between the predator and his prey.

"You are not going to get past me easily, Tragin," Justin says, evenly.

"Fine, then I'll just go through you," Snowpuff retorts.

Snowpuff grabs a chunk of earth and rips it up with an angry sound. He swings his new club at the dark lord. Justin slices through the club causing Snowpuff to make a sound of surprise. Justin then takes the Tragin's head off with a back stroke. There is a look of surprise on the leopard's face as the head falls to the ground. The body turns around to search for the missing cranium, finds it, and places it back on the shoulders. Justin frowns at the beast as the head reattaches to the rest of the body.

"That was not nice," Snowpuff snarls then attacks using his claws.

On top of the roof, Brion and Neil watch Justin defend himself against Snowpuff as Dwayne treats Zaria's wounds. The shiadokat curses then groans as she simply sits there and takes the treatment. Vicki notices that the claw marks from the Tragin are deep and that

Zaria has lost a lot of blood. Oliver makes a whining sound as he places his head on the shiadokat lap. The pooch is rewarded with a gentle pat from his feline friend. Sonja looks up into the sky with Dysis, as if trying to figure out what is making it so bright. Even the clouds are unable to form due to the unnatural heat.

"Zaria, are you still with me?" Dwayne asks as he finish packing a few more wounds.

"I'm here," Zaria said through gritted teeth. "Still blind but alive. If someone can take care of this infuriating light, it would be greatly appreciated."

"I think I see what is causing the unusual amount of light," Dysis informs, still looking up. She noticed a bird fly into something, bump it and then fly around it. "I think it's mirrors. There is a ring of mystical mirrors surrounding the city."

"What?" Brion looks up and squints as he tries to see the obstacle. "I think I see them,"

Reflecting the sky in all its glory, the mirrors appear to be as big as buildings, reaching as tall as a tower. The sunlight bounces off each one of them and aims both light and heat directly towards the center of the city. Dysis concludes that if they destroy the mirrors, she will be able to bring in the clouds to block the actual sun and make it as dark as night. Vicki judges the distance of the mirrors then shakes her head; it is too far for her to throw her weapon.

Brion concentrates on his sword and mentally launches it into the sky. He tries to direct it to the mirror but it seems to not obey his commands. Dysis stares at the blade as she feels a tingling sensation around her body. She looks at her hands to see that they are glowing a very light blue. Dysis takes a breath in and lets out a sharp sound of surprise when a lightning bolt arcs from her to the levitating sword.

The blade illuminates white moments before hundreds of lightning bolts erupt from it in all directions. The bolts hit the mirrors and instantly shatter them. Snowpuff looks up when the sound of the shattering glass reaches his ears. He sees shards of the mystical mirrors fall to the ground then evaporate into nothing but a mist. The daylight starts to fade back to normal strength.

"No!" Snowpuff roars.

The Tragin breaks off the fight with Justin and bounces over to the building as the clouds begin to roll in. He takes a single leap and effortlessly lands on the rooftop. Sonja meets the charging beast first but finds herself grabbed and tossed from the rooftop altogether. Justin rushes forward to catch the girl before she hits the ground. Snowpuff jumps over the Dresden siblings but does not account for Vicki's whip. The weapon tangles around his leg, causing him to fall hard. Snowpuff yanks his leg, snatching the whip from Vicki's hands. He shreds the weapon and casts the remains to either side before he brings his focus back to Zaria.

Oliver snarls, his shortened hair bristling, as he stands in front of the shiadokat protectively. Snowpuff leaps and Oliver responds by jumping up and catching the Tragin's arm. Snowpuff grabs the dog by the back of his neck and tosses him to the side. The clouds darken considerably, becoming a menacing dark green color, as the winds pick up. Zaria stands up and glares at the Tragin as she jumps back, fading from sight.

Snowpuff lands on the spot she has been sitting and emits a mighty roar as he leaps from the building and tries to make his way back to the castle. Twilight plunges into absolute darkness as the Tragin lands on the ground. The town square seems to shift, reorientating itself into something very unfamiliar. A large claw rakes

Snowpuff, digging out large chunks of flesh. Still, the Tragin does not bleed.

"Cowardly shiadokat!" Snowpuff yells into the darkness. "Face me without your veil of darkness. Fight me feline to feline!"

The wind rustles the fur upon his back as a lone figure walk toward him. The absolute darkness slowly lifts back to twilight. The lighter environment reveals the owner of the footsteps. She is an Elven woman with long black hair. The whites of her eyes are dark blue while her pupils remain black. She is nearly six feet tall and healthy, instead of the more familiar five-foot, emaciated form she usually travels in. She wears a black toga with what appears to be an equally dark cape draped around her shoulders. The cape suddenly opens behind her as A'drianis spreads her dragon wings and focuses her angry stare upon the Tragin.

"You are not worthy of a cat fight, simpleton," A'drianis said coldly.

"You finally reveal yourself and are hardly anything to be afraid of," Snowpuff retorts and shows his teeth. "I will destroy you!"

Snowpuff vaults into the air then dives toward his prey with all his claws extended. The next instant, he is upon his back, pinned to the ground as a giant panther stands on his chest. His arms are detached from his torso. A'drianis hisses at him as she swats him towards Milea. The Tragin grunts as he tumbles into the binding seal. The nubs where his arms had been lit up green before new ones sprout from his body. Snowpuff unleashes an angry bellow as he charges towards A'drianis.

The shiadokat, once again a woman, stands in place and folds her arms across her chest. Snowpuff jumps and slams into a shield, sliding down slowly until he once again touches the ground. Symbols light up around him as he stands back up. He looks around and panics, attacking the shield in order to try and claw his way out. Milea smirks when she senses the struggling Tragin and increases her concentration to keep him in place.

Standing on the back of one of many grotesque gargoyles cropping out from the clock tower, Justin looks down upon his intended target. The clock starts to toll the hour, yet the bell seems to be louder and deeper, as if marking the time of death for the Tragin. Snowpuff whips around and charges towards Milea only to slam into the shield once more. He claws at it, unable to reach his new target or break her concentration.

The clock's vibrations rattle the air as Justin causes his spear to appear in an eruption of dark flames. His eyes change from sage green to mustard yellow as an evil grin spread across his features. Justin takes a step then crouches and jumps from the back of the gargoyle with a mighty yell. He shifts his spear to point directly down, aiming right at the Tragin. Snowpuff looks up just in time to see Justin but does not have enough time to move.

The Tragin hits the ground, landing on his back one final time, with the spear through his chest. The weapon glows menacingly as Snowpuff tries to grab hold of it to pull it out. Justin shoves the weapon deeper, pinning Snowpuff. The clock chimes once more as the Tragin roars in pain and anger, shaking the entire city with his rage before going silent.

Justin pulls his weapon and takes a step back as the body of an emaciated snow leopard cub now lies in the mud. A strange green glowing spirit hovers above the body. It speeds towards Justin only to be blocked by a large hand. Justin takes another step back as the hand grabs hold of the Tragin spirit and drags it into one of the symbols upon the ground. Justin nods, it is appropriately the rune of Oswind.

The body of the snow leopard cub levitates then bursts into fine snow. Snowpuff is no more. The clock finishes with a loud and defining bong, signifying the middle of the day. The dark clouds start to dissipate as the circle fades. Milea stands up and stretches as the daylight returns to normal. A'drianis nods to the sorceress as she too fades in the daylight.

"Is she going to be alright?" Justin asks as Milea stands next to him.

"She will be fine, I think she is going to the ship to rest in darkness for a while," Milea answers.

"How far up did you jump from, Justin?" Sonja asks.

"Jump?" Milea arches an eyebrow.

"The method of destroying a Tragin varies from beast to beast," Justin explains. "The one I used to get rid of Snowpuff is not the safest and should only be used if you know exactly what you are doing. I, however, did not have the time to come up with a better strategy at that moment."

"How far up did you jump from?" Milea reiterates her daughter's question.

"Just the back of that gargoyle," Neil answers and points up as he, Vicki, Brion, and Dwayne with Oliver approach them.

"We all saw him do it from the rooftop of Dwayne's shop." Dysis said, joining the group.

"That's not so far," Sonja looks up at the statue. "I think I could..."

"Absolutely not," Both Milea and Justin said as one.

The funeral pyre is set ablaze for Madame Hawthorne an hour after Snowpuff's demise. Milea watches the flame for several minutes then turns and walks to the ship. Neil, Sonja, and Vicki follow, silently saying their goodbyes. Justin nods respectfully to the fallen priestess and trails after Milea and her company. Brion is last to depart, but not before he says goodbye to Dysis. Oliver whines as he watches his friends go but does not follow. Dwayne pats the dog on the head and provides comforting words to the saddened pooch.

Dysis watches as Brion gets onto the ship and the boarding plank is pulled up. The Lady of the Night pulls anchor and pushes off from the docks. Oars stretch out from the sides of the ship and row the vessel out to sea. The sails unfurl to catch the winds, increasing the speed of the craft to her next destination. Dysis continues to watch until the ship disappears over the horizon. She wipes a tear from her eye, finally realizing that she will miss her new friends.

The funeral fire is all but out by the time Dysis enters the castle to retrieve a few things before departing to the forest to heal and learn her new abilities. A pungent odor of decay smacks her sinuses as she nears the throne room. Dysis pauses as her senses go on high alert, something does not feel right, and she needs to get out. Frowning, she turns to retreat outside but finds the way blocked by two large Sierge warriors. Dysis backs up from the dragon men as they take threatening steps towards her. She ends up backing into the throne room.

"Welcome to your trial, traitorous weather witch," Koro announces.

Dysis whips around to face the thrones. Koro has taken his seat as king. Wyntre is sitting, comfortably, in the queen's throne. Qwest is standing next to his father, along with a white-haired stranger. She does not focus much on the visitor, but knows that he is not from Selcros, nor is he anything she has seen so far in her lifetime.

"The only traitor in this room is you, Koro," Dysis counters. "You betrayed my trust, broken promises and who knows what else you have done."

"Silence!" Koro bellows. "You allowed the red devil forest witch into Selcros's innermost sanctuary. She does terrible things to my children while you watch, and you even stoop so low as to become one of her disciples. As queen, your first and most important duty is to protect the future of Selcros. You failed at that, miserably."

"You are speaking madness, Koro," Dysis defends. "Know that your children brought whatever disasters they encountered upon themselves."

"Why didn't you stop her from changing me into an ass?" Qwest demands.

"You are still an ass, Qwest, that much has not changed one bit," Dysis retorts. "Why didn't you heed the warning signs?"

"You allowed her to threaten me. She stole my true love by placing him under her wicked enchantment," Wyntre nearly shouts. "Father, I think she should be executed!"

"If you are referring to Brion, you had only met him, as an adult, when they landed," Dysis corrects. "He also gave you his very strong rejection. You, apparently, do not understand the common tongue very well."

"Hold on, now," The stranger interrupts any rash decisions. "First, we must learn why Milea Sirus of Selvast Forest visited Selcros. She is a warm weather sorceress. We also must know if she is still here."

"From my understanding, Xandous, that red she devil came up here to kill me," Koro concludes. "She stages a battle to try and slay me but it did not work. Then she sends this worthless woman to do it instead."

"I have a name, curmudgeon," Dysis said as the room starts to plunge in temperature. "You killed the Great Bear, thus breaking any bindings I have with you. Why did you break your promise to me? What other secrets do you hide? Did you have a hand in Chastity's death?"

"Grawl, kill this insignificant terrorist!" Koro demands, pointing to his ex-queen.

Dysis causes the room to immediately plunge to freezing. The Sierge shrill in surprise as they lose their footing upon the ice now covering the floor. Dysis slides over to the window and breaks it with a powerful blast of wind. She then jumps out of it, landing in the courtyard and surprising the few soldiers left in Selcros. Without hesitation, Dysis grabs the nearest horse as Koro shouts for her head. The stallion whinnies as he rears up and bolts. He reaches his top speed as they exit the courtyard. Dysis looks behind to see that the Sierge is now running after her. Their speed soon become apparent as they start to close the gap between themselves and their prey.

The chase soon enters the deep pine forest, with the stallion still charging ahead. Dysis hears her pursuers behind her and quickly turns the horse toward the river. She figures she will use the water to freeze her pursuers. Dysis takes a breath of surprise when she sees a cliffside instead of the banks of a mighty river. She swears and pulls on the reins of the stallion, causing him to rear up as he slides to a stop. He dances a little on his hind legs as he walks backward then places his forelimbs on the ground.

Dysis turns the horse and pauses when she realizes the Sierge have trapped them. The dragon men hiss as they pan out and surround the former queen. Dysis glares at the Sierge before her mind suddenly goes calm. She relaxes as a soft wind blows in the trees. The stallion dances in place as he feels a strange energy from the woods. One of the Sierge starts and is grabbed by a branch of the pine he is standing under. The tree tosses the Sierge warrior into the river, a distance below the cliff. He hits the water and screams in surprise, then goes silent as the river drags him under. Two more Sierge meet a similar fate, all the while Dysis is simply staring into the distance.

The rest of the Sierge turn and run back into the woods. They do not get far as the roots of the great pines lasso their legs and pull them underground. Their screams of surprise and pain are cut short as the earth buries them. Dysis swoons a little as she breaks out of her trance and holds her head. She looks around, slightly confused. Dysis looks back at the castle and decides that it is not a good idea to return. Instead, she instinctively heads north to get as far away as she can. The stallion whinnies and starts trotting in the direction his rider wishes to go.

Weeks later, the north wind blows gently as the midnight sun blesses the blooming tundra with life-giving heat and light. Liev walks out of his yurt and gazes upon the nomads that have adopted him into their ranks. He takes in the environment with his left eye, the right lost in a battle with his brother, Koro. Liev recalls the battle every day and does not know if he is lucky to have lived or if he should have given in to the shadows of death. Alerts go off as Faul and his group finally return, much to Liev's relief. His son has been gone a long time on his secret mission. Liev jogs down to meet the group then stops in his tracks when he recognizes one of their members.

Dysis looks up and stops in her tracks when she sees her lost love. She recognizes him, even if he is slightly disfigured from a battle she knows nothing about. Dysis places a hand over her mouth and tries to take a step closer to him. Her knees give way, but she does not fall to the ground. Liev wraps an arm around Dysis and helps her back to her feet. When she cannot walk any further, he picks her up and holds her in his arms. Liev instructs his son, Faul, to retrieve the healer as he takes Dysis back to his yurt. A family of dragons flies overhead as he closes his door.

Seabirds call out, heard above the echoes of the ocean as the Lady of the Night sails south toward the tropics. The addition of oars makes the trip even faster since the enchanted ship can row without fatigue. The weather has warmed considerably from the northern seas as they pass several ports. They had stopped at the last port in order to change into clothing for warmer weather. Neil had said nothing when he discovered that the port they had chosen is under Selcros control, and seeking news from their sovereign. Instead of sticking around, the group had decided to head back out to sea as soon as they could.

Milea brushes her hair as she listens to the laughter of her friends on the other side of her door. She smiles at it, remembering that the joyful sound had been very absent during their stay at Selcros. She chuckles a little to herself when she recalls the whip Vicki lost to Snowpuff, sitting upon the deck of the ship as if it has always been there. Zaria reminded Vicki that the whip once belonged to Keela, and it is unknown what mystical gifts might be a part of its makeup.

Milea stares at the door for a while as she listens as Neil finally fulfills his promise of dagger lessons to Sonja. Someone clears her throat, causing Milea to turn back to the mirror. She swears quietly as she jumps to her feet. The sorceress then identifies the person in the mirror and calms her reaction as she sits back down.

"I see why you told me not to do that, Maya," Milea notes. "I was about to contact you but see that your mystical abilities have returned. Amadahy actually listened?"

"It would be a blizzard in Dorma if she did," Maya said, honestly. "No, I broke her hold on me after fighting Nul."

"He came to Dorma?" Milea frowns at the news. "Nul visited Selcros as well. We chased him to the Ruins of Yedis. I am told that he has horns and a tail. Did he have those when you battled him?"

"No, he developed those after he ate a cursed dragon," Ra'jil chimes in. "It happened during the time you were buried, Maya." A few moments of silence fill the air as the twins focus on their friend.

"Ra'jil, can you please sit next to Maya," Milea requests. "I want you both to tell me everything, starting from the beginning."

"Gladly," Ra'jil says as her image appears in the mirror next to Maya.

Milea ignores the soft tap upon her door as she listens to Maya explain the plight that she and Ra'jil found themselves in weeks before. Justin enters the room quietly just as Maya finishes explaining the Temple of Krast to her sister. He closes the door softly as Ra'jil relates, in vivid detail, the strong sensation of rage as she battled the Witch of Sentical as well as the Tragin, Weyma. Maya admits that she managed to send Weyma to Ublivorion and explains how she did it. Milea smiles at her twin, impressed with her ingenuity.

Justin senses someone else at the door and opens it before the person could knock. Zaria gives him a curious look when he motions for her to be silent as he beckons her in. The shiadokat cautiously walks in and pauses when she sees and hears Maya in the mirror, as the woman continues to explain the happenings in Dorma. Milea's posture changes and she sits up when her sister and friend conclude with news of the presence of Tandon councilwoman, Taigi.

"What is Taigi doing there?" Milea asks slowly.

"From my understanding, a diplomatic thing," Maya answers. "Amadahy even agreed to send her daughter, Aldona, to Tandon with Taigi. In exchange we have Taigi's daughter Paige. The girl is nothing like her mother."

"Hate to say it but that is minor compared to the most recent event," Ra'jil says as she leans back in her chair. "One named Jasmine Underak has threatened to attack Dorma, with the dead of the jungle."

"She gave Amadahy until tomorrow night to surrender or face the consequences," Maya adds. A small silence once again fills the room. Zaria frowns as she quietly leaves the room. Justin closes the door behind her.

"Has Amadahy made preparations?" Milea leans forward a little.

"Amadahy believes it is a bluff, and in her own words has refused to do any unnecessary preparations," Ra'jil summarizes. "She even yanked Kay's rights and privileges then banished me from Dorma. I must be gone by nightfall."

"She did what?" Milea asks, anger trickling in her words.

"Breathe," Maya gently instructs her sister, noticing the flames dancing in Milea's eyes at the mentioning of the punishments.

"I'm breathing," Milea takes another deep breath in and slowly exhales it as she focuses on her calm once more. "Maya, have you entertained Amadahy's request for a test of skills?"

"I have not," Maya answers. "However, she insists that I have three hours of rest then a small meal before I take this test of hers.

Since I've got my abilities back, I do not want to accidently change her into something or send her to dad's front door."

"She still might go there, the old-fashioned way," Milea nearly grinds then once again breathes calmly. "Ok, I want you to accept her challenge and request the style as 'free-for-all'. I will be there within the hour."

"Will do," Maya grins a little. "I cannot wait to see you, sister. You have been missed. Take care."

"Both of you stay out of trouble until I get there, do not give Amadahy an opportunity to know what is coming," Milea instructs. "I have missed you too, Maya and Ra'jil. I cannot wait to be among you once again. Bye for now." The mirror fades back to normal.

"Jasmine being in Dorma is a bad omen," Justin says, causing Milea to whip around and face him.

"How long have you been in here?" Milea asks, suspiciously.

"I have been here since they were explaining the battle with Weyma," Justin answers. "I've originally come to fetch you for dinner."

"Ah, I need to talk to Neil, Vicki, and Brion anyway," Milea muses as she stands and moves to the door.

"Excellent idea, we are going to need their help in Dorma," Justin agrees. "Best to get them prepared."

"We?" Milea pauses in her departure to face Justin.

"You do not expect me to let you go to Dorma, with its current threat, by yourself?" Justin scolds mildly as he approaches her. "I will not do that."

"What about the device they placed near your heart?" Milea asks as she touches his chest. "I cannot afford to lose you during this upcoming struggle."

"And I do not want to lose you," Justin counters and gently touches her cheek.

Milea meets his gaze as she catalogs the information, known about battles with the Underak. She quietly admits to herself that Justin's powers will be an asset against the enemy. The risk is that if he dies or falls back under Jasmine's control, the battle would tilt greatly in the Underak's favor. Milea crosses her arms and walks over to a window, her features reflecting her displeasure. Justin comes up behind her and pulls her into his arms as he kisses her on the top of her head.

"Do not take this as a defeat, my red queen," Justin said gently. "I would conquer all of Bri'al for you if you so desire."

"I know," Milea responds as she turns to face him and quickly kisses his lips. "But it does not lessen the blow. Let me inform the captain of our impending departure. Then I will contact Keela to speed our journey."

"Tell them about the happenings at Dorma, and let them make their own decisions," Justin suggests. "You will need all the warriors you can get. Those who have experience with the undead are priceless."

"Very well, I will give them a brief overview since I gave myself only an hour to get to Dorma," Milea reluctantly agrees.

Justin politely opens the door for Milea. She nods her thanks as she walks out onto the open deck. Justin trails and closes the door behind them. Zaria, sitting on a coil of rope, pauses her conversation as she looks past her audience. Vicki, Neil, and Brion all turn and greet Milea warmly. Sonja is a slight distance away practicing the technique she had just learned from Neil.

Milea waves a greeting back and calls Sonja over to the group as she begins her explanation of events. Neil crosses his arms and tilts his head up to the sky as he listens. Brion arches an eyebrow when he hears about the Underak. Vicki scratches her neck and rests her hand upon her coiled whip.

"I've already volunteered to go," Justin said. "I told her she needs as many warriors that are skilled in fighting the undead as she can get."

"I'll go with you, mom," Sonja chimes. "I can't wait to see Lady Kay and Queen Zoe again."

"Well, you know I'm going," Zaria stands up. "Not only to help you, Milea, but also to hunt down an annoying arachnid that has escaped me over time."

"Are the spiders as big as the ones on Cyenzie Island?" Brion inquires.

"The one I'm hunting is much larger, yes," Zaria answers.

"I don't know about my brother, but I'm going with you." Vicki said. "I'm not going to miss the opportunity to meet Ra'jil in person."

"That's right, I recall making a bet with Neil about that very legend," Brion said. "I'm in."

"I suppose I have no choice but to also go," Neil said. "I want to lay eyes on the legendary Pirate Queen myself."

"Going to Dorma this time will be dangerous, the risks of becoming a part of Jasmine's undead army are extremely high," Milea cautions. "However, I do not have time to argue or to convince you a different way. I must get to Dorma within the hour."

"I thought we were two days from the range of your teleportation spell," Neil said with a frown of confusion. "How are we going to get there within an hour?"

"Come with me, all of you," Milea said. She retreats to her cabin. Her company complies with her request.

A short time later, Milea is standing on the bow of the ship looking out over the waves. They are now in the tropics, thanks to the assistance from Keela. The island of Dorma looms into view quickly as the Lady of the Night increases rowing speed to get to the shallows as quick as possible. Zaria stands and stretches in preparation to use the shadows to take them directly to the queen's home.

The corner of Milea's mouth turns down a little as she realizes that she has to deal with an ornery Dragonigena when she arrives. The sorceress reminds herself not to kill Amadahy, or at least to wait until after Jasmine's defeat. The anchor drops, catching Milea's attention. They are in the shallows of the island as well as the deep shadows of the jungle itself.

"Everybody ready?" Zaria asks.

"Let's get this done," Neil responded.

"Glady," Milea said and starts to walk. "I have been waiting to confront Amadahy for a very long time."

www.ingramcontent.com/pod-product-compliance
Lightning Source LLC
Chambersburg PA
CBHW060510300726
48975CB00008B/2725